Colorado State of Mind

An Anthology by the

Colorado Springs Fiction Writer's Group.

The characters and events portrayed in this book are fictitious. Any similarity to real persons, living or dead, is coincidental and not intended by the author.

"Marrying In" copyright 2007 by Carrie Vaughn, LLC. Previously published in Asimov's Science Fiction, June 2007

All other stories copyright 2016 held by the author

Edited by Kari Wolfe

Cover design by g.griswold.

ISBN: 978-1-945632-06-8

A CSFWG publishing release.

Contact CSFWG

http://www.csfwg.org/
(719) 393-3168
https://www.facebook.com/Colorado-Springs-Fiction-Writers-Group-127414032955/

Table of Contents:

Trials of the Moon

by Nicole Godfrey

The arrow hit its mark with a sickening thud. Wood splintered and flew through the air as the elk crashed to the ground, eyes wide like black discs, and foam bubbled from its open mouth. Makya stood from his crouched position and ran as he drew his bone knife. The animal still twitched, its great side heaving to take in air.

Before the elk suffered too long, Makya buried his blade and silenced its beating heart. He hung his head and gave a prayer of thanks to his brother elk for giving its life so that others may live.

Whooping and yelling brought Makya to his feet in time to brace himself for pats on his back from his fellow warriors.

"You have brought down the largest one. Our families will eat well this night."

"So much for small rabbits! The cold season is truly over."

"Sequoia will be pleased by your show of skill."

"So will her father."

They all spoke in succession and Makya could only smile in response. His heart sang at the thought of impressing the father of his intended.

"Enough talk. No one can be pleased by the kill if it is not properly cleaned soon." The head of the hunting party handed over his own knife. "For your true aim, you have the honor of choosing."

Smiling wide, Makya bowed his head as he took the knife and used it to remove the liver.

Before taking a bite, he raised the offering to the sky, thanking the Great Spirit for the gift and the elk for its sacrifice by sharing the blood. More whooping ensued. The elk was then quickly cleaned and tied to a stripped tree branch. With some strain, they hoisted the branch to their shoulders and began the trek back.

The woods near the mountain camp were too dense for the women to follow safely, so the carcass had to be brought to them to be broken down. Some of the hillsides were still covered in snow, making the journey treacherous and slow. The sun barely peeked over the mountains as the band returned. Children gathered around them, giggling and reaching out their small hands to touch the soft side of the elk. Women followed, exclaiming over the size of the antlers and hooves. Sequoia stood at the back of the crowd, head down, stealing brief glances at Makya through thick lashes. Her full lips pulled back in a shy smile, making his chest tighten. He took a step toward her before he remembered the elk.

The band was greeted by two of the elders, the head of the council and Makya's grandfather. Silence crept over the crowd as Fox Runner inspected the prize, then he turned to Makya's grandfather, Proud Feather, and nodded his approval before walking away. Without any other command, the women took over and began to break down the meat and bones.

Makya approached his grandfather, trying not to appear eager. Proud Feather put his arm around the young brave's shoulders and guided him away from the commotion. With respect, Makya waited for his elder to speak first.

"The council is greatly pleased with your ability as a hunter, and even more so by your bravery in battle when our enemies sought to rob us of our food this winter. In reward, we have decided Sequoia will be your bride. You must bring a final offering to her father and ask for his blessing." The man's tone stayed even, but when Makya looked into his eyes, they held a proud gleam.

A smile spread over Makya's face, heart soaring. With a shout of joy, he ran back to the group of people surrounding the elk and grabbed the beautiful young woman that would soon be his by the hand, leading her beyond the shelters to a stand of trees. Once there, he gathered her into his arms and kissed her hard. His excitement flowed over as he picked her up and spun her around, his lips remained pressed to hers. When he put her down, they were both breathless.

"My prayers have been answered. The council approves our joining." His hands cupped her face and he watched as her expression went from dazed, to shocked, and finally, to happy.

She threw her arms around his neck and laughed riotously as he picked her up again.

"I will bring your father the heart of the elk and ask his blessing." Makya held Sequoia away from him, his smile fading when he saw her wide-eyed expression.

"What if he says no?" Tears filled her soft brown eyes.

"He would not go against the wishes of the council. Strong Bear waited too long." He clenched his jaw at the mention of his rival.

"Yes, but my father and his father have been friends since they were boys." She bit her lip, looking around the tree as if speaking of her father would make him appear.

"And White Cloud saved your father from dying of illness during the last cold season." Makya didn't mention that his own father also brought her parents together when they were young.

"Let us try then." She took his hand and they went to fetch the elk's heart.

When they approached Sequoia's family shelter, a raised voice drifted in the air.

"You swore that nothing would stop you from giving Sequoia to me!" Long black hair swept over Strong Bear's back as he made wild gestures at the aged warrior in front of him.

Black Bird stood tall with arms crossed, and face like a stone carving. He saw Makya and Sequoia first, walking hand in hand, and cut off the words of the ranting brave with one gesture of his hand.

Strong Bear stepped back, glaring at Makya with half-lidded eyes and a hard set to his mouth.

Makya spared him a glance and then bowed his head to his elder. "I bring you the heart of the brave elk that fell by my arrow today. It's accompanied by the blessings of Fox Runner and Proud Feather."

Black Bird stood quietly for several moments, but Makya knew better than to look him in the eyes while he decided what to say.

"Strong Bear just made his intentions known, but I see he was too late." His voice rasped, an after affect from the illness he'd suffered. Then he turned to his daughter and took her hands. "Daughter, which of these warriors would truly make you happy? Take a moment to think. I want you to be sure."

She shook her head. "Father, I do not need a moment. When I was a child, Makya brought me flowers and feathers woven together. He has always been there when I needed him, took me fishing, taught me to swim, and you and Mother both think of him as a son already. Strong Bear is an impressive warrior, but I am not the one to complete his spirit."

"Then it is done. I would have let them compete for your hand, but I will not fight the wind." Black Bird accepted the elk heart from Makya and nodded. In doing so, he gave his blessing.

Strong Bear stayed silent before walking turning and walking away.

The moon hung, large and glowing bright, just above the mountains. Ceremonies took place throughout the day, meals were eaten, dancers moved to the beat of the drum for many songs, and the newly married couple ended the festivities in each other's arms, surrounded by friends and family in their new lodging.

Makya gazed down with an open grin as his bride slept against his chest. An overwhelming sense of happiness warmed his whole body and he slid his fingers through her soft black hair. She stirred at his touch, but only to pull closer to him, which made his smile widen.

In the distance, a low, mournful howl rose into the night. The sound was sweet at first, but then gained in volume. As it continued, the howl grew into something more menacing, a grating and hollow sound. When the sound reached its peak, it was a roar like that of a bear mixed in with the yowl of a mountain lion.

Sequoia stirred again, but this time her brow furrowed and she groaned pitifully. Her hands clenched against Makya's bare skin and he wrapped his arms more tightly around her. *What demon could make such a sound?*

The next day brought bad news. Scouts reported the usual passage lay buried beneath a rock slide. Makya and his hunting party joined the scouts to seek out a new path for the tribe to take down the mountain into the plains.

"Take us to the rock slide. We can start from there." He looked to the council members who nodded in turn.

A high-walled canyon led through some of the taller peaks in the area, making a single file line the only means for Makya's people to travel, but the path could hardly be seen beneath the dirt and stone that filled the opening. *Nothing could move such a large amount, except the Great Spirit.* Makya ran his fingers over deep marks in the piled rocks that looked like a bear used them to sharpen its claws.

"We should go now." The scratches made the hair on the back of his neck stand up. He looked to the scouts, who nodded back, and then they were moving.

They slipped through the trees like shadows and made no sounds, only gestures, to communicate. Following the wall of sheer rock down the slope led them to a passage much further away. Trees clung to the sides, barely able to get purchase for their roots, but the center was smooth rock and could fit three people across. Silence lay heavy in the air, almost as if the animals wouldn't go near the area. Sunlight also retreated from the stone, blocked out by the trees above. The wind picked up and swept down the canyon with a low moan.

"This should make travel easier." The scouts nodded in agreement with the brave who spoke, but Makya just stared.

Another prickle over his skin gave him pause, but he found no words to express the feeling.

"Let us return and have the council decide." Makya turned and ran back up the hill, the rest followed close behind.

The tribe gathered around as the scouts told of the new path. A lot of heads nodded and the feeling of dread crept deeper into Makya's heart. His wife found him and slipped her fingers through his.

"Makya, you seem to doubt this new direction." It was Fox Runner who spoke.

"I think we should find another way down the mountain." Shouts of disapproval rang out from the gathered people.

The elder raised his hands and silenced them. "Share your fear, brother."

Makya looked around at the angry faces and faltered, his throat dry, but then the small hand clutching his squeezed and gave him back his voice.

"Last night, I heard the sound of an animal that I have never heard before. I fear none of my animal brothers and sisters, but this one is unlike them. Then today, I found large claw marks on the stones filling the canyon, larger than any bear we have seen. Now we find an open path, one the Great Spirit has not shown us in all the years we have traveled to the mountains for the cold season. I feel we risk too much."

"So, now you are a wise man? That can interpret signs from the Spirits?" Strong Bear stepped away from his companions. His father, Dances in the Storm, stood to his right with muscled arms crossed over his broad chest.

"No, I claim no wisdom. Only the instincts of a hunter." Makya faced the man, accepting his challenge.

"All of our people have the right to speak. On your word Makya, the council will gather to decide the matter." Fox Runner said and the crowd dispersed, leaving the two challengers in a silent battle of wills.

Sequoia brought it to an end by pulling on Makya's hand and leading him to their shelter.

"The council could be a long time in deciding." Her soft words played over the young man's skin and made him shiver.

Using one hand, he pulled his wife to him, and with the other, he untied the flap to cover their door.

The sun lit the sky before the council came to an agreement. Makya rolled his shoulders while they waited for the rest of the tribe. His dreams kept him from a sound sleep. His mind telling him he heard grunts and growls outside in the night. When he woke, his muscles were knotted from tossing and turning.

"The council agrees, even though there is a strong voice against it, we need to try this new path in order to reach the plains in time to follow the buffalo. Please begin to pack for our journey." The elder avoided eye contact, but Makya didn't blame him for the council's decision. Makya had done his duty. At least he had tried.

With a heavy heart, he walked hand in hand with Sequoia to start packing.

By the following morning, the camp had been broken down into a mobile caravan. Most of the horses carried supplies and shelters, and those that were left carried the eldest among them. All able bodies walked alongside the animals and led them through rougher terrain. Some of the women took up a song of safe travel, and it wasn't long before almost every voice joined in.

Makya still felt uneasy, but the song lifted his spirits and he even sang what words he knew. When they came to the gully, its trees still hugging against the rocks, it appeared a little less threatening. The sun shown down on the trees above, casting dappled light onto the ground. Birds sang in the branches and it smelled like the soil had ripened to breathe new life into the woods.

Perhaps the Great Spirit heard my prayers.

Keeping that thought in mind, Makya paced his steps with the line. He left Sequoia to walk with their joined families, and took position in the loose formation the braves made around the others.

The sun dipped low, bathing the mountains in a soft orange from its fading light. Nothing unexpected had happened, not even when they passed dark and wet caves that could hide any number of things. Maybe he had read too much into the things he saw.

With a light sprinkle of rain, the gray clouds reached over to cover the last bit of sun before it could fully descend behind the peaks. The travelers trudged on until one of the scouts spotted an outcropping of rock that could fit the whole tribe beneath it. Makya helped tie the horses to the crags in the back, glancing over his shoulder to catch a glimpse of Sequoia while she helped the women get a meal going.

As the remaining supplies were removed from the last mount, a familiar roar shook the rock walls. Pieces of the stone roof fell and people began to scream. Makya leapt over packs, trying to push bodies aside without hurting anyone, and searched the terrified faces for his wife. She no longer stood where he last saw her, and there were too many running about for him to see the whole scene. Finally, he broke through into a gap and his blood turned to ice.

There, with several fallen bodies before its giant paws already, stood a massive beast. Its large head had a long snout, dagger-length razor teeth dripping gore, pointed ears laid back against its skull, and wide, blood-shot, yellow eyes. Gray fur dangled in clumps from behind its ears and under its powerful jaws. Its back had the same matted fur covering it, as well as its arms, and its giant paws sported claws twice the length of a full grown grizzly.

Makya took all of this in with the eye of a hunter, but all he carried was a bone knife. That mattered less when the creature bent down and took another mouthful of the already mauled woman beneath it. The blood-curdling scream spurred him into motion and he threw himself at the neck of the beast with knife in hand. Not knowing how the creature was built, Makya hit its shoulder hard and slid his knife over its flesh while he fell off.

Another roar, louder and shriller than before, ripped through the air. Some of the other warriors found weapons and began jabbing at the creature, and Makya stood up. As he did, he caught a glimpse of Sequoia standing on the other side of the circle, her hands covering her mouth while she stared at the beast. Then Strong Bear blocked his view by stepping in front of her. The lunges of the man's spear were off-balanced, causing him to step too close to the creature.

The spear flew from Strong Bear's hands and the creature charged. Screaming in fear, he turned to run, then grabbed Sequoia and threw her into the beast's path.

Makya vaulted onto the creature's broad back and began stabbing furiously. The only thought that penetrated the haze in his mind was to save his wife. Blood gushed everywhere, making the fur slick, but he wound his hand into the longer fur at its neck and continued to plunge his weapon repeatedly into its flesh.

Snarling viciously, the beast bucked and jumped, trying to unseat Makya while the other braves jabbed spears at it during the distraction. It finally turned and ran from the alcove, taking Makya with it back the direction they had travelled. It jumped, hit the rock face with its paws, and tumbled to the ground back first. The blood coating its fur made Makya slip off as soon as it started to turn and he jerked out a huge clump of gray fur as he hit the ground, jarring his shoulder. He jumped back to his feet before the creature slid to a stop. Rolling back onto its feet before it lost all momentum, the animal charged back toward him and forced Makya to lunge out of the way.

Searing pain ripped across his stomach and thigh before he landed on his injured shoulder. The pain intensified, almost causing him to pass out, and he lay there for a moment just trying to breathe, with his eyes clenched shut. When death didn't claim him immediately, he opened his eyes and found the beast facing away from him. More warriors, young and old, had taken up spears and were rushing toward the creature.

The beast roared at them with its teeth dripping with gore and spittle and then, with a snap of its jaws, ran back up the mountain side.

His family and friends made it to him as Makya pulled himself back to his feet.

"My son, let the healer come. You will only make your injuries worse." White Cloud put a hand on his son's shoulder.

"Sequoia...." Makya reached his hand toward the outcropping.

"She lives. Her wounds are being treated. Let us do the same for you."

He couldn't tell who spoke that time, his vision narrowed to the area around the fire. Taking two more steps, he fell to his knees and darkness greeted him before the ground could.

There was no accounting for time passed when Makya woke again. Blurred visions of horrible things plagued his mind and pain beyond belief wracked his body. His eyes felt crusty and someone was burning sage nearby. A gentle hand bathed the sweat from his brow.

"Sequoia...?" His hand found the one touching him and he opened his eyes with some effort.

The woman before him had seen many winters and wasn't his wife. He let his eyes close again and swallowed around the dryness in his throat. Water touched his lips even before the bowl and he drank deeply. When there was nothing left, he asked again.

"Where is Sequoia?" He opened his eyes when no answer came.

Her brown eyes wouldn't meet his, then she grabbed up some bowls and herbs before quickly leaving.

Makya tried to sit up, but the pain in his shoulder denied him. After much struggling, and a fresh sheen of sweat, he lay on the pile of skins, panting from effort.

Voices raised in conversation met his ears before the flap pulled back and Fox Runner walked in to stand in front of him. Bushy white eyebrows bunched between his small, black eyes, and his mouth drew down in a deep frown.

"Please, where is Sequoia? Where is my wife?"

"She lives. Her wounds were different, mostly scratches and a bite on her arm. You stopped the beast from killing her." The old man's voice sounded drier, adding years that he didn't have. He licked his lips and swallowed several times, as if parched.

"Then she is safe." Makya felt dizzy with relief.

"Alive is quite different from safe."

Ignoring the pain, Makya rolled to his side and used his uninjured arm to prop himself up. "What do you mean? She lives—that means she is safe."

The elder sighed heavily and sat down by the young man's feet.

"You have been walking the dream paths for many moons now, but not long enough to have mended as much as you have. Your wife is fully healed. The attack has changed you both."

Makya finished sitting up, gritting his teeth the whole while, and looked deep into the eyes of the most respected man of his tribe. He felt no lie in his words, but he had to know. So he flung back the blanket, and tore at the bindings around his thigh and stomach. Smooth pink scars were all he found underneath.

"Your shoulder was the worst injury. The bones shattered and your skin was covered in angry marks. The marks are gone, and even though the pain remains, I am certain the bones have mended. For the safety of the tribe, we must know if you or your wife will take the form of the beast."

"How?" Makya rubbed his sore shoulder.

"The moon is almost at its fullest and then we will see if the moon heat brings out the demon."

"I thought that only worked for those who are mad?" Makya remembered the stories, but didn't understand how they fit this situation. The others willingly kept their madness from the tribe, secretly consuming the flesh of people to take their strength. The full moon forced them to reveal their true nature. He and Sequoia weren't *Wendigo*.

"Yes, it works for them, but might be our only hope now. The Great Spirit willing, we will prove that you both are not cursed."

"So why are you here alone, if I could be a beast?"

"I believe that it can only surface at night. The beast tried to come back for us the night after you were injured, but we were ready and drove it back. There has been no sign of it since."

Makya thought for a moment and nodded. "So we wait for the trial of the moon."

Fox Runner nodded. "And the tribe will be praying until then."

Family members came to pray, friends told him to be strong, but all Makya wanted was to see his wife. No one would speak of her, not even her mother when she came to smudge sage. Being separated, even for the few days more until the moon filled, tore him apart inside. Like a hot ember being twisted in his gut.

Finally the day of the full moon came and so did the warriors. Makya stood, completely healed, to wait for them with hands held out in front of him. He shifted his weight from foot to foot, unable to stay still as his heart beat with the speed of a rabbit's. They hesitated, but tied his hands and led him out of the shelter. Camp had been set up in the foothills, only just out of the mountains. The tall, snow-covered peak could barely be seen beyond the mountains they'd stayed in all season. Makya shuffled after his friends as they led him beyond the light of the campfires and into the forest. They came to a clearing where most of the tribe gathered around two large trees set a good deal apart from each other.

His heart thumped painfully against his ribs at the sight of Sequoia bound to the base of one of the trees. Lying limp against her shoulder, her head tilted at what looked to be an uncomfortable angle, her arms pulled back and tied behind the tree with straps. She still wore the torn dress she'd had on the night of the attack. Blood stained the beautiful buck-skin where claws had rent her flesh.

Anger at how she'd been treated burned in Makya's body and made him growl. The warriors attending him turned. Their looks of sadness and understanding deflated Makya's rage. He couldn't be mad at them if they were only following the commands of the elders. Still, every blood vessel in his body pushed him to go to his love and fold her into his arms where she would be safe.

"The moon calls and asks that the blood be tested. Here to answer—our warrior brother, Makya," A murmur began from the people as Fox Runner raised his arms toward where Makya was being bound to the tree. "And also our sister, Sequoia." He gestured to the other tree and its captive, but only silence filled the air.

Makya didn't understand this reaction from the tribe. *Why are they acting like her soul is already lost?* His anger toward the whole situation found a spot in his heart and smoldered, his chest heaving from the effort of breathing through the heat. If he couldn't get it under control, he'd burst through his restraints and take Sequoia far from the judgment awaiting them.

Thoughts of being isolated from his family and all he held dear were the only things that kept him in place.

So he focused his energy on his wife, his eyes roving over every beloved detail, even down to her filthy toes. He ignored the fact that her beaded moccasins were missing, the ones her mother had given her for their wedding, and locked his gaze on her serene face. She appeared so peaceful in her slumber and he tried not to think of how or why she had come to be in this state.

Time stretched out like a bowstring as the full moon crept higher in the sky. Light filled the clearing and bathed the couple in a soft glow. Shadows covered the rest of the gathered faces, lending to the tension heavy in the air. Makya only marginally noticed these things at the edges of his vision, and waited to see his wife's beautiful brown eyes.

When they snapped open, Sequoia gasped hard, as if she'd just come up for air after diving into the mountain lake. Her gaze locked onto his and he saw panic in the depths of her eyes, making his own anxiety overwhelming. The ball of heated anger rose and expanded.

Sequoia struggled against her restraints, groaning and whimpering pathetically. Some of the braves stepped forward, their weapons held low in white-knuckled grips as the bound woman thrashed before them.

"Get away from her." The words rumbled low in Makya's throat, more guttural than intended, and the pensive men stopped their advance.

The heat in his chest throbbed in the veins just below his skin, causing an erratic beat in his heart that pounded against his eardrums.

His reaction felt more intense than it should be, and when a spasm wracked his muscles, he knew something was wrong. A haze covered his eyes, making the images around him swim and blur. Leaning back against the tree, Makya tried to breathe through the pain and get his body under control. The fire in his blood had other plans, and he screamed as bones snapped in his limbs, followed by the feeling of being stretched. Breathing became impossible once his ribs cracked, and the sound of ripping leather could be heard over his grunts and moans.

Just as the pressure threatened to suffocate him, the heat vanished and the contorting stopped. He sat there, head down, panting, and realized he was no longer bound to the tree. Instead, he looked down at what should have been his hands. Huge gray paws, like that of his brother wolf, nestled among the leaves and debris on the forest floor. Makya moved his arm and the paw followed the motion. He opened his mouth to speak, only to be greeted with a lupine whimper.

This is not possible. The Great Spirit, in all his wisdom, would not do this to one of his warriors!

"Ma—ky...a." Sequoia's low plea brought his attention across the clearing.

Her doe eyes were fixed on him, but every other part of her couldn't be recognized. The features of her face were twisted, eyebrows straight up and mouth stretched back toward her ears, ears that had lengthened into fur covered points. That elegant line of her jaw had disappeared, drawn back in on itself so that an elongated snout took its place. A large black nose rested at the tip and sniffed the air wildly. When Makya brought his eyes back to his wife's, they'd turned a sickly yellow and were much larger.

The tethers that had held her to the tree now lay in a heap, along with the remains of her dress, at the clawed feet of a beast. One that mirrored the beast that attacked them in the pass.

Gasps and cries came from the gathered onlookers, causing the pale eyes to swing in that direction. The warriors formed a line in front of the rest, keeping the new beast at bay with sharp jabs and loud shouts. Their goading seemed to enrage Sequoia and she reared back on her hind legs.

Great Spirit help us, she could rip them to pieces. It could cost his life, but Makya faced the beast that was his wife and howled. He poured his pain and anguish into the sound, and silence filled the clearing once his cry trailed off.

Sequoia leaned forward and put her front paws back on the ground, her sides heaved, but she did not advance. One clawed foot moved to the side, as if she wanted to sidestep around him. He moved with her. Another step back to where she started and he followed again. Her lips curled back as she growl, and Makya bared his teeth to show he refused to back down. Her growl deepened and Makya stepped forward. She immediately stepped back.

Shuffling sounds came from the warriors behind him. Makya turned so that his body was a wall between the group and his wife, but made sure he kept both in his line of sight. He snapped a barking growl at his fellow braves. The sound made them jump back. He maintained the sound as he turned his head back and forth. One step at a time, he drove Sequoia away from the clearing toward the trees.

"Makya, wait." White Cloud tried to push through the warriors, his eyes wide and fixed on his son.

The snarl left Makya's lips and his ears perked forward as he stared at the man who had given him life. Emotion weighed heavy on his lupine heart, but it registered differently. What he would have once considered sadness or regret felt more like separation.

Movement on the edge of his vision made Makya snap at Sequoia who had inched back into the clearing while there was a distraction. She stopped and bowed her head low. Her eyes avoided his gaze and the profile of her mass blended with the shadows. Without looking back, Makya nudged his wife's side with his shoulder. Spurred on by his touch, she ran off into the trees. His smaller shadow flanked her every move.

Early morning light woke Makya from a deep sleep. Only broken shafts filtered down through the roots that twined above him. The bitter taste of copper lingered in his mouth and his face felt coated with war paint. All he could smell was the strong scent of rich soil mixed with the smell of both animal and woman. His arms were wrapped tightly around the naked form of his wife. But he couldn't remember how they came to be in a hollow beneath a tree.

Images flashed through his mind, a blur of events that made no sense, until his memory finally rested on the clearing and the trial of the moon. Sequoia groaned in her sleep and curled in on herself more, almost as if she sensed his distress. Her back pressed against his stomach and he rested his cheek against her matted hair.

I must return to our people and talk to them. They are our family—surely they will want to work with us to find a way to live together. Makya ran a hand over his wife's brow to soothe her. She moved into his touch and whimpered. *How can this be the same woman who changed into a beast?*

The woman in his arms was the one he had loved since they were children. The one who was quiet and shy. She cared for all those who needed it, old and young. She could never hurt a soul. But the creature she became last night could. Its yellow eyes had been filled with the need to kill. Something only Makya's wolf-self could have known.

His wolf. That was a whole other matter. *Why did I take the form of my brother wolf instead of the beast? Why do I feel the need to protect instead of the urge to kill? And who can answer these questions for me?*

Only the beast that attacked them would know about these things. Before he attempted to speak with the tribe, he would try to locate the lair of his enemy and get answers. Hunting in human form was engrained in his soul, and he would need those skills more than ever.

Pushing himself back against the earthen wall, Makya shimmied out from behind the still sleeping Sequoia and crawled out into the sunlight. He stretched, reaching his arms up toward the sky, and closed his eyes as he enjoyed the heat on his face. A soft breeze stirred the air, bringing with it the smell of blood. He opened his eyes to look around.

Behind the hole they slept in was the carcass of a young bear. Understanding quickly replaced surprise when he reached up and brushed dark red flakes off of his face. Bending down, he saw that red blood smeared across Sequoia's face as well. She also bore several claw marks on her arms and chest, though they looked a few days old.

Instead of trying to figure out how it happened, Makya found a cluster of rocks and made himself a rough knife. Then he went about cleaning what was left of the bear. Not much meat remained, but he saved what he could. *More of my brother, the bear, should have been picked off by scavengers, but I give thanks to the Great Spirit the pelt is still intact.* The remaining fur would make a blanket, though he might use some to cover himself before he spoke to anyone.

"How did you take down a bear?" Sequoia's question came from behind him as he finished cleaning away the gore and he turned. Skin smeared with dirt, she stood with her arms wrapped around her middle. Her usually smooth hair hung over her shoulders in tangled clumps and covered her bare chest.

Nothing could have been more beautiful to him. She was alive and whole. "I did not take him down. The Great Spirit has provided for our needs."

"Why are we here, naked? And you have dried blood on you." Her hand touched her face, brown eyes going wide.

"You do not remember?" he asked, more out of surprise than need.

She shook her head and her hand slipped down to her throat.

He stood and walked to her with the skin in his hands. "It is still a little wet." Slowly, he draped it over her shoulders. She didn't even flinch. "We will make this work, my heart. I swear to you that I *will* protect you."

Turning her head, she looked at him as if he had lost his senses. "What are we making work? I do not understand and I want to see my mother."

Makya's throat tightened, a lump forming. "You can not see her right now. I need to speak with the elders and get some issues cleared up. Then we can go home."

"Why just you? Should we not face them together?" Her voice shook and he pulled her head to his chest.

"I want you with me, in all things. They do not trust us, and I can only defend you from a few people at a time. The tribe would overwhelm us in numbers. I can not see you in bonds again." He closed his eyes against the anger that flared up at the mere mention.

"But why do they not trust us? What happened? I don't…." Her anguish burned at Makya's nerves. He knew he must tell her the truth, but he hated being the one to hurt her.

"We have been marked. You by the beast and me by the wolf. I have no reason to give as to why it affected us differently. The moon decided. It is out of fear that they lack trust." It was the simplest way to explain what he still didn't understand either.

Sequoia didn't move or speak for several moments. He thought she handled the news well until her body began to shiver. Then he realized she wasn't breathing.

"You have to breathe, my love. I am here." He rubbed his hand up and down her back while holding her close.

For several more moments she remained silent, her whole body shaking violently until she expelled a burst of air and words. "How can they do this? We are family! That thing attacked everyone! Why are we being punished?" Then she pulled away from his embrace and tears started to fall.

"I plan on talking to them about that very issue. I agree—none of this is fair." Makya cupped her face and tried to soothe her.

She jerked away with a sneer. "They will talk to you because you turned into a wolf instead of a monster. That is why you want me to wait here."

His heart sank as she stepped out of his arms. "Yes." He refused to lie.

"So, you are better than me? What did I do that was so wrong?" The tears flowed freely, but her chin tilted at a proud angle.

"You did nothing. This is not your fault," he said.

She turned her head and looked down the mountain. "Go. Speak with the tribe. I doubt they will take us back, but perhaps they will take you."

He shook his head. "I will not give them that option."

"You would be a fool to turn them down," she whispered.

"Then I guess I am a fool." He didn't give her the chance to respond before he turned and walked away.

Makya had to walk back to the pass. It didn't take as long as he'd expected because the burrow they'd slept in was further up the mountain. He accepted that his brother wolf could scent better than he, and asked for his help. Whether he answered or not, the harsh smell of animal assaulted his nose. The smells of the tribe were distinctly familiar, as if he'd known their marks all along, but the scents hadn't been strong enough to pick up until now.

Taking careful steps since the trail wasn't fresh, he worked his way down the gorge. There were scratches along the rock that were new and he stopped to examine them. Inches deep, they exposed the heart of the stone for the world to see. His fingers traced each one, feeling the pain in the earth. *I would heal you, if I could.*

The trail led him to an opening in the rock face. He inhaled, noting a stronger smell mixed with blood, and stepped inside. *Chances are that the beast will be found within.*

Each step echoed off the walls. Makya's heart thumped inside his chest. He kept his breathing even. He swept his gaze back and forth. The palm of his hand grew moist around the knife he held tightly. Nothing moved in the dim light even though it felt like a thousand eyes watched him.

His nostrils flared. The smell was stronger than before. Covering his nose with the arm that didn't have the knife, he stopped himself from gagging at the stench. A tingle of familiarity crept through his mind. Mingled with the smell of animal came the scent of human. Not just a human, but one Makya had seen every day of his life.

A bend in the tunnel led to an alcove. Bits of bone were scattered about. Against one of the loose rocks sat a bundle of skins. Makya stepped toward it, swatting flies, and picked up the bundle. They were cleaned buck skins. Torn to shreds, but no trace of blood. As he unfolded the pieces, a waft of air carried a more distinct smell to his nose. *Strong Bear's father.*

The skins slipped from his fingers and he ran back down the tunnel. Sunlight still filled the canyon, but the angle of the sun was lower now. Makya didn't stop—he simply ran, praying to the Great Spirit he could make it to the tribe in time to warn them.

When he finally reached the encampment, both the last rays of daylight and winking stars fought for dominance. He noted the white globe of the moon peeking over the horizon and sped up his pace.

He stayed on the outskirts of the camp. A few people were moving around and he wanted to speak with his father first and get some clothes. The designs that marked his family's lodging were further in than he wanted to go, but he didn't hesitate, keeping low as he moved from lodge to lodge. Two warriors appeared around one of the lodges and Makya ducked in the opposite direction. He turned and came face to face with a pudgy-cheeked child.

Wide, dark eyes looked up at him while the child gnawed on his small fist. Makya smiled and held a finger to his lips to tell the little boy to be quiet.

"Ma! Ma!" The boy cried and ran off.

After the boy disappeared and he'd checked to be sure no one had seen him, Makya slipped into the home he had shared with his family.

White Cloud stood at the sight of his son. Fox Runner sat at the fire beside White Cloud, but simply puffed on the pipe in his hand instead of standing. There was no one else inside.

"You have returned," White Cloud said.

"I have. Father, I must speak with you. With both of you." Makya inclined his head to Fox Runner and the elder nodded in return. "May I cover myself first?"

His father nodded and sat back down.

Makya quickly found some of his hide clothing among his family's belongings and dressed. Then he sat across from the two men he respected most in the world.

White Cloud opened his mouth to speak, but Makya held his hand up. "Before we discuss the obvious reason I came here, I need to warn you that Dances in the Storm is the beast that attacked us in the pass. I found a den with his scent all over it."

Fox Runner continued to puff while White Cloud looked into Makya's eyes. "You could...smell him?" his father asked.

Makya nodded, holding his hands close to the warmth of the flames.

"Then your spirit guardian, the wolf, has truly blessed you." Fox Runner's words were accompanied by a plume of smoke.

Makya closed his eyes. "I do not see it as a blessing."

"How can you not?" His father's words made him open his eyes. "To have the keen senses, strength and speed, like that of our brother, the wolf… that is nothing less than a blessing."

"And what of the gift given to Sequoia?" Makya spoke the words softly, so as not to be offensive.

"The beast marked her as his own—she can not be saved. The Great Spirit chose to let you remain honorable. We have no place arguing with that decision." The elder placed the pipe on a rock next to the fire. "We do need your help. You are the only one with the power to face Dances in the Storm. If he truly is a beast, he is a danger to everyone."

"The rest of the elders will want to know of this." White Cloud gestured to Makya. "What do you choose, my son?"

Makya looked deep into the flickering fire. There was only one choice, only one path he could follow. But being this close to the only life he'd ever known made him pause. The mingled smells of burning wood, the smoke from the pipe, and the individual scents of his loved ones pulled at his soul. To not be a part of the tribe, to not take part in the hunt, felt like being torn in half. Then Sequoia's face flashed in his mind's eye. Her smile, her laugh, and everything else he loved about her.

"I will defend the tribe. When that is done, I will take my wife and leave." He stood and the two older men flinched. Then he realized he'd moved with great speed and was next to the entrance.

"Makya, you can not leave your family. Not for a woman." White Cloud slowly got to his feet.

"I will not forsake her father. Her or my heart. She is my wife." Makya stepped aside and motioned for his father and Fox Runner to leave ahead of him. Many voices joined in a constant murmur outside. If he focused, he could make out familiar individuals. Most of the voices, though, held an odd tension, while others trembled in fear.

When they stepped out in front of the gathered people, silence fell. Fox Runner took a few steps closer than White Cloud and Makya, and held up his hands.

"My brothers and sisters, family and friends, Makya has returned and agreed to lend us the strength of the wolf in order to make our people safe once more. I would like to ask Dances in the Storm to step forward." Though he didn't speak loudly, there was no doubt everyone heard Fox Runner's words.

Heads turned, looking at those who stood close by, and soft whispering spread through the crowd. Toward the back, people began to part. Makya swallowed around a lump in his throat, waiting to see the face he knew the beast wore in human form.

Strong Bear walked through the gap. "What do you need from my father?"

"That is for your father to know. Where is he?" White Cloud crossed his arms and stepped up beside Fox Runner.

"He said he needed to rest. My father enjoys time to himself." Instead of showing respect, Strong Bear scanned White Cloud from head to foot and smirked.

Makya's blood boiled in his veins.

"We wish to speak with him. Would someone, other than Strong Bear, please go ask Dances in the Storm to join us?" Fox Runner lowered his arms and looked up at the tall brave. Even being shorter, Strong Bear still took a step back. Makya smiled.

"You will not find him," Strong Bear said.

"Why not?" Makya couldn't help but speak up.

Strong Bear's lips thinned and a scowl creased his brow. "He always goes out when the moon is at its brightest. He told me he likes to run." Each word came out through clenched teeth.

"Then it is true." White Cloud rubbed his forehead and began to pace.

"What is true?" Strong Bear's scowl vanished, his eyes widening.

"Your father is the beast that attacked the tribe in the pass." Makya hadn't meant to blurt out the truth, but he saw no reason to lie.

Again, silence crept over those gathered. Strong Bear's mouth opened and closed as he glared at Makya, as if he couldn't form words. One person stepped away from Strong Bear, then everyone scrambled to put distance between them and the young warrior.

Makya lost sight of Strong Bear as people swarmed around them. He turned to make sure his father still stood next to him. White Cloud blocked Fox Runner from the panic with an outstretched arm. With a jerk, Makya was spun around by the shoulders to face his rival.

"You are a liar! My father is no beast. First you took Sequoia away from me, and now you wish to take my only living family." Strong Bear pulled his arm back and clenched his fist.

The simmer in Makya's blood reached a flash point. Everything around him seemed to slow as he bent his knees and drew back both arms. Time caught up the instant both of his fists impacted Strong Bear's stomach. The warrior went flying into the moving throng and knocked several people to the ground with him.

"Makya!" White Cloud stepped between his son and the rest of the tribe. He raised a hand toward Makya. "Calm yourself, my son. The moon calls you, but you can control it."

Looking down, Makya found he had fur rippling across his arms. The call, every fiber of his being reaching for the wolf inside, but instead of fighting it like his father said, he closed his eyes and welcomed the change. He looked back up at his father and had to keep looking up. White Cloud lowered his hand, the corners of his mouth turning down.

Wavering light from multiple fire pits distorted Makya's vision. The screams from women and children hurt his ears. Smoke, fear, and so many other smells overloaded his senses. He shook his head, a growl and a snort coming out where he'd intended to groan.

I need to find Dances in the Storm. The thought brought focus amidst the chaos. With one final look at his father, who still stood there staring at his wolf son, Makya loped off into the night.

On the outer edges of the hills, he came across a scent he'd recognize anywhere. *Sequoia.* Worry seeped into his bones until he whined from it. He turned up the slope to head back to the burrow they had slept in, but the further he went, the more faint the scent grew. Shadows played over further ground as he circled around. When he found the right direction, Makya took off at a run.

There was no doubt where the trail led once he entered the canyon. His sure-footed paws gave him better purchase than feet and he stood before the opening in the rock face in no time. Breathing deep, he took in the combined scent of Sequoia and Dances in the Storm. Both in human form and bestial form. Something else hung in the air as well. Musk. *They mated?*

Makya gagged, the sound echoing off the stone. The overlapping scents told him neither were inside anymore, but he'd only just missed them. Betrayal and rage warred within his chest, but he didn't wait to know the victor before he was moving again. He followed the trail that looped back away from his approach and headed back down the mountain. Even before the screaming began, he knew where they'd gone.

Flames ravaged the dry wood and treated leather that made up most of the tribe's lodging.

This can not be the same place I left tonight.

Bodies lay scattered across the ground. Blood seeped into the dirt and gathered in puddles. Open eyes stared vacantly back at him.

These are not my people. They can not be.

On silent paws, he moved farther in. This time, there was no child to spot him and run for his mother. There was no one there to scream at all.

He finally found the source of the only noise left. A beast, Sequoia or Dances in the Storm, their scents still mingled in his nose, sat amid several mangled bodies. The pile had to be at least four deep. Blood oozed from its jaws as it feasted on flesh and bone alike.

Glowing yellow eyes fixed on him as soon as he stepped into the open. The beast's lips drew back over massive canines. It snarled. Blood sprayed from the open mouth like crimson rain. Then it bit down on the neck of its victim. White Cloud's head rolled down the pile and stopped a short distance away from Makya.

In response, Makya bared his own teeth and snarled. He flattened his ears and held his head up. Slow and sure steps brought him closer. As he moved, he let the volume of his snarl increase until it could be heard in the surrounding forest.

The beast on top of the bodies seemed to respond to Makya's behavior. It stopped eating. Lowering its head, it shuffled back and crouched low to the ground. Then another form came from around one of the burning heaps of shelters. A much bigger form.

Makya flinched at the revelation. His demeanor fell for a split second. The larger of the two launched forward. Its speed belied its size. Makya ducked under its legs, but still felt its claws graze his flank.

He didn't have time to stop. The massive body twisted and came at him again. His paws scraped at dirt and he found himself facing the wrong direction. One giant paw caught him while his back was turned and Makya went rolling. His head still spun even after he stopped moving.

Teeth dug into his back and he flew through the air. He let out a cry from the bite that cut off as he landed hard. His legs shook, but he stood and faced the charging monster.

The smaller beast cut the bigger one off before it reached him. A more high-pitched roar filled the air. The sound had a definite distinction from that of the beast in the pass. When the larger one roared back, Makya had all the confirmation he needed. He moved behind the bigger of the two while they focused on each other. Then he darted in as fast as his aching body would allow him. His jaws closed around the flesh of its thigh and a bitter metallic flavor filled his mouth.

The big beast stumbled forward with a screeching whine. Blood gushed from the back of its leg. No matter how many times it tried, it couldn't stand up.

I have to finish this.

When the beast tried to rise again, Makya went for its throat. Blood filled his mouth once more. He kept his jaw locked while the beast shook to dislodge him. Pain radiated through his teeth and the muscles in his neck strained from the exertion, but Makya refused to let go. With one last push, the monster tipped on its side and hit the ground. The impact jarred through the wolf's body. He let go and flopped onto his haunches.

The beast's sides heaved from laboring to breathe. Dark blood drained from its wounds in rivulets. One last stuttering exhalation and its yellow eyes rolled back, all of its limbs going slack.

Makya sat and stared at the body for several minutes. It didn't move again.

He tried to regain his footing, only to fall back to the ground. Everything hurt, inside and out. He couldn't even find a measure of relief from the fact the creature lay dead.

A soft whine drew his gaze to where the other beast sat. It watched him intently. Makya tried to stand and its ears perked up. He sat again, heavily. Another whine. One last effort and, finally, he placed his legs securely under his weight. The beast, who he now knew to be Sequoia, stood as well. When he tried to approach, she backed away. He tilted his head and stepped forward. Again she backed away.

She rubbed a clawed paw over her muzzle and sneezed. Then she looked around. Makya followed her gaze and took in all of the bodies. His heart felt heavy with their loss. When he looked back, Sequoia was disappearing through the trees. He tried to follow, but she ran faster than he could. His injuries prevented him from keeping pace. So he returned to the camp and waited for daylight.

No black outs came to relieve him of his pain. He stayed awake until the burning in his blood took over and he ended up curled in a ball on the ground as a human once more. His tears and anguish flowed freely a moment before he stood on his aching legs. Even without the wolf's keener senses, the smell of death hung heavy in the air.

Still covered in muck, Makya gathered all the bodies of the fallen in one place. Then he used fire to send them on the Spirit Path home. They would walk the skies while the lonely warrior waited to join them. He watched over the pyre, not willing to give up his vigil while smoke still rose into the air.

When it eventually stopped, the sun shone down from directly above him. He cleaned himself with slow movements and gathered as many supplies as he could carry.

There was no sign of Sequoia until after the moon completed another cycle. He came across an odd stone structure held together by mud and the trunks of trees. The whole thing struck him as clunky and useless. There was no way to break down all those pieces and take them to a new location. Inside, the mess matched what he'd smelled. Blood-soaked bodies. He'd never seen a tribe with such pale skin before, nor dressed in such odd garb.

A wide-rimmed basket sat close to a man's head and his bloodied shirt was not made of animal skin. The coverings on his feet seemed to be a hard leather of some sort, but they had a thick bottom like wood.

Sequoia had kept her advantage by staying ahead, and these people had paid dearly for it. Though why she'd attacked them in their home, he couldn't say.

The further ahead she got, the longer it would be before he took her down.

As he lit the structure on fire to send off the spirits of the dead, Makya accepted the fact that his world had completely changed. Forever.

He followed the trail left by his beloved along the foothills, toward the tallest peak still covered in snow, and then out toward the empty, open plains where the buffalo gathered.

I will find you, my heart, and together we will join our families among the clouds.

Nicole Godfrey

Nicole loves to write about love in all its manifestations. She goes to conventions and workshops constantly, and works toward becoming a better writer every day. Nicole Godfrey is a writer who calls the beautiful city of Colorado Springs home, along with her furry children. She was born in Omaha, NE. and has lived in Florida and Tennessee. Her writing career started with poetry at a young age, leading to her first publication at the age of twelve. Poetry eventually evolved into the love of storytelling, and any good story, no matter the genre, is open to her creative mind. She has two short stories published through Colorado Springs Fiction Writers Group; A Page Lost in An Uncommon Collection, and The Power of the Word in Remnants and Resolutions: Tales of Survival. When she's not writing, Nicole actively participates in Amtgard and loves to play table-top RPG's. Art has also been a part of her life since a young age, so she spends as much time as possible playing with different mediums.

Driver

By Jason Dias

Regina huddled further into her coat, wishing the zipper hadn't broken two years ago, and tried to see the bright side. At least Colorado was dry. The cold was tolerable because it didn't have moist fingers to reach into clothing, into bones. Not like Atlanta.

She looked up the road, where the headlights should appear, waiting to hear the distinct noise of air brakes. The bus only came once an hour anyway, and it was late. Which meant she'd probably miss her connection when she finally arrived at the station downtown and have to wait another half hour there. The bright side was harder.

Cars went by on the road and she tried not to look at them. Their headlights were painfully bright in the early darkness of Colorado winter. But she would much rather be driving than waiting for the bus. She remembered a time not that long ago when she had her own car. Not much to look at, just an old Buick with a leaky head gasket, but it had broken down five years ago and she had no money to fix it. Five years ago. That was when things had started to go sour.

One car came on slower than most and she thought, for a second, it might be the bus. But it was clearly too small to be the bus, headlights close together. It made hardly any noise as it slowed into the bus lane, stopped a little past the bench. Regina watched the thing roll in without looking straight at it, healthy curiosity tempered by discretion. The car did not discourage curiosity, though.

It was some old bit of art-deco work from a bygone age, the opening decades of the twentieth century, when cars were still made by carriage-makers. It was long with a hood that stretched out into the distance. The cab in back had two doors on each side. It was chromed out. Whitewall tires. Running boards. Big, sweeping fenders that gave the impression of horses pulling the car from the front. Deep paint, maybe black, hard to say in the dark. It looked like something Cruella DeVille might have ridden in.

The driver got out, came around the front of the car, stood by the back door. "Do you need a ride, ma'am?" she said. She was tall for a woman. Her uniform jacket hung on her like a sail, flapping open to reveal broad shoulders, narrow waist and hips. Scarecrow hair was restrained by an old-time driving cap. Not young, not quite old: frown lines, grooves around her mouth like brackets, no sign a smile had ever passed across her face.

Regina knew better than to take rides from strangers. But this was a very strange situation. She thought: *Is this a real person? She looks like a ghost.* Her skin tightened with old dread at the thought of death, of ghosts, and she seemed to hear the sound of tires crying out against a sandy roadway, against forces of momentum and gravity.

At the same time, she was looking at forty-five minutes to the station, thirty minutes to the stop nearest her street, another fifteen minutes of walking to get to her apartment, and never mind waiting at the station for the next bus. Hour and a half, minimum.

"Ma'am?"

"I'll be right there." She gathered up her belongings. Caution to the wind. If nothing else, she'd have a story to tell. The driver opened the rear door - it opened backwards - took Regina's bags, shut her into the car. Went around back and stowed Regina's gear in the trunk. Got into the front.

"Where to, ma'am?"

Regina gave her address, looked around the dark interior. It smelled of old leather, not unpleasant. There were no lights from the dashboard, the car being of a vintage long before such conveniences. The seat in back was a long low bench, leather, dark and rich in the wash of headlights from a passing truck. There was wood all around, in the door panels, consoles, floor. She bet it was mahogany though it was too dark to get any evidence. The front seats were a mile away. There was what looked like a mini-fridge between the front seats facing backwards.

"Help yourself, ma'am," said the driver, as if able to follow Regina's gaze.

She opened the fridge, saw a couple of sandwiches, a couple of Cokes in the sexy old-school glass bottles. Two champagne flutes. She took a sandwich and a coke.

The roast beef had mustard and onions, just like it should; nothing extra.

"Roast beef, ma'am," said the driver, again as if following her gaze or thoughts. She stretched the word 'ma'am' as if she wanted to pronounce the 'd', say 'madam.' "I hope they are to your liking." No accent. Not Midwestern, just no accent. Almost old-worldish. Deep voice for a woman.

Regina kept quiet. She had a hundred questions but was too tired and wary for any of them. She tucked the second Coke and roast beef into her coat pockets. Things weren't so good she could pass up free meals.

The car did not move fast, just whispered along at its stately pace. It rode smooth, smooth enough that Regina felt OK pouring some Coke into one of the chilled glasses and sipping it like a person of privilege. The miles rolled by steadily and suddenly they were outside her building. Ninety minutes by bus reduced to twenty by car. She looked around for a door handle, couldn't find one.

"One moment, ma'am," said the driver. She came around the front, opened the door, gave Regina a hand out. Went to the back for her bags. Regina went to help. "Not to worry, ma'am. I'll bring these in for you."

Regina wanted to argue, wanted also to be indulged. Why not? So she led the driver into the building, to the stairs, up to her floor, down the hall to her apartment. At the door, the driver set down her bags, tipped her cap, and set off back down the hall. "See you in the morning, ma'am," she said, and was gone before Regina could ask any questions.

Regina let herself into her apartment. Her room-mate, Cassie, was watching NCIS on the TV. "You're home early," she said.

"Yes, and you won't believe why."

The next day, Regina hadn't forgotten, exited her building warily, on-guard for some kind of scam. She was a person to whom good things did not routinely happen.

And there at the curb was that old limousine and its unusual driver. The vehicle turned out to be blue, a deep midnight blue that looked purple in some light. There was gold or silver flake in the paint, maybe both. All Regina knew was that the paint job probably cost more than her last car. And the engine cowling looked like mother of pearl.

"Good morning, ma'am. May I take your things?"

Regina gave up her bag but kept her purse. She had been planning to ask some questions first, but the driver made this all seem so natural that she was ensconced in the car before she could - or wanted to - mount any protest.

"Where to today, ma'am?"

"Work," she said, and gave the cross-streets where the Denny's was located.

"Very good, ma'am."

The driver wore fingerless driving gloves, black kid leather. Her fingers, as far as they were visible, looked pale and skeletal. This morning her hair was tied back with a black ribbon into a loose pony tail that hung out the back of her driving cap. It still looked like straw, just orderly straw.

Regina summoned some courage, risked a question. "What's this all about?"

"Ma'am?"

"Why are you giving me rides? What's the angle here?"

"No angle, ma'am, but one can appreciate your skepticism. This must seem an unusual situation. It seems you have a benevolent sponsor, ma'am. They own the vehicle. I was sent to find you. I will be your driver for the next three days. My services are compensated by the sponsor. I am to accept no payment, tips, gifts or other forms of gratuity from you. Please relax and enjoy the ride. You're in good hands."

Regina thought this over. She checked the refrigerator, found a pair of foil-wrapped items that were probably breakfast burritos. An urn balanced on top contained coffee. Again, the ride was so smooth, the items barely wobbled. "Who is this sponsor?" she asked, peeling back foil. She sniffed. Burrito.

"I am neither permitted nor able to answer that question, ma'am. The sponsor enforces their confidentiality with quite expert secrecy. I have met only an intermediary."

"I don't understand. You don't know who you work for?"

"That is correct, ma'am."

She sipped coffee and nibbled on the burrito. It was as tasty as the roast beef had been.

"How did you know when I would be coming out of the building?"

"I did not know, ma'am. When I am not driving, I am waiting curbside to anticipate your potential needs. I will notify you in advance if this service is temporarily unavailable."

"You mean you waited outside all night?"

"No ma'am. I waited an hour and then came back at six-hundred hours."

Here was the first slip in the driver's language. Probably a veteran, maybe a cop. Regina was of an age to have some good reasons to not trust cops. She was just a little girl when her parents had marched at Selma, but she kept her ears open and listened to the stories. Her dad's busted nose hadn't been an accident.

They were almost to the restaurant. Time for questions was running out. Although, because of the directness of her travel, she would be as early for work as she was early getting home last night. "So, you wait outside for me, drive me where I want to go?" The driver indicated yes. "So, where all will you take me?"

"Ma'am, I will take you wherever you want to go that can be reached by car."

"Can I take this second burrito?"

"Yes ma'am, the food is always yours to do with as you wish. Any leftover food is donated to the homeless; the sponsor is clear that nothing is to be wasted. If you have preferences, please do indicate them, and we will attempt to accommodate you. Otherwise we will attempt to anticipate your needs as best we can."

"We?"

"Sorry, ma'am. I cannot discuss this matter in more detail, only assume one means 'we' in the royal sense. The sponsor will never directly communicate with you, but I have been asked to convey their wishes that you enjoy their largesse and hospitality."

"Don't tell me you're royalty?"

"No ma'am, only in elocution, and that only aspirationally. If I may, ma'am, it is in my contract."

"I only graduated high school," Regina said, "and not at the top of my class, if you follow me. I'm sure I don't always understand what you say."

"Yes, ma'am. We're here, ma'am. Shall I wait for you here?"

"You mean, wait in the parking lot all day? I won't get off work until four."

"Would you like me to come back at that time?"

Regina thought she had been clear. "That would be fine," she said. "You said I can take this? You don't want it?" meaning the burrito.

"Of course, ma'am. I do not eat."

Regina did not attend closely to this comment. "And what if I asked for some salmon pate or some caviar for the ride home?"

"Of course, ma'am. We will endeavor to accommodate your preferences."

"It's going to be a good day."

"Yes ma'am."

The driver let her out, carried in her bag for her. Her co-workers gaped, but Regina felt good for the first time in, well, as long as she could remember off-hand.

She walked into work with her head high and her back straight. Yes, it was going to be a good day.

The driver came to meet her promptly at four, take her things. She ignored Regina's companions, efficiently stowed her and her things in the car, got into motion. Regina noticed for the first time that the windows in back were tinted out, affording her complete privacy. Her co-workers gawked from the front doors and the day's few remaining customers stared at the car from their window seats.

"Home, ma'am?" said the driver.

"No," Regina said, suddenly inspired. "You know, it's a pretty night, not even dark yet. You know anyplace pretty?"

"Of course, ma'am. Cheyenne Mountain State Park is attractive and will not be crowded this time of the season. If you like, it also affords nice views of the city lights as evening sets in."

"That will be fine, just fine," she said, increasingly pleased. Cop or no cop, the driver was certainly efficient and accommodating. She looked in the fridge, found a cocktail glass of caviar, a small plate of crackers, a tiny spoon. A little glass dish of paté. Also a pint of Haagen-Dazs ice cream.

"I took the liberty of adding some pecan ice cream to your repast, ma'am. I hope you don't mind. Most people, when they try caviar for the first time, find it to be an acquired taste and need a palate cleanser."

She was right. Regina ate some of the salty black eggs on one of the crackers and found it to be bitter, unpleasant. She ate more than she wanted just to be contrary. Then she was forced to concede the Haagen-Dazs had been a good call, thoughtful even. The pâté was pretty good, and she ate some of that.

"You got my back, don't you?" she told the driver. "I don't even know your name. What should I call you, anyhow?"

"If it pleases you, you can simply call me 'Driver.' I have no other name of any importance."

"Well that's mighty mysterious, but suit yourself, Driver." They were climbing up now into the foothills, engine whispering, smooth as could be. Regina caught some glimpses of the white rectangle of light that marked the low entrance to Cheyenne Mountain Air Force Base, that great mountain vault reminiscent in her mind of places Dwarves might live in a fantasy book.

"Yes, ma'am," the driver offered. "Indeed, I am here to look after your interests to the extent they coincide with my duties. I hope to be of the best service that I may."

"Were you a cop or a soldier?"

"One might say I was both in my way and in my time, ma'am. But now I merely drive the car."

"You don't seem to have any accent. Where you from?"

"Ma'am, that subject is complicated for someone like me. I do not have a simple or cogent answer. Many places, but no place really. Again, the answer is of no real consequence."

Personal questions did not seem to be getting Regina what she wanted, so she switched tracks. "What sort of car is this, anyway?"

"It started life as a 1939 Daimler saloon. The engine is original to the automobile, with some minor modifications such as a fuel injector to manage the altitude changes inherent to Colorado driving. The frame and body have been modified extensively for style and function, including a substantial stretch and custom interior. I hope you find the ride comfortable and even. I have never driven anything so smooth."

There was almost emotion in her voice as she said this last. She found a good spot to pull over, turned the car so that Regina could watch the city start to light up as the last of the sunshine left the sky. The mountains made the horizon high, brought on dusk early, especially this close and especially in winter. The evening was clear but not too cool, and Regina had a sudden impulse to get out and look at the stars.

Her door opened. She had not noticed the driver get out and come around. Must have been woolgathering. She hopped out as though it were completely natural for this gaunt stranger to hold her door or read her mind. The view of the stars was completely worth it.

After a few minutes, the driver pointed out a comfort station behind them. "If madam needs it," she said. Regina did.

Not long later, safely ensconced in the limousine again, she wondered aloud, "If you were me, Driver, where would you ask to go?"

"Ma'am, if I may say, one suspects you wish to explore the limits of this arrangement, to do everything all at once. But I will come around for you again tomorrow, and the following day, and so forth, until the contract has elapsed. You have plenty of time to rest, relax, and think how best to fully avail yourself of the services you have been offered. To that end, I would elect to go home."

"I like that advice, Driver. Take me home, please."

"Of course, ma'am."

"I don't have to work tomorrow. Maybe I'd like to go someplace special."

"What time should I collect you, ma'am?"

"Let's get an early start. Make it eight o'clock."

"Of course, ma'am."

There was no more discussion that night.

"Good morning, ma'am," said the driver from curbside. The car sparkled in the morning light, as though it had been there gathering dew through the hours of darkness. She opened the door for her client.

"I've decided where I want to go," said Regina. "First to a flower shop. And then up to Denver."

"At once, ma'am," said the driver. "We took the liberty of preparing you a fruit compote for breakfast, and some fresh crescent rolls."

"They look delicious," she said. And they were. She decided against pursuing the "we" question again, being preoccupied with her own business for now.

At the flower shop, Regina bought all of the day-lilies she could afford. That turned out to be about three dozen. The driver helped her arrange them around the cab where they wouldn't shift around - not that anything seemed to shift around much in there - and then returned to her station.

"What part of Denver, ma'am?"

"Hm?"

"What part of Denver are we going to, ma'am? Our choice of route depends on our final destination."

"Fairmount Cemetery."

"Very good, ma'am." The driver gave no impression of any emotional reaction. She just drove the car.

The ride was as always smooth and stately. The old Daimler was not fast. They stayed off the highway as much as possible, but some driving on the interstate was essentially inevitable. The car floated along in the right lane, newer cars zipping past as though the Daimler were standing still. Some drivers beeped their horns in approval, many slowed to get a better look. Regina was self-conscious for a while, then remembered the tinted out glass. All the passing drivers would see was their own reflections.

She checked the carafe balanced on the refrigerator, wondering for the first time exactly what kept it perched there. It never shifted an inch, half an inch, even when they went up a steep incline into the passes. Never even appeared to tilt. There was coffee, piping-hot. A bit rich for her taste, but she supposed she could get used to it. She drank sparingly. At her age, coffee just went right through her, and she was still a touch shy about telling the driver she needed to toilet.

Even at their stately pace, the road wore away beneath their tires. Monument was in the rearview, then

Larkspur, then what seemed like a thousand miles of open range. Castle Rock loomed, swallowed them up for a few minutes, then joined the rest of the distance in the rearview mirror. Soon enough, there was Denver ahead.

The driver took the first opportunity to get off the highway as they were creating a minor traffic jam. They skirted through a newish neighborhood along the Front Range, full of giant houses called 'daylight ranchers' by estate agents and 'McMansions' by common folk. Everything was gray and somewhat similar. Regina imagined being rich, living in a neighborhood like this. *How,* she wondered, *would I ever find my own house? I'd have to plant a cherry tree, or something else that could blossom to point the way.* Not that such good fortune was ever likely to be her lot. *God is good,* she told herself reflexively. *God is good.*

The newish neighborhood faded away into foothills, and then an older neighborhood took its place. Houses both smaller and larger, but each with their own character. Some Victorian survivors, eccentric holdouts that were new long before the Daimler was conceived. And then, suddenly, walled off with high evergreen bushes, the cemetery.

It never occurred to Regina to wonder how the driver found this place. Driver seemed to never look at a map or an atlas and there was no obvious navigation system in the car. When the car pulled up alongside the right series of plots though, she had to ask. "How did you know just where to go?"

"This was high on the list of probable visits, ma'am."

"I don't understand."

"A good driver anticipates the wishes of their client, ma'am. Perhaps I can help you carry your flowers?"

"No," she said. "I need to do this myself." She had to take three trips, back and forth. The grave was about two hundred yards from the curb, and the ground was soft and damp. The well-tended grass kept it from being muddy. Really, the place was parklike, which made her happy. Davy was gone, could not appreciate the beauty all around him now, but nevertheless she remembered how much he liked running and playing in the park. His short life over so quickly, so quickly. On the second trip she started to tear up. By the third, grief flowed freely.

She remembered the first time Davy had seen a lily, before he was even old enough to proclaim his wonder. It was in his eyes, though, in his grasping hands. His momma let his hair grow out and it formed a halo around his head. Everyone who saw him told him what great hair he had. It was like a lion's mane, though he was too young to be much of a lion. *Still just a cub. Just a baby. My baby's baby.*

She placed the flowers around his little headstone. Even back then, things hadn't been so good. His little life deserved more than the cheap bit of rock marking his place in the soil. The flowers helped. It didn't look like anyone had come by recently. There were no older flowers to sweep away, little evidence of human activity except that the grass was mown. At least the church took good care of the place. Grass, trees, birds, sometimes rabbits, all profligate life in this place of loss.

A candy wrapper marred the view, caught in a tree not too many steps away. She wandered over there, snatched it down, stuffed it into her purse.

She wished there were a bench to sit on, some place she could rest and think and feel her sadness undistracted by the insistent demands of the mortal coil. Her feet hurt and her back ached and the damp soaked into her stockings. But she stood the best she could, did her thinking with one hand resting on the cheap stone. *If I had a thousand dollars, I'd fix him up something better, if his momma would let me.* And there was the rub, the real rub. *Not my daughter, not no more, justhis momma.*

Time passed irresistibly. She had done all she could here. She didn't feel better exactly, but maybe she felt worse in a way that mattered. She plodded back towards the car, saw a hearse pulling in at the front gate, three more limousines behind it. A procession. Always more customers, and never mind the economy. Less than an hour had passed since they arrived.

God is good, God is good.

Soon enough, she climbed into the back of the car, with a little help from the driver. "Home, driver," she said.

"Of course, ma'am."

God is good, God is good.

Another day, another ride.

"Where to, ma'am?" asked the driver.

"Church, if you please."

"Very good, ma'am. Which church?"

"I'm sure it doesn't matter. Where do you go?"

"I am what you would call 'lapsed,' ma'am."

Regina nodded. "I guess you could say I am, too. I never turned away from God, no, but I stopped going to His house. Sometimes I feel like He turned His face away from me. It's hard to accept at times that His plan involves pain for you, the suffering of children."

"Yes, ma'am."

"Seems you know a lot about me. Do you know where I used to go?"

"Yes, ma'am."

"And do you have enough gas to get us there?"

"Yes, ma'am."

"I'll assume it was 'high on the list of probably visits.' Then let's go, shall we?"

"Yes, ma'am."

The drive was a long one, more than a couple of hours. Regina fell asleep on the drive, lulled by the motion of the car, the gentle road noise, the silent honesty of her driver. When she woke up, dry-mouthed and aching in the neck, the old church was looming up on her left. The driver turned across traffic efficiently. Other cars made way for the stately old Daimler.

She parked efficiently also. Wherever the Daimler went, good parking always seemed to be available. Even if it were not, Regina supposed she would be dropped off curbside. "Rock star treatment" was the phrase these days. She found herself wishing they might have parked further away. She was suddenly not eager to go back into that place.

She said so. "I'm suddenly in doubt as to whether this was a good idea. It was a nice nap, but now that it comes to it, my nerves are sapping the strength from my knees."

The driver responded, "Yes, ma'am." Somehow, it was less than helpful - but, in a way, also very, very helpful. It gave her space to think in. Simple acceptance without judgment.

"It's judgment that leads me here, to this place now, today," she finally said. "And it's because of that judgment that I don't really want to go inside. And it's because of judgment that I suppose I have to do it."

"Yes, ma'am."

Driver still sat patiently in the driver's seat. The engine, off, ticked gently as it cooled, another few dozen miles of history sounding off in those ticks.

"I suppose we have come all of this way," Regina muttered, and then Driver was there, opening her door. Was there any other way she could be there before the intent had been voiced all the way?

Regina clambered out of the car feeling like an old woman. It had been comfortable to get out of before, just the right height, but now seemed too low for her bones. "I expect there is more gravity here than elsewhere," she murmured.

Driver gave her obligatory response: "Yes, ma'am." Incongruously, she also offered, "I've been instructed to assist you in whatever manner seems needful."

She clambered to the door of the place as she had clambered from the car: old and tired, heavy. *It's only my heart that is heavy*, she thought, and kept on trudging.

Through the overly heavy oak and glass doors. Along the hallway, decorated with placards shouting psalms, with the pious artwork of children, with pictures of parishioners in far-off places. Missions to Asia and to Africa. Good Works, all of them. Yes, those folks got Bibles - but they also got electricity, running water, a few strong backs to dig irrigation trenches.

My back hurts, she thought distractedly, sullenly.

In the main chapel, a man she didn't know stood on a small stage talking to a group of people dressed in their best funeral black. The women were all crying, one outright sobbing. The men held their women's hands and sat with straight backs. The speaker was a White fellow in a seersucker suit, shiny at the knees and elbows. He was too tall and too thin, bent over a little at the hips. The folks gave him their most rapt attention, even through their tears and stoicism.

"He's gone on to his rest now," the man said, "And that is good. All our lives are suffering, his more than any of ours. God saw fit to try him with disability, to afflict him with retardation. He surely never wanted to be a burden to anyone, and surely he suffered each and every day of his life."

"That's not right," Regina wanted to say. "Being different doesn't hurt. It's being *treated* different that hurts." But she held her peace.

"Mark was innocent, in a way. He was not born into sin as the rest of us are. God blesses fools and little children, holds them innocent; Mark could not know God, or good, or evil, or sin. But it is from sin that he was afflicted. We are all sinners."

"Amen," said the mourners.

"The world is full of sin. Only one man was ever born perfect.He gave His life for us, to wash away the blood of our sin, but only when we die and join him at his right hand. Until then, we strive for impossible grace. We cannot know God, or grace, or good, any more than Mark could. The difference is that we know it, that we are accountable for it. And that God will judge us for it. And from this judgment, from this world of sin and fallen-ness, come the poor ones like Mark: the broken, the disfigured, the afflicted, the tormented.

"One day, after Megiddo, we'll all be born again into perfect grace, just as it was in the Garden." Some murmurs of approval greeted this pronouncement. "Then there will be no disability, no madness, no retardation, no sin. Until that day, we bear these burdens.

"Today and ever after, Mark and his loving parents are freed of his burdens. May he find peace at the right hand of our Lord Jesus Christ. Let us pray."

"Sister Regina? Is that you? I thought it was a ghost, a Holy Ghost, come back to haunt me!"

The pastor had popped out into a hallway behind her like a magician. What had alerted him to her presence? Perhaps her too-heavy footfalls. "Yes, it's me, Francis."

Francis did not correct her, and looked only briefly crestfallen at not being addressed in the style of pastor. "Welcome home. You've been away so long. I am so, so glad to see you again." He started to lead her down the corridor, towards his office. She knew that office well. He had counseled her a great deal once

"Who was that man?" she asked when they were far enough away not to disturb the service.

"The deceased had some family from out of town. They brought their pastor. Daniels, his name is. Interesting fellow. Likes just to be called Daniels, military-fashion. But what is it we can do for you? When you left, you gave us the impression it was permanent - not that we are unhappy if you have decided to change your mind."

"I don't know what I came for," she said, and that was right. Nothing more honest might have escaped her lips at that time. "I'm afraid I'm not so glad to see you. I feel like you are judging me again, even though you've scarcely said a word as yet." Even so, she put her hand on his arm and they walked this way down the stairs. He ducked to avoid a low rafter. She didn't have to.

"God judges," said the pastor. "You heard Daniels. But come, come sit down with me. We'll have some tea, and you can catch me up on what has been happening in your life."

He was so solicitous she could scarcely refuse. Minutes later, she found herself in a dreary little office under the church, sipping weak tea with lemon and spilling out the story of her life since Davy. A divorce, a lost job, a lost daughter, loss compounding loss.

"We live in such a sinful world," Francis intoned when it was all out there. "God is with you through all these trials."

She knew then it had been no mistake to come back to this place. "That's what you said before," she said, "and it is why I stopped coming. Daniels. They didn't have to bring him all the way in from wherever they came from. That was the same speech, more or less word for word, you gave us about Davy when he... when I... when he passed." She folded her hands in her lap, wishing for a purse to clutch to hide her white knuckles. "Davy, he was just a baby. He still is, here in my heart. My baby's baby, my baby. He didn't die for sin. She didn't stop calling me for sin. I can't believe that, and I can't believe in you. Thank you for the tea. You know, it's very cold in your office. You should consider warming it up a little bit."

I have sinned, she thought on her way out. The pastor was saying something, not letting go, trying to rationalize. *I have sinned, but we are all sinners. This much is true. The Bible starts with 'thou shalt not kill' then says who we must kill: Canaanites and witches to start with. We cannot know the mind of God and so we must sin. But they blamed me for Davy. They blamed me, my soul, for Davy. It was just a mistake. Anybody could have made a mistake.*

"Yes, ma'am," said Driver at the car, although Regina hadn't said a word yet, just sat silently in the back. Her back hurt worse and worse until they were well away from the church.

In her dream, the car had a Northstar V8. Also in the dream, her back didn't hurt. That was amazing, and she almost cried. The lack of pain felt like something positive rather than a mere absence of something, like joy or elation over an absence of sorrow. *I never want to wake up,* professed some hidden recess of her life that knew she was dreaming.

She was asking a salesman about the car. "It has a 13:2 compression ratio," he said. That seemed to make sense in the dream. Like so many things in dreams, it would lose its meaning later. The salesman's name was Daniels. It said so on his blue work shirt. He was too thin and his hair wafted around in the breeze like dandelion fuzz.

"Speaking of compression," someone said. "You should stand up straight."

"What?"

It was a weird little person, not identifiably male or female, child or adult. It had hair that was always changing, skin that wasn't easy to categorize as black or white. It stood on a yoga mat. One foot was on the mat, the other pressed against its own leg, and its hands were pressed together over its head. Regina had never tried yoga. It looked uncomfortable.

"I said, stand up straight. It's all bowing you over. No need for that. Align your spine to the Sun and the Earth. Your spine is on a string, and your head is hung from the Sun, and stand up straight."

"Do I know you?"

"I should think so," said the being. "I am with you always. I am with everyone. Most folks don't choose to talk to me, though."

Not God, she thought. God doesn't do yoga. Francis had been sure yoga was blasphemy somehow, but she could never piece it together how for herself. So no, not God. That made sense in the way such logic does in dreams. She knew it then, what this thing was. "Sorrow," she said. "You're sorrow." You're Sorrow? Your sorrow?

"Close," it said. "I am the Star of Sorrow."

"Oh," she said. And then she noticed another be-ing, another presence. It was hard to see. It was more than one place at a time, squamous and shifty. Dark in the darkness, light in the light. "And that?" she asked, dread suddenly in her heart.

"You know who that is too," said the Star of Sorrow.

And it came to her that this was the Star of Blood, of Pain.

"Are you not the same thing, then?"

The two stars chuckled, and she awoke.

Her back hurt as bad as ever now, a shock after the painless dream. Some of the dread of the dreamscape remained, and Regina thought she would welcome all of the dread back if she didn't have to feel the pain coursing through her body. Most of her dreams slid quickly away, but this one lingered. For a while, at least half of the long drive home, she wondered which Star was driving the car.

The fourth day. Regina knew she had today and tomorrow and this strange blessing would be out of her life. *So what do I do with it?*

For now, all there was to do was pack up her things and go to work. So she placed her keys in her purse, a change of clothes in a bag, along with sneakers for whatever would happen later. Waiting tables was hard on her feet. Then she left, making sure to listen to the door to know it was shut all the way.

Down stairs. Three flights. At least they were inside stairs, not outside ones like pricier apartments had now. Missing Joe, she trudged down. *Joe was always good to me.* And then into the parking lot.

Regina didn't look up to see if the Daimler was there. She knew it would be. Something about Driver made her know it, made her know Driver would always be exactly where she said she would be, and exactly when.

"Ma'am, I'll take your bag for you."

Regina gave up her bag, allowed herself to be stowed in the back of the limousine, now hardly seeing the soft leather and fine wood. "What good is it?" she said.

"Ma'am?" said Driver from the front seat. The engine came alive, hardly a vibration marking the moment through the cabin and floor.

"All of this luxury. What good is it, Driver?"

"I don't know, Ma'am. I think the owner of the vehicle feels the same way."

Regina looked for Driver's eyes in the rearview mirror. Driver watched the road, though. "You said you never met... him?"

"True," Driver said. "But I spend a lot of time driving around with not much to do but think. And I think, this car must have a value of over a million dollars. And I know what I am paid to drive it, a not insubstantial sum. The owner is a person of means, ma'am, who eschews this particular luxury."

Regina thought, her attention drifting off the rearview mirror and out the window. Town slid by outside, clean and orderly, green in the morning light. Ahead, the mountains glowed pink in the peculiar light of sunrise.

Whoever owns the car is looking right now at that same sunrise. The thought came with no emotions, no rush of revelation, no comfort.

"You will have to decide for yourself, ma'am," Driver said.

"What?"

"What good such luxury is, ma'am. You will have to decide. We are almost at your destination now."

"It's too early for work," Regina said. "I keep planning for how long it would take by bus. I still have a whole hour to waste and I don't want to waste it there."

"Very good, ma'am. Where else, then?"

"I don't know. Liquor store, I suppose. All the money I'm saving on food, I can have me a glass of wine tonight."

Driver signaled a left turn past the highway, u-turned back over the overpass. Moments later she pulled the car into a space in front of a liquor store. Bottles of wine glowed yellow in the windows.

Regina stepped out when Driver opened her door. She shuffled into the shop, the bell tinkling overhead. The register was unmanned. She walked past it, deeper into the shop where the lighting was not so good. The floor was grimy off-white tile, not mopped lately. Sand crunched underfoot from a recent snow.

I haven't bought wine in so long, I don't know what I'm even doing. She looked around for someone to help. There was nobody, though. So Regina picked up a bottle of white that was in her price range, with a picture of a fanciful angel on the label, and carried it to the register.

There was a bell at the counter. *A bunco bell*, Regina's mind told her, remembering better days. Bunco night, cards with girlfriends, whoopie pies. The bell rang with a high, clear sound.

But nobody came.

Maybe I should just leave cash on the counter...

Finally, a sound from the back of the store, a door to a stockroom. Someone came through. A man, tall, head covered with a ski mask.

"Good morning. Can you help me?" Regina said.

And she knew already that he wasn't there to help her. His hands were sticky with blood. He had a little purse-sized bag she recognized as a cash deposit bag. And in his other hand, he held a butcher knife.

"Oh," Regina said. "Oh."

The man turned to look at her, gray eyes hazy with emotion – fear, panic. He raised the knife and stepped forward. "I wish you hadn't seen this," he said in a toneless voice.

He took another step forward.

And the bell over the door tinkled again.

"Ma'am, I'd advise leaving the wine and stepping outside."

"Driver?"

"Yes, ma'am."

"He has a knife. I can't leave you here with him."

"I'll be fine, ma'am," Driver said. She held the door and Regina stepped through, out into the cool pink day.

She felt like a coward, less than nothing, leaving that woman to fight her battle – but also very grateful. She looked around for a payphone but, of course, there weren't many of those left anymore. Everyone had cell phones now, smart phones with GPS in them and all the databases in all the world. Great, unless you didn't have one and wanted to call the cops.

Another car pulled into the parking lot. A little white pick-up truck on giant tires. A guy started to slide out, saw Regina standing there wringing her hands.

"Something up?" the man said.

"In there," Regina said, pointing to the door. She went back to wringing her hands. "Murder."

"Shit." He fumbled around in his pockets for one of those smart-phones. "Shit. How do you call 911 on one of these things?"

Regina left him to sort that out and went back into the store. *God is good, God is good.*

The man in the ski mask lay sprawled on the floor, blood seeping through the wool where his nose was. Driver sat on the floor a short distance away, her right leg on the other side of the man's body, her trouser leg empty.

"What?" Regina said reflexively, trying to process the scene.

"Ma'am, perhaps you could pass me my leg? This gentleman managed to kick it out from under me."

"Excuse me?"

"My leg, ma'am. It is a matter of some dignity. And I imagine there is a telephone in the back room, if you can stand the sight of blood. We should obtain medical help for this gentleman and his presumed victim as quickly as possible."

The leg. It was a prosthesis. Regina picked it up, trying to not touch it as much as possible, and handed it to Driver. "That's really your name, isn't it?" Regina said. "Driver."

"First lieutenant, U.S. Army, ma'am. The phone?"

"Got it covered," said the man from the parking lot, jingling into the store. He saw Driver fumbling with her leg, looked away as though he'd seen her in the toilet. "I'll check the back."

"Ma'am, it looks like you are going to be late to work today."

"Here. I'll help you up." Regina put out a hand and helped Driver to her feet. "I guess we ought to wait for the police to show up."

"Dignity," Driver said.

"Yes, I can see how a lady showing more of her leg than she meant to--"

"No, not my dignity now, ma'am. The answer to your question of earlier. The use of so much luxury is dignity."

Regina leaned against the counter. From the back room came the sounds of retching. "You've been so tight-lipped to now. Given me space to think in. A strange kind of solitude, really, a quiet place. With no roommate, no traffic noise, so little conversation. And now you're just about chatty."

"Yes, ma'am. At this time I think you have seen for yourself and there is no harm in venturing an opinion." Driver leaned too, suddenly favoring that artificial limb more than previously.

"Dignity," Regina said, trying the word out. "Dignity is something we carry with us, isn't it?"

"Perhaps," Driver said. "I felt undignified on the floor with my vulnerability showing. My... unwholeness?"

"And I feel undignified on the bus, watching cars go by... Fifty-eight and I have a roommate. And sometimes I have to pay for groceries on a food stamp card."

Now Driver offered no opinions, no eye contact. She seemed to be mentally inventorying the wine all around.

"Well, he's dead," said the guy from the parking lot, coming back from the stock room. "Stabbed in the neck, bled out all over the floor."

"You're tracking blood," Driver said, not looking.

Then the police arrived and there was no more talking, not between Driver and Regina.

Regina reclined in the back of the car. The whole day was gone, used up on police statements, interviews with the press, and a long conversation with her shift manager about whether being involved in a murder investigation qualified as no-showing for a shift. Now winter darkness curled around the car and a few flakes of snow drifted listlessly in the air.

"What would you do?" Regina said.

"Please clarify, ma'am." Driver was back to her unflappable self, steady and calm.

"One more day. Today was wasted. Tomorrow is the last day I have this largesse, as you called it once. What would you do? Go to work as usual? Maybe do something else? In the end, what good is dignity, after all?"

Driver was quiet so long Regina thought she would not answer at all. But then she did. "I was a logistician. Supply master. Counted things – loaves of bread, bombs, bullets, shoelaces. Set up storage, resupply lines, routes. Scheduled people to unload things as they arrived, to drive trucks, whatever. In Afghanistan.

"One day I was out with a convoy looking to secure some warehouse space, a staging area for incoming materiel. The trucks they gave us... the first few years, the body armor was weak, especially under the chassis. And that's where IED's strike, under the truck where the armor is flimsiest.

"I lost my right leg, my left breast, two ribs, about an acre of skin, and all of my dignity."

"I didn't mean," Regina started, but Driver cut her off.

"I know you didn't. You couldn't, ma'am. But I lay in a bed, what was left of me, for three months. That was just the beginning of my recovery. I laid there in a paper robe. I pissed through a catheter. A nurse had to take away my urine in a bag, and my feces, too. Most of my intestines stayed in that wrecked truck. When I had a period, a nurse had to deal with it. I was completely broken, completely dependent. I couldn't even eat. I still don't eat. I take in food directly into my stomach through a PEG tube."

The car continued for some time more, so quiet Regina could hear herself breathing.

"I'm sorry," she said at last.

"Sorrow is of no purpose," Driver replied. "Women tend to apologize to grease the social wheels for things that are not their fault. But there is no need. I found something in that bed, with its antecedents in the truck, in the explosion. Some of me made it out, you see. The others in that truck, they all died. Instantly killed, turned into... but I came through. I lived to suffer. The pain, the indignity. And I found that dignity is a quiet thing. It always lives inside, right next to your heart.

"You're always well, Mrs. Polk. But sometimes life is so loud and confusing and hurried that you forget that. You get caught up in life and forget you are alive."

"One more day," Regina repeated then. "One more. What would you do with it?"

"I would live," Driver said.

Another cold morning. Regina's breath fogged up the window glass, obscured the world outside.

"To work today, ma'am?" Driver offered.

"Well, let's say I had a little chat with my shift manager. Turns out she needs me more than I need her, you know? And after being involved in a violent crime, it doesn't seem unreasonable to skip a day. Wouldn't you say?"

"Yes, ma'am. Where, then?"

"Denver, I think." Regina cracked open the mini fridge. A small bowl of fresh fruit waited, a tiny fork next to it.

"Address, ma'am?"

"I think you know the address," Regina said.

"That may be true."

"It wasn't my fault. I didn't kill him. It was an accident. A busy street, a distraction, then it was over. All over but for the crying, as they say nowadays. And him just a baby. Well, someone had to be to blame. I've carried that, shouldered it, oh, these ten years now."

"What about forgiveness?" Driver said.

"Suppose I've no more use for it, Driver. I can't ask my daughter to forgive me, and I can't forgive myself. I have to live with it. Dignity isn't found in letting go of guilt but in shouldering it. Of being big enough to carry it."

Driver was silent. Regina slowly got the sense that the silence was heavy, pregnant with something.

"Driver?"

"They all died," Driver said. "I was in charge of that convoy. My call, my team. They died because of me. I should have died, too."

"But you didn't," Regina said.

"So I have to live. Anything else is a disgrace." She sobbed, an incongruous sound from a stoic face, in this leather-upholstered dream.

"I know," Regina said. "I understand now. It's a nice car, you know?"

"What?"

"The Daimler. It's a nice enough car. Beautiful. A work of art. A masterpiece, even. Your boss -- he just doesn't want it locked up in some garage someplace, gathering dust. He wants it out in the world, doing its job."

"Yeah," Driver said. Then she corrected herself: "Yes, that seems probable."

"Well, I've hid my light under a bush long enough, I suppose. Gathered dust. It's time to get out on the road."

Driver took a right, eased the car up to highway speed – as close as it would go. Outside, the sky spit icy little flakes of snow at the ground. Silence reigned inside the car while life happened outside in all its noisy glory. Trucks tore past at dangerous speeds, cars of every color, people in a hurry to get wherever they were going.

Larkspur slipped by unnoticed. Castle Rock. Then, south Denver. Driver took the turns with confidence, knowing the way, sliding the old car through neighborhoods like it belonged there. And then, at last, she pulled to a stop outside a house.

It was a 1950's property, a small house on a big lot. The yard was brown, having shed its summer color for winter hues. A single tumbleweed sat drying in the dead grass. The house had new vinyl siding, a dull beige, and a jaunty green door.

"Here we are, ma'am," Driver said, letting the engine idle. She made no move yet to go around to open Regina's door.

Regina peered at the house through the foggy window. With one sleeve, she wiped away the condensation. There was a garage, and no cars in the driveway or on the street outside. "Who's to say she's even home?"

"This is the day," Driver said. "There won't be other days. Today might not be perfect, might not be the best possible day, but it is the day we have."

"Yeah." But Regina still didn't move, either.

Drapes moved aside in one of the front windows. A young face peered out, full of curiosity, eyes wide. Then the drapes opened all the way and there she was, picking up her little girl.

"I didn't even know. She never told me. Oh, the lost time..."

And then the door opened, Driver standing there by the curb in her cap and jacket, clothes flapping in a December wind. There were tears on her face.

Regina climbed out, straightened her own clothes. *Stalling. Too old for any more stalling.* Then she said, "Take the day off, Driver. I think I shall stay here a day or two."

"How will you get home?"

"Oh, I shall find some way, sure. And Driver."

"Yes, ma'am?"

"Dignity isn't something you have or don't have, or something that lives in your heart waiting for you to be well. It's what you are."

Regina walked away, away from the old car and its strange driver and towards the house where her granddaughter lived with her daughter. She waved to the little girl through the window, then walked up to the door. Another moment of hesitation, just a moment, a passing weakness, and then she used the little brass knocker to tap on the door.

Jason Dias

Jason Dias is the author of the high fantasy, For Love of Their Children. His first love is science fiction.

Dias is a doctor of clinical psychology living in Colorado Springs, Colorado. He teaches college and writes incessantly, mostly for a New Domain.

Presently, he is working on a number of book chapters concerning psychotherapy and no fewer than four novels. And you can follow his work for *a New Domain* here:

http://anewdomain.net/author/jason_dias/

A Moon Divided

By Todd A. Walls

Part 1

The Colorado district of the Moon stood out like a drab scattering of boxes and towers sitting on a monotonous plain, which is to say not at all. A few settlements hypnotized visitors with colors and shapes, like Tsuki Tokyo, and a few dazzled with neon, like Lunar Vegas, but the majority were standardized colors and shapes, mostly gray. The Colorado Springs complex, where I lived, was so colorless it sometimes made a girl want to gouge her eyes out. I had moon fever—bad.

There were only a handful of buildings and antennas on the surface; most of the Colorado complex was underground to protect people from radiation. Since there was no atmosphere to scatter the light, shadows were black in the vacuum. The nearest silhouette etched a razor-sharp curve at my feet, matching the nearby police dome. Sunlight carved the ubiquitous dust around me in distorted shapes like a mutant Thanksgiving turkey. I had never been claustrophobic on Earth, but here, the monochrome landscape drove me nuts.

Holding up a pressure-suited hand to block the glare of the sun behind the police dome, I peered into one such shadow, hoping to find my inside man. My faceplate slowly lightened in response. The police dome was really the center of all city government, not just law enforcement. Even that symbol of authority was a sardine can of cross-training. Nobody had only one job on the moon.

The whole city only had a couple of full-time police officers. The rest were part-timers who worked as needed, which was rarely. Not a lot of crime on the Moon. Misdeeds mostly revolved around drunk and disorderly and the occasional petty theft.

Once you got over the novelty of being in space, it was a crappy place to live. Most women who ended up here were overachievers and far too straight-laced for my liking. There was a lunar-wide poker tournament going on, and gambling was my current lifeline to sanity. In a safety-obsessed world, I craved a touch of danger.

There, leaning against the police dome, lounged the shape of a pressure suit. A shock ran through me when I recognized the shoulder patch. It was a police shield. With a belly no suit could conceal, it could only be the police chief. I had been making money betting against Chief Kurc all week.

He raised an honest-to-god projectile gun, not the regulation stunner he would use in an official capacity. The gun was pointed at me. At his feet lay a convulsing body sucking vacuum through a shattered helmet, presumably my inside informant who had spiked the Chief's drinks with downers all week. My blood ran cold. Did a regular gun even work in a vacuum? With one final shudder, the newly minted corpse proved the point; it was as deadly as it needed to be.

The chief sighted his gun, bracing one hand with the other. It occurred to me that I'd never viewed a gun from this angle before. The barrel shrank to a surprisingly small circle, and the man behind it grew into a monster.

I rode a bull. Once. Eight seconds can seem like a lifetime. I hiked a volcano after college. Sat on a stick of dynamite all the way up into space, too. It suddenly seemed a tragedy that I never got to skydive. A hole formed in my chest in preparation for the bullet, and I realized that my heart was empty. No one would miss me much. More than anything else, that was the tragedy of this moment.

I'm not one to believe in miracles. Mathematically speaking, one-in-a-million coincidences are guaranteed to happen with clockwork regularity, but miracles require divine intervention and I don't think the universe cares enough to intervene.

Today, the universe delivered a doozy.

The Chief's midsection erupted into a geyser of blood droplets that arced in a wide slow-motion spatter. Several puffs of dust exploded from the nearby ground. The gun pulled a cartoon gag, seeming to spin in place while the Chief fell backward like an old oak tree, stiff, bounced off the dome wall and slid to the ground.

Crystals of blood were already forming around the gash ripped into his stomach. My radio came to life long enough for two words before going dead.

"Stupid. Dyke."

Breath thundered in my ears. It took a moment to realize it was my own. All I could think of was that I wasn't dead.

Turning and scanning the horizon, I saw nothing. No one.

Looking back at the chief, my throat locked up mid-gag. You don't throw up in a moon suit. You just don't. The entrails of my would-be murderer were oozing out into the lunar soil, puffing up like a grotesque balloon animal made by a demonic clown. The back of my throat stung from bile. I swallowed. Hard.

Crouching in my pressure suit, I looked at the hole in the Chief's suit, then clenched my teeth and squeezed my eyes shut while a wave of nausea bowled a strike in my midsection. Slowly, I stood and looked away before opening my eyes again. Facing death one minute and someone else's the next made me want to crawl into a hole. Then reality set in. Was there another shooter?

Scanning the horizon in all directions revealed nothing. Nobody was in sight. Not alive, anyway. *I don't know what happened, but everybody on the moon is so hypersensitive right now, I might not want DNA evidence on me. This could have been caused by a small meteorite, but it might as well have been a bullet.*

Training took over. I've been many things in my life, student, cosplayer, dungeon master, math teacher, and I even spent a couple of years as a crappy private eye. Now I'm Jaz Moser, semi-famous as a lottery winner, astronaut, and lunar resident. I may have a weakness for taking chances, but I'm no murderer.

Investigator reflexes kicked in. How guilty would I look? I examined the circumstances.

Means?

Maybe. I don't have a weapon on me, but all it takes is a hole in a suit and the vacuum of space does all the damage. Odds are both bodies are still armed—not to mention what's probably an unregistered and illegal firearm lying in the dust. I got enough means for a dozen fucking murders.

Motive?

Duh. I got 200 Kays in the bank, won by one victim's losing at poker and the other victim's cheating. No hiding that shit now. Money is a common motive.

Opportunity?

I'm crouching here in the shadows with two bodies, the Mark and the Partner. It's a classic double-cross and disposal of witnesses. Come to think of it, that geyser of blood probably coated everything in sight with little droplets, including my suit.

Physical evidence tied me to the scene.

Means, motive, opportunity, and physical evidence.

I was screwed.

Part 2

Authorities already deported citizens whenever they got the chance because the competition for a posting on the moon was fierce, not to mention political. Colonizing the moon had been a messed up affair from the beginning.

At first, nations planted flags, claiming first come-first served. But imperialism was frowned upon. The

United Nations stepped in and divided the moon among all recognized nation-states. It was an over-politicized formula based on land area, population, and perceived historical victimhood.

Standing there, staring at the bodies, I was paralyzed with indecision. The authorities would evict me, sent me to Earth in handcuffs. Going back to Earth wouldn't be so bad, but not as a felon. They might even consider a punishment harsher than prison for killing the chief of police. I didn't want to think about it.

There was no time to hide the bodies. The tournament was finishing up for the day. I could hear a lot of chatter on my suit radio on the proximity band. Other people with moon fever or claustrophobia would be suiting up and wandering out on the surface soon.

What can I do?

Connections between settlements were mostly underground tunnels. All of them would be locked down within minutes of discovering the bodies. Overland could buy me some time. With supplies, I might hide out for a few days, but the moon had satellite and GPS coverage as complete as that on Earth. Footprints in the lunar dust lasted for centuries. The only place I had a chance of hiding was inside.

But where could I go without being seen? Entrances were covered by security cameras. The Chief knew he was going to kill two people. What was his plan? He probably wanted to set this up to resemble a shootout between two criminals, both suits punctured. That's plausible. What was the Chief planning to do afterwards? He would want to distance himself from the crime scene. But how?

My eyes fell on a nearby maintenance hatch. We chose this meeting place because it was a blind spot for surveillance. Heedless of DNA evidence now, I rummaged in the Chief's outer pockets. There were two sets of keys, one of which was labeled, "Environmental Services. Do Not Duplicate." I also grabbed his RSA soft token and the gun—just in case. The gun had been modified with a large trigger guard to accommodate bulky suit fingers. The Chief had actually planned to use it in a moon suit.

You don't modify an illegal gun on short notice. What was he thinking?

Shoving the key into the maintenance hatch lock, I turned the key. *Phew!* It opened. Somehow, I didn't have enough elation for a smile. Locking the door behind me, I flipped my helmet light on to reveal rows and rows of batteries for the solar panels.

Along the far wall was an old manual airlock. There were no computer controls on it. This must have been one of the original buildings. No computer, hopefully, meant no electronic records of opening and closing. I opened the inner airlock door and left it open. Safety interlocks would prevent anyone from coming through from the other side.

I hesitated. Maybe I would be better off staying here until I had a plan. No telling what alarms I might trip inside the government building, and I knew no good place to hide. I had to think.

Digging around in lockers and crates, I found plenty of old rations, oxygen tanks, and tools. They had tossed everything old or outdated in here, since nothing was ever thrown away on the moon. Lift costs from Earth made this junk pound for pound more valuable than gold. Using the airlock as a temporary atmosphere, I could do suit and body maintenance as needed, which would be soon. Of all the wonderful inventions that made life on the moon possible, they still hadn't designed a decent catheter for female anatomy.

Now I needed a plan. First step was to fix the airlock door so that it couldn't be operated from the other side. The hinges resisted movement as I pulled it open. Old, and in poor repair as well.

Somebody's not doing their job. More than one, it seems, since routine inspections should reveal the shoddy maintenance. Maybe this chief was corrupt in more than one way.

I took stock. The equipment area was airless, less corrosion on equipment that way. I hated working in airless rooms, though, with a fat-headed suit. It was a limitation you just got used to, if you lived here.

That was the whole problem with the moon. Like people living on an island, people felt hemmed in with no place to go. It was called 'island fever,' or 'moon fever.' I was sorry I ever entered the lottery. Why I agreed to go into this extraterrestrial rat cage, I couldn't recall.

Many postings to the moon were determined by committees, then once chosen, through training, tests, aptitude, and desire. Affirmative action influenced some percentage of those postings. One in ten obtained a slot through political influence, and another one in ten from publicized lotteries.

Lotteries were the appeasement to the claims of nepotism, corruption, and eugenics. Lucky me, I was a lottery winner. I was the fairness factor and I probably should never have been allowed to set foot on that rocket. The only other ways to get to the moon were government service and a waiting list. Those waiting for permanent assignment were randomly chosen from all the other selection methods.

I sat on a dusty bench and shook my head. Three unlucky bastards were about to get a text message inviting them to the moon. I would consider them unlucky, but a lot of people wanted what I had to the point of obsession.

Three lucky bastards!

I sat up, grasping at any chance of a way out. That was a motive. Anyone on the waiting list had a motive. The scene from moments before replayed in my head. *…a geyser of blood…, …low gravity…, …puffs of dust exploding from the ground…, …dust settling…, intestines oozing out, puffing up like clown balloons…, …body slumping to the ground. Puffs of dust.*

Puffs of dust, like a scattering of meteorites. Small rocks orbited all over the solar system. That was no surprise, but rarely in clusters so close together.

If it was a small meteorite, it wasn't natural. Could one of those people on the waiting list somehow arrange for meteorites to hit the Colorado moon settlement? It's a wonder one of them didn't hit me.

Powering up a nearby maintenance tablet, I saw the previous user had not logged off. *So much for security awareness training. Someone should be more on top of these things.* A twinge stopped that train of thought. The person in charge of that was dead, now.

The date of the last command on the terminal was over three months ago, so this area wasn't used very often. On the other hand, using the computer now might draw unwanted attention. Instead, I pulled out my phone, hoping for a good signal through the structural and electrical interference. I had two bars.

As I was looking up some facts in astrophysics on the Moon's version of the Internet, I felt a vibration through my boots. I turned and there was a deputy sheriff peering through the maintenance hatch, still holding onto a key in the lock.

They found me.

Part 3

The deputy was Kelly Scott. She looked like the movie version of a deputy, too; the long-haired, long-legged beauty who never seems to advance the plot, but looks damn good in every scene.

I had dated her. A few times, anyway.

Our eyes locked in recognition; there was surprise, shock, and then suspicion. Kelly was a deputy investigating a double homicide, and I was standing right where the murderer ought to be.

Why did it have to be her? Of all the stupid luck.

At the same instant, she reached for her stunner and I dove for the open airlock.

Cursing my luck for the bodies being found so fast—along with my stupidity for not blocking the maintenance hatch—I started cranking the airlock door shut.

These manual doors are so freaking slow!

Somehow Kelly missed her first shot, impacting the doorframe about six inches from my head. I wanted to think there was some remnant of our intimacy that skewed the shot. Even if there was, I couldn't guess if the miss was from affection or anger.

Does she love me or hate me at this point? I never did figure out what happened, and why she was partying with those bitches from immigration.

I got the door slammed shut before another shot could get through, and started cycling air. After an eternity of waiting for pressure equilibrium, the Cycle Complete indicator changed from red to green. I turned another wheel to open the other side of the lock.

With a loud, rusty squeal, the inside door burst open. I left it open to block pursuit. The airlock wouldn't cycle while one side was open, and this was a manual door.

What now?

I had spent one night in this place after a few too many at Phantom Crater Brewery. The hallway led—I recalled—to a supply room, a couple of jail cells no bigger than a walk-in closet, and a duty desk for a guard. They never had a guard on duty.

Upstairs, there were a few government offices and a couple of administrative cubicles. Outside of business hours, the building might be completely empty. The structure wasn't very large, being one of the oldest ones.

The underground garage had to be somewhere to my right. That was the quickest way out. I hurried down the hallway to my right and opened the door at the end. Inside was a storage room full of vehicle parts and a spiral stairway down into darkness.

At the bottom of the stairs, I flipped on the light to reveal the old rover I sometimes saw around town. Refitted with a platform, it was mostly used as a cargo hauler around the Colorado Springs Annex, like a moon-style pickup truck.

What I hadn't expected was a moon bike. Fat mesh tires made of woven steel wire took up most of the bike, with an electric motor on each wheel and a gyroscope in the middle. It appeared functional, but with a homemade look about it. The welds were rough and still sported the black wounds of electrical arcs. There was a police shield decal on the side of the gyro unit, with the name Kurc painted below it.

"Woo! The chief's been holding out on us! This baby's too sweet to sit in a garage,"

There wasn't much crime, here. As far as I knew, the chief had committed the only extraterrestrial murder in history. There was no key, just three switches, two brakes, and one throttle. There were no gyro controls other than an on/off switch. Crude, but effective.

I sat astride the large electric motorcycle, checked that it was level, and flipped the gyro switch. There was a kickstand on both sides to maintain relative levelness while parked. If you turned on the gyro while the bike wasn't level, it would stay crooked until you adjusted for it, only I didn't see any adjustment controls.

Flipping on the front motor, I eased the throttle enough to pull up into the garage airlock. It was big enough for the truck and then some. I hopped off and punched the cycle button, but a display and a touchpad lit up. It wanted strong authentication. *Crap, this is one of the new upgraded security pads.*

Pulling out the RSA token, I punched in the chief's name and the rotating key shown in the window of the token. The key on the display changed every ten seconds, ensuring that only someone with the token device could authenticate as the chief. But it needed a PIN, too. PINs could be anywhere from four to eight digits, all numbers. I had a similar token for access to the construction office. On the Moon, I was just basic labor, a builder.

What would the chief have picked as his PIN? Let's see, he was big into poker, big enough to be in the tournament, anyway.

I punched in four ones, which would represent four Aces. The panel responded with a soft beep. No go. Three strikes and the panel would lock out for fifteen minutes. Somewhere, I was sure, an alarm would be going off as well.

Long enough for Kelly to figure out where I am and stun the bejesus out of me. So, it isn't four aces. What's the best poker hand?

I tried to figure out how a Royal Flush would be represented in numbers.

What is a Jack? An eleven? That would make an Ace a fourteen. That just doesn't sound right. Then there's a flush and a straight. A flush would be all even or odd numbers. That can't be it. A straight is numbers in sequence, but what numbers?

Then it hit me. I had studied all the players in this year's tournament. The chief's big win had been back on Earth, several years ago. What was his winning hand?

He won with an eight-high straight. That's it. Straight to the eight.

I pressed eight, seven, six, five, enter.

Beep. Strike two!

Three strikes and I'm a dead woman.

Just because most people used a four-digit PIN doesn't mean the chief did. The tourney final game is usually Texas Hold 'em. There are seven cards in play, but a player's best 5-card hand wins. The Chief's PIN should probably have five digits, and the cards would be laid out from low to high.

There were a lot of possibilities, but no time to mull them over. If I didn't get out of here fast, I'd be behind a different kind of locked door. I slowly — carefully — pressed, four, five, six, seven, eight, enter.

The airlock door closed behind me, and a pump sucked the air out. I hadn't realized I was holding my breath and exhaled in sync with the airlock. Two breaths later, my chest tightened again with anxiety. A peripheral display told me I was using oxygen at an accelerated rate. The suit had about an hour left and the nearest recharging station was behind me in the garage.

There's no way this ends well. I have to do something while I still have my freedom. But what?

The outer door slid sideways. A dirt ramp with concrete sides curved up and out of sight, like the ones I built in the newer areas of town. It would go up quickly to ground level, and I needed to know what I was doing before I came out into the sun.

The moon was divided among all nations of Earth, as well as a few non-nation ethnic groups. The United States' allotted area was further apportioned between state and federal land. Strangely enough, the habitable land area of Earth was not much larger than the total land area of the moon, so Colorado on the Moon was almost as big as Colorado on Earth.

Even with bleeding off its acreage to federal and world governments—not to mention the UN committee's opinion of fairness adjustments—Colorado's annex of the moon was still almost fifty thousand square miles, most of it unused. Despite all that space, I couldn't think of any place to go.

No time to sit around with my head up my ass. Once I start running, I can't stop.

The door started to close, signaling that someone inside was cycling the lock. I flipped the rear motor switch and gunned both motors. I must've thrown a bucket load of dirt back into the airlock as I peeled out all the way up the ramp.

As I exited the ramp up to level ground, I went airborne for about thirty feet. Low-grav jumps were magnified from what you expected growing up in Earth's higher gravity. I headed north between an observatory and the community center. Several people had come outside after the last poker hand of the day. One person pointed at me. Did they have an alert out already?

Of course, by now anyone could be on my tail. Kelly would have alerted all law enforcement, such as it was, plus all the volunteer deputies.

Darting between a dome and an antenna array, I broke free of the downtown area. There were a few remote buildings still ahead, but it would be smooth sailing up the crater to Rim Road.

After the initial thrill of powerful moonbike acceleration, my subconscious thoughts finally bubbled up to the surface. My brain was studying the problem of how the Chief had been killed. I had started on it before, but it would take a much more powerful computer than my smartphone to work out the probable roots of the equation. If I could figure it out, the answer might save my skin.

I need to get to CU-Moon in the Denver District. That's where I can figure this out.

On the Moon, the Colorado Springs and Denver districts are a bit closer together than they are on Earth. I only needed to go about ten miles.

Rocks and dust flew by faster than I had ever traveled off Earth. No amount of twisting in my seat would allow me to see if I was followed. Space suits have always been inflexible. All I could do was hope no one was gaining on me. Four empty bolt holes suggested that there was supposed to be a mirror on the handlebars.

It was dangerous, but I twisted the throttles all the way open on the undeveloped ground between districts. Most loose surface rocks near developed land had been harvested to make concrete, but the further away I got from civilization, the bigger and more numerous they became. Still, I couldn't imagine I'd managed to leave town without a tail.

Topping a small hill, I dodged to avoid a rock the size of a helmet. The straining gyroscope vibrated against my legs. I hoped it would hold up at this speed. An LED indicator on the dash started flashing.

The big Theophilus crater was dead ahead. Theophilus "F", the home of Moon Denver. Roads spiraled up the crater wall ahead. I went off road, hitting it straight on, momentum pressing me hard into the seat. I had no frame of reference for speed, but I was moving far faster than safety would normally allow. The dash had holes where dials and gauges should be, a kit bike that somebody never finished putting together.

The wall got steeper as I climbed. The tires, made of wire mesh, were wide and cross-treaded to grip the dust. Despite that, the bike was loosing traction, digging a rut into the lunar grit. That's the thing about electric motors: great torque. Those wheels kept on spinning, digging. Just as I thought it would stall, the wheels caught solid ground and catapulted the machine forward.

I popped over the rim. In this gravity I never even touched the Rim Road, flying over it and splashing down on the steep inner crater wall. Gathering speed down the hill, I headed directly for the Moon Denver Complex.

On Earth, Denver was skirted by the Rocky Mountains. Theophilus, the largest crater in Moon Colorado, surrounded the Denver moon complex in a jagged wall equally as majestic, if a bit less colorful, than the great

Rockies. It rose about eleven thousand feet above the domes of Moon Denver.

Moon Denver was almost ten times larger than the Colorado Complex, being the oldest of the settlements. It had one of the largest Helium-3 extraction ovens. The crater floor was near bedrock, attracting mining activity for rare earth elements.

In the center of the crater rose the shining gem and claim to fame of Coloradans everywhere: the great green dome of the Moon Denver Botanical Gardens. On the surface, the gardens represented a haven of biodiversity protected from any natural calamity that might take place on Earth. It provided about ninety percent of all pollinating insects for crops the moon over, like bees and butterflies.

Below the garden, so I had read, was the greatest seed vault of them all. Where better to protect the genetic treasure of heirloom species than deep under the Moon's surface?

My destination was just to the east of the garden. It was the Asimov High-Capacity Computing Center (AHCCC), right next to the Colorado University Moon campus.

Oh, no. Looks like somebody smacked a robotic beehive.

About a dozen beach balls rolled out across the smooth plain of the crater floor ahead. They weren't beach balls, of course, but the resemblance gave them the nickname. These specific robots were usually called bee balls, due to their distinctive black and yellow stripes. Functionally, they were designed for GPS mapping, mineral sampling, and crust density surveys. Mining bots.

Right now, they were, most likely, keeping me under surveillance. Wherever I went, they could follow and report back both my location and activities.

Then it occurred to me what was going on. I was a spectacle, like a fugitive high-tailing it down the 405 with a bunch of police cars on my ass. For the Moon, Moon Denver was a major city, and it was just in time for the evening news. Pulling out my phone, I punched up the news feed. My stomach sank.

On screen, I saw a close up of my face. I could read my own lips, and they were saying words people weren't supposed to say on public media.

Part 4

"Hey, gorgeous." My radio finally came back to life. It was Kelly's voice.

I answered, "I was never the gorgeous one, you know. Besides, I thought the whole moon was on radio silence."

"Silence? You kidding? The whole system is buzzing about the first murder in space, and this is a double. They'll be talking about this for decades. It's just you. We put your suit radio on remote lockdown."

"Hey. What if I had needed help?"

"No, Jazzy. We can hear you, but you can only broadcast on law enforcement channels, now. You just can't hear the normal bands."

The hint was clear. This was not a private conversation, and anything I said would be used against me in a court of law. Her concerned tone left me wondering if she was trying to protect me, though, in her own way.

The situation made more sense now. "Oh, so only the cops can hear me, and they voted you to talk me down off the ledge. I'm sorry to be such an embarrassment. Again. Did you follow me all the way to Moon Denver?"

I had been driving downhill, but the crater was almost flat at this point. The bee balls closed around me in a strange sort of escort. I could almost hear the behind-the-scenes discussion my question must have sparked. After about a minute, she answered.

"I'm about a half mile behind you in the municipal truck. Keeping up with that homemade crotch rocket has been a bitch, but my batteries'll last about ten times longer than yours. Why don't you slow down and let me catch up? You can tell me all about what happened, and we can figure out a way to help you."

It almost sounded like she was calling me a bitch, and I wasn't sure if I should be offended.

"Yeah, right. You'll help me into an electric chair, or a stroll to the hole at the very least."

The last time I saw her, Kelly was dancing on a table in a bar, thrusting her crotch over a dickhead's twenty-credit. I was no stranger to getting wild in a bar, but Kelly didn't answer my calls the next day. She had acted like she didn't know me for two days before, and I hadn't seen her since. She better not be saying I'm the bitch.

Kelly said, "You're just a person of interest at this point, but when you ran, we had to pursue. I had no choice. Are you saying you didn't commit any crime?"

"Come on, Kelly. You know I'm not the innocent type, but I sure as hell didn't kill anybody. I ain't stupid."

The radio went silent again. They were probably chatting about the best way to bag the cop killer. Reaching the outskirts of Moon Denver, I eased off the accelerator.

No sense in killing myself before they have a chance to light me up in the Chair.

The buildings here were decidedly more industrial in nature. Fewer domes. More blocky concrete. It was a mining town with a side order of education. If you flunk out of the University of Colorado Moon campus, at least you'd have a ready job in the mines. A lot of people do it the other way around, though, and work the mines to pay for school.

I moved into what passed for a downtown, here. The only way to tell was the dust had been swept into smooth areas. Dust gardens, I guess. To the left and right of the main path, they had put up signs, "Do not walk on the Dust."

"You gotta be shittin' me. What a bunch of idiots," I laughed. Then I remembered they were listening to me. I bit my lip. The whole world was watching and listening.

Anything I say can be used against me…

The true center of activity was underground. Topside was deserted. They were probably all sitting down there watching me on big screens in the bar. Feeling acutely self-conscious, I was glad when the computer center came into view. Waiting until the last second, I hit the brakes, expecting to slide up to the door in a very cool spray of dust.

Nothing happened.

Damned half-ass bike.

I had no brakes.

Part 5

What kind of idiot puts together a bike and leaves the brakes for last?

The answer was pretty obvious.

A dead one. And I might be joining him in a few seconds.

Scanning the area, I saw the door I had aimed for. On the moon, outside 'main' doors were not fancy like on Earth. It was just a simple door. Most intra-building travel was underground, and outside doors were not used a whole lot. The second floor was set back, smaller than the ground level, and covered by a clear dome. Several welded sculptures littered the yard, remnants of bored students with too much time on their hands.

I leaned heavy on the steering and aimed for the stairs to my left, leading to the second floor catwalk. Momentum fought the maneuver, and I slid into the turn, churning up a spray of dust through the dust gardens.

Being heavy and hard to come by, metal was used sparingly on the Moon. The stairs were narrow, made of thin steel bands welded in triangle shapes for strength and filled in with concrete. I should know—most of my jobs here had been in construction.

This was not an Earth bike. With the gyro, you can't lean into a turn. The gyroscope housing between my legs hummed and vibrated into the turn so strong, its screams gnawed into my thighs. A light on the dash turned yellow and then red in quick succession.

I gritted my teeth, gripped the handles, and braced for impact. It would be just enough of a turn. I was going to hit the middle of the stairs, but would they hold?

I got my answer in a cloud of debris, sort of. The fat front tire, being almost as tall as the bike, crushed the first few steps, throwing concrete shards in every direction. The welds in the embedded steel held up, though, and the demolished front tire climbed each step, absorbing as much energy as it could.

Despite my attempt to hold on through impact, I fell forward. My helmet's faceplate smashed into the dashboard, but my face didn't stop there. The rest is a blur of pain and disorientation.

Pressure suits are designed for safety. You don't think about it much, but inside the helmet is a web of fibers. If you stretch them too far, the fibers shatter and expand into a cushion. Once exposed to oxygen, the cushion decomposes into dust, and is cleared out by the suit's environmental system.

The next thing I knew I was looking up into Kelly's face through a splatter of blood. I was laid out on the catwalk on the second level, head in her lap.

"Oh, babe," she said over the suit radio as I stirred. "You flew up and landed on the dome, and then slid down. So limp and lifeless. I thought I'd lost you."

Through my shock-blurred vision and red-spattered helmet, I was lucky to see anything. I could hear them, though, I could hear the tears in the cracking of her voice.

They made me mad.

"You don't deserve to call me 'babe'. You dumped me and never even had the guts to break up." My voice was slurred, but clarity began to return along with my repressed anger. I must have hit that dome pretty hard.

"No," she wailed. "No! I was on an undercover case. I'm not just a deputy. I mean, I am, but I'm on assignment. I'm a fed. Undercover fraud. Somebody was embezzling."

"You acted like you didn't know me." I struggled to sit up.

"Just wait for the doctor, babe."

"Stop calling me that!" I rolled over and got on my hands and knees. As soon as my head stopped spinning, I needed to be on the move.

"Listen, my mark was a man. He wouldn't have understood us. It would have blown my chance to get inside information. I needed him to, you know, to think he had a chance with me. It was just a case."

Three more suits came running, stunners out. I grabbed at my tool pouch and pulled out the chief's old bullet gun. I straightened, and pointed it at Kelly.

Kelly's eyes widened, and then hardened. Pointing a finger at my face, she said, "You will *not* aim that thing at me."

She was right. I couldn't do that, so I aimed it at my own chest. "Listen. You think I had moon fever before. You put me in a cell—away from any color or any distractions—and I'll hang myself. I'll go nuts. I can't take that right now. I'd rather die."

She backed up two steps. "What do you expect me to do, then?"

Quickly trying to figure out a way ahead, I finally said, "I need the computers inside. I need to run a simulation. It'll take some time, but no matter what the outcome is, I'll surrender. Until then, this bullet has my name on it."

"I can't do that. I'm a federal agent, and you're a potential cop killer."

She paused a moment, during which I couldn't help but notice how good she looked in her moon suit. My suit was flat-chested and baggy in the crotch. She looked like some kind of space amazon action hero. I shook my head. I must be half-delirious. Things look different when you're facing death.

"Listen," I heard Kelly in my ears, along with the telltale beep of encryption. "We're on a private channel, now. There's no way I can convince them to let you in there. One guy said I should open your helmet while you were unconscious. They think you're a cop killer and aren't thinking clearly. I'll consider myself lucky to keep you alive long enough for a trial. Sometimes these stunners short out the suit controls. You could die in a matter of minutes if that happens. Please don't make me shoot you, Jaz."

My head was clearer. The hurt in Kelly's voice was almost too much to bear. Maybe she *had* been undercover. What happened between us made sense through that lens, I supposed. Maybe she still loved me after all. Desperation made me consider anything, though, no matter how much it might hurt.

"I'm sorry," I told her. It broke my heart all over again to have to do this. I wanted Kelly to love me, but she would hate me forever, now. I was ready to die rather than face the rest of my life without her, knowing I had betrayed her. "I'm really sorry." I tightened my grip on the gun and aimed it right at my heart.

Part 6

"No!" Kelly jumped at me, but I was ready. I chopped the stunner out of her hand by hitting her wrist with the heavy gun. Then I grabbed her arm and twisted it behind her as far as the suit would allow. Reaching around from behind, I put the hard, metal, muzzle of the gun up to her transparent helmet.

Please forgive me.

I used her as a body shield, and put her gorgeous body between me and the other cops. We were about the same height, but I was lanky and had the kind of training you get from a checkered past.

Feeling her press up against me created a different kind of ache. This would probably be the last time we would be so close. I cursed the thickness of the space suits that held her soft skin away from mine.

"Please forgive me," I gasped, aloud this time, near tears myself. "But I can't think of any other way."

"Shut the hell up," she said.

I heard the beep signifying the drop of the encrypted channel. Radio controls were usually changed with a combination of chin and tongue, so she must have done that while I held her arms pinned.

A voice was already speaking over the open channel. "…shoot you now. I repeat, drop your weapon and lie face down on the ground."

"Sorry, I won't shoot unless somebody jumps us." I answered, knowing every law enforcement agent on the moon would be listening. "I'll surrender if you let me into the computer facility first. Let me set up a couple batch jobs. You can disconnect the computer from the Internet. I don't need outside connections, just the mainframe."

"You let the officer go first."

"If I let her go, you'll shoot me."

The nameless policeman answered, "You already killed one of us. Two people. What's going to stop you from killing another one?"

"I…" I started to answer, but couldn't think of a good story. All I could think of was the truth. "I'm innocent. I didn't kill anybody. But I'm also desperate. I think I can prove my innocence inside the computer center. It's all I know to do. Without that, my life is over. I might as well let you shoot me."

They didn't answer, presumably strategizing on another radio channel.

"Let me do this," I continued. "And we'll all get what we want. Nobody else gets hurt."

A different voice came on. "This is the Moon Denver chief of police, Chief Olivaw. I won't pretend to know what you're talking about, but I want this over with no more bodies."

"Okay. Good." I answered, not believing it one bit.

"What is it you need?"

"First thing is, I need you to clear the computer center, but leave one screen logged in. It needs to have access to at least one fifth-gen optical processor, an orbital mechanics compiler, and an intelligent database engine."

Chief Olivaw answered, "Would you like a helicopter, too? Maybe a plate of Chicken Cordon Bleu? A glass of forty-five year-old Chateau Mouton-Rothschild?"

I didn't like his mocking tone, though a glass of wine did sound pretty good about now. I had a headache that I was afraid might put me in the hospital sooner than later, and if the shock ever left my muscles, I'm pretty sure I would find a few broken ribs somewhere under there.

Let him get under a microscope like I am right now and see how he likes it. Instead I said, "No." *You asshole.* "But I could use a bottle of aspirin." *No sense in antagonizing the only man who can help me.* I bit my tongue to keep from cussing him out. Out loud, anyway.

There was a slight movement at the edge of a roof across the courtyard.

It was a sniper.

Part 7

It was too much. Too many pains from too many places, both physical and emotional. Kelly had me on a damn roller coaster. I wanted to love her, I wanted to slap her for not trusting me, and I wanted to kiss her. Most of all, I wanted to die for betraying her. I wanted to tell her I would never hurt her, but instead I held a gun to her head and said her life wasn't worth shit. Later, I would probably die from a panic attack, or maybe a broken heart. For now, I had to stop thinking about it.

Kelly whispered, though it was a whisper heard round the world, "Do you actually know what to do with that stuff?"

"I was a math teacher in high school. You have to learn computers to stay a step ahead of the students. Yeah, I can plug in an orbital equation set as well as any ninth grader. Although, I've never had access to an optical processor before. I can do a multiple regression matrix about five levels deep with that kind of hardware."

Olivaw answered, "I only heard about one word in all that. Aspirin. That it?"

"One last thing. Open the door. I'm getting an itchy trigger finger out here in the crosshairs of a sniper."

All Olivaw said was, "Hmmph."

It seemed like forever, but they finally let us in. After rounding what I'm sure was intended to be a 'soothing' curve in the corridor, Kelly pointed up. Standing pretty as you please on the transparent dome above our heads was the dead Chief's bike.

"I guess I didn't blow out the gyro, or it would have fallen over. That must have been one hell of a bounce off those stairs."

"It was." Kelly sounded strangely monotone.

We were silent the rest of the way. I wished for the ability to set up a private line to Kelly so we could talk. Was she angry? Frightened? I wanted to know and to soothe those feelings. I wanted to protect her, but I still held the gun. I would never pull the trigger, but they couldn't know that or it would all be over.

Kelly led me to a console in the center of the computer room. It was exposed, very visible. Of course. On the table sat two bottles, one of aspirin and one of water.

There was only one chair. I moved it to an open spot about ten feet away where I could watch her while I worked. I motioned her to sit. She sat, popped the seals, and took her helmet off. Then Kelly crossed her legs, which is a real trick in a typical ill-fitting suit. I couldn't figure out how she could possibly look so sexy in a space suit.

"Did you have that suit tailored? Or something?"

She smirked. "Girl's got to have a few secrets."

I wanted to take my helmet off too, but I wasn't sure. There was no taking aspirin unless I took it off, but that would leave me vulnerable in many ways. I wanted to swallow the whole bottle to end this headache. It was probably a concussion. Instead, I held the bottle up and raised an eyebrow.

Kelly didn't speak, didn't move her head, but she focused at the floor, then back up. I got the message. The aspirin wasn't safe, or it wasn't a good idea to take off my helmet. Or something. *Crap.* I left it on, but set the gun down. It was hard to think with this headache, and I was beginning to suspect that aspirin was not going to help. My hands were shaking.

"I don't think it needs to be said, but I see any movement in this room that I don't like, I'll pick up this gun and shoot it. I'll figure out what it was after it stops moving. Don't say I didn't warn you."

The console worked. All the software I could wish for was right there in the system. This API used the latest Android Next schema emulator, which was good thing. Android Next anticipated my needs and guided me through the necessary data links. The room was getting brighter and brighter, with distracting flashes and sparkles. Something seemed to be wrong with my eyes. I knew Kelly could easily overpower me in this state, but I didn't know what else to do.

Fortunately, many of the data elements were pre-populated, like coefficients of drag in the Earth's atmosphere based on altitude, the mass of every major planetary body, moons, and even the larger comets and asteroids. Naturally, it had a built-in function for current gravity well coordinates, so that was a no-brainer. I had to make common-sense judgements for maximum and minimum variable boundaries. After thinking on it a bit, I added a few dummy variables, which would weed out billions of unlikely solution sets.

I set it to multi-thread on all available processors, touched 'Execute' on the screen, and then I didn't know what to do with myself. Looking around, I realized I hadn't paid much attention to the room. The interior here actually had some color. Shipping a crate of paint up here was expensive, not to mention a total luxury. I shook my head, imagining an endless series of bake sales and ice cream socials to pay for the paint. I was impressed with the concept, but not the execution.

"Uggh," I said. "These pink and blue baby colors make me want to puke more than the gray, did."

Kelly answered, "I kind of like it. And it isn't pink and blue; it's Rose Quartz and Serenity. Very fashion-conscious."

"Oh, my god. Please tell me you don't have a subscription to *Color Trends* magazine."

"Hey, it's about the only color I get to see around here."

"Yeah, tell me about it."

Our eyes met in a strange mix of signals, and the moment of levity was over. I was apologetic, scared, desperate, and unsure. Kelly was more steady. Her eyes held a mix of freak-out and menace, not a good combination. I would rather have seen anger, or compassion, or something I could work with. Instead, she gave me the impression of a wild animal trapped in the city. Unpredictable, and poised to attack. I had never seen her so hard.

Neither one of us could manage another round of small talk. I started pacing. The worst thing in the world for anxiety was plenty of time to second guess yourself. My head started feeling woozy. I needed to sit, but I had given the chair to Kelly, so I leaned against the table.

A flashing yellow indicator in my helmet gave warning that I was dangerously close to hyperventilating.

Part 8

"Jaz?" Kelly singsonged uncertainly, like an adult trying to calm a child. "Someone's coming in. Don't be alarmed, she's a journalist."

Sure enough, there was a woman just inside the door. I hadn't noticed. In fact, it was hard to think. I couldn't tell if my head hurt anymore, and I swallowed nausea. I didn't want to be sick, especially not in my suit. I desperately wanted my helmet off, and finally popped the seals and tossed it on the floor. For a moment, I drank in the fresh air and tried to get my head clear again.

I motioned her over. She started talking, eyes still locked on mine, with a tiny camera velcroed to her shoulder.

"This is Valerie, from *A Slice of Truth,* here in the Asimov High-Capacity Computing Center with a fugitive named Jazzy Moser."

Jesus, she's on air.

"Jazzy, or should I call you Jaz? The world wants to know what you hope to accomplish here and why you struggled so hard to reach this building. Why don't you just let the police take you into custody? You can't possibly expect to escape."

I was flustered. "You, you asked more than one question."

Valerie reached up and gently tapped the side of her forehead.

My hand felt the same spot on mine and came away with fresh blood. Looking down at my collar edging the helmet frame, I saw it was soaked in red. It must have been seeping down out of my helmet into the suit ever since the accident. That meant. Something. What did it mean? I had a head injury that had never stopped bleeding. Vaguely, I recalled that was a bad sign.

"You need a doctor," the reporter said. "Has it occurred to you that you might be a little delirious? In shock?" She nodded at me.

I wiped my face. Hands coated in red. *Crimson. Kelly would say crimson.* I tried to wipe my hand on my shirt and my face on my sleeve, but just managed to smear blood on the outside of my suit.

"Listen, it wasn't me. I didn't kill anybody. That guy. The poker player. He was spiking the drinks of his competitors. The chief. The chief of Springs, you know. He was a player, too. He probably found out. Check his blood for narcotics. Not to knock him out. Just enough to make him play stupid. The chief killed him. With…." I scooped up the gun. I had already forgotten it on the table. "With this gun."

Valerie stiffened and put her hands out. "Whoa, whoa. Be easy with that thing."

The computer terminal chimed. It was a welcome distraction that cleared my head. The data was in. I typed a command to list how many rows were in the output database. Millions. I had expected no less.

"Mind if I take a look?" Valerie asked, edging closer.

I glanced at Kelly, who seemed rooted to the chair. Remembering the gun, I held it up, pointed at the ceiling.

"You're a cop. I've seen you in the news. That drug bust last month. Really cute little nose."

I realized how stupid that sounded and shook my head. That was a big mistake. Stars exploded in my vision.

"Don't worry. We all have two jobs here." The journalist cop soothed like a banana trying to calm a gorilla. "I'm here to find out the truth, not to sucker punch you or something stupid like that."

She moved up, and I clutched the gun to my chest. It was threatening, but not an active threat.

"Okay. I did a bunch of math here, and I got millions of answers." I pointed to the number on the screen.

"Now I'm going to filter out the solution sets that're highly unlikely." Even to my own ears, the way I said 'highly' sounded like I was high. With my free hand, I punched in a filter. "This will remove starting vectors with too much initial energy. That would crush the payload."

The number on the screen dropped to just over a million. I typed in another filter.

"This removes any trajectory that goes twice around the Earth or Moon. It's too uncertain a path for no course corrections."

I didn't wait for questions, but typed in another one.

"Can't have it burning up in the atmosphere. This one removes those with too much atmospheric velocity over too long a time."

The number dropped to six digits, and then five with the last one.

"Still not enough. I'm going to have to guess a little. I'd say there's no point in pushing full escape velocity. So this'll cut anything with more than the minimum push to get to the Moon."

I smiled. The number dropped to five.

"Ha! See?"

Valerie shook her head. "No. Not really. I have no idea what that means."

"Don'cha see?" I vaguely realized the woman was too close, that I wasn't paying enough attention, but I had to get the words out and couldn't spare the concentration. "Somebody at one of those points back home shot the Chief. It wasn't a shot heard round the world. It was the shot *made* round the world."

"You got to be kidding me," said the reporter. "Are you saying that somebody standing on the Earth pointed a gun into the air and shot a man on the moon?"

"I know how it sounds, but you can prove it." I spread my arms out and gestured at the racks of computers like an actor, or a politician. "You can prove me wrong in front of the whole world, right here, right now."

"Okay, how can I do that?"

"You hook me up into that super fancy satellite stuff you got. I need footage from Earth over the last—um—48 hours or so. Department of Defense-level resolution, not that crap you feed to the public. You know, the stuff from the National Reconnaissance Office, or the NSA, or whoever does that. The super-secret spy satellites."

Valerie snorted. "I can't get that. I don't even think it exists."

"I used to date a colonel. Besides, I watch the History Channel. I know what we got, and Kelly's gonna get it for us."

I looked at Kelly, who I hadn't noticed until then was right next to me looking at the computer screen.

"Actually, I can."

Valerie said, "Bull."

Kelly looked at me with a whole new kind of respect, then over at the reporter. "I'm a fed, and I was recently granted special access for a case." She walked over to a nearby terminal with a red keyboard. "This is sipper-connected," she announced, pointing to an emblem on the side of the monitor that said SIPRNet. "Universities often collaborate on government projects."

Kelly logged in, opened a browser, and typed in a hard-coded address, the kind used in the dark web. This was a dark web on a secret government network. Another set of credentials got her into a screen asking for coordinates. "Voila'."

I had already printed the final five numbers, picked it up off the printer, and handed it to her.

"I think you should type them in," I said, not sure of my typing abilities at this point. I could barely see the tiny freckle that I knew Kelly had just above her right eye. One tiny blemish on an otherwise angelic face.

Kelly said, "I'm probably getting into trouble for letting you get a video of this." She typed in the coordinates one by one. The first three showed nothing but ocean.

"That's expected," I said, getting anxious all over again. "The Earth is three-fourths water."

The fourth number was in the middle of a desert. There were no signs of human presence. The fifth number showed a wide open field of cut wheat. Widely spaced rural houses dotted the edges around the field.

"There ya go," I was giddy with relief. At least it was on land. "Zoom in on that puppy." On the edge of the field was what looked like a large red propane tank.

Valeria asked, "Where is that field?"

"You're never going to believe this. It's Aurora, Colorado," said Kelly. "Right next to Denver."

Phone in hand, the reporter stared at the mobile device. "PunkinChunkin Colorado starts in two days. Right there in that wheat field."

I grinned. "Fire in the hole! Somebody's a couple days early to the funeral, somebody who wants to come to the Moon."

Kelly punched more keys, each time zooming in closer to the red tank. Soon, it became clear the red tank was a PunkinChunkin air cannon, plain as day.

Kelly said, "Could somebody modify an air cannon to shoot bullets? Or be so accurate they could shoot somebody? But how would they even know ahead of time where the Chief would be standing?"

"They wouldn't," Valerie said, "but somebody on the waiting list gets bumped up no matter who gets whacked. All they have to do is pepper a populated area of Moon Colorado with rocks and somebody'll get hit eventually. It was timed right at the tail end of the poker tournament, when folks would be going outside."

Kelly nodded. "Odds are one of the next few people on the waiting list will be a known pumpkin-chunker. What a heck of a shot, though."

"Not bullets," I said. "All you need is a sticky ball of gravel with a popper inside to spread 'em out like a shotgun. Lot'sa shots. Look jus' like micro. Micro. Meteor. Things." I couldn't express myself. The words weren't forming right.

I collapsed into Kelly's arms, too dizzy to stand any longer. As she lowered my head into her comforting lap, I looked up into her eyes. This time, I saw something much better. I saw that she cared. It was more than I dared hope for.

"Arrest that pumpkin," was the last thing I remember saying to her.

Part 9

One year later:

I awoke to a pain in my ears. It was my new ringtone.

Gotta change that to something that wakes me up without drilling a hole in my head.

"What is it?" I answered.

The damn thing rang in my ear again. Ahhhck! I punched the touchscreen again, and put the phone hesitantly back over my ear.

"Hello?"

"Ms. Moser?"

After a short conversation—during which I woke up considerably—I hung up and stared at the clock.

"Who calls at five o'clock in the damn morning?"

Kelly said, "Hmm?" and rolled over to face me, coming half-uncovered in the bed sheets, but her eyes were still closed.

I sat up, rubbed my eyes, and playfully tugged at the sheet until my imagination had nothing left to consider.

"You up?" I asked.

Kelly answered, "Hmm."

That was a 'maybe,' at best. I gave Kelly a full body scan. She was all soft, everywhere, from silky curls, to a sensuous mouth, and down a long supple body. Even her feet somehow looked soft. Actually, I knew exactly—intimately—how soft they were.

I'm damn lucky.

Instead of talking again, I used a different tack. By this time, I was more than awake. Aroused. I scooted back down in the bed until our lips were close, her breath tickling my face. Sliding my hand over her waist and down to the small of her back, I firmly pulled her to my waiting mouth. Oh, yes. Kelly was awake, playing the gazelle to my lioness move.

Her kiss set delicious things in motion inside my body. It was one of those half-asleep kisses that moved like a vessel on the waves of a great lake, rocking, sliding, in a dream-like motion that seemed like it would never end. Two or three times, we reflexively withdrew tongues to swallow without breaking contact.

Sometimes I wondered if Kelly had mental superpowers and could read my mind, know what I wanted, synchronize our tongues and our breathing with the expertise of a clockmaker. But I knew the truth. She spoke the language of the body. I was no stranger to sex, but until Kelly came along, I had never experienced this kind of poetry.

A number of new skills were coming into my life, and one of them started to intrude on the mood.

Once she could speak again, Kelly asked, "What is it, Jazzy?"

I backed away until my gaze could focus on her deep gray eyes, and I almost lost myself again. "Uh," I licked my lips, still tasting the kiss. "The governor of Nevada wants to meet with us. Apparently, they have this high-profile murder thing and they don't quite know what to do with it."

"Oh? Somebody needs the great Moon detective to hold their hand?" The way she emphasized Moon make it sound a little corny, like it was in quotes. "I can relate."

I shook my head. It was hard to believe, but I was the most famous detective in human history. At least, the most famous non-fictional one. Holmes still gave me a run for my headlines whenever a new movie came out.

"Well," I said, batting my lashes innocently. "I did solve the first extraterrestrial murder, ever."

"Not to mention the first interplanetary murder, where the shooter wasn't even on the same planet." She reached up and cupped my neck, caressing my earlobe with a thumb. "Hold on, did you say Nevada? Moon Nevada?"

"Lunar Vegas, baby."

Kelly sat up in bed and tugged the sheets back over her breasts. "Road trip!" She grinned wide.

"What. Don't you trust me in Vegas alone? I'll keep you on speed dial." I sat up as well, looking away in mock annoyance.

"Of course I do, but you still need a bodyguard," she pouted, then bit her lower lip.

Jesus. That woman plays me like a fiddle. The ache returned. I wanted to go nibble that lip myself.

"You think I need a bodyguard?" I asked, teasingly, leaning back against the headboard.

"No. My lioness can take care of herself just fine. It's all those other predators that I need to distract for you, to keep your head in the case. Besides, they appointed me as your parole officer. You can't leave town without my permission."

"You are one hell of a distraction," I muttered, looking away again.

It was her turn to move in, straddling my legs, pressing me into the mattress. Kelly sat back on my legs and pouted again; it was her classic passive-aggressive move.

"I plan on guarding this body," she said, eyes locked intently on mine.

Kelly's hands started on her thighs, slid together between them for a moment, then moved down to my legs. God, her fingers were warm and gentle. They slowly traveled north.

We were a few minutes late for our meeting with the governor, but I don't think anyone minded.

We were on a case!

Todd Walls

Todd A. Walls is a writer as the result of a truce. The stories that keep clamoring for attention will calmly await their turn, as long as Todd keeps writing them down. With the calm and quiet of Colorado's eastern plains outside—and the majestic Rocky Mountains marking the horizon—Todd's characters speak to him of their dreams and accomplishments, along with their failures and shame. Todd's imagination is a conduit to the end of time, riding the many failures of humanity to their impending outcomes, and embracing the heroic efforts of those who refuse such a fate.

Todd is the Vice President of the Colorado Springs Fiction Writers Group (CSFWG.org), and first became a member in 2000. He has professional technical certifications in engineering and computer security. He currently works as an Information Security Consultant in the finance industry.

Contact Todd A. Walls:
www.toddawalls.com,
todd@toddawalls.com
https://www.facebook.com/Todd.A.Walls

Tweeture

by A.M. Burns

The cell-phone on the bedside table chimed softly, indicating the arrival of a text message. Julie Tinsdale rolled over and snatched the phone, her sleep broken by the insatiable need to stay connected with her friends at all hours. After all, the message could be important.

With sleep-slowed fingers, she pressed the spot where the text icon flashed over the Colorado College background on her phone. The message opened. It was from "Tweeture." She didn't know anyone by that name. There wasn't an avatar next to the name. The message read: '*Hey sexy.*'

Julie rubbed her sleep-filled eyes. It must be a wrong number. She set the phone back on the bedside table and rolled over. Her cat, Queen Pudding, blocked her with a soft purr. She pushed the cat aside and settled onto her side so she could get back to sleep.

Before she could drop off and return to her dream of the CC quarterback, Byron and his broad shoulders, the phone beeped again. Queen hissed softly.

Hoping for something interesting this time, maybe even a message from Byron, Julie snatched the phone again.

'What's the matter, sexy? Not in a conversational mood tonight?'

Julie stared at the phone. Her groggy mind tried to place the name 'Tweeture.' She couldn't remember the name, but she knew a lot of people and, now that she was in college, seemed to meet more every day.

'Who R U,' she replied.

The was a slight scratching, like claws on hardwood, even though Queen Pudding was on the bed, right before her phone beeped again to let her know of the new message.

'A friend of a friend. Tony said you are fun.'

Julie paused, looking at the screen. She knew several Tonys, and at least one Anthony. One of them was Byron's tight end.

'Tony?' she replied.

The scratching came again, somewhere in the distance. She couldn't imagine which of her housemates was up and moving around. She tended to be the night owl of the house. Queen Pudding stared toward the floor, like there might be a mouse or something under the bed.

'Hey Sexy, got to dash. Catch you later. #tweeturefeature' Tweeture responded.

Somewhere in the hall, a floorboard squeaked. She swung out of bed and went to her door. Queen Pudding hissed from the bed. The door opened without a sound. The empty hallway was cloaked in darkness. Could one of her housemates had been playing a trick on her? It wouldn't be the first time, and probably not the last.

The next night, Queen Pudding's hiss woke Julie. "What is it, Queen?" Julie rubbed sleepily at her eyes. She couldn't tell how long she'd been asleep, but it didn't feel like very long.

Her phone beeped with a new message.

She stroked the cat's orange fur while hitting the message indicator.

Another message from Tweeture: *'Hey Sexy, what are you doing.'*

'SLEEPING,' Julie typed, irritated. Off in the distance there was a muffled beep.

'Sleeping is good.'

The cat hissed, swatting at the phone.

"Pudding, stop it!" Julie pushed the cat toward the edge of the bed.

The orange tabby growled as she dug her sharp claws into the pink comforter to keep from sliding off the bed.

'Who R U?' Julie glared at the cat as she typed.

'Tony said you looked nice today.' Nearby a floorboard creaked.

Which Tony had she seen that day? It might be some guy from one of her classes, or was it some customer that came into the coffee shop she worked at in downtown Colorado Springs? Maybe "Tweeture" was really named "Tony." She'd lost track of how many guys she ran into who had been more than a little creepy.

Queen Pudding waddled over and stretched out across Julie's chest, demanding attention.

'I bet you're wearing a slinky pink nightie' came Tweeture's next message.

Julie glanced down at the clingy pink silk across her sleek body. She shivered. Who was the person? How could they know what she was wearing? She never wore the same nightgown twice in a week. It had to be one of the girls in the house. She never showed off her best lingerie to any of her boyfriends. They didn't stay around long enough to deserve her best.

'WHO R U?' she typed more forcefully than she intended, her hands shaking as a cold sweat ran down her back.

Queen Pudding hissed again, her claws digging through the sheer silk of the nightie before her paw knocked the phone out of Julie's hand. The phone clattered to the floor. "Damn it, Pudding," Julie snarled as she shoved the cat away so she could bend over the side of the bed to recover the phone.

In the soft moonlight coming in from the window on the other side of the bed, the ruffle on the far side of the bed moved slightly. Julie's heart raced.

"Queen Pudding?" Had the cat jumped off the bed?

A floorboard creaked again.

Julie spotted the phone lying just under the edge of the bed. She snatched it from the shadows. Her fingers chilled as they grabbed the metal case of her phone under the bed.

Queen Pudding lay curled in the middle of her pillow, contentedly licking her right front paw, just like she did after catching a mouse.

After three nights of messages from Tweeture, Julie called a house meeting to speak to her housemates about the texts, and see if anyone acted guilty about the prank. The four of them gathered around the kitchen table with a big tub of ice cream, each with a spoon..

"What's this that's been keeping you up all night?" Margo, the owner of the house, asked.

"I've been getting these strange messages," Julie said, reaching for a spoon. "Coming from someone who calls themselves 'Tweeture'."

"What kind of name is 'Tweeture'?" the very blonde Cindy asked, shoveling a spoonful of chocolate ice cream into her delicate lips.

"If you didn't put the number in your phone, it should just show as a number. Have you checked to see if you put the name in your phone?" Sally suggested.

"I think I would remember entering a name like 'Tweeture'." Julie said, pulling her phone out anyway. There was always the possibility she had added it at a party and she'd been too drunk to remember.

She pulled up the phone's address book. She hit the 't' button and scrolled through various friends and family to find 'Tweeture' listed in her phone. She stared at the listing, trying to remember when she had put the number into the phone. "Well, here it is," she muttered more to herself than her housemates. She pulled up the listing, which included a phone number, email address and a website.

"Well, what did you put in for it?" Margo asked,.

"No notes from me. But there is an email address and a website," Julie said. She clicked on the website and her phone brought it up. On a black background, across the top in dripping red and gold script, were the words: "Tweeture Feature."

Julie read over the main page of the website. It didn't contain much, just a weird write up on how much you could learn from people while hiding behind curtains and looking through windows. Along the left side, there were buttons to a blog, and a few others stating to follow Tweeture on-line.

"What does it say?" Cindy asked after she finished her mouthful of ice-cream.

"Here look for yourself. Definitely sounds creepy to me," Julie handed the phone over and shuddered. How did the weirdo freak get her number, or more to the point, how did *she* get his information? Maybe last week-end when they had the massive party and most of them ended up too drunk to remember anything the next morning?

"Wow, he has over a hundred thousand people following him on Twitter," Sally said, leaning over Cindy's shoulder.

"So?" Julie muttered.

"So? Julie, my dear, this means you are texting with a celebrity. A celebrity who thinks you're sexy," Sally chided.

"How do you know he thinks I'm sexy?"

"It says so right here in his tweets: 'been texting with Julie. She's sexy. But her cat is mean.'" Cindy read, then frowned. "I don't think Queen Pudding is mean. She's one of the nicest cats I know."

"When did he write that?" Julie snatched the phone back from Cindy. A feeling of dread spread over her.

"Last night," Cindy said and reached for another spoonful of ice-cream.

She recalled the messages last night. Like the ones from the previous nights, they had been highly suggestive, without Tweeture coming right out and saying he wanted her for anything in particular. When she stopped and thought about the repetition in the encounters and the vagueness, it all felt much more sinister. Queen Pudding had been extremely agitated as well. She scanned his Twitter feed from the past couple of nights. Apparently, he had a pattern of the people he texted. Each night, the entries were in the same order. Last night, before he contacted her, he contacted someone named Jonathan and chatted about masturbation. After that, he chatted with 'Sue' about her psycho-ex.

Somehow, finding the website made Tweeture's contact with her made her skin crawl. He was blatantly stalking her. Julie suddenly didn't want to be alone. She had never had a stalker before. If he was watching her through the window, he could easily climb in. There was a trellis outside her window. It wasn't old—anyone could probably climb up it.

"What should I do?" she wondered aloud. "Should I call the police? Should I call him and tell him to never contact me again?"

"What can the police do?" Margo put her arm around Julie's shoulders. "He hasn't done anything yet. Delete his number and forget him. Don't answer the text if he tries again tonight."

Julie pulled up the entry in her address book again. She stared at it for a second, then hit delete. A feeling of anxiety crept into her that no amount of ice-cream could cure. Her hands shook so badly that she put her spoon down. For the first time in her life, she didn't want any more of her favorite treat.

It might've been the moonlight coming through her sheer pink curtains, or her fear that Tweeture might text her again, but sleep proved elusive as she clung to Queen Pudding that night. The cat's purr comforted her in ways it had never done in the past. For three hours, the two lay together on the silk comforter, Julie not even thinking about getting under the covers. She didn't want to risk falling asleep and having something happen.

Queen Pudding hissed and growled right before the phone chimed indicating a new text. Julie ignored it, clutching Queen Pudding to her as the cat began to squirm.

The phone chimed again. Julie ignored it again.

On the third chime, Julie snatched the phone off the nightstand and stared at the flashing text indicator. Almost against her will, she fingered the button to bring up the messages. Three new messages waited for her, all from Tweeture. How could his name be showing? She definitely had deleted his entry. Could her phone be playing tricks on her? It should be showing a number—not his name. There was no way the phone could show his name if she had deleted his entry.

While she stared at the list of messages, trying to work up the courage to push the button, another message came in. "Leave me alone!" Julie shouted as she threw the phone across the room.

The phone lay quiet long enough that she began to think that she may have broken it.

A floorboard squeaked nearby. The cat hissed again.

Julie started to get out of bed. Queen Pudding lashed out, snagging the cuff of her dressing gown with a soft growl.

She wanted to yell at the cat, but the look of fear etched on the cat's furry face stopped her. Queen Pudding's ears were pinned back and her wide eyes nearly hid her whiskers. She reached down and rubbed the soft orange fur. "It's okay, Pudding, I'm just going to get the phone."

Her fuzzy pink slippers settled silently on the plush rug at the side of her bed. A floorboard squeaked as she took her first step toward the phone. It sounded just like the noise she and the cat had heard moments before. It couldn't have been. How could two different boards make the same exact sound? She stared down at the floor, as if the rug would provide answers for her.

At the sound of scratching on the bed, her heart thumping in her chest, Julie spun around in time to see

Queen Pudding sliding under the head of the comforter. Maybe the cat had the right idea. She felt cold and alone standing there in her bedroom.

Julie laughed nervously at herself. What could happen to her in her bedroom? She was perfectly safe. Anyone, or anything coming after her, would have to get through the whole house to get there, or come up through her second story window. One of the reasons she'd picked the room was that it was on the second floor and she felt safer there. There was nothing for her to fear.

She squared her shoulders. She walked over to the phone lying against the far wall and picked it up.

When she returned to the bed, she lifted the covers and revealed a worried looking orange cat. "Slide over, Queen Pudding," Julie said and slid into bed next to the cat.

The new message chime shattered the silence of the room.

Julie jerked in surprise and fumbled the phone almost hitting herself in the face, but managed to grab it just in time. She stared in disbelief at the screen and the new message from Tweeture.

Without her clicking on it, the new text opened: *'Why so angry sexy girl?'*

Julie stared in horror at the screen. How could Tweeture know she was angry? He had to be watching her somehow. Her curtains were pulled and her lights were out.

She grabbed at the knob of her bedside lamp so hard that she nearly toppled it. She had to reach out with

her other hand to steady it as the light pushed the shadows away.

Nothing appeared out of place. Julie tried to think
about anything new she had brought into the room recently. Maybe there was a camera or something hiding
somewhere in the room. How else could Tweeture know
she was angry? The idea he'd been in the house made her
even more nervous. She wiped her sweaty palms on her
comforter, but the satin fabric didn't do much to help
remove the moisture accumulating there.

The bed creaked. Neither Julie nor the cat had
moved.

The phone chimed. *'Trying to see into the shadows?'*
the next message appeared on her screen.

Julie resisted the urge to throw the phone at the
wall again. *'LEAVE ME ALONE!'* she replied.

'I can't do that now.' Tweeture's message came faster than Julie thought possible. What was Tweeture? How
could anyone answer a text message before it had been
sent? Her hands shook so badly she could barely see the
screen on the phone.

Queen Pudding shot out from under the covers
with an angry yowl. Julie jumped and pushed herself
against the headboard of the bed, jerking the comforter
up to her chin, and stared at the cat now clawing at the
closed door.

The phone beeped again. *'You know these pink slippers are really cute.'*

Something at the foot of the bed moved.

Julie threw the covers off the bed, yanking her feet up under her. The lamp went out, plunging the room into darkness.

A weight landed on the foot of the bed. "Queen Pudding, is that you?" Julie whispered as her pulse raced. She could still hear the cat scratching at the door.

Julie reached for the lamp, putting one foot on the floor for balance, finding the familiar knob in the darkness. When she turned it, nothing happened.

Something soft, and fur-like brushed against her ankle. She jerked the foot back toward her. Her heart pounded like crazy and she tried to catch her breath that came in short gasps.

Before she could get her foot underneath her again, sharp claws sank into Julie's leg. Julie screamed, but couldn't move. The soft glow from a cell-phone screen cast light onto the bed. The creature's large green eyes reflected the light from the screen. There was a sharp metallic smell. Somewhere in the distance, she heard Queen Pudding screaming. The creature's phone fell on the bed. Another set of claws dug into her shin as the thing climbed along her body. Blood—her blood— shining in the odd green light, running across Tweeture's large bulbous nose was the last thing she saw.

"I wonder if you'll taste as good as Tony did?"

Minutes later, a Twitter post appeared on the website, *Tweeture Feature*. It was short. *Had fun with Julie tonight. Found out she's a screamer, and so is her cat. #tweeturefeature*

A.M. Burns

A.M. Burns lives in the Colorado Rockies with his partner, several dogs, cats, horses, and birds. When he's not writing, he's often fixing fences, splitting wood, hiking in the mountains, or flying his hawks. He's enjoyed writing since he was in high school, but it wasn't until the past few years that he's begun truly honing his craft. You can find out more about A.M. and his publications at:

> http://www.amburns.com
> http://www.facebook.com/authoramburns
> @am_burns on Twitter

The Offering

by R.E.D.

Allen sat by the window, looking out onto the driveway. He'd always felt like an easy target at Palmer High School. He wasn't as pretty as most. With average looks and being slightly overweight, school was a constant battle. He hoped that, by reaching out, he might be able to prove himself to Tim, the quarterback of the football team. Since telling his ghost story a few weeks earlier, a lot of his classmates had suddenly become interested in him as more than just a punching bag. If he could get Tim on his side, everyone else would fall into line and things would get easier for him.

Being a little past noon, Allen expected to see Tim's SUV drive up at any moment. His camping gear was already by the front door, ready to go so he wouldn't make his potential new friends wait.

Allen's mom came out from the kitchen. "It's so nice to see you finally making some friends at school. Don't you do anything to lose them."

"I know, Mom." Allen kept most of the truth about the camping trip a secret from his mom. He wasn't going down to Durango, but up north to Caribou, a ghost town near Nederland. He had told the ghost story of the old mining town at the end of year bonfire, and Tim had dared him to go up there with him to prove he wasn't scared. If Tim's step-sister, Amy, hadn't been there, Allen would have had no problem refusing, because it was all crap. There was no such thing as ghosts.

Allen cheeks grew hot as he smiled at the thought of looking cool in front of Amy. His crush on her was obvious and Amy knew how to play him, mostly to get a reaction from Tim.

The mid-sized red SUV pulled in the driveway, so Allen grabbed his gear and headed outside. Tim got out of the car along with Francis. Tim was big, as any football player should be. He wore his number six team jersey.

Francis was the Goth foreign exchange student. He wore black studded clothes and red contact lenses giving him an eerie appearance. Allen had a few classes with him during the past year. They had gotten along, but they weren't exactly friends. His French accent wasn't as heavy as it had been when he first arrived. "Hey, Allen. Ready for some ghost hunting?"

"Keep it down," Allen whispered. "My mom doesn't know we're doing that. Remember?"

"*Oui.*" Francis laughed. "*Je suis désolé.*"

"In English please?" Allen asked.

Tim popped the hatch, which was crammed with everyone else's camping gear, flashlights, video cameras and enough food for the weekend. "Would it kill you to learn another language, Allen? He said he's sorry."

"Just because I don't speak French doesn't mean I'm not learning another language, Tim." Allen retorted.

Tim shrugged. "Whatever. Let's just load this stuff and get going."

"Yeah." Allen muttered under his breath "The sooner this is over, the better."

It looked like Tim was playing Tetris with Allen's gear, trying to get it to fit. Once it was secure, Allen opened the back passenger door. Francis got in on the far side, meaning Stacy was in the middle. There was hardly any room for him to sit comfortably, but Allen crammed himself in. He pushed against Stacy trying to buckle up. The floor in the back was littered with fast food bags and wrappers, and bottles and cans of various soda, making it difficult for Allen to find a safe place to put his feet.

Amy sat in the front passenger seat. From her strawberry blonde hair to her hazel eyes, she was damn sexy. She looked back at him and winked. "Hey there."

"Hi," Allen said.

Tim pointed at Allen as he turned the car on. "Watch it." Then he put in a CD and turned the heavy metal music up.

They made it to the highway and headed north.

"So, ghost boy," Stacy asked. "We need something to burn, right? For like some weird ass ritual or whatever?"

Allen turned to look out the window and rolled his eyes. "If ghosts were real, yeah. Something human-shaped like an effigy."

Stacy screwed up her face. "What's an effigy?"

"Don't worry about it," Francis said as he fiddled with his phone. "Whatever you brought will work."

Allen sighed. "It'll be a bust. You'll see. Ghosts aren't real."

Francis chuckled. "You just haven't seen one yet."

"You told us at the bonfire, but what's the story again?" Stacy asked.

Allen looked at Stacy. "Caribou was a small mining town a long time ago. Supposedly there had been a bunch of murders, people being burned to death."

Stacy jabbed her elbow into Allen. "Skip that part. It's making me sick just thinking about it.

"Whatever." Allen tried to lean away from Stacy. "They caught the guy who claimed he was following the orders of a ghost in the mine. No one knows how, but that night the jail cell the man was in caught fire and, as the fire spread, most of the town burned because of it. They say you can awaken the ghost if you go up there and burn something like an effigy. It's just a story though."

"Ghosts or no ghosts," Tim said, as he accelerated past a slow semi. "I'm going to prove how much of a chicken you are."

"There's nothing to be scared of, so good luck with that," Allen said. He turned back to the window, just as they reached Denver, passing by buildings of all shapes and sizes. Tim was so full of himself, thinking he had to prove something like that, but Allen didn't have anything to be scared about.

They made it through Denver, and Boulder came into view. The buildings were smaller and there were far more trees than in Denver. The tall mountains grew larger as they drove through the small town.

Stacy groaned more dramatically than necessary. "Tim, your crap music is giving me a headache."

"Hey! Don't diss my music," Tim said.

Stacy put her hand to her head. "It hurts my ears. Can't you play something better? Got any Country or Pop?"

"Sorry, but I like my musicians to have talent," Tim argued.

Amy slapped Tim on the back of his head. "You wouldn't know talent if it came up and bit you on the ass. Put the radio on Magic or Nash FM."

Allen shrugged. "Those stations won't come in well, up here. At least lower the volume."

Tim lowered the volume. "You're all hating on my music, so there." Tim pointed to a sign on the road. "Look. Nederland. We're almost there"

Tim turned on the first left through the forest. The aspens and pines were tall and numerous, but as they continued down the winding dirt road, the forest thinned. Tim turned off the a/c and cracked the window. "I want some fresh mountain air."

Tim's 'fresh' air smelled rank. Allen wrinkled his nose. "I wouldn't call that fresh."

Further down the road, the trees became equally dead as they were sparse. Eventually, the only trees were broken stumps, black and decaying, giving a clear view of the surrounding mountains There was no sign of life in any direction

They reached the clearing filled with burnt and rundown building. Only a few of them still had decent structure to them, but most were without roofs and had crumbling walls. Tim drove around the ghost town. The dead trees formed a makeshift perimeter around Caribou. "Okay, Allen, even you have to admit this place is creepy.'"

Allen nodded. "Worse than it looked in the photo, but that doesn't mean ghosts are real."

Tim drove the car to the center and parked the car. "Alright, everyone out, and let's get set up."

Allen got out of the car and looked around. Apart from the five of them, there were no signs of life anywhere. "Let's just get this over with." He pointed over to a few buildings that still had large enough walls. "We should make basecamp in those buildings. There should be enough space for us. We can use the walls to help block the wind and other things."

"What wind?" Tim asked.

"Just because there's no wind now, doesn't mean there won't be wind later," Allen said. "Boy Scout thing, always be prepared, right?"

"I'll get started on building the fire," Francis said, walking away from them. "There should be enough wood around here for it."

Allen grabbed his stuff and carried it to the space in the buildings between what was left of the crumbling walls. The wooden floor was mostly intact and covered by a thick layer of dust. Earlier when he'd checked the weather, there wasn't any rain in the forecast, so he left his tent and sleeping bag to one side and set up his chair and video camera. He grabbed a bottle of water from his bag and took a drink. He looked up. Because of the mountains, the sun would set earlier. He grabbed his video camera and went to go help Francis with the fire.

Francis kneeled next to the fire pit, his video camera lying just outside the stone circle. He had a decent wood structure for the fire built in a pit surrounded by large rocks. "Damn it. And I didn't bring a spare," he muttered, trying to light his lighter.

"Need some help?" Allen asked.

Francis shook the lighter. "Can't start a fire with no fluid in my lighter."

"I know a few tricks." Allen set his video camera down, reached into his pocket, and pulled out a large bag filled with dry pine needles. "My old Boy Scout troop called this Pyro Grass." He loosely stuffed the pine needles in the center of Francis' structure. Then he pulled out flint and steel. Allen got on his knees and struck the flint and steel against each other until the dry needles caught the sparks. He blew on the sparks until the fire grew and was able to burn on its own.

"Wow!" Francis applauded. "You're good at that. I thought Boy Scouts used two sticks."

Allen chuckled. "That way works too, but I can do it faster with flint and steel." He picked up his video camera and stood.

Francis looked up. "Just in time too. The sun is about to go down."

The fire blazed brightly as the sun set.

Tim came up to the fire, camera in hand. He pointed to the building with the tallest walls. "Got everything set up in that building. Nice job on the fire, Francis."

"It was all Allen with the flint and steel," Francis said.

Amy was next to arrive with her camera and flashlight. "Nice work, Nature Boy."

Tim clenched his fist, giving Allen a good reminder that he shouldn't do anything to piss Tim off, while they were in the middle of a ghost town. If he could just make it through the weekend and prove himself, he wouldn't have to worry about Tim messing with him again.

Stacy called from behind the group. "Hey, so, I got this…"

Amy turned. "Ugh! What the hell is that thing, Stacy?"

In one hand, Stacy had her camera, but in the other, she held onto an ugly ragdoll. It was torn in several areas, with stuffing coming out from various holes, and had an eye missing. "This thing has always given me nightmares. I'm so freaking glad to be rid of it. Finally."

Amy backed away from Stacy. "It's so hideous. I don't want to touch it. Why do you even have it?"

Stacy shrugged "I found it when I was like five, but it freaked me out to much that I was too scared to get rid of it. I always thought it was cursed."

Tim laughed. "That's so crazy. I mean, yeah, it's fugly, but cursed?"

Stacy gave a nervous chuckle. "I know, right? It's not really cursed, but it's definitely super creepy."

Allen moaned. "What a load of superstitious shit."

Stacy stormed up to Allen raising her fist fast, but Allen flinched away. She smirked at him, and then went to go stand by Amy. "Whatever. Let's just burn the damn thing. Do I just throw it in, or is there some kind of incantation or stuff to the ritual?"

"There's no incantation, as far as I know." Allen said.

The five teens glanced at each other in silence. It was so quiet, Allen could hear himself breathing. The glow from the flames flickered off of each of them. Allen hated the eerie feelings the fire gave off, but as long as he proved Tim wrong, he didn't care what happened.

"Maybe we should each put a few drops of our blood on it. It would make the spiritual invitation appear even stronger," Francis sounded too eager.

"How the hell do you know that, Francis?" Tim asked.

"I'm a ghost fanatic, but you don't need to be one to know that," Francis said.

"I still think this all a bunch of bullshit, and it's pointless, but might as well," Allen said, walking over to Stacy then pulled out his pocket knife. He took the doll from her and turned to Francis. "Come here. I can't cut myself and record at the same time."

Francis walked up to Allen and took the knife. Allen gasped as Francis pressed the blade into his thumb in a slow sting of sharp pain. Allen dripped his blood onto the doll. He handed the doll back to Stacy. "You next."

Stacy held her finger out. "Do I really have to cut myself? I'm really squeamish about blood."

Amy took the knife from Francis. "No, just let me prick your finger, so you won't bleed for long."

Stacy shrieked as Amy pricked her finger.

"Good grief, Stacy," Allen said. "It's only a small drop. Just rub your blood on the doll and pass it along."

Stacy's hands shook as she touched the doll with her bloody finger and passed it on to Amy. "I-I-I guess you're next."

Staying calm as she did it, Amy pierced her finger and pressed her blood onto the doll. She handed the doll and knife to Francis. "You're next."

A little too eager, Francis sliced his palm quickly, letting as much blood as possible drip onto the doll. He walked over to Tim and passed him the doll and knife. "You're last."

Displaying no signs of pain, Tim cut his hand and smeared his blood onto the doll. "What now? Do I just throw it in there?" He handed the knife back to Allen.

"I guess," Allen said.

Tim threw the doll into the fire.

The fire burst up in a quick flash, then died. A rush of cold wind surrounded them. Even though it had been a warm summer evening, their breaths became visible.

Everyone turned on a light, either from their camera or a flashlight. The illumination did little to chase away the chill that settled around their circle.

"What the hell was that?" Stacy asked.

Allen rubbed his arms. "Should have brought a jacket."

Francis looked around with wide eyes. "That was *merveilleux*."

Tim readied his video camera. "Alright, let's go find some ghosts. We'll split up to cover more ground."

"Are you sure we should split up?" Allen asked. "It might be better if we went in groups of two or something. I could go with Francis or…"

Tim mocked Allen. "Come on, Allen. I thought you were the brave one."

"I'm not scared or anything." Allen retorted. "It's just that, you know, what if people get lost? I mean, who would want to go to the mine alone?"

"Stacy will go." Amy winked at Stacy. "Won't you, Stacy?"

"But I…" Stacy said.

"Come on. It can't be that bad. Won't you do it for me?" Amy asked.

From her trembling hands, it was clear Stacy didn't want to go, but she took a deep breath and nodded. "Okay. I'll do it."

"See?" Tim asked. "Go alone, and don't be a bitch about it."

Allen turned around. "All right whatever. I'm ready."

Everyone went off on their own to explore the ruined town.

Allen walked towards a group of burnt-out and tumbled-down buildings near the edge of the ghost town. He took a few deep breaths before walking into the first building. Its remaining walls only came up to his waist. There were piles of broken and decayed wood that could have been furniture at some point. The air had stayed cold and the occasional gust of wind made him shiver. It seemed like he was alone, but as his video camera swept back, a strange form appeared on the screen. It was blackened and curled up on itself, cringing in the corner as the light crossed over it. Allen lowered the camera, trying to focus the light on the corner, but there was nothing there. Maybe it was a smudge on the lens, but there wasn't enough light to check. He raised the camera to get a second look, but it was gone. "Must have imagined it."

Allen poked around a little more. He was bored, so he picked up a small stick and whittled it with his knife. When he finished, he tossed it aside, left the buildings, and headed towards the basecamp.

Upon returning to basecamp, Allen found Tim and Francis were already back. He hadn't been gone for too long, but for both of them to be back before him, probably meant they didn't even try. Considering how much Francis was into ghost hunting, Allen would have thought he'd be the last to return. Tim was reviewing the footage from his video camera, while Francis reclined in a chair with his feet up.

Allen took his seat. "When did you all get back?"

"A little while ago." Francis said. "I got nothing."

Allen turned his head to Tim. "You find any ghosts?"

Tim looked at Allen for a moment and shook his head. "Naw, maybe some weird sounds, but no ghosts." He turned back to his video camera.

"What are you looking at?" Allen asked.

Tim kept his attention on the video camera. "I thought maybe I heard something in one of the buildings. I felt like I was being, you know, watched the whole time. Worst part was the wind. Kept thinking someone was breathing on the back of my neck." He rewound his video camera and watched it again. "Did you hear anything out there?

Shaking his head, Allen replied. "No, nothing. I mean it was creepy, but maybe you heard the old buildings groaning as they cooled off or whatever." He turned the video camera to himself. Almost inaudibly, he asked, "Who's the bitch now?"

Allen played the footage he recorded. Everything seemed fine, until the dark figure appeared, a loud guttural noise came from the video.

Francis and Tim looked up.

Tim put his camera down. "What the hell was that?"

Allen quickly rewound the video. "I don't know. I didn't hear that when I was out there."

Francis rushed over to Allen and looked over his shoulder. "Play eet again."

Allen pressed play. He glanced at Francis. His eyes widened and his jaw dropped as the strange growl played again.

"There is defeeneetely sometheeng there." Francis reached for Allen's camera and played it again. "Lucky. I weesh I had found that."

"Found what?" Allen asked. "It was probably just a wild animal or something."

"What aneemal makes a noise you hear on a video camera that you deedn't hear out there?" Francis asked.

Allen got up from his chair. "What's with your accent? You were talking normal earlier?"

"Sorry. It happens when I get excited or overemotional," Francis said, looking down and shuffling his feet.

Amy came in, but she kept quiet, as she took her seat.

"Did you find anything?" Tim asked.

Amy shook her head.

"Everything all right?" Allen asked.

"She hates scary movies, probably just got too scared being on her own," Tim said.

Amy didn't respond.

Allen checked the clock on his camera. It had been a few hours, but Stacy still hadn't come back. Francis paced around inside. Tim watched Amy, as she got up every five minutes to look outside. Allen kept to himself, watching the footage on mute over and over.

"What the hell?" Amy said. "She should have been back by now."

Francis looked at Amy. "Maybe she got lost in the mine or something."

Allen turned his video camera off and stood. "I told you it was stupid to go alone."

Tim got up. He grabbed a backpack. "Alright, everyone, calm the hell down. Let's just go look for her."

They set out from basecamp again, this time as a group. Allen took his video camera and turned it back on, in case something happened. The screen cut out sporadically on their walk to the mine. Maybe it needed new batteries. Allen aimed the video camera towards the town. It felt like something was watching them from the darkness.

Tim, Amy, and Francis led the way uphill on the dirt path to the mine with Allen following from behind, kicking at the few pebbles along the smooth ground. The lack of trees gave them a full view of the town. As the grew closer to the mine's entrance, the area became bare, with nothing but dirt and rocks surrounding them

"You sure it was this way?" Amy asked.

Tim pointed further up the path toward a hole in the mountain, "Yeah. That hole up there is the mine. It's kind of obvious. Stacy's gotta be lost inside of it. Just watch your step."

"Let's just find her and hope she's okay," Francis said.

Tim slowed his pace. "Stay close."

The mine was pitch-black and dusty. Their only sources of light were Allen's video camera and Francis' and Amy's flashlights. They each took turns calling out for Stacy.

"Why isn't she answering?" Amy asked.

"Didn't they used to worry about bad gas and stuff in these old mines?" Allen asked. "Like you'd just be working one moment, and then this gas would come from out of the ground and kill you."

Francis glared at Allen. "Allen, man, that's not helping." He paused and sniffed. "It might be my imagination, but it totally smells like smoke."

Allen sniffed the air. "I don't smell anything."

"He's right," Amy said. "I think it smells like smoke too."

They wandered further into the mine, sticking together. Allen's filming caught the various twists and turns of the mine tunnel and its branches. Metal tracks on the ground were worn down and rusted. Piles of broken old wood were what remained of the supports. In the midst of calling out for Stacy, Tim hushed the others. "Shh, shut up. I think I heard something."

"I didn't hear anything." Francis whispered.

Tim looked around. "Like a voice or something."

Allen's video camera screen went snowy. "Damn video camera, batteries must be dying."

"Dude, are you really filming right now?" Tim asked.

Allen shook his video camera. "How else am I gonna prove that I'm not scared here?"

"Damn eet! Why would she have gone een so far?" Francis asked.

Amy looked around. "I don't know, maybe she was scared and got turned around."

Allen turned the video camera toward the deeper area of the mine. Stacy came into view along the tracks. "There she is."

Stacy stood alone, but her video camera lay on the ground. She appeared to be listening to something. Her head was tilted, but suddenly jerked towards her shoulder. She shuffled to face the other four, not moving her head.

Amy picked up Stacy's video camera. "Something's wrong. Stacy?"

Stacy didn't say anything.

"Stacy, can you hear me?" Francis asked from behind Allen.

Stacy opened her mouth, but no sound came from it.

Tim set his bag down. "We can't stay here. Something is obviously not right." He walked up to her and tugged at her arm. "Stacy. Come on, Stacy. Let's get out of here."

Allen froze. A tall gangly shadow appeared on his screen, standing as still as a statue next to Stacy. He looked up, but didn't see the source, so he double-checked the screen. Whatever it was stood over Tim.

Tim gasped. "Oh god."

Tim picked Stacy up and ran. Everyone panicked at Tim's outburst and ran screaming after him. The little bit of light they had bounced wildly down the mine shaft, creating terrifying shadows from the rock and wood around them. When they burst out into the moonless night, the patterns of light and darkness danced around them, making it impossible to tell what was real and illusionary. They ran all the way back to basecamp.

"What the hell was that?" Francis gasped in ragged breaths as he put his hands on his knees.

"I don't know. I thought maybe I saw something," Allen said, trying to catch his breath.

Francis stared back at the mine. "Everyone just started screameeng and runneeng, and I deedn't wait to look."

Allen was still trying to catch his breath. "I don't know. Maybe shadows playing tricks."

Tim helped Stacy to her chair. "That was no shadow." He gently slapped her face. "Stacy, come on. Snap out of it."

Stacy lay against the back of her seat with her head tilted. She whispered, "Burn… burn… burn."

Their flashlights provided enough light for them to barely see each other.

Amy held up Stacy's video camera. "Let's check this, and see if she found something."

Allen, Tim, and Francis gathered around Amy as she rewound and played the footage.

The image was shaky. Stacy could be heard muttering to herself. "I can do this. I can do this. Amy can do this. She wouldn't be scared. I can do this." Inside the mine, the view swung back and forth. The light from the camera was dim at best, barely able to illuminate anything "It smells like smoke in here, but where's the fire?"

A guttural voice similar to what they heard on Allen's camera growled, but Stacy didn't seem to hear it. She continued walking into the mine, whispering, "For Amy. I'm doing this for Amy."

The raspy voice growled louder.

Stacy froze. "What was that?"

The camera swung again. A tall gangly humanoid appeared. It lashed out. Stacy screamed, and dropped the video camera.

Amy dropped the video camera, screaming.

Tim grabbed the video camera and looked over the footage. "What the hell was that?"

"Was that the ghost of the mine?" Francis asked.

Allen rewound his video camera. "Or some lunatic. It's a good thing I was filming back there. Check this out. That, guy, whoever the hell he is, showed up." He showed everyone a freeze frame of the shadow.

"How do we know this is the same thing?" Tim asked.

"Eet's the same size and shape," Francis said.

"I say we just leave everything, get out of here, and get Stacy some help now," Amy said.

"Agreed," Tim said. He looked around. "Let me just get my keys." He paused for a moment, before his eyes widened and his jaw dropped. "Oh shit! My keys are in my backpack!"

"Where's your backpack?" Francis asked.

Allen played the video from his camera again, trying to get a better look at what he found. "Tim freaked out and left it in the mine. Why did you even put it down? You're big enough you could have had it on your back and still be able to carry Stacy."

"I don't know," Tim said. "I'm not really sure why I put it down, but why didn't you think to grab it?"

"Right," Allen scoffed. "Like I would risk you beating me up for touching your stuff. It's your bag so you go get it. If that creep is still there, there's no way I'm going back. Who knows what he did to Stacy."

"Like some random guy just leeveseen the mine. Eet's totally a ghost." Francis paced around inside base-camp. "We should wait unteelmorneeng."

Amy raised her hand. "I'll go. You all heard it. She wouldn't have gone there if it wasn't for me." She looked out towards the mine. "Oh God!"

Amy turned to head out, but Tim grabbed her hand. "There's no way I'm letting you go back there. You stay and keep an eye on Stacy, until I get back."

"Can't let you go alone." Francis rushed after Tim. "I'm comeengweeth you."

Tim turned to Allen, fist raised. "Do I need to dare you to come with us?"

"I'd be going either way, so screw your pathetic dare," Allen said. He followed Tim and Francis out of basecamp, and back to the mine.

Tim and Francis stopped at the entrance of the mine. Allen walked past them into the mine.

Tim grabbed Allen. "Wait!"

Allen wrenched his arm free and pushed Tim away from him. "We wouldn't be up here, if you weren't such an ass trying to make me look like a loser. So if anything happens to Stacy or anyone else, it's on you. If I really needed to, I could hike my way down to Nederland—" He jabbed his finger at Tim"—and leave you to clean up your own mess. It's a long way on foot, and there's no way any of you could last that long or even find the right way to go. Let me put it like this. If you can't find your keys, you need me to help everyone get back to town and look for help. Now, pull your shit together, and let's go get your keys." He took out his pocket knife and flipped it open. "Probably won't be much help, but some defense is better than nothing."

Francis stepped away from Allen. "You can't stab a ghost, Allen."

Allen kept his right hand ready to attack while he continued recording with the video camera in his left hand. "If I cut him and he doesn't bleed, I'll start believing in ghosts." He turned and walked into the mine, aiming the video camera from side to side, hoping to spot the backpack. He couldn't remember how far they'd come. With the fright he'd received, the details were lost to Allen. A sharp, burning odor filled the air, making him wrinkle his nose. "Now that I'm here again, I'll agree. It smells like smoke in here."

Tim and Francis followed behind with heavy footsteps. Tim kept his voice low, but Allen could still hear. "You don't think it's really my fault, do you, Francis?"

"How do you say… I plead the fifth," Francis said.

"You're not really American, so you can't do that," Tim said.

Tim's denim backpack came into view on Allen's video camera. Allen reached down and picked it up. "Found it."

"You did?" Francis asked.

Tim jerked the backpack out of Allen's hand. He opened one of the pockets, digging through it. "Come on, come on… Yes! Got my keys. Let's get out of here."

The three of them left the mine and headed back down to basecamp.

Tim rushed into basecamp. "I found my…" he paused, "keys. Amy? Guys get in here."

Allen followed closely behind him. He paused and stared in disbelief. Everything was in shambles. It was obvious there must have been some sort of struggle.

Dark blotches in the dirt led outside. Allen bent down and touched one. It was cooled and slightly congealed "This is blood."

"What?" Tim grabbed Allen's hand and yanked it up. "Whose blood is this?"

Francis came inside. "Blood?"

Allen freed his hand from Tim's grasp and showed Francis the blood-stained dirt. "You think… maybe, being all out of sorts, Stacy attacked Amy?"

Tim shook his head. "No. She may be obsessed with Amy, but she wouldn't hurt her."

"Maybe she would, if she was possessed by the ghost," Francis said.

Allen went back outside to look for a trail. "Stacy was obviously having some kind of panic attack. That mental instability could have caused her to attack anyone without really knowing she was doing it. If there is a trail, we don't have enough light to follow it, and the sun won't be up for a little while. Let's wait until it does, then we'll have an easier time."

Tim came outside, pushing Allen out of the way. "How the hell do we not have enough light to follow a trail?"

Regaining his balance, Allen pointed at basecamp. "For one, the ground inside there, is different than the dirt out here. Blood soaks into dirt better than a dusty hard floor. Also blood is red meaning it's on the lower end of the visible spectrum and doesn't reflect light well. If we had stronger flashlights it might be possible to find a trail. If there is anything you should trust me with, it's that we don't have what we need to see the trail."

Tim raised his voice. "I don't care. We're going to look for her now!"

Okay." Allen held up his hands in surrender. "But we'll cover more ground, if we split up."

"The hell I'm going by myself!" Tim retorted.

"Francis can go with you, and I'll go off on my own." Allen started to walk off to search on his own. "But the more ground we cover, the better chances we'll have of finding them." How hard was it for Tim to understand that simple fact?

"Just come with us for now, Allen," Francis said.

Tim, Francis, and Allen left basecamp together and walked around the ruins, calling out for Amy and Stacy. No matter which way they went, they couldn't find any signs of where either girl might be. Where were they? Allen did what he could to keep himself calm. As long as he kept calm, he could focus on making sure everything worked out.

As the search continued, the strange raspy voices incoherently whispered for a moment, but fell silent. It had been so quick, Allen wasn't sure what it was or where it came from.

Francis quivered so much the beam from his flashlight danced across the ground in front of them. "Deed you hear that?"

"Hear what?" Tim asked.

The voices were louder the second time.

"That!" Francis cast his light around in an arch, like he was trying to illuminate the source of the spectral sounds.

"Yeah, I heard it that time." Tim turned to Allen. "Did you?"

Allen looked around. "It was probably just a wild animal. They're usually more afraid of us than we are of them."

The voices were even louder for the third time.

"That's not an animal," Tim said.

"Well, eet's not human," Francis said.

Allen moaned. "I'm getting sick of all this superstitious crap. I'm gonna go off and keep looking for Amy and Stacy on my own. Cover more ground. I'll meet you guys back at basecamp."

Allen set off on his own, and when Tim and Francis were nowhere in sight, he attempted to follow the voices, wondering if he could find Amy and Stacy by doing so. A hunched shadowy figure appeared in the doorway to one of the buildings, but when Allen looked again, it was gone. He walked over to the rundown building. The air grew colder with each step. He looked inside, but there was nothing.

The voices fell silent. "I should head back." Allen said. He swung his video camera from side to side, trying to find even the slightest clue. As he passed the mine, he found a video camera on the ground. He picked it up. *Maybe it'll have some clue to where Amy and Stacy are.*

When Allen made it back to basecamp, Tim sat huddled in the corner.

"Where's Francis?" Allen asked.

"Francis. I told him not to do it, but he dropped his video camera and went into the mine."

Allen rewound the video camera and watched the screen.

Francis' voice was frantic, "Tim, don't go eento the mine!" The screen shook as he ran to catch up to Tim. Francis' hand reached out to Tim, but Tim turned and punched Francis, making him drop the video camera.

Allen looked down. Blood was spattered on Tim's shoe. Tim seemed distracted, as though listening to someone. Allen backed slowly out of basecamp, whispering. "What did you do, Tim?"

Tim snapped his head toward Allen, leapt up, and tackled him, punching him repeatedly.

"We're friends!" Allen balled himself up, screaming in between blows. "You can't betray me!"

Tim continued striking Allen, until his screaming went silent.

Allen was dazed but not completely out of it.

Tim stood and grabbed Allen by his leg, dragging him towards the mine, shouting, "We were never friends!"

Deep in the mine, Allen came out of his daze. Tim had his back to Allen as he attempted to light a fire. Sparks flashed every few seconds as the familiar sound of the flint and steel striking filled the quiet darkness of the min.

Somehow, Allen's video camera was still in his hand. It caught movements from the further down the mine. The flashes from the sparks illuminated the disfigured faces of Stacy, Amy, and Francis. They appeared as if they had been dead and decaying for years. Their eyes shined briefly on the screen. Behind them even further down the shaft, countless blackened dead faces watched.

As panic surged through him, Allen fought it back and stayed quiet on the ground, adjusting the camera so it had a better view of the horror. Several pale humanoid forms melted back into the darkness, arms, hands, and eye-shines of unknown people crawling backward on the ground, up the walls, and on the ceiling. Each of them looked exactly alike, with no features to distinguish them from the others

With the fire started, Tim turned back to Allen. Again strange voices were heard in brief snatches. Tim appeared distracted and turned away.

Allen mumbled, "I wouldn't pick Tim. Tim wasn't first."

One voice, smoother than the others, whispered in Allen's ear, "He'll kill you if you don't get him first. You know he deserves it. Do it!"

Allen scrambled for a large rock visible in the fire-light and grabbed it. He dropped the video camera and got to his feet. Tim turned towards Allen as he raised the rock, striking Tim in the face. Tim fell over. Allen leaned over Tim, raising the rock over his head. With both hands, he continued to beat Tim. Every strike with the rock sprayed Allen with Tim's blood. In his mouth, it tasted of salt and rust.

After killing Tim, Allen sat beside the body for a moment, panting, before coming to and standing. Instead of heading towards the mine's entrance, he reached down and dragged Tim towards the fire. Allen dropped the body into the fire and squatted beside it.

Allen let out a mirthless laugh. "You were right, Tim. We were never friends, but I wasn't talking to you." He turned to look deeper into the mines. "I've done it. I brought them to you."

Several hands reached out from the darkness, taking turns as they gently caressed Allen's face. Then they grabbed him, pulling him deeper into the mine.

Allen panicked. He twisted and writhed, trying to break free of their grip, but for every hand he broke free from, another grabbed. "Wait! What are you doing? You said I'd be free and never have to come back. Please. Stop!"

Allen turned to run, but one hand caught his ankle, making him trip. Before he could get up, multiple hands snatched him, jerking him violently into the darkness.

R.E.D.

R.E.D. started writing in college on fanfiction.net thinking, "If they can do it why can't I?" Soon after, he began writing original stories based on his extremely vivid dreams. He is often asked what goes on in his mind to have dreams like that. He simply says, "Hey, it works when it comes to story writing. It feels like I live my stories through the main characters, and I simply put it into words later."

Marrying In

by Carrie Vaughn

Alice leaned on the immigration officer's counter until he scowled at her. She straightened.

"How long did you say you're here for?" he asked for the third time, staring at the data on his scanner.

"Um. . .I'm staying." For the rest of my life. Forever. She hardly believed it herself. "I've got the visa, the immigration stamp should be right there."

"Let me scan you again."

She offered the back of her hand and the officer scanned her chip yet again. This time, something must have pinged right because his eyes lit up.

"Oh yes--here it is. Marriage visa, immigration stamp, it all checks out." He clicked a button, uploaded her pass into her chip, and gave her a bureaucratic smile. "Welcome to Colorado."

She repeated to herself, had to be nice, couldn't yell, couldn't growl. He was only doing his job. Her smile was strained. "Thank you."

The reward for her patience was finding Tom waiting just outside of immigration, before she even reached baggage claim. She lunged at him, and he caught her in his arms, laughing.

"You made it! I can't believe you're finally here!"

Neither could she. They'd married six months ago. She hadn't seen him since their honeymoon in New York City. It had taken a year for the visa to come through, and she hadn't wanted to risk coming on a tourist visa, then having her immigration application shuffled to the back of the queue when her time ran out. She'd contacted Colorado immigration every day for the last month looking for reassurance that her application really was on the track for approval. None of the department's email replies reassured her. Finally being here in Tom's arms seemed like the end of some monstrous quest.

So there they stood in the walkway outside customs, arms around each other, kissing like the characters in an old movie while the crowd pushed around them.

Within an hour they were on the tram heading for Pueblo, where Tom was from, where his family had lived for almost two hundred years. They had Pioneer status, which gave everyone in his family free residency. That was why they'd decided to move her out here, rather than move him back to Maryland. She wrote ad copy, her job was portable. She'd join the ranks of the state's many telecommuters. His residency didn't transfer. If he moved out of state for more than five years, barring school or military service, he'd lose his status.

They'd decided they wanted their children to be born here, so they could make that choice for themselves when they grew up. It was much easier leaving the state than getting in.

"You don't have to do this," Tom said. "I'm perfectly happy telling her to wait a couple of days. You should come home--I want to show you the house, you can tell me everything I did wrong with it. Rest up after the flight. You don't have to see her straight off the plane like this."

Tom's mother had invited them over for dinner tonight. Alice had only met Tom's parents and the rest of his family once--at the wedding, back East. She hadn't had much contact with them then. They'd had a rowdy buffet reception, certainly not enough of a chance to sit down and get to know anyone. Tom seemed to assume they wouldn't get along, the old mother-in-law cliché. Alice didn't know why he was so worried.

"No, it's fine. I'm looking forward to it." Might as well get it over with. . .

Tom frowned, clearly not looking forward to it. She squeezed his hand and tried to be reassuring.

Together they leaned toward the window and watched the scenery pass by: mountains to the west, past the rolling green prairie, sharp, uneven smudges on the horizon. They both repelled and beckoned, like a fortress wall. She hadn't seen mountains like this since a family trip to Aspen when she was little. She hardly remembered.

"What do you think?" Tom said, with obvious pride, like he'd painted the scene himself just for her. Like a child with a new creation, he was desperate for her to be pleased.

"It's so different," she said, immediately realizing that wasn't right. Not enthusiastic enough. Not happy enough. "It's beautiful. I can't wait for you to show me around."

He kissed the top of her head. This was right, she told herself. Coming here was definitely the right thing to do.

Tom's older brother Chris was waiting for them at the tram station with the car. Without leaving the driver's seat he opened the back, so Tom could throw in her luggage.

"Is that all you brought?" Chris said at Alice's one suitcase and shoulder bag. Not even a hello first.

"The rest is being shipped," Tom said.

"I figured there'd be steamer trunks. We could have taken the bus."

She had no idea what to say to that. "Don't bring more than I can carry, that's the rule."

"Huh. Maybe she will survive out here," Chris said to his brother.

Alice stared at Tom, trying to initiate one of those silent conversations that married people were supposed to be able to have: *what is he talking about?*

Tom kissed her and hurried her into the back seat, sliding in next to her. Apparently they hadn't been married long enough for the telepathy to start working. It was just the time apart. They had to get used to each other again. They loved each other, everything would be fine.

They set off.

"How was your flight?" Chris looked over to the back seat. "No trouble?"

"No, none at all." She had an accent, she suddenly

realized. She sounded different than the brothers: more clipped, softer R's. She'd never noticed it before.

For the rest of her life--or as long as she stayed here--she'd be the one with the accent.

Tom's parents lived in a newer part of town, which meant their house was fifty years old rather than a hundred. Tom had told her some of the history of the place, the stringent growth controls that made building permits as hard to get as immigration visas. Finding any construction younger than about thirty years was hard. Businesses had learned to adapt and use existing structures. Colorado had rebuilt its economy to strike a balance between business and preservation. The whole state was a carefully maintained park, now. It had also become a status address for the wealthy, who paid for the privilege of living here.

Upon entering the well-kept ranch-style home, Alice was mobbed. A couple of big dogs barked and jumped, a handful of people yelled at them to get down, and everyone in the living room stood, calling out and saying hello. Tom waved back, Chris pushed past her to herd the dogs away, and Alice froze, stunned. Then Tom's mother Connie appeared in front of her and hugged her.

She'd acquired a whole new family.

Tom introduced her to the various aunts and uncles and cousins she hadn't met yet, and the only reason she remembered names was Tom had prepped her beforehand. He'd been talking about these people for as long as she'd known him.

The scent of cooking she couldn't identify filled the house. Dinnertime revealed roast chicken and mashed potatoes, three different vegetables, and a Jell-O salad.

For some reason Alice had expected something more rustic. More exotic. Slabs of venison maybe.

After dinner, the family retired to the living room for coffee. This was when the real conversation started. Alice sat close to Tom on the sofa.

"Alice, you ever been to Colorado before?" one of the aunts, Katie, asked.

She was happy to answer yes. "When I was about twelve my family came here for a ski trip."

Katie's husband, Joey, snorted. "That's not really Colorado. Probably took the shuttle straight there from the airport and never left the slopes. Where'd you go? Aspen?"

She found herself blushing, because he was right. They had taken the shuttle, and they'd never left the town. "Um, yes."

A cousin, who was either Pete or Paul, Alice suddenly couldn't remember, said "I thought that was the way everyone wanted it--show the tourists the ski resorts, then herd 'em back to the airport, and leave the good stuff for the rest of us."

Tom leaned in to whisper to her, "This is the obligatory political argument. Happens every time." He wore a tight-lipped grimace that was probably supposed to emulate a smile.

"That's right," Joey said smugly. "Now we finally have the water and infrastructure to support what we have without worrying about what it's going to be like in twenty years."

"I think some of you would be just as happy going back to the frontier days."

Some of them practically had. Alice remembered Tom's stories: Joey and Kate owned a ranch and raised cattle. Chris managed an organic food distributor, and Pete/Paul was a back country pilot. Tom was a biologist for the forest service. Most of the state's jobs were in agriculture, service industries, or small business. This had become a state of entrepreneurs--people made their own jobs. It all seemed like an adventure.

Joey said, "You're too young to remember what it was like. Believe me, this is better. We finally have things under control."

"It's a damn socialist state is what it is--"

Tom interrupted. "So, Aunt Katie, how's Stuart liking school? He's at Boulder, right?"

Katie opened her mouth, but Joey spoke first. "Damn straight. Didn't think he had to leave the state like some people."

Tom glowered. He and Alice had met as students at Harvard.

This sounded like a long-running argument. Alice wasn't the cause of it, only the current catalyst. She had to keep reminding herself that.

"You kids just don't remember what it was like," Joey grumbled again.

"At least we stopped the Texans from coming in," one of the older uncles, Harry, said. Half the room--the older ones, Tom's parent's generation--laughed.

It hardly seemed fair, when states like North Dakota were paying people to move in. She knew better than to say that out loud.

"Marrying in's practically the only way to get residency without paying the fees anymore," Connie said to Alice. "You're very lucky you met Tom."

Yes, she was, she wasn't going to argue with that. But Tom's mother made it sound like she'd married him just to get into Colorado--not that she was only here because of Tom. She already missed the ocean.

"I told him that would happen when he went to college out of state," Connie continued, inevitably. "I told him as soon as people found out he's from Colorado, the girls would swarm him trying to get in."

Tom was clenching his hands in his lap. His knuckles were white.

Connie's older sister Jane was close enough to pat Alice on the knee. "Don't mind her, she always hoped Tom would marry that Doyle girl from La Junta. Never expected him to drag back an Easterner."

Tom was right. They should have just gone home from the airport.

His family didn't know how long she and Tom had discussed her coming here, how many pages they'd scribbled out the pros and cons on, all the hair-pulling, tearful late nights. They didn't know how much she'd given up. They only saw people clamoring to get in. They only knew their pride in their place. Their pride in their history.

"This all started with those Pioneer special interest license plates," Tom muttered. "You start marking people, giving them status, it all goes down hill from there."

"I had ancestors on the Mayflower," Alice said weakly.

Jane smiled. "Sorry, honey, that doesn't mean anything here." She stood and went to the kitchen for more coffee.

Connie sighed. "At least you came here instead of stealing him away. That would have been hard to take."

Alice set down her cup of coffee. "Would you excuse me a moment?"

She went outside, to the back porch. Culture shock, that was all it was. She didn't have to like Tom's family. She and Tom had a place of their own, a house downtown that had belonged to his great-grandfather. She'd have her own office, her own space. She could start rebuilding her life.

Pioneers, they called themselves, even now, when they had indoor plumbing and power and wireless, when they'd been rooted in the same spot for two hundred years, when they'd turned their state into a New Frontier triumph. Didn't they realize, she was the real pioneer? She was the one who'd left everything behind to start fresh in a strange place. Even the air smelled different here: dry, dusty. Half a mile away, the neighborhood ended and the prairie started. The wind from there was sharp. She could just make out the gray smudge of mountains to the west, where the sun had started to set. The door to the back porch opened. Tom emerged and joined her on the railing.

"You regret it already, don't you? Me dragging

you out here, into the middle of a family you don't know and a place you don't like."

"I have to say, it's a bit of an adventure," she said. Tom bowed his head, disappointed. He really wanted her to like it here. She didn't want to disappoint him. She hooked her arm around his. "I didn't say I didn't like it, Tom. It's just different. People told me that coming out here is like traveling to a different country. I guess I didn't believe it."

"We'll take a drive tomorrow. Into the mountains. I'll show you the good stuff."

"I'd like that."

The sun set further, and the light changed, becoming more golden, more diffused, reflecting off and filtering through a few puffy clouds that had gathered around the mountaintops.

Tom said, "Back East--you have cathedrals, monuments, history. That's what people go there to see. Here--we have the land. That's all we have. The families who've been here a long time take a lot of pride in that. They don't like the idea of people coming in and taking it away from them."

The colors of the sunset changed: the clouds turned orange, pink, purple, lighting up in vaporous wisps, all glowing. They were the colors of a Maxfield Parrish painting, pure and joyful, splashed across a vast, huge sky. Alice had never seen such colors in life. And then, after only a few moments, the sun dropped a couple more degrees, and the colors faded. Just like that, the sunset ended, all gone, leaving gray clouds.

Tom sighed, and Alice wrapped her arms around

him. He held her close. That sunset--that was the welcome she'd been looking for, the one she'd hoped to find.
This felt like coming home.

Carrie Vaughn

Carrie Vaughn is the author of the New York Times bestselling series of novels about a werewolf named Kitty. She also writes for young adults (her novel STEEL was named to the ALA's 2012 Amelia Bloomer list of the best books for young readers with strong feminist content), the Golden Age superhero series, and other contemporary fantasy stories. She's a contributor to the Wild Cards series of shared world superhero books edited by George R. R. Martin, and her short stories have appeared in numerous magazines and anthologies. She's a graduate of the Odyssey Fantasy Writing Workshop, and in 2011, she was nominated for a Hugo Award for best short story.

An Air Force brat, she survived her nomadic childhood and managed to put down roots in Boulder, Colorado, where she lives with her fluffy attack dog, a miniature American Eskimo named Lily.

Visit her at www.carrievaughn.com

Inner Fire

by Fatma Alici

I'd always felt trapped inside. My skin was like a cage holding me in. At night, I'd wake up gasping for air, as if I couldn't breathe. There was no good reason for me to be this way. There were no horrible events in my life. I was happy. At least, I thought I was.

It was one of the hottest days I had ever experienced in Colorado Springs. At seven in the morning, the sun had only poked its head out, and already the temperature was in the seventies. As I pulled up in my rust-bucket of a car, Liddie closed the windows in our rented townhouse. She kept the windows open at night to let the cold in. A window A/C unit wasn't in the budget.

Opening the front door, I let out a heavy sigh. As I exhaled a white cloud bellowed outward. *That doesn't seem right.* The radio told me—not a minute ago—it would be hot again today. I sucked in a deep breath and let it go. The white cloud flowed outward once more. Puzzled, and a little bit disturbed, I opened the door and went into our home.

Liddie looked up from shutting the blind in our tiny kitchen window to smile. "Zack, off work a little early today? You want some cinnamon rolls?"

"I know you like baking Liddie, but isn't that a bad idea to do in this weather?" Liddie worked as a baker, and even baked at home, but in this weather, it was ridiculous.

Liddie picked chipped plate with a slightly misshapen cinnamon roll on it. As she brought it close to me she bounced it. "You know you want it."

I sighed and took it. The dough was flaky, buttery, and filled with delicious cinnamon. It hit the spot. "Still, you know I'm right."

"They're mess-ups from work. They're all a bit lopsided. The boss was going to throw them away, but I talked him into letting me have them." She gave me a look over. "What's wrong?"

"Nothing. I was imagining things before I walked in." I chewed on the cinnamon roll, feeling a little better after the long night of cleaning out freezers. "By the way, isn't Carl supposed to be off by now?" All of us roommates worked the night shift. It paid extra, and nobody else wanted to do it.

"Zack, tell me what's going on." Liddie put her hands on her hips, she tossed her head to the side sending a cascade of rich, corkscrew curls over her shoulders. The look in her hazel eyes told me not to argue with her.

"Well, umm, I can see my breath." It seemed silly. "That's what I thought when I was outside anyway, but I don't think I can see it now."

Liddie crunched up her forehead as she tilted her head up at me. "What do you mean? When did you see your breath?"

I set the plate on the counter, then let out a long breath. Again, my breath showed up as if it was a cold day outside. Giving Liddie a shrug, I picked my plate back up, "Weird."

She walked up to me, and put the back of her hand up to my forehead. A second later, she jerked her hand back. "You're freezing."

"I feel fine." I took another bite of cinnamon roll.

Liddie huffed, her hands back on her hips. "I don't see how you can eat right now. This seems serious—seeing your breath and your forehead is freezing." She stopped talking. "Wait a minute," she said and rushed off to the tiny bathroom in the small connecting hallway between our two bedrooms.

When she came back, she handed me the old-style thermometer. "Put this in your mouth, under your tongue."

I swallowed the bite of my roll I had been chewing and eyed the thermometer. "Is that really necessary?"

"Zack, if you're sick, we need to take you to Urgent Care." She glanced over at the clock above the oven. "Soon too, Urgent Care will fill up once it opens."

As I stuck the stupid thing in my mouth, Carl burst into the house.

"Damn, it's already getting hot out there." Sweat glimmered on his broad, dark forehead. He rushed to change into his lounge clothes.

After a minute, Liddie looked at the thermometer and let out a gasp. "Your temperature is ninety degrees! That's so not normal. We have got to take you to the hospital."

Carl barreled into the room. "What's this? Zack looks fine to me."

"His temperature is really cold." Liddie rounded on Carl. "You know he'll ignore it unless we make him do something. He's stubborn."

"He isn't a-wilting," Carl said with a rakish grin.

"Why am I bothering? Both of you are the same, stubborn as mules." Liddie's face got all squinty. That was never a good sign.

"He's tough, Liddie. Calm down." Carl gave me a sympathetic glance before stepping back from her. "All right, all right, we'll take him in. But, do we have the money for that?"

That made the whole discussion shut down for several minutes. Even with all three of us living together, it barely was enough to pay the regular bills.

"Well, I did get a bit of extra cash fixing the neighbors car. Not a lot, but I can put some in the bucket," Carl said after a few minutes.

I nodded. "I have a small amount of rainy-day money."

"I can throw in some too. We'll have to stop by an ATM to get the cash out," Liddie said before turning to Carl. "Get out of your lounge clothes. The Urgent Care will be opening in less than an hour. If we don't get there right away, we'll be waiting all day."

Carl rolled his eyes but with a smile on his face. His dark eyes twinkled as he disappeared back into the bedroom.

It wasn't much later we all piled into Carl's generously sized car. Mine was a two-seater with only the illusion of a back seat, and Liddie didn't have one. The car bounced up and down on all the potholes on the way to Urgent Care. The roads were quiet as we arrived at the Urgent Care before it opened.

Fortunately, the cheap, barely padded beige chairs were empty so early in the morning. An old couple stood next to coffee pot, arguing over how much creamer one of them used. The receptionist gave me a weary smile before handing over the paperwork.

I sat down next to a window and started to fill out the forms. A deep ache pulsed at the base my skull. Every second that went by, it got harder and harder to focus. The ache worked like a lightning bolt, shooting its way up my skull. Letting out a stifled noise, I spread my hand across the clipboard the paper was on. To my horror, frost rippled across the paper to the edge of the clipboard. A sharp pain stabbed at the base of my spine. The clipboard dropped and the frost melted almost instantly, turning the paper wet.

"Holy…" Carl trailed off.

I looked up at him, his dark eyes wide and round. They were fixed on my hands.

Liddie glanced over. "What's wrong? Is he worse?" She leaned closer to peer at me.

Carl tightened his lips and gave a sharp shake of his head. "Let's go outside."

"What on earth are you talking about, Carl?" Liddie's voice rose in clear annoyance.

Carl gave her a grave stare, something he almost never did. It silenced her. He got up and motioned for us to follow. Together we went outside.

Carl tugged me around to the edge of the building and behind the dumpster. "What was that?"

"I don't know. I can't believe I did that. This couldn't be happening. Did I cause frost to form? How could that be possible?" Yet, I couldn't drum up the emotion to be terrified—the emotions felt far away from me. Like the shock and terror were to big for me to feel.

Carl gave several swift nods. "You are really cold now. I can feel it coming off of you." His gaze flicked to the dumpster. "Do it again."

"What are you two talking about? I saw Zack flinch in pain and then you rushed us out of there. Away from the doctors, I might add," Liddie snipped.

"It couldn't have happened." How could it have? It didn't happen. That's all I could rationalize.

"It did happen. We need to accept that. Otherwise, we can't move forward. Ignoring this isn't going to work." Then Carl jerked up my hand, pressing it to the dumpster.

It didn't frost over. "We only imagined it."

Carl shook his head. "I don't think so. Maybe you have to try to do it, to think about doing it."

"Why would we want to try to do that?" It would be a lot better if we could just forget any of this happened.

"I still don't know what the two of you are going on about. Let's go back inside." Liddie crossed her arms, tapping her shoe against the cracked asphalt.

I pressed my hand harder into the side of the dumpster. "Forget it. We should both go inside."

Before I could lift my hand, Carl held it there with his. "C'mon, concentrate, for a second."

Fighting the urge to really lay into him, I turned to the dumpster and focused on my hand.. The sidewall became coated in frost. Large icicles connected me to the dumpster like an ice sculpture jutting between me and it. I jumped back and my hand broke away as ice shards hit the cement and melted. I stood there staring at them for a moment before sitting down. "It *is* happening."

Liddie let out a sound. "Did I…?" She swallowed. "Did I just see that?"

Carl looked between the dumpster, Liddie, and me. "Yup, you did."

"I don't understand." I held out my fingertips. Ice started to spread out like webbing between them. "Is it a power?"

"Seems like it. Really odd side effect of a disease otherwise," Carl shrugged.

Liddie let out a gasp as she stepped toward me, her feet crunching on the ice. Each moment seemed to take a long time as she extended her hand out to my head. "You are colder now." Her fingers came away covered in frost.

Carl let out a low whistle. "This is some freaky shit." He grabbed Liddie and pulled her back. "Wait a second, we don't know if he's safe to be around. What if he freezes one of us?"

My heart thudded at a rapid pace. Everything seemed to fast and to slow at once. I sank down into ice. "I'm a danger to everyone."

"No." Liddie shook her head and stepped forward. "Zack would never let anything happen to me. He's always been there for me."

"He won't *want* to hurt you. Obviously, he's got some stuff going on. Stuff we don't know nothing about." Carl pulled her back again. "Best to not get too close."

"You guys should head home." Carl and Liddie had my back since I'd found my way to Colorado Springs. When I had no money for food, they kept me fed. Never once had they held it over my head. The idea of accidently hurting or killing them scared me more than anything else.

His hand still clutching Liddie's arm, Carl said, "I don't feel right about leaving you, but we really don't know if you're dangerous. You're turning things into ice. What if you turned one of us into ice? What then?"

"We aren't letting him deal with this on his own." Liddie twisted out of Carl's grasp. He might be a man, but Liddie was tall and in good shape from hours of labor at the bakery. "If you try to get me to let you handle this on your own, Zack, you have knocked something loose in your head." Her eyes shifted back to the Urgent Care building. "Let's get you in to the doctor."

I didn't think the doctor could do anything. Ice powers weren't something they probably learned to deal with at med school.

"No, wait." Carl jerked his head to the side. "If people find out about his powers, well, you know how it turns out. The government—or some other organization—will try to seize him. Use him for experiments. He'll never be free again."

"What are you talking about?" I frowned. Did he know other people who could freeze things?

Carl looked down and thought for a bit. "In superhero movies and stuff, people with magic powers get whisked away by secret organizations or the government. Especially powers like yours—scary stuff. If others find out, they'll think you're dangerous and try to lock you away. We better keep this quiet."

Huffing out a breath, Liddie rolled her eyes. "This isn't a movie."

"You really want to risk it?".

"Do you want to risk that this is some odd disease that might kill him?" Liddie tapped her foot a few times. She pointed back at the Urgent Care.

"He seems fine—other than turning everything to ice." Carl glared at her.

"Oh yes, because turning things to ice and being extremely cold are normal things. Of course, he's all fine and dandy. Don't know why I was concerned in the first place." Liddie's whole posture went stiff.

"You really gonna fight me over this?" Carl's eyes went wide and incredulous.

"Both of you stop it." I'd had enough. "It's my life. Don't I get to make any decisions about it?'

They turned to stare at me. Carl winced and looked away. Liddie might have blushed. It was hard to tell under the shadow of the building.

"Right." I massaged my temples. "I don't want to go away to some kind of government agency, I don't want to be sick, and I definitely don't want to put you guys in danger. I think it's best if I pack up and strike out on my own. Maybe after a few months I'll have this powers thing settled and I can come back. Then, together we'll figure things out."

"Zack," Liddie's eyes turned glossy as a tear trailed down her face. "Don't leave us. You're my best friend in the whole world."

I wanted to take her hand in mine, but I didn't want to risk hurting her. "You know it's for the best."

She gave a slight nod and looked away from me as she rubbed the tears out of her eyes.

"Well," Carl said, "let's get you home."

We got back into Carl's car—this time, I sat in the back. The seats iced over as I slid in. As the car pulled out of the parking lot, I ran my fingers over the window glass. It iced under them, making frost patterns that melted in the early morning sun. My breath was visible every time I breathed unless I kept it shallow.

As we pulled into the gravel side yard we used for parking, Carl let out a half-laugh, half-sigh. It was nothing like his regular loud over-the-top chuckle. "We didn't have to turn on the AC. That's something, I suppose."

Liddie let out a sob. She wrenched the car door open, fumbled with the lock on the house and stumbled inside.

"Maybe, save the joking for later," I said.

Carl gave me a sheepish look in the rearview, and shrugged before getting out.

I followed them into the house. Right away, I went to my bedroom to pack up some things, but I left my rainy day money. They'd need a way to cover my part of the bills for a while. I wasn't sure I'd survive this whole ice powers thing to begin with. Zipping up my beaten duffel bag, it finally hit me. I was abandoning my friends, my home, my job, everything—because I had ice powers. I might be dying, for all I knew. "Dammit," I said and sagged down in front of my twin bed.

My whole life I'd had to crawl out of one bad situation just to land in another. My parents died when I was born, my foster parents had returned me after a year, and I'd never done well in school. Finally, things had started to look up. Now this. Why didn't the world want me to get ahead?

It sucked. There was no point in denying it, but, at least I wasn't dead. Shoving my duffel to the floor, I climbed on the bed, standing up—it wasn't as if I had to worry about the laundry anymore—and looked out the small window. Looking a bit to the right, you could see Pikes Peak. The mountain's serene, cold, fresh beauty always sung to me. At least I could stick around here and see the mountains every day.

Pain burst in the base of my skull. It was so quick—it took me to my knees. I fell on my side as everything was dwarfed by that pain. Everything in my vision turned blue and white. Pain screamed down my spine—even the tips of my toes sparked in agony. My throat closed and I thought, for one moment, this was the end.

Then everything fell away. I stood on a mountain ledge, rubble all around me, the world spread out as green carpet beneath. The sky seemed bluer, wider, and more wonderful. My back stretched and shadows spread out from behind me. A voice—where it came from, I don't know—echoed in my head. **"Go there. Be born."**

"What?" I asked as my eyes popped open. Then I let out a gasp. My room was covered in a thick layer of frost, beautiful complex patterns across every surface. "Oh god," I managed before sitting up.

The door flew open. Carl and Liddie stood there. Liddie's hands shook as she gazed at the ice. "You screamed. Are you okay?"

She began to step in but Carl grabbed her arm. "Liddie, I wouldn't do that if I were you." He tapped the floor with his foot. "You're wearing socks and that's solid ice."

"Both of you back up. I need to go—leave Colorado." Pain cut me off, the image of the mountain cliff etched in my vision. It was the top of Pikes Peak. I knew I couldn't leave Colorado—I had to go there first.

Still holding Liddie's arm, Carl's dark gaze flickered over me. "What's the matter, man? You look pale—even for a white dude."

The words poured out of me. "I have to go to Pikes Peak." Afraid they would insist on coming, I grabbed my duffel bag, using it to push them back. *I need to get away from them.* Before I finished the thought, throbbing agony arched across my back. My legs gave out, leaving me in a heap on the floor.

"Zack?" Liddie's worried voice asked me from above. "What's going on? You keep making these terrible noises. What can I do to help you?"

"Carl, can my car drive up Pikes Peak?" My body wasn't letting me *not* go up there.

Carl shook his head while leaning against the door frame "Your brakes and transmission are already iffy in that old beater. Way too easy for something to go wrong at that height."

"I guess I'll take the cog railway." If my car couldn't go up, at least, that could take me.

"Zack, you're freezing things. What if you freeze the train? You might kill everyone on board." Liddie sounded outright horrified by the idea.

Carl clicked his tongue. "That and, during the summer, it's way too busy to buy a ticket last minute."

My head swiveled to look in the direction of Pikes Peak, even though I couldn't see it. "I have to go up there."

"Why?" Carl said with a snap to his voice.

My friends were amazing people, but even they might worry about me hearing voices in my head. Yet, if I wanted their help, they needed to know the truth. "I had a vision. There is a place up at Pikes Peak — I gotta go. I know it sounds crazy."

Liddie shifted back and forth. "All of this is crazy."

"I'll take you." Carl held out his hand to me.

It was a gesture of friendship and trust, yet I didn't dare. These powers, whatever they were, might kill him. Instead, I pushed myself up. "What if I freeze the car? You and Liddie could die. I don't want to risk your lives like that."

"What are you going to do instead?" Carl asked in an overly matter of fact way. He always talked like that when he thought Liddie and I were being stubborn.

I thought it over. "Maybe, I'll take some of money—enough for a car rental."

"You got no credit and a bad driving record. You had that car accident last year, remember?" Carl tapped his hands together.

"That wasn't my fault. That idiot rammed into me." The whole thing irritated me. The skinny, nervous sixteen year old shouldn't have been within ten feet of a car. Yet his parents had bought him a sleek, shiny new machine that smashed into my previous junker.

Liddie rubbed her hands nervously. "I hate to side with Carl when he's like this, but it's still on your record. The rental people probably wouldn't be likely to sign out to you."

Another reminder that living this close to the edge was not easy. "It isn't safe. I'm sure what all this ice stuff is, or how to control it."

"It isn't." Carl rubbed the back of his neck. "But, can you make it safe?"

"I don't know." My skin itched. I wanted to be on my way. "Maybe, like focus my energy like I did at the dumpster? Still…, what if something happens and I can't control it?"

"You got in that fight outside my shop to protect me," Carl said. "That guy had a knife, but you backed me anyway. That wasn't safe."

Liddie stood still, finally, and looked me in the eye. "You threw my boyfriend out when you caught him hitting me. I even screamed at you not to touch him." Her eyes welled up with tears. "You saved me from myself."

"None of those are ice powers." As far as dangerous and crazy, these powers took the cake.

Carl gave me a crooked grin. "Just because you're turning into a cartoon princess doesn't mean you need to get all dramatic."

I let out an annoyed sound in shock.

Liddie made a stifled sound that turned into a laugh. Her hands clapped over her mouth in a futile attempt to keep it in.

The tension of the last hour hit us all at once. Laughter bubbled out of us and we couldn't stop. Every little noise, every attempt to shush each other, ended up starting another round. We all ended up on the floor, wheezing to get our breath back.

"You need us," Liddie said. She was the first to recover.

"No fighting. We got your back." Carl said with all the bravado he could muster.

"Let me try something first. Before you drag me out to the car, that is." A sharp sting grew at the base of my skull. "Out," I said.

Reluctantly, they slinked back into the living room. Bracing myself, I held out my hands. The webbing formed faster, exploding between my fingers and outward. It thickened faster than I could follow. Then, it cracked. The ice around me turned to slush. Heat hit me like a slap in the face.

"Did that help at all?," Carl said from the living room.

"A bit," I said, before stepping out into the hall. "I'm still not sure how much control I have over it."

"Zack, let us help you, will ya?" Carl grinned.

"All right, fine, but at the first sign I'm losing control, I'm jumping out of that car, whether or not it kills me."

Liddie's face tensed but she gave a terse nod.

Carl gave me a smug grin. "I'm not stressing."

"What is wrong with you, Carl?" Liddie whipped around to rail into him. "This is serious. Take it seriously; everything is a joke to you."

Carl cocked his head to the right. "I am. Zack has had my back a hundred different ways. Today, I'm deciding to trust him. Even if he doesn't trust himself."

All the warm sentiment was making me uncomfortable. "Let's go. The quicker we do this, the less time there is to have something bad happen."

"We should grab coats. If Zack keeps making things cold, we'll need them." Liddie switched to her "hurry" mode, gathering coats, drinks, and snacks. Carl went out to check the car for the drive up the mountain.

I stood in the middle of our box-shaped living room, trying to get some more control over myself. Holding my fingers slightly apart, I imagined ice connecting them. Slowly and surely, ice spread across my fingers. It didn't feel cold—it was comforting, like a cold glass of water on a hot day. *Maybe if I keep generating ice, I can keep it under some kind of control.*

"**Be born, be free**," the same voice said, echoing in my head, overwhelming every other sound.

Carl cracked open the door. "Car's good. Liddie, you done?"

"Water and muffins." She held up a small cooler. In the other hand were our jackets.

I took long strides to the door. "My power feels weaker. I feel a bit warm. Let's take advantage of that."

We piled into the car and drove off. Mountain peaks jutted out of the early morning sky, still frosted with snow. They took my breath away. The more I looked at them, the more rushed I felt. Even as we headed in that direction as fast as the speed limit would let us, it didn't feel fast enough. Yet, I couldn't look away.

"You doing okay, Zack?" Liddie asked from the front seat, her face pinched up.

"I'm not sure." Wrenching my eyes away from the mountains, I tried to give her a smile.

Her eyes teared up. "I wish I understood what's happening."

Liddie always felt better when she could feed people. Everything was better if she could stuff someone full of food.

"Can I have a drink?" I asked, more to have her do something than because I was thirsty.

Unzipping the cooler, she pulled out a metal bottle, handing it over. The second my fingers closed over it, I had an idea. Focusing my energy on it, I attempted to cool the bottle. A thin layer of frost formed around the outside. "See, it's not so bad. I'm a bottle cooler."

Carl whooped from the driver's seat. "Next football party, Zack can chill all our drinks."

Liddie pressed her lips together, her gaze looking somewhere between us. "Thanks for the effort. People aren't supposed to be able to chill things, you know."

"That's weird," Carl said in a quiet voice.

Liddie rolled her eyes and looked at him, a smirk on her face. "Yes, that's what I've been saying this whole time."

Carl shook his head. "Not that. There's a long line to the Pikes Peak Highway. I know it's usually busier in the summer, but I didn't think it was this busy."

A long line of cars winded off the entrance. The road wasn't even open yet. It was still early in the morning. "Yeah, that is weird," I said. Though, for some reason, it was less weird now that I could freeze things and see my breath in the heat.

Liddie rubbed her neck. "Was there an event or something today? I sort of remember something being said on the news a few weeks back."

None of us could remember. As our car inched forward in the line, tension thickened the air. I had to get to the top of Pikes Peak and I needed to be there soon. Yet today, of all days, the road was packed to the brim. Could it really be a coincidence?

We finally reached the entrance where Colorado Springs city personnel collected the entrance fee. Carl flashed his big friendly smile. "Real busy today, huh? Something going on?"

The guy gave a nod and sort of half-smiled back. "You didn't see on the news? Fort Carson is doing a special half-price day with some activities."

Liddie's face went pale.

Carl went along as if nothing was wrong. "Oh wow, well that's pretty lucky then? That saves me some money."

The guy nodded, took Carl's money, and waved us on through. Once past the sight of the kiosk, the friendly smile left Carl's face and his face tightened. "That's a little strange, don't you think?"

"The military being here? Why? Sounds like they announced it a long time ago." Liddie shook out her curly hair. "I really doubt one has anything to do with the other."

"Zack, you feel you have to be on the summit, right?" Carl asked.

The idea of leaving made me pant as my heart pounded in my ears. My skin felt clammy. "Yeah, I gotta go there."

"The day you get weird powers, the military happens to have some kind of event exactly where you need to be." Carl carefree demeanor slipped away as he talked. "I don't like it. We gotta make sure we avoid them. If they see you doing the stuff you're doing, well, it won't be good."

"You're being paranoid," Liddie scoffed from the front seat. "I'm not even sure what the military would use ice powers for."

"It isn't something everyone has." Carl glanced at me from the rearview mirror with narrowed eyes. "That's reason enough."

Liddie glanced back at me. Deep concern had etched its way into her soft brown features. "Carl, is there something you aren't telling us?"

"I know how the military works. Let's just leave it at that." His tone was flat.

Liddie reached across to rest her hand on his arm. "I'm here for you."

Carl's body relaxed a bit. "You're the best, Liddie. And I don't just say that because of the free food either." He shot her a smile and went back to watching the cars in front of us.

The lane cleared up a bit as we ascended through numerous switchbacks to the top of Pikes Peak. It was slow going, but the views were wonderful. I'd never been up there before, but there were trees, drop off cliffs, and animals all over the place. There were also military vehicles and guys in uniform scattered about handing out free swag. Carl didn't stop at any of them. However, everytime he had to slow down, he let out another curse and tightened his grip on the wheel.

As we climbed, tension continued to grow inside me. I felt jittery, nervous. It was unsettling because I didn't feel that way very often. Each mile, each moment we went higher, it felt worse. My breath showed enough that I laid down in the back seat, cramped as it was for my bulk, so no one could see it.

Trees started to fall away, leaving only scrubby bushes and clumps of straggly grass in their place. "We are pretty high up, huh?"

"It's getting kind of hard to breathe." Liddie gave her head a rough shake. "I'm feeling kind of sleepy."

"Altitude sickness, most likely. Take some aspirin in my glove box and drink a bottle of water," Carl instructed. My eyes were riveted on a cliff, lonely, sprinkled with a light dusting of snow, no parking nearby. My thoughts racing too fast, I opened the door in a panic.

"What are you doing?" Carl hollered from the front seat.

I couldn't answer. I didn't want to answer. The ground hit me hard. Cracking, sharp pain split across my body as I rolled off the road toward the cliff. Everything slowed to a crawl as I made my way to the cliff. "**Be born, be free**." The voice was louder now.

My breath was visible and ice formed under my feet as I walked. The frost pattern spread out from me, crusting over the rocks further away. I tossed off my heavy jacket as I stood there. Then I ripped off my sweatshirt. I didn't feel hot, but I couldn't stand to have all of that on me either. My thin cotton shirt felt right.

Behind me, a car rumbled over the rough surface on the dirt pull off. I'd seen several as we went up the mountain. Carl said they were for cars whose brakes had overheated. *Carl, that's right, he's here too.*

It took all my focus to turn back to see both him and Liddie scrambling out of the car. Carl ran at me. "Get back in the car." He peered off in the distance. "Before one them sees you."

"I need to be here." Looking back at the cliff, I headed in that direction.

A calloused hand grabbed me. "You're so cold." Liddie jerked my arm, making me turn to look at her.

"Liddie, I need to be here."

"You aren't yourself. Look—you're bleeding. Your other arm looks broken."

For the first time since I jumped from Carl's car, I looked at it. The shape didn't look right. The bone pressed up against my skin. Blood welled up from scrapes across it. "It's fine. It doesn't hurt."

"Is he in shock?" Liddie asked Carl in a trembling voice.

Deep inside my mind, I knew this wasn't right. Liddie was right. My arm should hurt. This should be terrifying. I should be upset. But I wasn't. Overwhelming elation drowned it all. Joy, need, and hope rushed through me, overriding any other emotion. That cliff was all that mattered. "Please, let me go."

Tears streamed down Liddie's face as a sob burst out. "What if he's dying? Carl, we should have taken him to the hospital. Look at him."

Carl stepped around her to peer into my face. His eyes met mine. After a moment, he gave a grim nod and took a step back. "Let him go, Liddie."

"Please, let me go." I begged. That cliff—I needed to be there. The feeling burned in every vein, a cold fire sweeping through me. Every part of me wanted to be standing on top of that cliff.

Another cry as as she tried to get her hand free. There was a slight tugging sensation as she managed to yank it off my arm. "Oh god, I was stuck to him! He's so cold—I was *frozen to him*," Liddie's voice began to rise to a hysterical level.

I couldn't think about that right now. Part of me feared it, but another part pushed the fear aside as I sprinted toward the cliff. Each time my feet struck ground, ice sprung up from under them. As the cliff grew nearer, I started to smile. I'd be there soon. Then something—whatever it was—would happen.

A burning surge shot through my limbs as I toppled to the ground. Electricity rushed through every part of me. I sucked in the cold air as my body contorted. Shocks danced in my fingertips. Frost rippled across my body as a roar started in my ears. An inner warmth spread through me. That feeling grew stronger with each second. It was as if my whole life, I'd never seen color, and now I did.

Something hard and warm snapped over me. My elation evaporated. Ropes burned like fire over me. Several people in military uniforms stepped out from behind the scraggy rocks. My head swirled around to see even more, surrounding us. Guns were held up to Liddie and Carl, herding them toward me.

"We got him," one of the military men spoke into a radio. He tipped his head in my direction. "We've been waiting for one of you to show up."

The words were hard to understand. The urge for something—that something, the reason I was here— seared through my body, overwhelming everything.

"What?" Even that word sounded too drawn out to my ears.

The man looked at me before motioning several more uniforms over. Red hot metal rods glowed in their gloved hands. "You don't even know what you are, do you?"

"Let me go." The words fought their way out of my throat. *I need to do something.*

"Sorry, we can't do that. You're a valuable military asset now. If we let you out of that special net, we won't be able to use you." He kept his gaze on me while speaking to the soldier next to him. "Let them know to come in for pick up. Set up a blockade temporarily around this location. We don't need anyone to see what's going on here."

Despair flooded me. Every fiber of my body was yearning for the change that had stopped with their arrival. My eyes flickered to Carl. His expression caught me. The warm, openness had been replaced with hardened resolve. Those laughing eyes were stones. He kept his gaze on the net around me.

He saw me looking at him and he nodded. "I've got you," he mouthed.

Rolling to the side, slapping the gun aside, he darted up to the net. Shots caught him in the leg. Blood splashed across the frost and snow. His hands yanked off the net anyway.

I reached for him but my body seized up instead. Frost shot across my arms. Cold wrapped around me. A sharp twist dropped me on all fours. The soldiers braced their guns and one of them dragged Carl back to where he had been. My face felt pulled on as my vision blurred.

Sharp pain crackled across my back. Then there was a rip and crack that shook me to the bone.

There were swirls of the sharp smell of snow, the harsh tang of guns, the tin smell of blood. The taste of fear filled the air. White snow whirled around me as everything blended together. Agony, joy, fear, and release happened all at once. A chill swept over me and soothed my aching heart. The snow collapsed in a perfect circle around me.

When I looked up, everyone seemed out of proportion. Rocks were too small, the people way below eye level. I tried to talk but my mouth didn't work right.

The officer in charge shifted his gun and pointed in my direction. "Don't try anything." All his men followed suit.

Liddie's brown eyes were wide-eyed, and filled with tears as her hands pressed a blood-soaked rag I recognized as part of the lining of her coat into Carl's leg "Sir, he's bleeding badly. Please, help him."

He ignored her, keeping his eyes on me. "Keep the roads closed—divert traffic. Say it was rocks falling or whatever. We don't need civilians up here." Several of his people took off running down the road. "You need to change back. And come with us—nice and quiet."

Change back into what? I looked down at my body and blinked. Instead of my worn-down jeans and white shirt, scales covered my chest and legs. Black, with a hint of translucence, they rippled with rainbows similar to an oil slick. Moving backwards, a heavy, unfamiliar weight on my back almost knocked me off balance. "What am I?" I managed to say after several attempts.

The man flinched at the booming level of my voice. "Don't play dumb."

"Oh my God, Zack, you're—" Liddie let out a sob. "You have to help them."

Carl's skin looked washed of color. Blood seeped into the snow around both of them. "Vein?" It was like talking around a bunch of hard candies in my mouth.

"If you change back, we'll take care of your friend." The officer kept his tone level.

"I don't know how to change. I don't know what… Carl might die." The words were getting easier to say.

The officer lifted both brows before shaking his head sharply. "Do you really not know what you are? We knew some of your kind had scattered, but this is almost unbelievable."

"You're a dragon, Zack," Liddie said through clenched teeth as she clamped her hands down tighter on Carl's leg. "Now, help him."

"We can't help your friend until this asset is secure. Anything could happen if we let it loose," the officer said to Liddie.

Liddie let out a cry. "He isn't an 'it.' His name is Zack. You already shot one of my friends. I'm not going to let you hurt anyone else."

The officer shook his head. "You're crazy. Don't you understand your friend's a monster? Just look at him!"

"He is beautiful. He always has been." Liddie didn't look at me.

"Carl," I said.

"You have to change back," the officer insisted again.

With every fiber of my being, I tried. Nothing happened—I remained in dragon form. "I can't."

The soldiers' guns lifted up in coordination with each other. "I'm not playing games now. We can't have an uncontrolled dragon running around."

Carl wasn't doing so well. That much blood loss, well, couldn't be good. Liddie looked afraid—more afraid than I'd ever seen her. They wouldn't help him. He had saved me from being their captive. Both of them had been there for me for years. I sucked in a breath, on instinct. Bullets hit across my body. Each one felt like being poked really hard by a blunt object.

A silent communication passed between me and Liddie. My claws stretched out ,wrapping around Carl and Liddie, pulling them against my body. Turning toward the soldiers surrounding the cliff, I let out my breath. White smoke laced with electric blue shot toward them. As it touched them, they turned into ice. Everything went still. They looked like perfectly carved sculptures.

The difference shocked me into leaving my mouth hanging open.

"Zack." Liddie lifted her head. Her hair frosted over, and tears frozen to her skin.

"Sorry," I said. Everything was wrong now. It was my fault for this.

Liddie shook her head. "It doesn't matter. You have to get him to a hospital. Pikes Peak Regional is the closest. He's dying."

My claw cupped Carl as I lifted off the ground. My head jerked to the cliff side. "Take the car home." In an act of faith, I leapt off.

There was a moment of terror as I started to plummet downward, the wind rushing by my wings. Blood pounded in my ears as I flailed my wings wildly behind me. Then instinct took over and they snapped out. The city spread out beneath my wings.

Inside my claws, Carl shivered, jolting me back to reality. Scanning with vision that was better than expected, the hospital was easy to spot. Tugging my wings in, I dove down, air whipping by me. At first everything seemed so tiny. The closer I got, the clearer I could see. Familiar places like the Hilton and the sculptures downtown grew closer. As I neared the ground, people started to notice. Cars came to screeching stops. A few loud bangs made me cringe.

When I reached the parking lot, I angled my body back, my wings going perpendicular to the ground with big, heavy strokes to slow down. My landing area was an abandoned section toward the back of the building. My speed was a bit too fast and the cement crunched when I hit. Holding Carl aloft, I did my best to navigate the parking lot without causing too much damage. A few car alarms went off and I accidentally broke off a few side mirrors.

People stared at me. A guy pulled out a handgun and aimed at me. Using a claw, I banged on the glass. Instead of coming out, people scattered inside. A few dived behind the large admissions desk in the center. Only one doctor stood, slacked jawed, staring at me. She was dressed like a doctor anyway. Stepping back, I held out Carl to the automatic door, opening it.

"Dying." My words frosted up the glass.

She shook herself off. "Are you real?" She scanned me up and down.

Using the tip of the claw to press on the automatic door sensor for wheelchairs, I opened the door. "Yes. We are real. Carl is real." Talking was getting easier.

Letting out a breath, she slowly stepped toward the door. "Put him inside the door."

Adjusting my arm a bit, I placed Carl down as easy as I could. "Gun shot to leg," I said. Sirens went off in the distance. Visions of Godzilla movies flashed in my mind. If I stayed down here, I was a sitting duck. "Please. Don't let him die."

She knelt down, examining his wound. "Get me a gurney. We need to get this bullet out." The others jolted up as she barked out the order. Giving me a quick glance, she said. "We'll take good care of him."

As I began to back up, a shot pinged off my side.

"You're not going anywhere."

My gaze shifted to the guy who had pulled the gun earlier. "Move. You're in my way," I said. I wanted to take off from the same deserted section of parking lot. These cars had already taken enough damage. I didn't want to make it worse.

"Nope, you're staying right here until the police arrive." He pointed the gun straight at me.

Spreading my wings a bit, I stepped toward him. All the color ran out of his face and he backed up several steps. Spreading my wings wide, I flapped them to make a breeze. He turned tail and ran, not that I could blame him. He was pretty brave standing up to me. The sirens shrieked closer. I walked slowly back to where I had landed. Flapping with large, heavy strokes didn't lift me up more than a few feet from the ground. I eyed the building. If I could climb the side, I could dive off the side the way I dove off the cliff. Without letting myself think about it too much, I dug my claws into the side of building, pulling myself to the roof.

I leapt off the side of building, flapping my wings furiously. Then I was in the air, going high into the sky. My back burned from strain of working my way higher in the sky. The world spread out before me in every direction. My attempt to laugh turned into more of the frost breath around me. For the first time, I felt free.

Fatma Alici

Fatma Alici is gamer geek turned writer who blogs about neglectful gods, magic gone crazy, tech that can save you or kill you, and – of course – aliens, lots of aliens. Each week she takes a slice off these realities and puts it up at:
http://www.fatmaalici.com.

Collared

by Jazz Feylynn

A throbbing pain radiated throughout my body. Right down to my nails—both fingers and toes. What began as a persistent headache, the undercurrent ache that invaded my life became a full-blown bodyache. The agony had escalated during the final for Ecology 202. The night class test trapped me indoors, away from my necessary connection to nature. The constant hum of dead, unnatural air filled the lecture hall at good ol' University of Colorado at Boulder. Go Buffs.

Ironically, I chose ecology so I would have a career in the "great outdoors." Classes weren't held outside, but in a restricted, drab-gray concrete structure. The lackluster, synthetic plastic chairs lined up in measured rows and aisles,. The room's foul taste coated my mind—creating anguish.

Recently, whenever I am isolated from nature's energy, the Green Man part of me tends to physically snarl. Rather painfully.

I'm a half-breed hybrid, mixed-up mess. When not surrounded by nature, the Green Man part balks. The human part could care less. It's a battle of human versus nature spirit played out, abusing my mind, body and soul, imprisoned in the lecture hall. Not even Mom—who passed me these genes—knows how I'll turn out. Then again, what mother does?

It was a time for my metamorphosis. You could say I was going through my "second puberty," the coming into my full Green Man alchemy. *Fantastic.* I could have done without the first, let alone the second, scenario. Not being full-blooded, I didn't know what power would arise. What I could do, and would be able to do within the laws of nature, most people would call magic.

I was told I take after my dad, the DNA human half; he didn't like being restrained or confined. Your basic control freakoid. I don't know much about "Dad." He died in a mysterious accident before I was born. Mom grew upset whenever I asked her so I stopped pestering her about my other half. I knew what normal humans were supposed to behave like, having hung around one-hundred-percent, pureblooded humans. I blended into their society, to the best of my ability, hiding the nature traits in plain sight.

The other students' tension circulated around the hall as time ran out added to my pain-filled haze. The clatter of a pen dropped nearby ripped through me. Pain so intense I barely functioned. I checked the last two answer boxes quickly, hoping the teacher, as usual, had formulated more C answers than A, B or D so I could escape the rack-filled torture.

Pages flipped and paper crinkled as other kids finished. I restuffed my heavy, abused backpack with the scratch pad and pens I used during the exam. The pack slung on my back, I dropped my answer sheets on the teacher's desk. My sneakers squeaked on the over-polished floor in my sprint to the door. *Crack!* I pushed hard on the room's door as if it were an emergency exit. Heck, it *was* an emergency. The cold metal bar burned my hand. I needed to see Oak.

A deep breath. Ah! *Relief.* I breathed in the fresh air rolling off the Flatirons. Earlier, scatter shower had cleared the air and filled my lungs. Boulder's unique city smell—more nature than industrial—mingled with the scent of the nearby forest. The torment from my muscles and joints diminished, receding back to my ongoing headache.

I bolted to my stout century-old friend I called Oak (for a lack of any better name) out in front of the stone-face hall. The interior and exterior were different as night and day. The building blended into a city that kept touch with nature. There were walking and bike paths tucked along waterways throughout Boulder. Living green surrounded the area, all within easy reach. The city's environment resonated deep within my soul.

I leaned my unruly brow against Oak's moist, age-roughened skin. Oak had gotten me through the spring semester. The bark's touch relieved the aches from my academic confinement. I relaxed within Oak's strong aura.

"Hello, Oak, it's good to spend some time with you." I whispered to the tree. The green branch canopy overhead surrounded me in a leafy hug. I couldn't keep a goofy smile away. To others, it must have looked like a breeze swayed the tree branches but I knew better. I always had a gift to communicate with the life forces of nature, and plants in particular. It's a "green" thing. "Thank you for helping me feel more like myself." Oak's mirth vibrated into me.

More students clamored out into the night, giddy, having finished the test. A dude walked close by on the sidewalk, spotlighted under the streetlight glow. He gawked at me chatting to a tree. I grimaced. I had left the shoving, the pounding fists and loathsome plots back in high school, hadn't I? Yes, I had, for the most part. Guess the jerk didn't get the newsflash that as a college student, he should act civilized. I'm not the same scrawny sapling anymore. I had filled out and up several inches since high school. He took a step towards me. *Damn.*

Dude—go away. Leave! I really needed Oak for a couple more minutes. Abandon your idiotic scheme. If not, I'd either have to take a hike or stand my ground. Don't make me hurt you or—god forbid—you hurt me. Make it easy on both of us. *Go!*

He stared, his eyes lit in recognition. His jaw clamped in a sneer and his hands became fists. Great, he remembers me. Ain't that terrific. He hesitated. Chad's (yep, I finally remembered the dolt's name) eyes widened. He brought his unclenched hands in front of him, signaling that he was backing off, then turned away. Humph. He'd never walked away before. I'm not one to complain about my good fortune. Good riddance, chump. *Adios!*

I wouldn't have had to be concerned about the skeptics if I could have mutated into plants, especially trees, unnoticed like Mom. However, being a half-breed, it was not looking good. I smiled with heartfelt affection that, at least, I could chat back-and-forth with flora.

"Hey, Connor."

I jumped and turned, knocking the hand off my shoulder and slumped heavily against Oak's trunk. Olivia took a step backwards, out-of-the-way, slipping her hands into her front pockets.

"Holy crap, Olivia." I sloughed off my backpack to the ground, allowing me to lean back and stay connected to my immobile friend. "Thanks for having a group study session last night over at your house. It really helped me with the test."

Olivia, like the tree she's named after, came in a short and slightly squat body. Her silvery blonde hair was bound up as usual in a ponytail. She wore the standard campus outfit of jeans and T-shirt. Her shirt matched her sassafras-green eyes. The energy aura surrounding her was a peaceful sea of green.

She tilted her head and raised an eyebrow. "Connor, you genuinely went pale and turned puke-green during the test. Even your hair had chunks of green tint. In fact, you're still a bit off color." Of course, she'd notice the minimal natural moss green running throughout my hair. The swamp water shade amassed more green pigmentation at the roots but most of the time, my off-color strands blended in, and nobody but a great artist like her would notice.

She reached up to rest her hand on my forehead, then shrugged and dropped it. "You're hot, but you don't have a temperature." Her grin filled her face.

Oak's shaded awning hid the raising heat in my cheeks. "Gee thanks. It's been a long day." I nodded towards the hall. "I'm doing better now that I'm out of the fortress of death." An oak leaf fell onto my shoulder and grass had grown up over my sneakers wrapping me in the outdoors. I couldn't stop the smile deep within that touched my lips.

"Are you a witch like me?" She twisted her hair around her finger. "I thought you might be . . . since you're able to make physical changes and all."

"Wow, a witch. That's kinda amazing." I crossed my legs as I scratched my jaw. "I don't know precisely what I am." A glance into the swaying branches overhead gave me a moment to consider. I hadn't mentioned my nature half previously to Olivia. Heck, this was as good of time as any to blurt it out. Usually, creative types were more empathetic to my predicament. "I do know I have some nature spirit in my background. Green Man, to be more precise."

"Awesome." She bounced on the balls of her feet a couple of times. "So, if you're better, a bunch of us are going to celebrate our release from Professor Eco's class. We're going to Joey's Microbrew for pizza and beer." She cocked her head. "You want to come along? I'd love to chat about our connection to the mystical aspects of life."

I ran my hand through my hair. "That sounds great but my day isn't over yet. I have a cere . . . gathering to go to. I can't get out of it." I would have tried to get out of it if I could, but Mom would have made chopped salad out of me if I had missed the monthly ceremony tonight.

Rarely did I get out of one, and this one was especially for me.

"That's too bad. Maybe you can stop by afterwards. It's likely going to be an all-nighter to end all-nighters and, most likely, land at my place." She swung her arms back-and-forth ready to launch herself to the pizza party.

"I'll keep that in mind. Hey, if I don't make it, would you be interested in going to Mom's next month's Hawthorn Moon Gathering?" As I pushed off the tree, I restrained from nuzzling the trunk with my cheek and patted the attentive tree goodbye until the next school year. I reached down and picked up my backpack.

"I'd like that. Call me and let me know the time and place." She gave me an unexpected quick kiss on the cheek as I started getting back up. She turned around and heading toward Joey's Microbrew, waggled her fingers back over her shoulder.

Hmmm, that was interesting. Could there be more than friendship brewing between us? Maybe and maybe not. Might be fun to find out.

I walked to class this morning, knowing full well I would need time to recover outdoors walking back afterwards. I hitched up my backpack and headed for the path that lead toward Canyon Boulevard.

Most people in town avoid paths and trails late at night. I never had any trouble. I hadn't come across any worrisome animals. Being half-Nature Spirit, I scared away the few folks who happen to be on the paths at night anyway. I wasn't sure why, other than I was big with a tangled mass of hair that went every which way. In the right light or lack of light, it had a tree-like quality.

At six feet tall with muscles that had filled out rather nicely, it gave me a huge silhouette in the dark. I'd been known to roar and grunt at odd moments too. It was part of the package.

Canyon Boulevard lite-night traffic cleared. I crossed at Fourth Street and headed towards Spruce. An afternoon shower had scented the air with pine resin. By the time I got to Mom's, the fresh outdoors would reduce my classroom misery back to a dull background ache at the temples.

Olivia's concern for me was nice. *Really* nice, especially her kiss. It was only a peck on the cheek but I'd never seen her kiss anyone, on the cheek or otherwise. She seemed to like me. Genuinely, *like* me? I could see us together. Was it possible for me to make a connection with someone other than Amanda? Although probably nobody would be quite as strong of a bond as the one I had with Amanda.

"Ow!" I rubbed my chest as another filament of Amanda's and my weakened energy ties broke. We didn't have many left. It felt like less than a half-a-dozen tattered energy fibers remained between us. Maybe it was time I moved on with my life. Two years had been more than enough time to give Amanda a chance to defy her parents and come back to me.

I'd see Olivia at next month's ceremony. I would tell her more of my tale and see how it goes.

Off Spruce, there was a little known trail. A savage gulley wound through acreage of older residential homes that met up with Green Rock Drive. A natural bouquet gust of wind assaulted me. The domestic and native encroached on each other in a battle for dominance at the edges of the cramped path's undergrowth. The tangy scent of wild onion and sagebrush intermingled with the verdant odor of wild geranium, blue flax, columbine and creeping pussytoes. The wild weeds spiced up the en-croaching grass turf and the tamed floral honeysuckle vines and lilac bushes.

I thrive in an environment of lush vegetation where others struggle. I never want to damage any plants by tramping on them unannounced. *Please, may I pass by?* It would've been rude not to ask the overgrown plant tops to bend back off the path. The overrun weeds flowed back out of the way. It was like walking on manicured grass at Wonderland Lake Park.

There's a drive concealed by an assortment of shrubs and trees before Green Rock intersects with Sun-shine Canyon. Around a small bluff was a little-known street community Gramps and his friend built in the late 1800's. They left New York in search of isolation and pri-vacy in or near forested land with a small group of like-minded folks. This location maintained its seclusion even in modern times with the same families. Being prosper-ous New Yorkers, they didn't want to leave behind their upscale homes and lifestyle. Therefore, they brought it along into the — at that time — mountain wilderness with homes that could have stood in uptown Manhattan.

On the warm, cloudless evening, the full moon shone through mature maple trees lining the street. Stretched out before me in dappled moonlight, there were twelve Victorian "painted ladies." Each home was unique. At the end of the lane, the most vivid one was my mom's house. The outdoor porch light blazed in wait for Mom's guests to show up for the evening festivities. The bright gingerbread lace siding and trim in lavender, pink, teal and blue stood out from all the other homes. After my dad's accident, she repainted the house to resonate year round with a summertime oasis in floral colors from the backyard garden—her ceremonial grounds—keeping her in her roots of greenness.

My shoulders bowed under the heavy load hoisted across my back. I had hauled my backpack for the last full day and night classes—which started before sun-up— over three miles back and forth,. I was dog-ear tired and had a hard time even remembering my name.

I had avoided my ex-best friend, almost-girlfriend and next-door neighbor, Amanda Westmore, for the last two years, ever since she agreed to her dad's sudden decree not to see me. I passed the house next door, and the storm door smacked against the wraparound porch wall.

Dang. No matter how quietly I sneaked—I, literally, can be one with nature—tonight, I couldn't get by our neighbors' sonic hearing. Amanda rushed out of her family's home.

Amanda's lithe body left the elegant Victorian. "Connor, have you seen my dog?" she yelled, crossing the lawn stomping up to me in a snit. A common question that any person missing their beloved pet would have asked. It was the most peculiar question I had heard out of her mouth. "He ran off without his collar. That big stupid idiot!"

I scratched my head. "But Amanda, you don't have a dog. Never have." I adjusted the strap on the backpack.

She looked up and down the sidewalk. Grass filled the tree root-cracks. Some fractures were small as a spider's web, while others were monstrous and irreparable. On her far side, mostly hidden behind her back, she held a massive leather band studded with metal pieces that clinked. I attempted to lean around her to see what it was the best I could and shuddered. I could still only see a part of a curvy edge. Maybe a whip? She'd gone Goth a couple of years before. She layered on black eye liner and wore black leather. No matter how tainted she had gotten, she was too kindhearted to abuse innocent animals.

"I mean, a two-legged dog." She chewed a black lacquer nail. She kept her obsidian nails long and never ragged. She hadn't had a jagged nail in years. I had assumed, it was a habit she ended long ago.

"Are you dating that asinine jerk again? You said you never wanted to see him after the last time he ditched ya." I understood whipping that jerk. Why would she consider him or anyone else? I was a better choice in every way—except maybe the Green Man-it is.

Our families were close. Mr. Westmore brought me up like his own son, Jessie. With my dad gone, he was a father to me in every way but blood. He had even gone so far as to say that he and my dad—before Dad died— had hoped someday their kids would marry. If they had any kids, that is.

However, for some reason, Amanda's dad never let us date. When I turned eighteen, he cut me off. "Stay away from Amanda." That same day Amanda complied. That's also the day our energy bond begun to fray, strand-by-strand. Happy eighteenth birthday to me.

Maybe my being a green nature spirit was the problem for Mr. Westmore. I didn't know.

We, Amanda and I, had always been best friends growing up next to each other. When I was in seventh grade, her in fifth, we bonded and became something more.

During our younger years, I felt protective of her and Jessie, her baby brother, from our territorial neighborhood bully. I never was sure why, but whenever I showed up he backed down. He was the only bully who ever did that with me. Sure, I was a little older than he was, but definitely not larger back then. He was a massive beast even as a kid. He took after his dad in just plain nastiness.

All I had to do was appear and he would leave. Kinda the way Chad had done earlier this evening. It could have been to keep their beatings out of the public eye. Both of them were *sneaky* little shits.

I squinted to get a better look at what she brought forward. It was a collar, not a whip. "You want the jerk to wear a collar? To keep him from running off?" I removed the backpack from my back and placed it on the sidewalk.

"Huh? Oh, you mean Tim. No. Good riddance. I'm talking about my twit brother, Jessie." Her tough gal look smelled of leather, makeup and sweet herbal-musky shampoo. "And no, the collar isn't to restrain him. But for his safety, in case he gets picked up by that darn catcher. Tho' that's not a bad idea, chaining him up. I *like* it." Her eyes had a wicked gleam, and one side of her mouth crooked up.

"You and your brother have had moments. Don'tcha think the collar's a bit much?" I could imagine Jessie hog-tied with whatever was at hand by his big bad sis. Wouldn't be the first time—and most likely not the last—that they would get into their sibling rivalry. I felt sorry for the guy but with the way he was growing, Amanda would have to watch out. "And what's this about a catcher?"

"No, I don't think the collar is a bit much. The brat is my responsibility while Mom and Dad are out of town at a business conference back east. Weasel is the catcher. You remember Weasel?"

"Of course, I remember the *bastard*." I still considered Jessie my younger bro. He didn't have anything to do with their dad's issues between Amanda and me.

"If Weasel gets him before I do, we'll be in trouble so deep—Dad will never let Jessie or me see you or anybody again this century." She stared between the houses. "Dammit, he's long gone." The chewed nail tapped her cheek. "I don't have much time and can't do this by myself. Tell you what. If you help me hunt-down the brat and promise never to tell anyone—ever—I'll tell you our family's secret. It would help you to understand what's gone down between us. And maybe—just maybe—there's a slim chance you'll get in my dad's good graces."

I arched an eyebrow. "There's no question I'll help. Can't let Weasel pound Jessie." It was too good an opportunity to pass up. Secrets and finally some answers. The prospects reenergized me. I wouldn't hold out for a reunion with Daddy Dearest, though. I wouldn't expect that much from him. "'Course I swear. I'll tell no one. Ever.

Unless of course, you tell me otherwise." There was no other answer I could give.

"Connor, is that you?" Mother's voice came from behind me.

I turned towards my house. My dainty and truly ethereal—far older than she looked—new age mother, dressed in a hippy tie-dyed dress, came up to me. These days, my mother, a Green Lady, exposed her natural cypress-green hair for all to see.

I tucked my hands into my back pockets. "Yes, Mom, it's me." The ceremony had faded into the background. Jessie's catastrophe was more critical.

Mom walked straight to me, ignoring Amanda, which was odd since she adored her. She placed a hand on each cheek, scanning deep into my eyes. "I can see classes were tough today. Bad headache?"

"More of a total bodyache. But I'm pretty much okay now. Just the usual pain residue that's been hanging around lately."

"A bodyache," she wrinkled her nose. "Ummm, I'm worried about you. I didn't have this much difficulty coming into my full powers. Embrace your inner green. That's why tonight is so important." She poked me in the chest.

Ow! Dang! My chest is sure getting a workout tonight.

"You need to relax and let go of being uptight about the power you're growing into." Mom gave Amanda a nod, grabbed my arm and attempted to haul me home. She gave me a couple of tugs. However, it was futile.

"Mom, Amanda needs me to help find Jessie. It's not safe for him out in the woods at night."

"It's safer for him tonight than for you." She glared at Amanda—a nonverbal communication of something I wasn't privy to.

"Whatcha talking about, Mom? Weasel . . . Tom's after him for some reason. Remember what he was—*is*—to Jessie and everyone else around? Jessie's not safe." I bent down and looked her in the eye. "I can't let Tom treat people I care about like that." I straightened up, "It shouldn't take too long. I'll be back before your Willow Full Moon Ceremony. I'll help you set up out back later. Okay?"

"You'll be back before the moon reaches its zenith? Tonight is the anniversary moon of your birth. That's why's you must attend."

With effort, I didn't roll my eyes. "Yeah, Mom." It would hurt her if I didn't take this as seriously as she did.

"We're wasting time, Connor. Let's go." Amanda glared at my mom—a glare Mom returned in full. Yeah, there was something between them. Quickly, Amanda scooped up my backpack with ease and walked toward her house. "Man, what'cha got packed in here?"

"My laptop and overpriced textbooks loaded with useless knowledge." I'm muscular and an inch taller than Amanda. My eyes widened and I rubbed my jaw; she shouldn't have been able to sling my bag as if it only had a paperback inside. Kinda, made me feel like the weaker sex.

"It's quicker if I toss this in my house's entryway." She pressed the lock and shut the door hard enough it rattled the beveled glass window. "I'll give details while we're searching for the lit' sh—" she whispered so my mom wouldn't hear.

Mom watched us from the sidewalk. She brushed her hair away from her face. The moonlight showed she was far from happy.

I followed Amanda's lead and cut across the lawn heading for Sunshine Canyon. "Mom, I'll be back soon!" I shouted over my shoulder, jogging to stay up with Amanda.

At the trailhead, the path was wide enough for us to jog side by side. "Which way, Amanda?"

"It smells like he went this way."

I turned my head towards her. Smells? Okay, I know she thinks her little bro stinks but that sounds like she's tracking him by his stench. That's just plain weird—even for Amanda.

"Here's the deal. Don't freak out on me."

When someone says "don't freak," wouldn't a person think that maybe they should freak? But I couldn't tell her that. "Wouldn't think of it."

"It's like . . . double dang . . . we're not supposed to tell anyone our family secret, but with you not being 'totally human,' you should be okay to tell. I'll be in big trouble if Weasel finds out about any of this and tells Mom and Dad before they get back and I can explain everything to them." She looked down at the path, moving down towards Wonderland Lake Park. She turned to face me. "I think you deserve to know. Darn it! You deserve to know. We're a family of natural-born werewolves. You've lived your whole life in a community of

Lycanthropes. Phewwww." She breathed deeply and relaxed her facial muscles. "I finally told you. Wanted you to know for at least a couple of years. Dad's the alpha. He forbade me to tell you. I can't go against my alpha, no matter what I want."

I couldn't tell if her midnight-blue eyes hinted at a joke or not. If it was true, maybe I should freak a little bit or a lot. "You frigging *serious*?"

"Yeah." Her blue eyes glowed headlight red into my leafy greens. Those eyes were freaky.

The path narrowed. Amanda took the lead following her sense of smell. On the other hand, I followed a werewolf who was leading me by her nose. Not sure which of us was crazier.

"Why now?" I dodged branches that swung back after Amanda passed in front of me. The thicket along the path grew thicker. *Friends, please move aside. Allow us to pass.*

"Honest. I've wanted you to know for the longest time. Dad said I couldn't date you because he didn't want me to accidently infect you with the virus making you a bitten versus a natural-born were."

A werewolf—oh my god. The hair on the back of my neck rose. I knew not to show fear to animals. They could smell it. That included the wolf next to me. I shivered, stopping for a moment. My hands on my thighs, I took two deep breaths to clear my head.

Amanda came to a stop, turned, and placed her hands on her hips. She waggled her eyebrows. "Mmmm?"

Green Men, the few that remain, are nature spirits. A werewolf would be in the realm of animal spirits. Animals do come under nature spirits and are a part of the Green Man's domain. There are fangs and claws involved. Yeah, in my world plants have thorns and spines . I'm used to dealing with them. I can control plant life but not as well as Mom can. But plants are stationary and I can get away. Quick.

"Give me a sec to catch my thoughts." I'd notice werewolves living next door, wouldn't I? All those years constantly in her company with puppy dog eyes. Maybe my leaf-green eyes shielded me from seeing certain stuff.

If anybody had asked, I would have said the Westmores were normal everyday people. Never had I seen her family—or anything else—furry in or around their house or the neighborhood, ever, ever, *ever*. Maybe there was a reason why there wasn't anything small and furry around. Except strays that always ended up at my house. Maybe that's why the Westmores never allowed any pets. Hard to keep them off the menu.

Resuming our quest, we jogged in a northeasterly direction towards Wonderland Park Lake.

"Hey, if you're a werewolf, don't you, like, *eat* everything?" As the path sloped downward, our speed slowed to a fast walk.

"We tend to eat more flesh and prefer that it's not cooked as much as humans like it."

I'd actually noticed that, but the Westmores didn't eat meat that much rawer than I did. Mom didn't know how I could eat such bloody subsistence. I only ate barely-cooked chow when she wasn't around. When she was,

I honored her Green Lady traditions of vegetarian dining.

"We have strict rules on what we can and cannot eat. Humans and pets are not allowed as snacks." The path leveled and widened out. We accelerated back to the previous jog.

I drew up next to her. "Umm. What about half-human and half-nature spirit?"

"Come on, Connor. We don't eat sentient beings." Another chewed fingernail went under attack.

"Amanda, you're not inspiring confidence with that statement. I believe plants are sentient. They think, not the way we do but they *do* think and feel. My mother can become any plant. I have a slim chance to transform into plants someday."

"Now you're being ridiculous. If your mom changed into a carrot, I would think she would change back before someone ate her, werewolf or not."

This was Amanda. Never once had I felt threatened.

"Connor, we good?" The onslaught on another nail, number three or four, was underway.

I lost count.

"Yeah, sure… sure thing. I trust you." I did my best to keep my voice steady.

She gave me a sly sideways look. "I'm glad you trust me. I don't want to lose you."

After some time thinking, I asked, "What's going on." I followed her through a hedge. My wobbly legs had gotten stronger as we trekked. Lilac petals scent filled the air as we passed by the last lone ranch.

"Dad was the pack's second until our last alpha died. Not *clear* on the details. But Dad took over as alpha being as he was the oldest generation wolf and had the most discipline over his beast. That's how we determine an alpha."

"You mean, you don't fight to the death or overpower and see who's weaker?"

"Used to be that way. Still is with some bitten or out-of-their-minds weres. We feel fighting for dominance actually shows weakness. It's much harder to hold back the wolf than to let it have free rein."

"I understand being in control of oneself. Is there anything else that I ought to know?"

"Loads. Werewolves have a conference every year with the alphas who rule the horde of wolves in the states. While the 'rents are attending back east, I'm left in charge of Jessie. That makes me the temporary alpha in our household. I'm using that as my loophole in getting out of the gag order not to tell you about us. Fingers you, claws me, crossed hoping Dad sees it that way.

"Jessie's sixteen and just started turning wolf a few months ago." She smirked. "He's in control of the wolf but doesn't have the greatest restraint not transforming during a full moon yet. That's one of the ways we can tell how much authority over the wolf a werewolf has. Lucky me. He still needs someone to keep an eye on him during this time of the month." She pointed up at the suspended orb glowing in the sky. "He said he was good, but when I got back from taking a shower, he had snuck out. Doesn't mean he's gone wolfy but he went without his darn collar. He knows better."

"First, is he safe? Am I safe? Heck, is anyone safe from his teeth? Or safe from being bitten until he has his turning under control?" From the rapid pace Amanda set, I was breathing hard. "Second, what's the biggy about wearing a collar?"

"Yes, everyone is safe, especially you. Jessie really cares about you. We're natural-born werewolves. And, as a general rule, we have more power and greater discipline over the wolf with each generation's evolution. Even though Mom's third generation, we took after Dad's fourth heredity level, making us fifth generation. We could tell by how fast I got domination over my transformation. Pretty stable, really. Jessie's still working out the logistics of holding his human form in control during the full moon. Either way, our human side is always connected and managed when we're in our wolf or human forms. We don't turn into a beast at the first moonbeam that hits us like a first-generation bitten. That's why Dad was worried and told me to stay away. He didn't want you to be a first-generation wolf. It's a nasty life. It's also why your mom was giving me dagger eyes and didn't want you to come out with me tonight. She didn't want to take a chance of you being infected."

I guessed her dad was taking care of me in his own way. He should have let me decide whether or not to take the risk. I would have for Amanda. I was ticked that Mom knew and didn't mention it.

"To give you an example of a first-generation werewolf, Weasel—"

"You mean he's *bitten*?" Man, that would explain a lot.

"No, but his dad was—*is*—first generation. Weasel got the blunt end of the deal. Like most second gens, his father treated him like crap. It's why his mom left when he was young. It's hard to believe she never got bitten. The werewolf virus doesn't always take when you only have one werewolf parent. I guess she stayed around long enough to find-out that her kid was infected. Then she split."

That did explain his sucky home life growing up but didn't excuse the way he treated others. Was there childcare for abused werewolves?

"Weasel is better now as he has Dad as his alpha. Dad couldn't take charge until Weasel turned the first time. No matter how much Dad smelled the werewolf coming." She pushed through a large dead briar bush.

A branch snapped back after Amanda passed.

"Ouch!" Man that stung my cheek.

Amanda stopped. "Are you alright?"

"Yeah, I wasn't paying attention. That plant didn't allow me passage because it's dead. With dead wood, I need to concentrate so I can adjust my efficiency for stored power instead of living energy." I wiped blood from my cheek with the back of my hand. "I'm okay. Keep going." I motioned with my hand to continue on the trail. "You haven't told me about the need for a collar yet."

"Right. Jessie's fine, without wearing a collar. As long as he stays a two-legged dog. On the other hand—paw—if he alters into a four-legged wolf and is without a collar, he's breaking pack law. The previous alpha insti- tuted the need to have a collar on anytime we're in wolf form to blend in—so people don't panic—so they will think that we're just *huge* dogs. Not big scary wolves. If the pound picks him up, there's contact info to get him home without having to turn into human form in front of people, keeping our secret safe. This little bit of leather around the neck keeps wolves protected." She tugged on the choker that hung around her neck. "But that's really not the worst part."

"There's something *worse* than an unknown werewolf in an animal shelter?"

"Yeah," she said. "Weasel's a Catcher. You know he's always been an icky thing but now he's a dog-wolf catcher for the pack. Weaselly Tom wants to rise up in pack status. He's taken it on himself to patrol and catch werewolves doing anything they're not supposed to do. If he catches any of the pack roaming without a collar, especially Jessie or me, he'll bust them—us. Being the Alpha's kids compounds the situation. Dad won't have any choice but to move him up in the pack."

Weasel's plan sounded like a free ride. Collecting two hundred bucks as he passed "go" or getting a hotel on Broadway then sucker punching everyone that goes by.

We came out of the woods near Wonderland Lake. The small reclaimed lake had a lower than usual waterline from the drought. The recent afternoon rain showers relieved some of the water shortage and created a muddy shoreline. Cattail clumps held the bank in mud-bog conditions.

Amanda turned as the shore came into view. "Be careful. The conditions are treacherous with mud-sucking tentacles pulling shoes and socks into the murky bottom while smearing grime on those who passed by. We had incidents with some of the younger pack kids." She kept away from the water's edge.

Water sloshed through slime-coated concrete pilings beneath a dilapidated wooden dock. Mud weeds poked through cracked broken boards of the precarious structure at the end of the lake.

"Damn, damn, DAMN IT!" Amanda stomped her foot. "There's Jessie's clothes. He's *on* four-legs!" Amanda frowned sorting through Jessie's clothes at the end of the pier. Having gone through the pockets, she put a cell phone and wallet into her jeans back pockets.

Amanda growled at the back of her throat. A howl replied. Her head whipped around toward the way we had come. Again with the freaky eyes. Nails became long black claws. I took a step back, unsure what had happened. No way would I be able to outrun Amanda if she turned wolfy on me.

"Cut it out, Connor. You're safe with me. I amped up my senses. Weasel is coming. We need to get Jessie. Quick."

"How do you know he's coming? Do you see or hear him?"

"You'll never see or hear him if he doesn't want you to. Lack of nature sounds: birds, small critters; crickets even will go quiet when there's a werewolf nearby, giving off a threatening energy. Weasel always gives off aggressive vibes. He's always been about having a dangerous badass wolf image. Plus, I smelled his nasty-ass scent." Amanda took off sprinting past the dock.

Amanda ran around the bank's bend and slipped in the squishy soil. She steadied herself. Then she flat-out sprinted for the strand of trees. I did my best to keep up.

A different howl let loose up ahead. Her wild race caused the dried-up ferns, thorny plants, and low-hung tree branches—away from the lake—to grab at our clothing in the mad dash over the narrow packed dirt through the trees. She glanced at me over her shoulder once more, snarled, and then sprinted faster than I could ever hope to keep up with.

She had stopped and stood in a grassy meadow when I caught up to her a few minutes later. The forest chatter shifted to deathly quiet from the approach of Weasel's malevolent intentions. Across the wildflower field, a large sandy-brown canine, the same shade as Jessie's hair with wolf markings around the eyes, the color of dark bark, crouched whining. In front of her, he lowered his wolf's head and tail. Amanda leaned in, nose-to-nose. "Jessie, being sorry doesn't help us one bit if Weasel finds you without your collar. Let me put the damned thing on you."

Jessie snarled, his teeth rapidly flashing as he chattered. He did a great job working up a teenage snit. Spatters of spittle flew during a deep chest rumble.

"I don't care if you hate wearing it. He's coming. *It's going on now!*" Amanda pawed the collar. Her large claws were awkward and unable to wrestle the leather strap and metal buckle binding.

Amanda's frustration and Jessie's tantrum were the only noises in the field of wildflowers, a wooded area usually enriched with the songs of nature. Goosebumps rose on my arms.

"Here. Let. Me. Do it." I grabbed the collar out of her mismatched hand-paws. I didn't do much better. My nerves did a jitter dance, stuck between two wolves. Standing next to one wolf—a friendly wolf—in the midst of teenage angst, didn't help my situation. Then there was the third and expected wolf, which definitely wasn't friendly. I fumbled with the leather. I counted out my breath. Jess isn't the big bad wolf. *He's not the big bad wolf, the big bad wolf, big bad wolf.* I really didn't need that song rumbling around my head right now.

"Rrrrgh." That growl was just for show.

Right, Jessie?

Finally, the collar opened. "Jes . . . sie, it's me . . . Connor," my voice quaked.

He rolled his deep blue eyes just the way Jessie would—they definitely were his eyes, but touched with wildness.

"I know. I'm obviously being an idiot, but so are you."

He snapped his teeth a couple of times, but didn't even come close to nipping me. I got a whiff of minty fresh breath. Definitely not, what I would except from a wild wolf. "Jasper Arlington Westmore, *do not* give me attitude. I'm trying to help you. We don't have time to play games!"

Jess whimpered. He lay down with his tail tucked. I wrapped the collar around his enormous neck.

I jumped away from Jess, my hands in the air. Woo-hoo, I did it!

The sight of a huge young man with broad shoulders, forehead creased, and a frown upon his mouth came silently around a boulder at the field's edge. I jumped back to stand next to Jessie, who stood up snarling. My hand grasped his huge ruff, my fingers tangled in his hair. The three of us glared at Weasel as the children's song continued whipping around my head—only now the dictation was for Weasel.

"Amanda, what's going on here?" The grainy voice fit the obnoxious hairy rodent. Weasel hadn't changed much since the last time I had seen him. Well, except that he was older and wolf traits like the menacing snarl swirled in with his ol' rodent idiosyncrasies.

"Hey, Tom. Just taking the dog out one last time for the night with my friend." Amanda's voice shook but she stood in front of her lit' bro.

"You should have that mutt on a leash." Tom approached Amanda, not paying attention to me. His hands wrung the air instead of Jessie's shaggy neck.

"Jessie needed to change and run. I didn't think there would be any harm this late at night." She flashed him her fangs, sounding stronger. "You remember Connor, don'tcha, Tom?" There was an undertone of irony to her voice.

He squinted and scrutinized me behind Amanda. His foot hesitated taking the next step before continuing. Tom nodded. "What's he doing here?"

I looked towards Tom's feet. *Grow. Stop him.* Grass tangled in his shoelaces and spurge vines wove up around his legs and gripped them in place. A grin was plastered to my face. That's a first—and I'm hoping the many of firsts to come—that I could command plants to restrain someone. In my opinion, it couldn't have happened to a better fellow.

Tom struggled, grunting. His nostrils flared and he clenched his fists. He tugged and tore at the stems and vines. Those plants weren't strong enough to secure him by themselves individually. Together they acted like stapling tape. Boy, he made a fuss. He tugged and pulled his feet against the plants, to no effect.

Red-faced, Tom's stared at me. Sweat ran down his temples.

Jessie whimpered. Amanda turned her back to him, snickering. Kinda looked odd, her extra long canines sticking over her lip.

"Enough. I'll leave." Tom attempted to turn and gave me a questioning eyebrow.

Release him.

The plants squirmed away from Tom's legs.

"Next time, leash him." Weasel huffed off back the way he had come.

I rubbed the back of my head. "Well, ain't he lovely?" I hoped I hadn't ticked him off enough to come after me in the dark of the night in some dim alleyway or trail. No, make that a night of a full moon. He would be at his worst, all fangs and claws.

Amanda grabbed Jessie's collar. "Man, that was close. Jessie. Home. And don't let Weasel catch you." She gave the leather collar a shake and let go.

Jess fled. A happy "yip" came from the edge of the trees.

"Idiot." She shook her head.

On our way back, I asked, "Um, Amanda, why did you need me to come along?" I wanted to understand. In a way, it had seemed like a setup.

"It would've been really bad if you weren't there. Weasel would have reamed us a good one back there without you." She went to put a claw in her mouth but it looked too thick to chew. She shook her head, and her claws and fangs went back to normal. "Plus, who else would have whipped the collar on that fast?"

"Oh, you back to calling him Weasel?" I nudged her shoulder.

"Yes, I can't go calling him Weasel to his face can I? Can you?" She nudged me back.

I rubbed my cheek. The plant's scratch stung like a burr had dug deep into my cheek. My hand came away blood smeared.

Back on their ornamental porch, Jessie sat on his haunches. The collar dangled from his smirking jowls. I swear his huff-huff sounded like canine laughter.

Amanda pointed to the back. "Get your ass through the dog door and open the front door for me. And don't ruin the collar!" Amanda placed her arms on her hips and her face had a mock frown, struggling not to smile.

Jess hightailed it around the corner of the wooden porch.

I looked at her hands. "Hey, your nails aren't chewed up. The nail polish doesn't look damaged."

"One of the benefits of transforming is repairing one's nervous habits. It's a nail thing. After my first transformation, my nails permanently changed to black. I went Goth to hide the fact it's an *unnatural* color for a human." Her wide smile without sharp canines looked really good—safe. There had been a moment when she looked like she might have taken a bite out of Weasel. "Thanks, Connor. You really saved our butts tonight."

The door clicked open. "Think you might need this." Jessie, naked, leaned out through the doorjamb held the backpack in his hand like it weighed nothing.

I no longer felt wimpy now that I knew where Amanda got her added strength. I grabbed my stuff. "Hey, Jessie, even without wearing the collar, do you still feel collared?"

Jessie scowled. He backed inside and slammed the door. I wouldn't have put it past him to lock Amanda out, but he didn't. I wanted to understand how he handled the strip of leather. I didn't mean it to be insulting. Instead what I asked apparently had came off as a low blow. I'd have to make it up to him somehow.

"Talk with you tomorrow?" Amanda stretched her muscles out after the night's romp through the forest.

"Sounds good." I lugged my tonnage back over my shoulders and turned. "Later." I really needed to dash home for the *big* ceremony.

"Oh, and Connor. When Dad gets back, he should be okay with me going out with a human, green-man hybrid. Seeing you helped us out and you now know our secret."

I kept going on my way back home. I blasted back over my shoulder. "Really? He'll let me go out with you?"

"Yep. He can't say a thing now that he owes you." A great big grin made her even more beautiful.

I would have given a backwards wave but my laptop and books dragged me down. The adrenaline rush that got me through the chase was wearing off. I didn't know how I was going to get through Mom's ceremony. Then again, I thought of what tomorrow would bring dating the werewolf next door. *Woof!*

Last month, when I got home after running through the forest, I cleaned and put antiseptic on the dinky cut I had gotten before helping at Mom's gathering. Mom fussed, making it a bigger deal than it was. It continued to burn as it healed. It seemed to take longer than usual to close-up. A thin white scar had replaced the wound. Even though Jessie didn't take a fang to me, I worried that I had gotten infected with all the wolfy spit coming out of his muzzle. That would clarify the increased being torn asunder I felt—since the moonlight chase.

Eyes closed, I lay in a pain-filled. haze. Every joint felt like it had been stretched and tweaked in unnatural ways. My hand circled in the meandering creek behind my home. The humidity brought living green to flourish in the backyard landscape. My khaki shorts absorbed the moisture of the damp ground.

Mr. Westmore came from the back of the house. How I knew? I'm not totally sure. Possibly his menacing wolfish presence was communicated through the groundcover plants. Excruciating as it was, I squinted through the pain at him.

As if on a mission, he barged straight to me. His appearance told me he hadn't come to talk to Mom. He hadn't worn his tailored business suit and his sandy-brown hair neatly combed. Instead, he wore a casual polo shirt buttoned at the collar and holey black jeans that barely kept his wolf contained and hadn't done anything for his wind tossed hair.

This couldn't be good. I hadn't gotten any feedback about seeing Amanda since her folks returned from the conference. I could tell this wasn't about wolf stuff either. It was about yours truly.

He squatted down. *Crack.* His knee creaked like an old man. His arms rested on those creaky knees. "My bones groan adjusting for the full moon tonight."

Go away.

He raised an eyebrow. "I'm not going away Connor. You're coming with me."

Why in the hell would I even consider going anywhere with you?

"Because it's *important,* Connor." He responded like he heard my spiel inside my mind, similar to what I did with plants. Yet I shouldn't be able to do that with him unless I was infected, right? I took a deep breath and swallowed. This definitely wasn't about my Green Man growth.

Westmore ran a hand through his hair, messing it up even more. "You need to come to the pack's cabin. Today. Now, in fact." He growled. Yep, growled. "I'll explain. You need to hear what I have to say. Unfortunately you don't have much time to hear it."

I was not feeling up to his games. "Remember we don't have anything to do with each other. You made that clear years ago."

I splashed creek water over my forehead. The cooling liquid was so refreshing. My hand dropped back into the flowing water.

More of my energy had shifted towards my metamorphosis in the field with Jessie before the Willow Moon ceremony than during the actual ceremony. Not sure if all the changes had been good either. The moon gathering had been a bust as far as my green alchemy was concerned.

"Anyway I can't. I'm preparing myself for Mom's get-together later." The grass crept around me. The blades flicked in the breeze and kept me comfy as possible.

With puzzled eyes, he scanned my body. "What are you doing?" He scratched his thick afternoon stubble.

"The aches and pains I'm experiencing from my Green Man mutation have gotten worse this past month." If I hadn't begun to admit to myself I was becoming a wolf, I sure the hell wasn't going to mention it to Westmore yet. I'd do my best to keep Amanda and Jess out of trouble too. "The only way to restrain the pain is to surround myself with nature. Hence, my shirtlessness." I waved my free hand over my body. "My back is in contact with the earth and plants, my chest with the air and the warmth of the sun's fire, and my hand in the creek's water. Connected to earth, air, fire, and water. I found that makes my nature spirit settle...."

He tilted his head. Eyes closed. What the heck? As expected, he was shutting me out. I drummed my fingers on the ground to keep from tearing at the grass.

Finally, he opened his eyes and stared at me. "That explains it."

"That would be?"

"Connor Alexander Konovich, you are coming with me!" He growled.

I did not feel the least bit threatened no matter how much grrrrr he put in his tone.

Grrrr, right back at you.

Creases at the corners of his eyes deepened. "No matter how much trouble my possible new alpha is giving me, I have to follow my old alpha's orders. You're coming, *now*."

"I told you I *can't*. Mom will turn me into a green smoothie mess if I miss all things Hawthorn Moon tonight. I can't leave. Especially since my friend Olivia is coming to her first gathering." After helping Jessie last month, I needed to be at the gathering for Mom. "Leave me alone."

"I've talked to your mother. She understands. She's *not* happy but understands."

The cool water was no longer refreshing and steam seethed off my forehead. "I'm an adult. I don't need Mommy's permission to go or not go anywhere."

I gasped as I stood towering over Westmore. Sweat broke out all over my body, muscle spasms complaining at the change of position.

His eyes widened and he gave a curt nod. "Good. You're coming into your own. That's why it is so intensely hard not following my new alpha's orders. I'm the one who needed your mother's permission. It's about your dad. And you. Your mom's agrees that you should be

with me instead tonight. And she'll take care of Olivia."
He heaved himself up and grinned a wicked grin. "I'll
have Amanda come too. I'll explain to both of you at the
same time when we arrive at the cabin."

"Why didn't you say so?" I shrugged my shoulders
straighter—*carefully*—pretending I didn't have an ache in
the world and would endure the worst pain for Amanda.
I led the way back to the house barefooted. My toes dug
into the living soil. "I'll tell Mom I'm leaving, grab my
boots and change my shorts." My stomach tensed in an-
ticipation.

"It's not necessary to tell her. She knows." He followed close behind me. "You're okay without shoes. In
fact, it's better if you come as you are."

"Huh?" My jaw clenched. "What's that supposed to
mean? All I have on is wet shorts."

"Trust me. I know what I'm talking about."

I glared. We were going to a higher elevation. In the
woods, anything could happen. Ticks could latch on to
bare skin but then again I guess I could always ask them
to take a hike—I had gotten better with my energy work.
Or everyone outdoors could be enjoying a sunny afternoon, then 15 minutes later, they're pelted with baseball
hail. That's just the way the Rockies roll. *I'm going prepared, all the same Westmore.*

"You'll be fine as you are." A grin crooked the corner
of his mouth.

Of course I'm going but not without a change of
clothes and coat in the ol' backpack.

"You won't need anything," he yelled as I charged into the house. "But if it makes you feel better, be quick about it."

I rushed as fast as my battered body allowed. Doors slammed, my feet pummeled wooden floors, rugs and stairs. There was an enigma about Dad. I wanted answers. I hoped that I would get them.

Amanda stood next to their family's gray Jeep Cherokee contemplating her nails.

Westmore and I walked up to her. "How did you know to meet us?"

"Dad told me to get out here on the double. Werewolves have a mind-to-mind connection. It's a wolf thing. Bit annoying, but can come in handy at times." She opened the Jeep's back door. "You know I kinda thought I heard your mumbling in the background in my mind. Could something green be happening to you?"

"Maybe it's a green thing or a wolf thing or a short-circuit thing. I don't seem to know anything." I climbed into the passenger seat and rubbed my sweaty forehead.

The trip contained a chill silence as Westmore drove over packed dirt roads—not much more than a trail the higher in elevation and closer to the national forest we got. The ruts knocked us about. I hunched in the bucket seat as much as the seatbelt permitted, keeping away from the plastic and metal as much as possible. The Jeep squeezed through overgrown trees and bushes. My plant communion was nil. I couldn't warn them away. Branches scratched the metal sides of the vehicle taking away more of the paintjob.

I scowled over at Westmore. His eyes forward didn't deviate from the off-road trail, his chiseled jaw gripped shut during the ride. He didn't release any sound of explanation until we arrived.

We pulled up to the rustic hand-hewn log cabin. Room additions had been added in a jumbled manner, I assumed, as the pack grew.

Amanda squirmed, "Dad, with the full moon, Connor shouldn't be at the cabin."

"No one else from the pack will be here tonight." He turned the Jeep off. His intense eyes glanced at her in the rear view.

Amanda sniffed the air and with a gaping mouth, she turned her wide eyes to me. "No way!" She moved a nail into the danger zone of being chewed.

"It's rude not to include me in the conversation. By the way, what do you mean 'no way'?" I guess the wolf in me is out of the closet. So to speak. "I got infected last month, didn't I?"

"No, I don't think you got infected last month." Westmore slammed the car door and walked to the front steps. "I'll explain when we get inside."

Good to know I hadn't turned into a wolf with all of Jessie's drool flying all over the field. I scrambled out of the passenger seat, hauling my backpack. *Creak.* Now who sounded old?

"Connor, I know you would prefer to stay outdoors. Best if you disconnect for the night. It will be easier on you if you let go of everything green."

Yeah, like that could happen. It's written in my genes. I dropped my pack on the porch while I waited on Westmore.

He pulled out a set of keys. "We never used to lock the place when your dad was alive. But the night he died changed that." *Click*. He pushed the plank door open. "Go inside." He snagged a funky, cheap lawn chair before striding inside.

There wasn't much inside. Besides the reek of soggy dog, a roughly constructed table, a few wooden chairs to match, sorta, and a wood slab that constituted a type of kitchen counter. All bulky with a distress look through heavy usage. No electricity, fridge, TV or a game console. I guess changing from human was enough fun and games for werewolves. Amanda lit the kerosene lanterns that hung from pegs around the room. A coat rack by the door held at least a dozen massive-sized multicolored collars in leather, webbing and metal. In the back of the cabin in shadow, there was a large cell—a cage.

I stared in the back. The hair on the back of my neck stood up and a shiver ran down my back. The door and the walk back home looked mighty good.

"Sit." He plunked the chair down across from a couch that had batting sticking through the fabric on its worn-out arms. "Connor, don't make me have to tie you down." I heard his molars grind out the threatened promise.

I sat, arms crossed, touching the plastic as little as possible. Westmore and Amanda took the semi-comfy looking semi-comfy tattered couch.

"Just before you were born, a natural-born werewolf created a bitten and abandoned him. He received severe punishment for going against pack law." He leaned forward with his arms on his legs, his hands clasped. "The bitten went rogue and spawned a large pack that used the cabin as their den. As usual, your mom got ready for her moon ceremony, her way to honor your dad each month during the full moon—she continues that to this day. Your dad—being our alpha—came here early to prepare for the pack's monthly run through the woods.

"He was ambushed by nine barely-controlled bitten wolves. Your father was my friend and being eighth generation werewolf, he was the most powerful alpha on the continent at the time. There hadn't been any wolf with that many generations behind them before. He took out eight wolves. The ninth wolf had only started his first transformation and wasn't in the fight. That was Tom's father."

Amanda stared opened-mouthed at her dad.

I tilted my head, dumbfounded for about six seconds. "*What?*" I jumped up and stood in front of him, my fists clenched. "My dad was a werewolf, not a human? He didn't die in an accident. Why wasn't I told any of this?"

Westmore stood and placed his hands on my shoulders. He looked me in the eye. His normally recognizable blue eyes held knowledge the depths of the ocean. "Yes, it was an accident, a terrible accident."

"I figured it was a car accident. Not...." I looked down and away from him. It was hard learning the horrible truth. *Shit!*

"The pack and I arrived soon after the attack. Fatally wounded, he asked me to care for his beloved family." He gave my shoulder a negligible shake, let go, and took a step back to give me space.

I put my hands on my head in an effort to sort out all the thoughts, lies, pain, and my bloody confusion. "Arrrrrrrgh!" I spun around and kicked the freaking chair across the room. I realized why the cabin was so barren and abused. Whenever a wolf threw a fit, even without claws, they could be destructive.

"Your mother and I didn't know if you would become a wolf, especially merging the Green Man genetics with your father's werewolf genes. No longer having a wolf figure in the home, your Mom and I decided to wait to tell you about werewolves until you showed signs of transforming into a wolf. If you did, in fact, become a wolf. Your dad changed after he turned seventeen. We figured with your added generation, you should have changed by eighteen. We pulled you away when you didn't. We didn't want Amanda or Jessie infecting you.

"The signs were there, but I didn't equate it to the wolf. Like Amanda and you bonding. You were so young, I thought it was a especially strong first love. You always prefer raw food. You didn't just eat the raw vegetarian diet of your mom but also the barely cooked meat of your dad. The pain you've been experiencing—like you, I thought it was the Green Man power manifesting.

"Earlier I noticed you using your strong nature spirit and the elemental energies to suppress the wolf conversion I smelled coming on." He rubbed his jaw. "It hasn't been your nature spirit causing you this discomfort but the wolf fighting to come forth.

"The fact you have alpha level control has also materialized earlier as well. Being able to keep the wolf back for this long and the combining of your two natures can only make you powerful." There was pride in his tone. "It's a battle that you'll lose tonight."

"Tom said he could never go against you. I guess he knew a long time ago that you could be an alpha." Amanda widened her eyes and scanned the ceiling, avoiding looking at her dad and me. I swear it looked like she wanted her words to slither around us and go out the door unheard.

Westmore shoved his thumbs in the front pockets of his jeans. "The first time it hurts like a bitch, but after that, it gets easier."

"After the last couple of months, I'm used to a high pain level. However, it's going to ramp up several notches during changing isn't it? What you mean is I'll get used to the pain. Not that it's not as painful after the first time. Not at all like the smooth shift of energy Mom has when she mutates." If the pain I'd felt not turning into a wolf was any indication, it is going to hurt like hell. *Kill me now!*

He gave a curt nod. "You could look at it that way."

"I'm turning into a wolf tonight?" I sat down on the gouged floor cross-legged, my head in my hands. "What am I going to do?" I mumbled and reached into the wooden floor felt for any plant comfort I could find. There was the stored energy of dormant buds in the uncured wood planking. *Grow.*

"Nothing you can do but let it happen. Amanda and I will help you through it." Lines etched around his somber eyes.

"It's not a lifestyle choice. It's who you are. This is a good thing, Connor." Amanda leaned over, staring a few inches in front of me. "What are you doing to the floor?"

"I'm talking with the leftover plant essence in the wood and it's coming to help me."

"I'm not sure that's a help." Westmore sat on the ground, crossing his legs. "Tell me how you communicate with plants."

"Hmmm, you know that everything is some form of energy. Each species of flora has their unique frequency range. Like animals. There's a signature, I feel from them. Like us, an aura of energy surrounds plants. I adapt to the plant's ambience I'm chatting with." I leaned back on my hands. "Thoughts, actions, emotions are *types* of energy.

"When I say 'hi' or 'goodbye' to you, there's a vibration to the word. Many words have emotion tacked on them. I commune more in the tone or mood of the energy in the vegetation's aura. When I come up to Oak, a tree on campus, I feel his welcoming 'hello.' I can say or think the word 'hello' and he understands it from the aspect of the energy impression for that word. It's the same for us using sound instead of feeling energy." I leaned forward. "It's more complicated than that. But that's the gist of it."

His chin in hand, he looked at me. "The way you talk to plants sounds similar to wolf mind-speak. You know how to mind-speak because of knowing how to speak to plants."

"Is that why I heard him murmur in the background?" Amanda looked at her father.

"I believe so." He got up and walked towards the door. "Stop being green. You need to disconnect from it tonight. It only gets worse the longer you hold the wolf back."

I let the plants fade back into the floorboards.

Westmore grabbed a brown weathered collar off a peg rack next to the doorway. "This was your dad's collar. Your dad instituted the collar rule. It's a good precedent." He handed me the leather band.

"The name on it is 'Ruff.'" I wrinkled my nose at the name and handed it back.

"It doesn't have the name 'Ruff' on it but 'Ruffles.' Your dad thought it best to have cute nonthreatening names. So your mom gave him the name 'Ruffles.'" He chuckled. "He kept rubbing the last letters off. He thought 'Ruff' was cute enough."

He unbuttoned his shirt collar. There underneath was an oversize dog collar with tags. "We wear collars any time we plan on being wolfish and on full moon nights even if we're not planning on becoming a wolf."

"Even Jessie and Weasel *always* wear a collar on full moon nights, just in case." Amanda put her hand over her mouth. A muffled "oops" formed around her fingers.

"Amanda, what are you *not* telling Connor and me?"

"I guess I let that puppy out. Jessie, Weasel and I planned the whole non-collar affair." She shrugged with a sorry smile. "I told you Weasel wasn't as bad as he used to be. Connor, you might even find that you like him."

I really highly doubted that.

Westmore frowned at Amanda. "Later I will talk with Jessie, Weasel and you about how reckless and dangerous that was to Connor."

"But it wasn't, considering Connor is actually a werewolf."

"You didn't know that. We don't understand how the virus works other than some basics. The cut on his cheek did swell up from the Lycanthrope virus. I wasn't there but I believe Jessie's saliva aggravated the virus Connor already has. Luckily, it came under control." He glared his well-practiced dominating wolf eyes—or maybe they're parental eyes—on her.

"How were we to know he'd get scratched by a plant? Connor never had problems with them before." She shrugged it off. "He deserved to know why we weren't allowed to see each other and the right to choose if he wanted to take a chance with me."

He shook his head. "It's time, son."

I choked up. He hadn't called me "son" in such a long time. Or it could be I'm scared shitless about what is about to happen. Probably both.

He grabbed my arm pulling me up. "It's just precautionary having you in the enclosure. It's not personal." He turned to the back of the room.

"You mean 'cage'." I pulled back. It sure as hell felt personal.

Amanda came up to me. "We call it a cage when you're being punished. It's the enclosure when you're changing for the first few times. Just to be safe. Everyone goes through the 'enclosure stage'. It's how we judge how much in control of the transforming beast you have." She smiled widely. "This is a good thing in the wolf world. It's a wolf thing. Even Jessie and I had to do it a couple of months. Oh, and Weasel especially had to do it several times proving he has to work at control. That should make you happy."

"You're not helping Amanda." Her dad scowled. "The enclosure lets us gauge the discipline you have over the transformation process. The less time you need to be in it, the more control you have over your wolf." He shoved me into the cage.

I paced back-and-forth on the gouged floor—clenching and unclenching my hands—for what felt like hours.

Clank. Westmore lifted the latch to the cage. Amanda stayed outside as her dad came inside. I stopped moving and wrapped my arms around myself.

"I know you don't know what to expect but you need to relax. How about you try to communicate with the wolf within you like you do with plants?" He looked out the window bars. "It shouldn't be hard. The moon *is* at its fullest."

I shook my head. "That's easy for you to say. But it's been like a hundred years since you went through this the first time."

"That would be about right." He sighed. "How about you take your shorts off and get comfortable?"

"I can't with Amanda standing right there."

"You'll get used to it," Amanda nodded through the bars. "The naked thing, that is. I see Dad and Jessie—the whole pack—butt naked all the time whenever someone is about to transform."

"Sit. Meditate on a time you felt safe. Anything that gets you out of your head about what's happening." Westmore had the freaky eye thing going.

I sat. Shorts still attached to yours truly's buns, I settled in for the long haul.

Westmore went to the other side of the cabin, leaving the cage door open, and took off his clothes. He got on all fours and from the grunts and groans, his transformation sounded painful.

Gnar!

Holy shit! I blinked a few times. Westmore had leapt across the cabin and was growling over me in his overbearing wolf form. He did that huff-huff thing that Jessie did last month. That laughing at me thing.

It took him a few minutes to changed back into a human. He came to sit on the floor in front of me. He was still naked. "That's more like it. Sort of. Just what were you thinking of before you changed?"

Huh? Me changed? I scratched my floppy ear, with my hind leg. *What do you mean, Westmore?* Yeah, I was mind-speaking and sitting on my butt and the hind leg kinda gave it away that I had managed to turn wolfy. But why was he staring?

"You should see yourself Connor. You're weird-looking." The ever-helpful Amanda informed me.

"See if you can change back into human form." He scrunched up his forehead. "Wait! Think of yourself changing back into your normal Green Man mode."

"What's the problem? I changed and changed back. It was quick and painless, actually." I sat on the floor still in my shorts that mercifully had not ripped into shreds. I looked down, my hand covering my eyes from the sight in front of me. "Amanda, go away."

"No way am I leaving this weirdness."

"What were you thinking as you changed?"

"You said to think of a safe time in my life. I flashed to when I held this beagle puppy in my lap. He was one of those strays that ended up at our house. I could feel how safe he felt. Don't know what happened to the little guy."

"That's why you looked like you did." He grinned. "You were a commingling of wolf and beagle. Let's try an experiment. Think only 'wolf' as you are changing into a wolf. Then change back."

My wolf-self heard Amanda's *Oh, my.*

What?

Hey, Connor, I heard that. You're clearly mind-speaking. Can you hear me?

I nodded and shifted.

"What happened?" I stayed on the floor after changing back. I needed the ground's support to keep from toppling over. Heat spread across my face. Don't think I could get any more embarrassed.

"You changed into Jessie's wolf." She kept staring at me. Could this get any more awkward? I snapped my head up to look at Amanda.

"Why Jessie's wolf and not mine or his own? What's the difference?" Westmore's elbow was on his leg and his hand cupped his chin in thought. Yep, I could get more embarrassed.

She didn't turn to answer him. "Connor touched Jessie's wolf. Not yours, Dad."

"Connor, do you know what a Russian wolfhound is?"

I nodded, my eyes towards the ceiling. "I've seen pictures of them. Why a wolfhound?"

"They're from your grandfather's native country. They're not a common breed. But you know what they look like and haven't come in contact with them. Correct?"

"Yeah. I'm not trying to be dense but what that's got to do with anything?"

"Just change already."

What the *heck?* I couldn't. I looked at Westmore in the eyes. It was the safest place to look.

"Let's head outside." He opened the barred exit wider, pushing Amanda and me out the cabin door. "Try morphing into your friend, Oak. A young 'Oak' if you please."

I saw where he was heading with this. I was so excited that I forgot my embarrassment. This was unexpected. Maybe I'd be able to become plants and trees like Mom after all. I just needed to figure out the mutation process now that I was able to transform into a wolf.

I dug my toes into the grainy soil. Nothing happened. No way. I turned to Westmore with pleading eyes. *Grrrr.* I never wanted to hit something so much.

"You know, Connor, you didn't transform like we do." Amanda turned her head towards her dad, a questioning light in her eyes.

"This is my hypothesis. You are smoothly and painlessly mutating like your mom and not the forced transformation of a werewolf. That's why your shorts weren't shredded—you mutated them when you changed. You're able to change into a wolf but not plants. In addition, you can change into more than the wolf species—just as your mom can mutate into different plant species—but only into animals with which you have had contact with. We need to find out if that's a condition for your Mom. It's basically taking the strongest part of the processes from both halves of yourself. Instead of mutating or transforming, I would say you're transmutating."

My life turned into a big question mark. "Whenever I turn into a wolf, will I always look like Jessie's?"

"I think building up your contact with different wolves in the pack and with some practice, you might be able to come into what your true wolf should look like. I'll show you some pictures of your dad's wolf to help you. Ask your mom if she has any of his fur. She used to have a locket with some. Your features are like him in human form. I would think you should be similar in wolf form as well." He tossed my backpack at me. "See you didn't need a change of clothes after all."

"Yeah only because I didn't actually 'transform.' Instead, I 'transmutated.'" I took a deep breath. All the pain was gone. I grabbed a shirt and my boots and put them on. I didn't need the contact from nature to keep the agony away anymore.

Westmore went back inside. He changed into his clothes and got ready to leave. When he came back out, he had a collar.

"Even though you have control over your transmutation—better than any other werewolf—it's still the tail end of the full moon." He handed me Dad's old collar. "You know it's a rule thing. Use your dad's until you get your own." A broad smile covered his face. "Ruffles."

I glared at that thin strip of leather with the joke of a name on it. A joke on my life is more like it. If I put that thing on, around my neck, it's going to suffocate on more levels than I can count. To satisfy Westmore for now, I slid the collar over my arm as I climbed into the Cherokee for the drive back home.

What was my father thinking creating that questionable law? If I'm like him—and I am—I'm not going to enjoy someone or something's authority over me. I make my own decisions.

Being a werewolf, an alpha more so, is not about being aggressive over others but controlling yourself, the wolf's wild virus inside my DNA, and emotions that comes with the beast.

There's a similarity between the two, the Green Man and werewolf. The war between my two halves, the two ways of changing, the two ways of being, created a balance between them. The wildness and all that it entails comes without disregarding the freedom of my connectedness to nature. The battle of Green Man's nature versus wolf had found a truce between both of my essences without the need for arbitration.

Sometimes being in control means letting change happen and going along for the ride. That way I can step up and direct the flow that change travels from here on. Not just observing in the background but also focusing on outcome. Not letting it take over and getting lost in the process.

Putting on the collar is taking charge of unexpected situations. Keeping humans from taking control from me. To tell hunters that I'm not prey. Not a trophy by wearing the collar. I looked at the circlet again. Looking deeper, I see not subjugation, but a tool of power to control my fate in the world of man that symbolizes my ownership over both my nature spirit and wolf-self.

We get a license to drive and I deal with the rules of the road. This collar thing is a rule for the license to live. I took the collar from my arm and slipped it over my head, knowing I would have to get my own that had a name I could accept.

Yes, my Dad collared me before I was even born. Nevertheless, he made me the one in authority of the collar and myself. I finally understood the question, I'd asked Jessie all those nights ago.

Did I feel collared even without wearing the collar? *Yes!*

Jazz Feylynn

The life changing universes of Jazz Feylynn writing mark the hidden energies that glimmer the beauty within the story soul. Author of Fantasy, Paranormal, Speculative Fiction and Creative Nonfiction.

Jazz Feylynn is a new explorer to the world of creative writing. She adds writer to colorful artist and interior designer, movie and anime fanatic, and avid reader of her many life favors. Who loves to travel throughout the world and beyond. With embellished adventures in the magical and mystical realms communicating with otherworldly beings: angels, fairies, and dragons. In her spare time from plants and critters that are her life, her projects include art, photography, textiles, embroidery, historical archiving, and herbology.

Jazz was born in Hollywood and raised in Southern California. The summer following her sophomore year during high school, she studied in France and then following summer worked in London, England across from Hyde Park. College years were spent in Pullman, Washington. She moved back to Southern California after Mount St. Helens' ash cloud covered the town of Pullman before heading off to New Mexico a few years later. After 19 years, at the end of 2005, Colorado became her home.

Bullets and Bookshelves

by T.B. Ray

The following is an excerpt from **We Killed Americans: A Memoir No One Can Read** *by Matthew Gearn*

We did everything we could to survive.

I'm not talking about avoiding bullets. That's a given. No one wanted to die, and so you survived any way you knew how. We stayed alive because of instinct, and training, and our buddies, and smarts, fear, courage, and sometimes just plain dumb fucking luck. And sometimes none of those things were enough.

But there was another kind of survival.

Just *living* with the war. Waking up with the knowledge that it might be your last day, and there wasn't a damn thing you could do about it, and crawling to your feet anyway. Your day to catch a sniper's bullet to the bridge of your nose like Galloway, your brains blown out in messy gray-pink-white bits through a hole in the back of your combat helmet. Your day to whine and moan and cry like Smith because two bullets cut through your guts and the battlefield was too hot for extraction and your buddies lied to you saying that everything was going to be okay. Your day to jump the wrong way after someone yells "Grenade!" and end up with a face and neck and chest looking like raw hamburger. Like Heffernan.

We did whatever it took.

We talked about home. We told jokes, especially when those jokes were in poor taste. We insulted each other, even though we loved the men and women next to us. We talked about the past and the future. Endosa played video games. Dean and Yan, who were probably closer friends than anyone in the platoon, played cards. Miers watched porn. DeMille had this small chess set and kept begging people to play even though no one in the platoon could ever beat him. Carter played with an ancient coin, rolling it over his knuckles. Reiser talked about God. Yeager destroyed things with his knife.

I read and re-read the same two books, real ones. One was a collection by Edgar Allen Poe. The other a memoir of a marine from World War II's Pacific campaign.

It was late February or early March. Maybe two inches of snow on everything. We weren't calling it the Battle of Denver yet, but we were calling it the Second Civil War. Funny how at the time you don't realize you are fighting in one of the bloodiest battles to happen on American soil. Hell, I didn't even think of it as a real battle. We were fighting a holding action against the Reds. We had orders to meet any advancement with heavy resistance, to at least delay a major onslaught for two hours and make the enemy suffer heavy casualties. Not much of a strategy but the only one we had because we knew we were outmanned and outgunned. At least temporarily. We had to hold Denver at all costs while new troops were trained back in California.

No idea if those troops would replace us or go off to fight some other battle. All we knew was the entire war, and the United States of America, depended on us holding our few blocks of territory. That's how the Army gets you. Convinces you to throw flesh in front of bullets and explosives.

Now that I think about it, it was definitely late February when one of those mini-drones we always worried about sneaked up on our position. Normally, we would receive a warning from the rear line about the approach of a drone and have an opportunity to prepare our counter measures. This time, one of the snipers up on the seventh floor heard its approach. We had about ten seconds.

I was ready to have a lot of my men die. If it hit the second floor, that would be eight dead. Ten, not including myself, if it hit the fourth. Only four up on the seventh. I stood near the windows looking for the damn thing. I had to know where it was going to hit. Don't know what I thought I could do. Any warning I could give wouldn't stop the thing from flying straight into the building and exploding.

As I watched, the drone whipped into the open park to the east. That park was the line between us and the Red platoons on the other side. A dark gray bird of prey, the drone appeared roaring down one of the streets. Then it climbed sharply from its low flight pattern and exploded into a brilliant ball of light right there out over the snow-covered, dead-looking park and I had just enough time to pull my left arm up in front of my face before the window in front of me burst inward in a wave of glass.

When I recovered from the blast, I looked up into the startling blue eyes of my second in command, Sgt. Sandersen. She was a stocky woman, her blonde hair in a tight braid, twice my age. A career Army sergeant with a husband and son back in New Hampshire that she hadn't seen since a couple months before the War started.

"Sir?" she asked like it wasn't the first time she had spoken to me. "You with me?"

"Sorta," I answered and tried to sit up. Thankfully, she helped.

My left hand felt weird. There was a stinging numbness in my palm, and yes, I realize that is a contradiction in terms, but that's what it was. The rest of my hand felt numb. I lifted it up in front of my face where I found a seven-inch shard of glass protruding from the center of my palm. It almost went all the way through. As I flipped the hand over, I could see where the glass pushed against the skin from the inside creating a little alpine mountain peak near the knuckle of my middle finger.

"Shit," I said. Blood soaked my hand and the sleeve of my jacket.

"Anything else hurt?" Sandersen asked.

"My ears are ringing."

"Everyone's ears are ringing."

I knew it could be worse. We all had ear buds for communication that also dampened any sounds beyond a certain volume, such as gunfire and explosions. This was modern warfare. Buds in the ears, contacts in our eyes displaying simple computer-generated images a foot or so before our vision.

"What happened?"

Sandersen shrugged her shoulders and said accusingly, "I had my head down like I was supposed to."

"Sorry." She never let me forget that I had only been in the war five weeks, still green but expected to lead a front line unit.

"Well, maybe that hand will make you remember in the future."

It does. Even today, I stretch the hand in just the right way and there's a pinch in my palm right where a straight scar cuts through my heart and head line.

"The others?"

"Everyone's reported in. No injuries beyond a few scratches. Korben's on his way up."

The medic arrived seconds later, dropped to his knees next to me and summed up my injuries at a glance. He didn't seem overly concerned, so I relaxed a little. "That's gonna have to come out."

"Sounds like fun," I said.

My left hand stitched and wrapped in a white bandage, I made the long climb up the dark stairwell to the seventh floor. There was no power in the building, so places like this stairwell with no windows were just as pitch black day or night. I used the small flashlight attached to the side of my assault rifle to find my way. The closed-in space smelled like urine where someone had used it despite orders to the contrary.

Yeager, one of the snipers, had a report for me. I left Sandersen in charge downstairs and made the trek all by my lonesome. When I opened the door on the seventh floor, I dropped to a crouch as I moved toward the northeast corner of the building. This level had been dedicated to some kind of office, so it was filled with cubicles and desks that provided good cover.

Soon, I saw a pair of combat boots sticking out from under a fallen blue cubicle wall and stopped.

"Yeager," I spoke into my comm. I had a direct link with the sniper team. "I'm here."

Movement to my right, about ten feet from those pair of boots, and I saw Ripton crawl out from concealment. Remaining flat, the skinny woman scooted like a snake across the floor until she reached my position. She handed me a large, boxy spotter's scope.

"You can take my place, sir."

Yeager and Ripton were a funny pair, but even Sandersen admitted they were one of the best sniper teams she had seen. Yeager was a lanky kid from West Virginia, not even eighteen, fighting for the Blues even though he came from a Red state. Fighting for the real America, as he put it. Ripton was a heavily tattooed black woman from the Bronx, intimidating in both appearance and attitude. She was my age.

I handed Ripton my rifle and then dropped to the floor. With the scope in my good hand, I crawled across the floor and found the little hole where the spotter had been hiding. It was a tight fit for me. Once I was inside, I saw the small opening in all the piled junk through which an icy breeze blew in from outside. Even from a couple feet back, I could scan the entire three-block span around the park outside.

"Right now, someone in a control room somewhere is probably gettin' hollered at real good, sir," Yeager said in his drawl. It wasn't as thick as I had expected from a country boy.

"What do you mean?"

I studied the park and the buildings on the other side of the open ground.

"Well, the pilot of that drone must of triggered it too early. Darn lucky for us. It blew up right out there over the park, like dead center between us and the Reds."

Except for the occasional "darn" or "shoot," Yeager was the only soldier in the platoon who didn't cuss. He caught a lot of flak about it from the others.

I had noticed the damage on my first glance through the sniper hole. Many of the windows in the buildings across the way that had been intact that morning were gone now. The only thing that mini-drone accomplished was the shattering of windows over a couple blocks. Great news for my snipers.

"Problem is, sir," Yeager said, "if those buildings over there look like that, then I bet ours got a lot of the same. We're gonna have to be more careful when we move around. Might have to even pick some new travel routes."

Shit, if this was good news for our snipers, then it would be the same for the enemy. We had designated safe routes through the buildings on this side of the park. We moved periodically to keep the enemy guessing, but the enemy did the same. It was like a game of chess as we each maneuvered in the hope of gaining some kind of advantage. Now, with countless windows shattered or cracked, someone on the move could unknowingly walk into a line of fire.

I opened a direct connection to my sergeant. "Sandersen."

"Sir?"

"No movement. We have broken windows everywhere. Put together three teams of two to scout out our evacuation routes and find alternatives if we have to. Tell them to go real slow. The tiniest crack in a window could be all a sniper needs. Take no chances. Real careful, okay?" I said.

"What about reposition routes?"

"One thing at a time. If the Reds throw a couple hundred men at us right now, I want a safe retreat."

"Yes, sir."

I returned my focus to the view through the scope.

I knew this area well. I should – I had been staring at it for five weeks. Now, the landscape was slightly different with all the destroyed windows. Dozens of small openings like little caves through which a monster could spring at any moment. I didn't like it.

Down on the street directly below was the snow-covered blackened wreck of a Red tank destroyed the week before my arrival. That was a close one for the platoon I now commanded. Half of them ended up casualties, including the experienced lieutenant in command. I was his replacement.

There were no bodies down there though. As I hear it, there had been a moment of peace called after it became certain the two sides slipped into a stalemate again. Small, unarmed teams entered the battlefield and removed the dead so they could be properly buried. Oddly, a moment of civilized behavior among the brutality. If we could agree not to kill each other while reclaiming the dead, why couldn't we create a general peace between our two sides?

Well, I was only twenty. I was stupid back then.

Finally, Yeager said, "Wanna see something weird?"

There was no ominous tone in the sniper's voice. In fact, it was like he had discovered some strange new insect and kept it in a bottle hidden away somewhere.

"Sure."

"North side of the park. Four-story building made of tan brick out in no-man's land but close to the Red side," Yeager said.

I found the building quickly. It looked like an apartment structure.

"Yeah?"

"Third floor on the east corner of the building. There's a window missing now."

I located the window, but my resolution was too low. I kicked up the zoom and focus on the high-tech scope until the jagged glass around the edges of the window framed my view.

I immediately knew what he was talking about. Books. Floor-to-ceiling shelves of hardbound books along one wall of the apartment. From this distance, it was impossible to count them, but there looked to be a few hundred. It was a decade since the publishing industry in America folded and resorted solely to digital publishing. No one wanted, or read, real paper books anymore and so publishers easily made the economical decision to save their business. No more printing. Since then, books tended to find their way into trash heaps.

Whoever lived in that apartment before the evacuation of Denver had obviously been a major collector.

All I could say was, "Wow."

For three days, I couldn't get those books out of my mind. Twice I even slipped to one of the higher floors, sneaking up to a hiding place near the windows, and stared at them through my own binoculars.

The rest of the platoon was busy scouting and mapping new routes through the western side of the park. The sniper teams took turns scouting out new positions that would give them good firing zones into newly exposed openings. It was slow and dangerous work.

Once, an enemy sniper took a shot at Ripton that missed her by inches. The next day, DeMille hadn't been so lucky and ended up with a bullet through his right shoulder. We evacuated him quickly to a medic team that drew him even farther from the front line. So far, we hadn't received word about his condition.

We weren't the only ones who took hits. Yeager claimed two confirmed kills and my other sniper,

Adams, scored a hit although he couldn't be certain his target received a fatal wound.

As for me, I went about my work always with the image of all those books in the back of my mind.

How did they get there? What kind of person filled an entire room with books but still lived in a lower middle-class apartment? And considering how much they obviously loved books, why did the owner leave them behind? I never learned the answer to those questions.

What authors sat upon those shelves. Shakespeare? Dickens? King? Asimov? Morrison? Vonnegut? Leonard? A hundred authors went through my mind and, with each one, my desire to touch the stiff, dry spines of those books grew. I wanted to look upon them with my own eyes. I wanted to touch them, smell the old pages and fan them in front of my face so I could feel the soft air on my skin.

But that was crazy thinking.

Sure, hardback and paperback books were disappearing quickly from this world and very few people seemed to care. In the digital world, paper books had no purpose. We could hold thousands of novels on a single device and read them whenever we wanted. We could even download old books from various digital libraries for a small fee. It wasn't like the words of Shakespeare and Dickens were disappearing from the planet. They were still out there.

But books! Real, honest-to-God, books that you could hold in your hand, smelled, heard, loved. They were different. They were something special and they were going extinct.

I didn't expect anyone to understand. Not really. Maybe this was my way of surviving this war. I had those two books in my pack, my comfort during those silent hours when there was nothing to do. Holding those books in my hands instead of a rifle was almost as important as the words on the page.

If that sounds stupid, I can understand that. But that wasn't the dumbest thought running through my head.

On the fourth day after my discovery, I was prone on the floor directly behind Yeager's feet talking in whispered tones to the sniper instead of using the comms.

"Seen any movement in the northeast corner of the park?" I asked.

"They're over there, sir. I can feel it, but they've been keepin' their heads down."

"Intel says we have two to three platoons on our position."

"Three or four is more like it."

I hesitated a moment before I asked the next question. "Ever seen anyone in that place with all the books?"

"No, but someone's been in there. Some of the books are missing," Yeager answered.

"Huh? Missing?"

"Yeah, a whole shelf is gone. Maybe they saw all that paper just sitting there. Maybe the Reds ran out of toilet paper," Yeager said. I could tell the thought amused him.

But the thought of a bunch of soldiers wiping their asses with *Hamlet*, or *The Shining*, or *Slaughterhouse Five* made my entire body tense.

"Shit, Yeager, why didn't you shoot them?"

"Didn't see 'em. Maybe I was asleep."

"No one slips in there anymore. Keep an eye on it," I ordered.

"I am, sir," Yeager said sheepishly. I knew he was doing his job as best as he could. Better than most in his position. It was impossible to watch every open window at once, even with Ripton's keen eyes on the spotter scope.

"Just make sure no one touches those books."

It wasn't until Yeager told me that some of the books were missing that I realized I had been planning to go over there ever since I first put eyes on those shelves. And now I felt a certain sense of urgency like I had to rescue those tomes from the enemy.

It was the 'how' that kept me from acting immediately.

I could take a team over there on some kind of sham scouting mission, claim I received orders, and bring back as many books as we could carry. Everyone would know I was deceiving them, but they wouldn't be able to do anything about it except privately complain. Sandersen would be the only one who would give me any shit, and that would be until the end of the war.

But every time I considered that plan, I wondered how I would feel if one of my men died because of a book. How do you tell someone's wife, or mother, or child that the one they loved died over some printed words on paper?

Around 0200 while I pretended to sleep, I realized I had to do this alone. I couldn't risk another person's life over something that only I valued.

Well, not only I. My entire family. My mother loved books almost as much as her children, and my father was a true traditionalist in every way. In my heart, I was only fighting this war because it had claimed the life of my older sister during the earliest days of conflict, and later my mother due to utter, crushing sorrow.

Today, I realize I know the real reason I became obsessed with saving those books, but I was only twenty then. Back then, I told myself I was doing it for a higher purpose, that I was saving something that mankind could not lose because of some stupid war.

The next night, when most of the city fell silent and dark as tar, I would slip away and find those books. That was all the plan I had. Sometimes we do what we have to in order to survive.

I received a call from surveillance warning about the approach of a drone shortly after 1700 the next day. The predicted route would be flying within our zone, and so everyone burst into action. Most of the platoon took cover and the sniper teams on the roof grabbed their countermeasures. Yeager would be operating the laser rifle as a last resort. It didn't fire the kind of sci-fi laser that could burn quickly through a man, but one designed to disrupt the systems of a completely artificial device like a drone.

Adams manned the directional signal scrambler and the two spotters attempted to direct the snipers toward the target the moment it appeared in the sky.

For two tense minutes, we waited for the attack. I teamed up with Private Endosa, a short, baby-faced Hispanic kid with a real talent for everything technical. He was a Colorado native, like me, so he was kind of fighting for his home. A dedicated soldier, and a funny kid too. He plugged into a radar feed from the rear lines and relayed information to the sniper teams.

The drone turned out to be a scout, or maybe a false alarm meant to put us all on edge. The Reds did that sometimes, flying a drone over the city in a random pattern to get us all worried and afraid.

I hated those fucking drones.

I didn't go out that night as planned because I had to keep in contact with command as they speculated about the drone fly-by, organized air strikes, and generally lit up the Denver sky line with orange artillery flares. After the first mini-drone blew up over the park, everyone wondered if this meant an imminent attack on our position. Now they were fairly certain the enemy was testing a perceived weak point in our defenses. As a result, Blue troops were moved into positions where they could support us more quickly if need be.

In a small way, it made us feel better. Until then, it had just been us against two or three times as many soldiers across a block-wide park. We always speculated that if the enemy mustered a massive assault, we would be dead. No way to retreat fast enough, and no way to defend our positions. For some reason, that hadn't happened yet and now the upper brass thought the Reds were preparing for just that possibility.

The next day, the pressure was still too hot and I needed to stay with my platoon in case something urgent happened. But then the Reds used the same tactic of flying a drone over another stretch of the city, teasing us with the possibility of an attack, and then withdrew. My superiors freaked out.

Everyone hears all about the deaths in the Battle of Denver, the major battles where thousands died in ground advances, air assaults, and artillery bombardments, but what they don't know is those peaceful days in between, when soldiers still died because they made a stupid mistake, but most of us just sat around and did nothing but worry.

Seven nights after I found out about the small library of books located so close to me, I finally found an opening.

Yes, I understand it was absolutely the worst thing a commander could do to his platoon, but I had to get those books. I had to.

And I didn't really consider myself a good leader anyway. I only joined because I was in a dark place after my sister was shot down and my mother ended her life. I wanted to strike back at someone—anyone—and my father wasn't there because he had fled to South America to avoid going to jail. I didn't even want to be a leader. I was in college at the time studying for a history degree and the Army put me into officer training school to meet my request to stay in Denver.

Soon, I found myself in command of my own platoon in the middle of a major war with zero experience. That's why Sandersen always looked at me with those suspicious blue eyes and it's why I did a really stupid thing on a seriously frosty late February night.

At 0100, I crawled up from my position at the edge of the sleeping members of my platoon. I stalked quietly to the door to the stairwell, opened it, and slipped inside. I stopped briefly on the third floor to find something I stashed in a custodial closet the previous day. I was traveling light. My rifle, two pouches of ammo, my side arm with two clips, the combat knife on my chest, two grenades, a pry bar. No body armor, no pack, no water pouch. From the closet, I pulled two large, empty duffel bags with shoulder straps and slung those over my back.

Down the stairs to the ground floor but toward the rear of the building away from the heavily trapped first floor. I walked out into the cold night air through the only door on this level that wasn't rigged to explode. All I had to do was deactivate the motion alarm.

It had started snowing yesterday. Sparse flakes still dropped lazily out of the sky when I stepped outside that door into a few inches of fresh white powder.

After a deep breath, I told myself to turn around and go back to the others.

"This is stupid, Matt," I said softly.

No one argued with me.

"They're just books."

My father's voice, my mother's voice, even my fighter pilot sister's voice all answered, "If not here, then where is the line?"

In normal times, you can walk a city block easily. In minutes. No problem.

In war, you have to watch every opening, every possible path where someone could put a bullet through your skull. Whether you are walking, crouching, crawling, or scurrying through the battlefield, you are a blind rat hoping no predator spots you.

That's why it seemingly took me forever, months possibly, to exit the building we were staying in, enter another and move through it, and then exit again and run toward another. We were forced to move like this because, even though we were on the imaginary front line, enemy sniper teams had managed to get behind that line on numerous occasions. A city was nearly impossible to secure. Simply too many places where someone could hide.

My thighs ached from crouching and stalking bent over for more than an hour. My eyes stung from trying to suck in every bit of light to see if the enemy was present, almost never blinking.

I moved slowly along the buildings on the western side of the park until I reached the most northern point. Now came a real dangerous moment. I would have to cross four lanes of open, abandoned city street where I would be exposed to sniper fire. This would be the one place where I was most vulnerable, and thus probably the place where I would die. Knowing this, I paused for almost twenty minutes watching the shadows and listening to the night. I think I was attempting to reach out with some kind of sixth sense to detect if anyone was watching.

Or maybe I was just trying to build up the courage.

I clenched and unclenched my left hand a couple times. It was still bandaged too thickly to wear a glove, so the fingers on that hand were starting to sting from the cold. Korben removed the stitches the day before and sealed the wound with medical glue so it would heal cleanly, but the injury was still too new for me to have full use of the hand. Good thing I was right handed.

Finally, I took a slow breath and broke from cover, jogging bent almost double across the street in a straight line toward the corner on the opposite side. At any moment I expected the impact of a bullet. I knew I wouldn't hear the shot that killed me. The bullet would already be passing through my skull by the time the sound reached me.

Miraculously, I reached the other side, slid the last five feet into cover against the wall of what had been a two-story building with a coffee shop on the ground floor. A window midway down the wall was missing. I could climb in there and try to find a way from one structure to the next on this side of the block. Almost all the buildings on the north side of the park shared walls. There was a single alley not far from my destination but it would be difficult to reach out in the open. On the other hand, I didn't have the time to dig my way through the sturdy brick walls common to all these structures.

So, I passed the open window while I approached the back of the building. I reached the corner, peeked around for just a couple seconds to study the path ahead.

Too much open space. The half a dozen vehicles on both sides of the road would provide some protection. The good news was, with the exception of rooftops and a few windows, there were surprisingly few likely sniper positions. As deadly as it looked, and as uncomfortable as it felt, this was my best route.

Making myself as small a target as possible, I crouch-ran to the rear of a white sedan, slid up against it, and realized I didn't have any unwanted holes in my body. So far, so good.

I ran to another car, and then another, and then into a recess in one of the walls with a sturdy metal door. There was just enough room for me to hide. My next leg was one of the longest and took me up to a panel delivery truck. I dove behind the large rear tires, thankful just to be alive and breathing. Heavily.

That's why I didn't hear the growl until the dog stepped out from under the truck and bared its teeth so close to my face that I could smell its fetid breath.

I was laying on my stomach with my rifle at my side. I froze.

The dog was black and white, a skinny and filthy medium-size mutt. I either woke it or it had a meal somewhere nearby. It didn't appreciate my presence.

"Easy, boy," I whispered.

The evacuation of Denver had happened so quickly and with such strict rules that no one had been allowed to take along the family pets. In many cases, people just opened a door or window and hoped their pet would find a way to survive. Some people brought what they felt would be a merciful end to the animals themselves. More sadness to add to a truly sad war. This pup was probably one of those who had been let free, but after so long on its own, it had gone feral.

Man no longer represented protection. Man was a threat. I was competition.

Slowly, I shifted my weight to my left side. I couldn't shoot the animal or the gunfire would alert everyone in the area. I certainly wouldn't make it to the books, and even going back to the platoon would be impossible. So, I released my hold on my rifle and slowly brought my right hand toward my chest.

The dog growled. Drool dripped from its mouth into the snow. Its entire body tensed as it dipped its maw a few inches closer to my face.

"Come on now. I'm not that ugly," I said it what I hoped was a soothing tone.

My heart pounded in my chest with the knowledge that the animal would attack at any moment. Despite the cold, my entire body broke out in a sweat. The canine was determined to run me off, uncertain of my intentions, and so needed to exert its dominance. It didn't know that I hesitated out of sympathy because it was an innocent animal.

Finally my fingers closed around the combat knife strapped upside down on my chest. My thumb snapped open the protective strap across the hilt.

The sound made the dog skitter back a couple steps. It barked once and prepared to pounce.

I drew the knife, rolled halfway back from it, and thrust the seven-inch blade upward as the dog's mouth snapped for my face.

Teeth clipped shut so close to my nose some of its slobber splashed my cheeks. My knife, however, entered the base of its throat and went all the way through. I had the animal speared on my blade, but it wasn't dead yet. It struggled to escape, pulling away in great yanks that had to be doing even more damage to the poor canine's neck. The claws on its hind feet scratched against the cement beneath the snow. I held onto the knife with all my strength, fearing what would happen if the dog broke free. Would it die, or would it attack again?

Hot blood soaked through the black knit glove I wore on that hand. The only sound in the night was the scritch of claws on cement and a soft moaning whimper from the dying dog.

I have no idea how long it took for the poor beast to die. A minute? Every second was pure horror. Finally the mutt weakened. It sat at first, staring wide-eyed with fear at me, and then it sort of melted onto the ground into a bundle of black and white fur.

I pressed my left hand down on its head and drew the knife from its neck, and still the animal did not move.

It was the first time I killed anything. Over the years, I have tried to make something of that dog's death. Some kind of meaning. No doubt it had been someone's beloved pet. It hadn't meant me any real harm. It was afraid. Just an animal trying to survive the war. Just like us. But there was no reason in the world for me to be there that night. I was on a stupid mission to rescue some meaningless books and the dog had to die because of it.

Was even one book worth that dog's life?

I still don't have an answer to that one.

The door creaked like something out of a horror vid. I was certain everyone in a ten block radius had heard the sound. Instead of running, I jumped into the darkness beyond and pulled it closed behind me with yet another loud, metallic scratching sound.

I was in the basement of the building with the apartment full of books. At the rear, I discovered a door on the ground level and a set of stairs going beneath the ground to a single metal door. I had chosen the latter because of the protection the stairwell provided while I worked the door open with my short metal pry bar.

Inside was utter darkness. I didn't turn on my flashlight. The slightest flash of light could alert the enemy. With my rifle dangling by its combat sling, I crept through the darkness slowly with my hands feeling out in front of me. My vision was only a canvas of shadows and darker shadows. My eyes adapted to the lack of light, but the human eye can only see so much. I found laundry machines, closets, scattered junk, and finally a door. Beyond that door was a set of stairs that I could only assume climbed up to the floors above.

The smart thing to do, the military thing to do, would be to clear every floor before going to my destination, but I already felt like I had been gone from my platoon too long.

I climbed the steps slowly. One step, pause a second to listen, another step. It was silent and black. Even though the temp was down in the single digits, a layer of still sweat collected under my fatigues.

"Sir?"

The voice in my ear made my skin jump completely off my body. At least, that's how it felt. I took a moment to catch my breath and, maybe, let my heart start beating again. Only then had I realized the voice had been that of Sgt. Sandersen speaking through a direct line.

"Yes?"

"Sir, what are you up to?" Sandersen asked, her voice revealing that she was more than a little annoyed.

She knew I was gone. Did she know why?

"I'll be back soon. You're in command until my return."

"Ripton spotted someone on the north side of the park. That was you?"

"Yes."

"Yeager almost put a bullet in you, sir. You're lucky he saw the blue arm band."

Dammit! All that time, I had been worried about the enemy putting a bullet through my skull and I nearly died by my own soldier.

What Sandersen didn't say is she had taken account of everyone in the platoon and found her lieutenant missing.

I sighed. They found me out, and part of me wanted to return now that they had. My responsibility was to my platoon. Now, I had an excuse to abandon those books so the enemy could use them for toilet paper.

But still a larger part of me couldn't do it.

"Sandersen, this is something I have to do."

"No, you don't."

"You have my permission to yell at me, or report me, or whatever you want, but not until I return. I am sorry."

"Sir, you are my responsibility."

"Not tonight, I'm not. The platoon is."

"What are you up to?"

I didn't know how to answer that question because I didn't really know myself. It's not like I could tell her I was risking my life to save a few books.

Instead of lying to her, I asked, "When your son was a little boy, did you read to him? Bedtime stories?"

"Of course. Dr. Seuss. He loved them."

"My mother had a few Seuss books. Actual books. I remember all the colors. I remember sitting in her lap holding one side of the book while she held the other and carefully turning each page. I would read one page and then she would read the next. My favorite was *Green Eggs and Ham*."

"My son liked the one with the elephant," Sandersen said.

"Horton."

"Yeah, that's the one."

"Did he hold the book?"

She was older than me. Maybe her son was raised with real books. Maybe she would understand.

But Sandersen said, "No, I had one of those digital readers that paces the words to help put your kid to sleep. It was supposed to be sort of hypnotic. All the doctors suggested it."

"I held the book. I can still picture it. My mom let me stay on every page as long as I wanted. I studied those awesome pics. Those crazy pics. I loved them. I think she loved them too."

"And?" Sandersen wanted to know what Dr. Seuss had to do with me running around in the middle of the night in no-man's land.

"Tell Yeager I'm going to the book room. He can show you. Now, let me do what I have to do. I need to concentrate on staying alive."

"Funny. You need to concentrate on staying alive in a situation where you put yourself in danger," Sandersen said.

"Just more evidence of my incompetence. Maybe you can use this incident to have me reassigned. Get someone with more experience."

"You're not incompetent, sir. Your head is just in the wrong place."

I didn't answer at first. I was ready to get moving again, but then I remembered something Sandersen said and ordered, "No one moves from their position. Hear me, Sandersen? Everyone is to maintain their current position until further notified. Do you understand?"

"Yes, sir."

"I mean it. No matter what happens over here. To me. You maintain your position."

"I am not deaf, sir."

Finally, the third floor. I pushed the door from the emergency stairwell open slowly. Thankfully, it didn't make much noise. I stepped into a hallway slightly brighter than the stairwell. My guess was the apartment was to my right toward the front of the building. To the left the hall went straight for about the width of one apartment and turned to the right. I pictured an L-shaped hall, elevator out of sight around that corner. I had climbed up the emergency stairwell in the middle of the building.

Again, I should have cleared this level first. Instead, I turned to the right and stalked down the hall with my pistol in hand. I planned to go to the last door on the left where I figured I'd find the apartment facing the front of the building. The one with all the books. I was maybe fifteen feet from the door when I noticed it hanging open.

At first, I tensed. Someone else was there. But then I remembered someone had already been in the apartment and taken some of the books. Of course, they would have had to break into the place.

Silently, I stalked those last feet to stand in front of the door. I could see where someone splintered the door jamb with some kind of weapon. The door would never lock again.

I keyed up a direct line to Yeager and said, "Yeager, I am entering the book room. Don't shoot me."

"All clear, sir," Yeager said, meaning he had eyes on the room and couldn't see anyone. What was Sandersen up to? I pictured her laying in Ripton's spot, watching me through the spotter's scope, that motherly frown of disapproval on her round face.

"What's going on over there?" I asked.

"Nothin'."

"Yeager?" I asked again. Yeager not only had an inability to cuss, but he was a terrible liar as well.

Ripton came on the line instead and said, "Sir, Sarge is waking everyone up in case the shit hits the fan. If you don't mind me asking, why are you out there all by yourself?"

"I have something I have to do, Ripton."

"I don't get it."

"Well, you're not alone in that. It's just something I have to do. Can't explain it."

"I told my mom that once after I broke a boy's nose in English class."

I laughed and said, "Then you understand."

"Not really," Ripton said. "It was stupid punching that boy. He was cute."

"I get it," Yeager said. "When I was a kid, my Pop-Pop had this real old truck. Weird yella color like an old banana. Kept that thing in pristine condition, always fussin' over it. Could only drive it like a mile once a week 'cause he couldn't afford the gas. This rich man offered to buy it once for more than my Pop-Pop could make in three years. He turned him down. No one understood why. You're like my Pop-Pop, sir."

"Yeah, something like that."

"Hey, Yeager," Ripton asked, "what happened to the truck?"

"Pop-Pop died and my dad sold it to some other rich guy."

Ripton chuckled.

I said, "Just don't kill me, Yeager. I'm entering the apartment now."

"Your funeral, sir," Ripton said.

"I hope not."

More books than I have ever seen in one place at one time. That's not true. I've been in stores that sold books, and a couple of the last libraries when I was a kid. But that apartment held more books than I had ever seen in one place as an adult.

The wall we could see from Yeager's position wasn't the only one in the room covered in book shelves. I crouched in the doorway to the room staring at all that was within. Three of the walls were covered in shelves from floor to ceiling.

The rest of the apartment had been sparsely decorated with only a few pieces of necessary and dilapidated furniture. It was obvious the owner spent all his money on books. Still, for some reason, he had left all this behind.

Someone had obviously been in this room, and not only once. They had been shuffling through the books on the shelves not visible through the window. They had stacked unwanted tomes on the floor, left some shelves with books leaning over after removing some of the volumes. If all the shelves had been full before the war, at least half were missing now.

I slipped into the darkest corners of the room not visible from the window and started reading the spines. Many were paperbacks with white-scratched spines. Still other shelves had hardbound novels in various somber colors. Some of these had titles on the side while others I had to pull out to discover the mystery within.

When I found a history of the Roman Empire, I realized I had to take it. I holstered my pistol, pulled one of the duffel bags from my back, spread it out on the floor, and opened it up. I dropped the book on Rome into it and returned to the shelves.

That's how I went through the room at first. I stayed away from the window, grabbing any individual tome that interested me and tossing it into the big duffel. There were autobiographies, biographies, novels, and collections of poetry. I took a variety of them all. I chose hard bound books over the less sturdy paperbacks, but sometimes the paperbacks struck my interest because of the rarity of the author or the content of the story.

The real treasure, though, was on the opposite side of the room near the window. A faint glow, moonlight through the thin cloud cover, streamed in through that window. Even from twelve feet, I could read some of the titles. I recognized a few that had been written over a hundred years ago, although the books were almost certainly reprints.

I needed a plan of attack. I couldn't sit in front of those shelves studying the books like I had in the rest of the room. If Yeager could see me in there, I had to assume that the enemy could see me too.

I opened the second duffel and slid it across the floor until it was resting on the ground in the middle of the shelves. There were maybe ten books I could see that I definitely wanted, but I couldn't be overly selective. I planned to grab those books and as many from either side of it as I could fit between my hands, and then slide them off the shelves into the bag. I guessed I would be out in the open no more than ten seconds, then I would drop to the floor and drag myself and the bag of books back into the shadows.

I opened the connection to Yeager and said, "Stepping into the open for a few seconds."

"Don't do it, sir," Yeager said with concern.

Ripton added, "You're gonna get a fuckin' bullet in you for this."

"I'll be quick."

And I darted forward.

I told myself not to read any of the titles, just grab a bunch of books between my hands, twist, drop onto the bag, repeat. The books filled the big bag a lot quicker than I had realized, so the last few I only grabbed a couple at a time. Then right at head level, my eyes caught the name Aristotle. I paused and read some more of the titles on the small books on that shelf, spotting the names of other philosophers like Plato, Nietzsche, and Rousseau. It was an entire shelf of philosophy.

I suddenly thought of my father, who had loved philosophy and had two small shelves on the topic. That is, before he left us. Before he fled the country never to return or contact his family again. That had been almost four years ago, leaving me to be the man of the house.

Leaving me to mourn the death of my sister, and then come home one day to find my mother's lifeless naked body in a bathtub filled with dark red water.

"Who are you?"

The voice came from behind me. I had been too focused on the books and my own dark thoughts that I didn't even hear the man step into the room. I even turned toward the sound in a daze before I realized it was the enemy.

The man wore the black, gray, and white fatigues of a soldier and pointed an assault rifle, identical to my own, at my chest. On the front of his combat helmet was a large red square with the letters CSA in white in the middle. Central States of America.

"Freeze!" the man blurted when he realized I was the enemy. My own helmet had the old United States flag on it, but we wore a blue band around our right biceps to differentiate ourselves from our opponents.

We stared at each other in silence for a long time. I was waiting for the man to kill me. When he didn't, I began to wonder why. Slowly, I raised my hands.

In my ears, Ripton asked, "What's going on, sir?"

I couldn't answer without alerting the man across the room, but Ripton and Yeager were watching and had to know I was in danger as I stopped moving and raised my hands.

"What are you doing here?" The Red had been standing in the entrance when he spotted me. Now, he advanced into the room. The barrel of his rifle never moved from my body. If he pulled the trigger, he could put a dozen bullets through my body in an instant.

"I don't mean you any harm." I somehow found my words. The line to my sniper team was still open, so they could hear my side of the conversation. The tiny mic taped to my throat was designed to only pick up my voice though.

"What are you doing here?" the Red repeated, taking two more steps forward. He was still concealed behind the wall of the building, but now I could make out more than the shadowy shape of the man. He was around my age, short with plump cheeks and a small blonde mustache. I could not yet make out his rank.

"I came for the books," I admitted. I decided to be honest since the evidence of my presence rested at my feet.

"The books?"

"I spotted them when your drone blasted out the window. Couldn't resist."

"Why?"

"I like books."

He said doubtfully, "You like books."

"Yeah."

My heart pounded in my chest so loudly I was surprised the enemy soldier couldn't hear it. I glanced around the room looking for some way out of my situation, but I was out in the open with no cover of any kind. Not only that, I was standing in plain view of the park, which meant at any moment one of the Red snipers might spot me. Time was not on my side.

"You came all the way over here for the books?"

"Yeah."

"What were you going to do with the books?"

"Read them."

The Red soldier stared at me, judging me. He didn't want to believe me. I could see it in his eyes. But in the end, I think he did. Suddenly, I knew why. He not only believed me. He understood.

"You're doing the same thing." The moment I said it, I knew it was the truth even before the man nodded. "You've been taking the books all along. By yourself. No one knows about it."

"I have. I've been stashing them until I can figure out a way to send them home."

"Where's home?" I asked the man, hoping to gain some kind of connection that might save my life.

"Iowa. You?"

"From right here in Denver."

"Sorry to hear that," the man said with genuine sympathy. Everyone knew what this city had suffered so far and knew it would only get worse in the future.

"Who got you started on books?" I asked.

In my ear, Ripton said, "Where is this guy, sir? How far in front of you?"

I realized my sniper team had a plan to save my life. The only way they could help though would be a blind shot through the brick wall of the apartment building. Sure, Yeager had armor piercing rounds, but how effective would they be going through a solid wall?

The Red said, "My grandfather."

"For me it was my parents. They were both into real books. I think that's what brought them together."

The Red suddenly remembered the situation, stiffened a little, and raised his rifle to point at my head.

"Drop your weapons," he said.

"Why?"

"I gotta take you in," he said.

"You do that, and your platoon leader is gonna wonder what you were doing out here in the first place. You won't be able to get any of these books," I told him.

He hadn't thought that far ahead, but I could see on his face that he was anguishing over his desire for the books and his sense of loyalty to his platoon.

I said, "You could let me go. I promise never to come back. Just let me take my bag with me and you can have the rest. Even the ones in the bag behind you."

He didn't turn around as I had hoped. I wanted to charge the man and subdue him. He was smaller than me and my hand-to-hand combat training was still fresh in my mind.

Maybe I shouldn't have tried to trick him because a deep frown fell over his face as he remembered he was my enemy even though we shared the same love for books.

"Let the rifle fall first. Then slowly remove the pistol," he told me.

"Don't do this. Let me go," I pleaded with him.

In my ear, Yeager whispered, "Just give me a number, sir."

"Do it now, or I'll kill you," the Red said.

"Have you killed a man before?" I asked.

When he didn't answer, I knew that he hadn't. He had probably fired his assault rifle many times, but never knowingly killed someone. I hadn't either, but in order to stay alive I had to speak a single number that would likely end the life of this man across the room.

"Don't do this," I begged.

"Drop your goddamn weapons now!" he said too loudly for the silent night. He was going to kill me if I didn't.

I hesitated. I didn't want to be a Red prisoner. I didn't want to abandon my platoon. I didn't want to die, but I also didn't want to say the word that was on my lips. But I did.

"Eighteen."

The man's eyebrows came together in a quizzical look trying to figure out what that number had to do with our conversation. That's all the time he had before the wall to his right exploded inward. I watched as the man twisted to the side like he had been punched in the lower ribs. He cried out in pain, retreated toward the door.

I drew my pistol faster than I had ever done before. Every action had been beaten into me during basic training until it became instinct. I raised my weapon in two hands, flipped off the safety with my thumb, took aim as my target turned back toward me, and pulled the trigger four times, center of mass.

The book lover fell heavily to the floor and didn't move.

"Get out of there, sir!" Ripton shouted in my ears.

With the pistol in my hand, I closed the duffel at my feet and lifted it onto a shoulder as I retreated from the open window. A bullet zipped through the room somewhere behind me. I knew that wasn't Yeager. He no longer had a target. So, the Red snipers were onto me.

I skipped the second bag of books and crawled from the room. Somewhere outside, a gun battle raged. Automatic fire filled the night. I heard two explosions between the time it took me to get from the apartment to the door to the emergency stairwell. Once inside that pitch dark stairwell, I shifted the duffel across my back so I could move quicker and still use my rifle.

"Sarge says to come back the way you went in," Ripton told me.

Whatever Sandersen had planned, I decided to obey. I holstered my pistol, held the rifle in my hand and turned on the small flashlight. There was no reason to be stealthy anymore.

It was a tense few minutes before I managed to get back behind the front line. Sandersen had disobeyed my orders and assembled a squad positioned at the open road I had crossed earlier. When I came into sight, they popped smoke grenades and laid down cover fire until I managed to cross.

Thankfully, there were no serious injuries on our side. Yeager claimed three more confirmed kills during the chaotic battle my platoon raged to distract the enemy from my retreat.

Later, I sat covered in sweat alone on the fourth floor with the huge bag of books next to me. Sandersen walked in, her narrow lips a thin line of disapproval. She stood silently for a long time. She just stared.

Finally, I said, "I had to kill that guy."

Sadly, he was only the first man I killed.

"It could have been you."

"That doesn't make me feel any better. He was just there to grab a few books."

Like me.

"Nothing makes you feel better about killing a man," Sandersen said and turned to leave. She only got a few steps before she stopped and faced me again. "He felt his life was worth a few books. What do you think?"

I looked at the bulging duffel and placed a hand on top of it before I lied, "They're just books."

"Good," the sergeant said. "Now, maybe you'll start fighting this fucking war."

Soldiers on both sides did what they had to in order to survive the war. Some watched porn, some played cards, and some read books. But in the end, we died for those things too.

T.B. Ray

T.B. Ray is the author of the <u>Zycho</u> apocalyptic action series and the soon to be published <u>Hour 13</u> sci-fi thriller series as well as the <u>Jack Dublin: The Adventurist</u> action serial available for free exclusively through his newsletter at *tbraybooks.com*. He's been a mercenary writer for decades writing just about everything thinkable, but now he has set out to compose for himself. All part of his evil plan. He once lived next to a crematorium in Germany and set himself on fire. Those aren't related, but wouldn't it be cool if they were?

Love in the Ashes

by Erik Johnson

The line at the pre-registration table shuffled forward another two steps. Darren shifted his backpack and unzipped his winter jacket. He decided it would probably be dark before Deanna got to the sign-in desk. Their line was a lot shorter than the line for the walk-ins that snaked out into the packed lobby. Talent auditions closed at 9:00 PM, but Deanna wanted to be done by early afternoon, and they had arrived at 8:00 AM. He wanted to get back over the mountains before sunset, so her schedule was perfect. Getting home assumed the van could make it, and the ominous weather reports were wrong.

Deanna had paid him to take her to the premier national talent TV show auditions in Denver, so no room for complaints. She brought along her younger sister Susan, her total opposite. Susan had a great smile. She laughed at his jokes and he was comfortable with her. Darren brought Stan in case he had trouble with the old van and needed help. He wished his jokes were as funny as Stan's.

After fifteen minutes on the road, Deanna had

complained with every breath. Darren had told Susan they should leave Deanna and Stan stranded at the next gas station. They'd then drive to Florida for a life of wanton passion under the sun. Susan said no, but Darren noticed she had to think it over for a minute. He had used that line on her at least a dozen times and her refusals had come back fast and hard, so he made slight progress this time. Maybe he should ask Deanna, instead. A life of passion with Deanna was the ultimate fantasy. You never know.

The lower downtown Denver auditorium, built over a century ago for vaudeville acts and concerts, still hosted similar events, like the TV talent show audition. The bleacher stands had been added for the volley ball league and, collapsed, they formed a hard wooden wall. Cheap metal chairs clustered on the wooden floor and on the raised platform musicians had used long ago. Chairs stayed filled, so everyone else stood around or sat in little groups on the floor. The din of several hundred people talking and singing made any conversation impossible without screaming in someone's ear.

Deanna hated waiting. Lines meant waiting, and Darren and Susan used to joke that two minutes was too long for Deanna. When she exploded, fifty feet away was the right distance to be. When Deanna wasn't angry or on fire, he tried to get as close as he could. She was worth it. You never know.

"Stay out of my way and let me handle the registration. I know how to deal with these people." Deanna snapped at Susan and Darren. She turned and gave the bald man behind the table her plastic smile. He looked up with no expression.

"Your sister is rather strong willed today," Darren muttered to Susan.

"This is nothing. She was worse yesterday," she muttered back.

"What do you mean, at noon?" Deanna screamed. "I got here early, and I have to wait until after every butt-head and their dancing dog has auditioned? This is outrageous."

She shook her head, and the tips of her short black hair pointed at the bald man like daggers.

"Your time is noon, take it or leave it," the man behind the table replied.

"I demand to talk to the manager. We'll see about this," Deanna shot back.

"I am the manager, and your time is noon. Anything else?"

He showed no sign of emotion, and his eyes became hard and unforgiving.

"I don't have to take your crap," she screamed. "Nobody treats me like this."

"You have one minute to present your signed forms, or you can leave."

She waved her finger in his face and narrowed her eyes. "You can take your shit forms and—"

He raised an arm and cut her off. "Security!" he shouted.

Deanna stormed away, screaming obscenities, and left Darren and Susan standing at the table.

The balding man dropped his clipboard to the table and in a firm, but bored voice said, "Next." Darren stepped aside as a middle-aged woman muscled in front of Susan and dropped a fistful of papers onto the table. She wore a cheap red wig, had a pound of make-up on her sagging face, and held a small squirming dog.

"We drove for four hours to witness her total bitch self," Susan said as they scurried behind Deanna to a bare spot in the center of the room.

Deanna jerked her electric piano keyboard case out of Darren's hands and stomped away. It reminded Darren of how a child throws a tantrum.

"I'm sorry I got you into this," Susan said, lowering her chin. "I shouldn't have asked for your help after mom refused to let Deanna use her car.Deanna promised to be pleasant this trip."

Darren put his back to the wall and slid to the floor. He pulled his knees to his chin and pushed his wire rim glasses up his nose with a finger. "Not a big surprise. She's always quite a handful. At least I don't have to haul that damned keyboard around all day. I suppose we ought to pack up and leave. Deanna can find her own way back to Grand Junction. It'll be a quiet ride home for the three of us."

Susan laughed and dropped next to Darren. She rested her hands on her crossed legs. "Don't worry. Deanna will find a way home. It was fun watching her meet her match. Anyway, it's exciting to be here and see lots of talent and real auditions. It's as good as watching the show itself. Remember the guy last year that sang opera and blew the judges away? What was his name?"

Darren rummaged in his worn backpack. "Kent, the used car salesman from New Jersey. He won a million dollars. I could use a million or two, then I could afford to get the van fixed." He handed Susan a chocolate almond bar.

She peeled the wrapper back and took a bite. "Hate to waste the day, so let's check out the audition rooms."

"Good by me," he said, and poked her shoulder with a light jab. "Hey, I just got a brilliant idea."

She pulled some hair away from her eyes. "You have a history of stupid ideas, and I'm in no mood for the next one."

He dropped his hands and stretched out his legs without looking at her. "You do an audition."

Susan shoved his shoulder hard. "That's not even remotely funny."

"Wasn't meant to be funny. We're here, you can sing, so go sign up for an audition."

"I can't sing. Deanna sings. I'm not very good."

"She's good, but you're better. I remember you cried for two days after breaking up with that moon-eyed creep with the scraggly beard. We could do 'Love in the Ashes.'"

"He was only slightly creepy, and my singing isn't what these people expect. I only did it to help you get the rhythm right."

"You don't know what they want to hear. My guitar's in the van, and I'll be your backup."

Susan faced him and scowled. "Sometimes you go way beyond being stupid. No way." She huffed and crossed her arms.

"Yes, way," he replied, "you have nothing else to

do today and I'll be back in fifteen minutes. The end of the audition line is at the lobby doorway, by the way." He pulled his stocking cap out of his pocket and draped it across his ears.

She stood and dusted off her dark pants. "I don't know about this."

"Go get in the walk-in registration line." He pointed to the line. "And don't wander off."

Two dozen people were ahead of Susan when Darren arrived, his classical guitar case dangling from two fingers. An hour had passed before their turn. At least they didn't have to stand in line outside in the snow.

"What is your act?" asked the thin blonde woman with a clipboard sitting behind the walk-in registration desk..

"I play guitar and she sings," Darren said.

"Do you have a video of your act?"

"No."

"Fill these out, bring them back, and then go to room seven. They'll call your number for the audition." She handed both of them a tan envelope full of forms. A paper clip attached a long white sticker tag bearing a number to the first page.

Darren slapped the number on his chest and dropped to the floor against the bleacher wall.

Susan wrote on the first page with one hand while dangling her number tag with the other. "Not sure auditioning is a smart idea." She signed her name on the last page.

"Not sure either, but if we're in the audition

process, we can watch a lot more acts than sitting in the holding area."

"Hadn't thought of that." She smiled and stood. "At least I know the words to 'Love In The Ashes'. Besides, anything else you play sounds real crappy."

"That wasn't very nice, but you have a point. I should be able to play six songs without screwing them up." Darren grabbed his guitar and stood. "Well, I'll drop off our forms and then we'll head to room seven.. Let's see how much damage we can do."

A narrow long pale green hallway with singers shoulder to shoulder along the walls led to room seven. Everyone warbled their own song. The hallway was hot, stuffy, and smelled of people long overdue for a bath, but at least the fat number seven taped to a door was easy to find. A long strip of cheap fluorescent lights bolted to the ceiling provided lighting. With no place to sit, they stood and waited quietly without joining the babbling chorus. One by one, a number was called, and the performer disappeared into the room. A few minutes later they came out. Those with sad faces headed to the exit door. The first screening must be quick and brutal. After standing for an hour, Darren's feet hurt, and his hands were numb from cradling the guitar case.

Susan's hair kept falling across her eyes, and she swept it away a hundred times.

A face appeared at the cracked open door and called their number. Darren let out a big sigh and followed Susan into the room.

The only furniture in the stark room was a couple

of metal folding chairs and a banquet table with brown paper taped across the front. Behind the table, a middle-aged woman in a sagging blue blouse flipped to the next paper on her clipboard. Her business-like auburn hair was pulled back into a tight bun. The overweight man sitting to her right had a gray streaked goatee. His ill-fitting brown jacket failed to cover a faded rock star T-shirt.

The woman pulled papers from the envelope Darren had left at the registration desk. Her eyes darted down each page and then handed then to the man. She looked up and motioned Susan to come closer. Darren's palms started to sweat and he took a deep breath to calm himself. It wasn't like being at a police station—these two people wanted an audition. While Susan answered a question about her phone number, Darren kneeled and unsnapped the guitar case clasps.

"Do it acappella," the man with the goatee said with no enthusiasm.

"What does that mean?" Susan asked.

"It means no back up. You sing solo without the guitar."

Darren closed the case and stood.

"Any time," the man said.

Susan bowed her head and, after a slight pause, began the first verse. Her warm contralto voice lifted the song from her heart.

> *Love is a fire that burns long and bright,*
> *It all seemed so good that long lonely night.*
> *You gave me your heart, and I gave you a lie,*
> *Love died in the ashes... without a goodbye.*

The lady dropped her pencil and it clattered to the table while the man looked up with his mouth gaping. Susan tilted her head up with eyes closed and hands clutched at her throat.

Tell me your secrets, I'll tell you my lies,
Tell me you love me, don't look in my eyes.
When there's no feeling, it all sounds the same,
Now I know love... is never a game.

The lady stood and waved her hand to stop her.

Susan's face fell with rejection. It wasn't 90 seconds.

The woman's lips tightened. "Could you stay longer for a full audition with the producer?"

Susan raised her eyebrows. "I suppose I could."

Going to another audition surprised Darren. Today's auditions were to weed out the inept and untalented, and the survivors would go to longer afternoon evaluations and the inevitable eliminations. A second audition in January with a few remaining talented survivors would be where the performers would be selected to appear on the show. Instructions on the talent show website said as much, but there was nothing about meeting a producer.

"Go to room one, please. He'll see you at noon."

They stood in the middle of the hall among the singers waiting to go in the room. The hall continued past the audition room and stopped at a stairwell with rough room number tags taped to the wall, including Room 1.

"What happened in there?" she asked as Darren peered up the empty stairwell.

"Not sure, but they didn't pitch us out the back door." Darren stepped aside as two men with grim expressions tore off their audition tags and pushed open the back door. "You must have done something right."

"I have a bad feeling about this. Let's go home," she said, sweeping the hair from her eyes.

"Don't be so hasty. We have two hours to kill, so let's go to the cafe near the parking garage and grab a bite. You don't want to sing on an empty stomach."

Deep blue carpet, comfortable chairs, and a window overlooking the gray snowy street put room one in the executive suite category. The room was quiet except for the gentle rush of clean dry air from the ceiling diffusers.

A man with hard blue eyes, crisp curly blonde hair, and what appeared to be an expensive navy blue suit sat behind a low polished wood table.

"Sing for me." He put his fingertips together. "I'd like to hear what you chose for an accompaniment."

Darren played, and she sang 'Love In The Ashes.' Sad words fell from her lips.

No emotion showed on the man's face.

Susan finished, and the producer tapped his fingertips together. He spread his hands on the table and nodded. "Look up more often and smile. On national TV, you want to look professional."

Susan took a deep breath and wiped the corner of her eye. "It's a sad song from the heart. I can't smile when I sing it."

"I know that, so smile when you're done. You only

have three minutes on stage to impact the judges."

"I'll be on the show?" Susan's mouth fell open, and her eyes widened.

"No guarantee," he answered, "but everything you're doing here is to prepare for that eventuality. Relax, and we'll do the interview. I'll ask you about your musical background, how you found Talent All Stars, and what your dream is." He pulled a large phone from his breast pocket and tapped it once, speaking into the microphone. "I want the camera crew in here." Then he lifted a thin brushed metal briefcase to the table. He popped it open with his thumbs , and pulled out a form. Susan sat and put her hands in her lap.

"Please read and sign this." He looked up as Susan read over the form while lifting a pen. "You with the guitar, get over here. There are two people in this act."

Darren sat next to Susan and the man slid a piece of paper under his nose.

Two cameramen slipped in and assembled the camera and lights at the sofa and coffee table in the far corner.

"Next we go to the big room and film you hanging out with other contestants."

Darren handed back the signed form, and Susan held up hers. The man snatched both and dropped them into the briefcase with a quick snap of the lid.

"No need for you to be at the January evaluation audition. We'll do a full live tape session in March. Should you be chosen for the show, I want you to have a song ready for each competition phase. Do you have an audition city preference?"

Susan turned to Darren who shrugged his shoulders. "Dallas would be nice."

"Do we have a problem here? Full auditions were in Dallas last September, Talent All Stars uses different cities each year. You should know that."

"Well, I don't want to be a problem," Susan stammered, "so I guess it doesn't matter, and—"

"Let's do it in New York."

"I suppose, but—"

"Fine, I'll see you in March. You'll get airline tickets to New York City, expense funds, hotel reservations, and full instructions in the mail." He stood and adjusted his red silk tie.

Darren and Susan followed him to the sofa and the waiting camera.

They stepped out of the way of people in winter coats and red cheeks entering the front doors. Susan took two deep breaths and leaned against the inside lobby wall.

"What happened in there? I'm not sure I did what he wanted."

He shoved his hands into his faded brown ski jacket pockets. "That was rather blunt. I figure they have either set us up as the big laugh on the show, or we might have a real chance to win a few dollars."

"The million dollars?"

"Remotely possible. Even if we win nothing, we get a free trip to New York, and it'll be one hell of an experience."

She laughed and took his arm as they watched the cars caught in the early afternoon rush hour. He pushed the door open with his shoulder, and a blast of cold outside air hit them full in the face.

Darren crammed hisbackpack under the airliner seat and snapped his seatbelt closed.

Susan giggled as she peered out the window at the cart loading the luggage. "Never been on an airplane. This is beyond exciting."

"I've been on lots of planes going to trade shows for the graphic design company in Aurora. Unfortunately, my travel adventures ended when I got laid off. It's a long flight, so sit back and enjoy it."

"Oh, I will. This definitely makes up for the hundred times your stupid van broke down."

Darren laughed. "In January, when the engine blew, they hauled the dead carcass away for the last time. I sure miss it but Stan doesn't."

Susan giggled. "You should have been there when I told Deanna I was flying to New York for a personal audition. She exploded in a rage like I've never seen. Mom had to wrestle her to the floor to protect me."

Darren raised an eyebrow. "You didn't tell about this in November?"

"No, I wanted to tell her when the time was right." She let out a satisifed sigh. "It made up for the hundred times she made me feel inferior to everything she ever did."

"Well, you can forget about your sister. Talent All Stars doesn't think you're inferior. Even if we don't make the show, the next audition is better than anything Deanna accomplished."

She patted his arm. "Thanks for reminding me. You're always there when I need someone."

He patted her white knuckles in a death grip on the armrest and pushed his head back into the headrest with a smile. She would totally panic when the engines started.

The producer from the room one audition met them in the lobby of the prestigious Rock-On Recording Studio. The reception counter curved in front of elegant pictures of a dozen rock stars who had earned golden disc awards. The polished tiles ended in plush pale blue carpet on all sides. Darren recognized the waiting chairs on the lobby left side were the same ones seen in the TV special on Italy's finest exports. The lady behind the counter stood and gestured to the expensive chairs. "Please be seated."

"Look at her." Susan squeezed Darren's arm. "She could have walked off of a movie set."

Before they sat a polished walnut wood door to the side of the counter opened and a man stepped out. He wore a dark gray suit that fit as perfectly as a suit could fit. Every blonde hair was in place. Darren was sure his shoes cost more than the used Ford he had bought to replaced the dead van. Now he remembered. The producer was the blonde guy who replaced the host that irritated Jerry Owens and got fired. He stood in the talent show stage wings and made funny remarks into the TV camera.

"Right this way," he said.

Soft white acoustic panels covered the walls of the small recording room. A large microphone hung from the ceiling. A smaller one on a short black stand stood near a low back chair and a guitarist foot stool. Darren noticed everyone was friendlier than the Talent Stars people in Denver. Paying for airline tickets and hotel rooms wasn't chump change, so this recording session must be serious. The control room behind the large glass windows was dark, but Darren could make out three forms, milling about.

Susan struggled to adjust the big headphones, and Darren tuned his guitar.

Coffee usually pulled Susan's nerves string tight and thinned her voice, so Darren had kept her from the hotel coffee bar. Susan had sung the song twice while in the taxi to warm up her voice.

A voice from the control room boomed, "Ok, folks, let's do a sound check. I want both guitar and vocal."

Darren played the first verse and Susan's voice sounded soft and perfect.

The overhead speaker clicked on again. "We're ready, so this is a cut."

She sang and he played. When her lush pained voice dropped to silence, and his last brush of the strings faded away, Susan turned in expectation and faced the control room window.

"The take was good," a voice said over the speaker.

"Have her sing it again," a second fainter voice said.

"No, that was perfect."

Darren had watched the recording session through the long thin window on the break room back wall. Susan left the sound room, and went straight to the silver and black coffee machine sitting on a long table in the break room. She filled a white foam cup and took rapid sips. When Susan entered the break room, he relaxed and remembered a box of jelly filled donuts sat at the end of the table. The man in the expensive suit entered and waved to Susan. Darren hoped the conversation wouldn't force him to use the man's name. He never thought to ask for it when they were at the Denver audition.

"Nice job, folks. You came well prepared. We don't always see that. Mr. Owens will be impressed."

Darren pictured Jerry Owens, the brash comedian with wild tangled hair who waggled his finger at the contestant when judging them with stinging words. Owens had a sharp eye for talent, even outside his world of hard rock, but could spew withering criticism at any mediocre act. Darren didn't care for the harsh words that often resulted in the audience stomping their feet and booing. He had to admire Jerry Owens when he said that someone was a rising star. It would surely happen.

Susan tipped her cup back to empty it. Darren reached for the coffee pot handle as the man came up to her side.

"We're done in here, so we need to go." The producer looked at his Rolex watch.

"I did it wrong?" she asked.

"No, not at all. Everything went just fine. We have

a clean tape for the production selection team. They evaluate the tapes and then decide on which performers will be on stage for the live broadcast."

"I thought everything happens on the stage in front of Jerry Owens and the other judges." Darren said.

Ted smiled and put his hand on Darren's shoulder. "We want the viewers to believe that, but it's too risky. You can have a walk-on talent show at a karaoke bar, but on national TV, we don't take chances."

"There's a chance we'll be on the show?" Susan asked.

"Same as in November."

"What if we get selected?" Darren asked, as he tapped the coffee handle. Two drops fell into his cup. He glared at Susan holding her third full cup.

"If selected, we'll get in touch."

"So, coming to New York isn't a big deal?" Darren asked, as he lifted his guitar case.

"That's right. Nothing special happened." He paused and took a quick glance at his tablet for recent messages. "The live broadcast is in June, so it's possible you might come back."

"Are we done?" Susan asked.

"Not quite. Now off to the video set to film you two in a mock rehearsal. One set is a living room. We'll have Susan sit on a couch talking with someone off-camera about a technical issue, like how close to be to the microphone."

"Could I have a business card, just in case?" Darren was handed a card from the man's suit pocket. In flowing scroll over a pale silver background he read 'Ted

Beckman'.

Darren and Susan sat waiting for the airport shuttle in the quiet hotel lobby. It was clean and the chairs were comfortable. The breakfast buffet was better than he expected and had way too many cups of coffee. If someone else on the flight back home had done the same, there would be a fight at the restroom door. A valet in a maroon jacket struggled with a rolling luggage cart to the front desk followed by two women in immaculate business suits. Darren sighed and touched the guitar case resting next to the couch. "Our adventure got a lot bigger than I expected, and it's almost over." He lifted a foot and rested on his suitcase.

"The end of our adventure, but it's more than I ever dreamed. Even a remote chance to be on a TV show is like winning the Colorado Lottery."

"Oh, I don't know. Pretty sure we could be on the show. You'll get a recording contract, adoring fans, countless TV show appearances, the usual stuff." He smirked. "I'll practice guitar for five years and then go to a try-out. Maybe someday I can be a star, too."

She laughed and punched him in the shoulder. "That's way too funny. We'll be lucky if we become stars on the local Grand Junction TV station."

He dropped his foot from the suitcase and sat up straight. "I really think we have an actual chance, considering the acts I saw on Talent All Stars last year. They gathered a mix of red-hot performers and people with dancing dogs for a balanced show. We don't have a dog, so it's blindingly obvious you're the red-hot performer."

She laced her fingers behind her head and looked up into the ceiling lights. "Oh yeah right, red-hot. It's more likely they'd need me to replace an ailing dancing dog."

Darren chuckled and reached for his suitcase as the white airport shuttle van pulled up.

Susan squealed when Darren entered the Sandwich & Book Nook. He almost fell over when she jumped into his arms and locked her ankles behind his legs. After a big unexpected kiss, she dropped to the floor with her hands around his neck. "I can't believe it. It came in the mail today. We're on the show!"

"I got a letter too, and..."

"Oh, I can't believe it!" She spun in circles with her hands held high.

"Okay, okay, calm down and let's sit. We have some serious planning to do."

"I know, I know, but..."

He pushed her into a seat at a table for two against the old brick wall. She bounced up and down and rapped her knuckles on the table. Her smile lit up the whole room.

Susan grinned at the waiter. "Russian cream sandwich, the Summer salad, and Sarasan Tea."

Darren smiled. "The usual for me, please. And thank you."

The Manhattan Imperial Theater backstage buzzed with nervous chatter. Contestants watched auditions on the stage unfolding on the wide monitors on the back wall. Susan took short shallow breaths and tapped her knuckles together. Her long black silk dress caressed the floor and accented her slim figure. His eyes focused on the red rose in her hair.

"Deep breaths, slow and easy," he said, adjusting the rose slightly. "This is it, the real thing on national TV. Play time is over."

She forced a smile, her eyes meeting his briefly. "Deep ones. Right."

Darren twitched nervously in his brand new dark blue sports coat with the guitar tucked under his arm. His fingers tapped out a rhythm on his upper thighs.

Ted Beckman put his arm across Darren's shoulders. He was surprised. Ted usually did that to calm a nervous act. "Relax, man. Don't go out there tight as a banjo string."

Darren chuckled. "Yeah, you're right. Cool, calm, and collected—like you were last week on the Allan Laker show, right? I laughed my ass off. I've never seen Allan actually rolling on the floor laughing." He put his arm on Ted's shoulder. "You talked about the crazy things you and your brother Larry did. The audience ate it up. You know, you should have your own show. Call it 'Me and Larry'."

Ted turned and looked into a camera carried by a roving cameraman, filming them. "Hey, he's a lot smarter than my agent. I better fire him and hire this guy. Yeah, my very own show." His rubber face lit up with a wild grin.

"Darren, Susan…you're next," the man wearing a

black headset said as he gripped the curtain and waved his hand.

Side by side, they walked onto the stage and aimed for the white 'X' taped to the floor, as they had been instructed to earlier. Darren smelled the tang of white lights in the dark and hot auditorium and then the musty smell of two hundred people. The crowd hushed as Susan stood on the X at the microphone and Darren sat behind her. He glanced at Ted in the wings, who give him a thumbs up hand sign.

Jerry Owens tapped the table with a long fingernail. "And who are you?"

Susan smiled and answered, "I'm Susan Abrams and this is Darren Chandler."

"And what will you two do for us this evening?"

"I sing and Darren plays guitar."

"Well then, show us what you have." He looked away, bored.

Claire Baker, a popular rock singer, sat next to him. Her pale green hair piled high and silver eyeliner sold as many records as her pitch perfect voice.

To her right, Jackson Miller, the flashy lead guitarist of the legendary rock band, Oblivion Forever, famous for his open shirt and muscular chest, fiddled with a pencil and stared at the ceiling. He didn't even look at Susan.

The lights dimmed and the audience grew silent. Darren ook a deep breath. Susan stood with hands clasped and eyes closed. The introduction notes flowed from his guitar, and Susan opened her eyes, ready for her first note.

Tell me your secrets, I'll tell you my lies,
Tell me you love me, don't look in my eyes.

At the place where Susan sang the chorus of the song a cappella, Darren glanced up at the awe-struck audience and the judges beyond the bright lights. Ted stood in the wings, silent and motionless.

Now I know love... is never a game.

She opened her eyes as the last guitar note faded and auditorium lights kicked on. Her jaw dropped at the sight of Jerry, Claire, and Jackson standing and applauding. The audience stood with wild cheers, and the standing ovation felt like it would never stop. Darren tucked his guitar under his arm and sat still. He glanced up and saw Ted gesturing wildly for him to rise and stand by Susan.

Claire twisted to face the audience and motioned for them to quiet down. She turned back to the stage. "Girl, that is the most powerful song I've heard in a very long time. Every once in a while, a singer and a song come together. That's exactly what happened here tonight."

More cheers and clapping. Susan blushed, glancing at Darren with a trembling smile, and held her wrist across her lips.

The judges sat and Jackson leaned forward stroking his chin. "I've been in the music business a long time. Good singers come and go in monotonous regularity. Some skyrocket and burn out in seconds and others just fade away. You are much more than that. Your voice is a rare God-given treasure."

Susan could only stand there with her hands over

her mouth, her eyes beginning to tear up, while Darren remained silent beside her.

"Where did you find that song?" Jackson asked.

She pointed to Darren and then put her hand back on her mouth. "Darren wrote it."

Jackson pointed at Darren. "Move closer. You're part of this."

He took a shy step forward.

Claire fanned herself and dropped both hands to the table. "You wrote that song? What else do you do?"

Darren looked at Ted, who flicked his hands in a sign to continue. "I have a dull job so write songs to cheer myself up."

Claire grinned. "You can play me a song like that anytime you want."

Jerry crossed his arms and Darren braced himself for the cutting onslaught.

"Suze, you have no idea how good you really are." he said, jabbing his finger straight at her, "But I can tell you this. Good singers are rare, and I just saw one of the very best tonight. Whether you win or not, a full and promising career lies ahead of you." He smiled, setting his hand down on the table. "I wish you well."

The audience stood again and continued to applaud. It felt like an eternity before they stopped.

"All right, time for a vote," Jerry said, facing Claire and Jackson.

"Absolutely a yes," Jackson answered, nodding his approval.

"Yes," Claire said and pointed at Darren. "And I want him to write songs for me!"

"My vote is definitely a yes." Jerry grinned and started to clap. "You guys get to go to Los Angeles for the Talent All-Stars Semi-Finals!"

They walked off the stage to more applause. With a wide grin, Ted punched Darren's shoulder, and a stagehand gave Susan a glass of cold water.

Susan put her arms around his neck and Darren put his forehead to hers. "We did it. We really did. It's only a dream and I don't want to wake up. I can't stop shaking."

Darren stepped back, holding her hands. "No, you did it. I only help you a little."

"Don't say that. We're a team, remember?" she answered.

"A team. I told you that way back, and I meant it."

Susan looked like a million dollars in the white silk blouse and trim beige skirt. The talent show makeup department had a professional hair dresser fix her billowing light brown hair. It didn't fall into her eyes when she turned her head anymore. Ted had suggested he dress casual but formal, so a gray turtle-neck sweater under a dark blue sport coat was perfect.

"Over here, please," a rail-thin lady with pulled back raven-black hair said. "We want to film you with Ted and the other semi-final contestants."

Darren took a step forward to follow Susan but two muscular men in gray sweatshirts blocked his way.

"Excuse me," he said, but they didn't move. "I'm part of the act. I play guitar for—"

The lady with the dark hair slid in front of him.

"We know, however, you won't be needed for the semi-final performance or for the final show. Miss Abrams will be backed by an orchestra and a piano."

"The contract we signed has us as a team."

"It also says that, at our discretion, we can replace backup musicians."

"I was in the audition in Denver, I flew with Susan to the recording in New York, at your expense, I might add. I am most definitely part of the act, part of the team."

"You should read the contracts you sign. I'm sorry. I can't do anything about it, so, if you'll excuse me…." Her pale face showed no emotion as she turned away.

Darren rocked back, stunned. He took another step forward and the two men again blocked him from getting near the contestants. The group of contestants went through the large green metal door, and it slammed shut. He stood alone, surrounded by scattered coils of light cables, wood boxes, and trash barrels. He tapped his back pocket to feel the LAX to DEN airline ticket and headed to the door with an 'EXIT' sign above it. The curtain had fallen on his part of the act.

The Reuben sandwich combo with dark Arabica coffee sat at the left side of the small table. Darren flipped the magazine page and munched another chip. A leisure morning in the Sandwich & Book Nook was the best way to start off a hot August day. He stopped at an advertisement for an upcoming jazz festival in New York City. It would be in October at the hotel where he and Susan stayed for the Talent All Stars audition.

Darren shoved the magazine to the side and then closed his eyes. That cold Denver Saturday felt like it had happened fifty years ago instead of ten months. Everything had unfolded like in a badly written romance story, though the ending had a strange twist. He took a sip of his coffee and watched a girl walk past the front window. Like Susan in a small way, she had an innocent smile and a strand of hair that refused to stay out of her face. He wondered if the girl could sing. Darren shook his head to clear his thoughts and opened the magazine to a random page. He didn't look up at the sound of the opening front door.

Darren took another sip of the coffee from his mug and glanced up at a white blouse and beige skirt on the other side of the table. He didn't recognize the face framed by fluffed light brown hair. Her eyes were hidden behind expensive dark sunglasses.

"May I sit?" she asked.

"Excuse me?" he said, squinting with suspicion before recognizing the voice.

"It's me, Susan."

He sat back speechless. He hadn't heard a word from her in four months despite sending emails and contacting her mother. She glanced around and sat. Her fingers lowered her large sunglasses. He thought he had known those green eyes, now cold and hard. Her confident stare reminded him of her sister, Deanna.

She crossed her hands in her lap. Her gaze drifted from one painting on the wall to another. "It's good to see you."

Darren tightened his lips and looked directly at

her, watching her avoid eye contact.. "What are you doing here? I thought you were on tour in Australia."

She squirmed and confidence drained from her face. "I wanted to see you again."

He ate another chip and closed the magazine. "Why?"

Susan lowered her eyes. She had won the Talent All Stars top prize over a year ago and her time was booked solid. TV appearances, a record album and rumors of a big movie role now defined her life. Why was she back in town? Probably to rub her success in his face. With Deanna, he was always sure. Deanna was cold but passionate in her own way. She never played games with him and he liked that. Cold passion was better than none at all.

"I suppose you need to know what's been happening."

"Not really."

"I owe it to you."

"You might owe me a lot of things, like a call once in a while, even if only to say hello. I don't need an explanation. You auditioned. I played backup, and it worked," Darren said and looked down at his coffee-stained napkin. "You could have said something, anything, that day they sent me home. You don't need me as backup anymore and I can live with that. and I'm happy for you. I really am."

The waiter came to the table and pulled out his order pad. Susan looked up with a strained smile. "A Russian cream sandwich, a Summer salad, and Sarasan Tea would be nice."

Darren held his hand over his mug before the waiter asked if he wanted a refill.

"Deanna tells me you two are a couple." Her eyes fell to the table, and a finger traced a mindless circle on the tabletop. "That's great."

"Not exactly a couple. I thought we'd make love sparks fly. I really try but it hasn't happened. It's like what Oscar Wilde wrote." He looked up into the rafters to collect his thoughts. "The only thing worse than not getting what you want... is getting it."

Susan touched her neck and nodded slightly. "Well, that comes as no surprise. Deanna is a beautiful porcelain doll you set on the shelf to look at but never touch."

Darren nodded his head in reluctant agreement.

Susan glanced again at the familiar amateur paintings hanging on the walls. She pursed her lips and stared at Darren's coffee mug. "I need to know something, and then I'll go away."

He laced his fingers together and looked into her eyes.

"For the semi-finals, I wanted to sing 'She is Always On Your Mind'. They told me you wouldn't let them use it because you wrote it. I thought you wrote it for me, so why not let me sing it?"

He shoved the empty mug to the side and leaned forward. "Talent All Stars stripped me from our contract, so I owed them nothing. The moment you first sang 'Love In The Ashes' on their show, they owned it. They own your rendition of singing it, too. It's spelled out in the contract fine print and I didn't realize they had done that to me. After that, anyone they want can sing or record it, and I don't get a dime. I don't get a dime whenever you sing it, either. Talent All Stars gets the dimes. I didn't want that taken away from me too."

"It's about the money, isn't it?"

"Yeah, and you sing for money. That's the music business. I have no complaints or hard feelings. Talent Stars got rather nasty with me, but Ted put me in touch with a music publisher. In fact, I wrote the theme song for his hit TV show, 'My Brother Larry'."

She forced a smile as the Russian cream sandwich arrived. "I didn't know that. I'm happy for you."

He spun his empty coffee mug between two fingers. "Music writers are invisible, but since it plays every week, I get royalties. Music Times Publishing wants me to write more songs, which I'll do. So, our Talent All Stars adventure is working out for me, too." He grabbed another chip. "How's your life going?"

She put her sunglasses back on and her lips trembled. Her voice shook with each word .

"My life was a total mess, but I was living my dream. I had a fight with a music arranger, and stormed out in a huff. I knew I was the greatest rising star ever, but when I stood in front of the mirror in the dressing room, Deanna stared back at me. That's when I woke up."

"You're red hot, and the world loves you. How do you wake up from something like that?"

"I woke up when I realized I was playing Deanna's game. The Australia tour is off. Every tour is off. I canceled plans for the album and told the record company to stuff it where the sun doesn't shine. I tore up the contract." Susan sighed and folded her hands together on the table. "The price I've paid is too high, and I want my real life back. I want to sing in the park on a Saturday afternoon—like we used to do. And go to Stan's house for hot dogs and watch 'Space Aliens' on TV."

"The public will never let you quit. Your face is on CDs in every music store on the planet. You can't turn back the clock." He smiled and touched her fingertip with his. "But you can reset it."

"Nobody can reset the clock of life. The past can't be rewritten. Everyone will forget me, and I'll be a faint memory within a year or less. Claire quit the talent show and dropped out of sight. I can do the same."

"She won't be out of sight for long. I wrote 'A Summer Without Your Love' for her, and she records it next month. She wants me to be with her on a tour in England next Summer."

Susan's shoulders slumped. "Allan Laker wants me on his show next month. He doesn't know it, but that's when I'll sing my goodbye song. I'm coming home to start a new life, a real life. Maybe you're right. I have to reset the clock."

He put his hand into his backpack resting against the wall. With a rustle of papers, Darren pulled out a single sheet of hand-scribbled music. He handed it to her. Susan placed her sunglasses on top of her head and studied it.

"I suppose you could use this one for your goodbye song. I wrote it while on the plane from LA back to Denver. I hadn't gotten around to trashing it, so what do you think?."

Her lips moved as her fingertip followed each note. She went over it for a second time to capture the melody. Tears came to her eyes as she hummed the tune. "It's beautiful. What's the title?"

"I call it 'Love Me Again Forever'."

"May I?"

He nodded and sat back. She sang it with the soft contralto voice he loved.

Even when you love me, in the deep of night,
you think of her, she is always there.
Love me again forever and I'll make it right,
I'm the one with love to share.

She didn't notice the cafe had fallen to a hush and heads turned to listen. The song belonged to her now, and each word poured from the wound in her heart. At the last note, she pulled her hands away, and the paper floated to the tabletop. The cafe burst into applause and people rushed up to tell her how great her voice was..

She pointed to Darren. "Applaud him. He wrote it."

Hands slapped Darren's back, and the happy crowd drifted back to their tables. She turned her head to avoid his eyes.

"I should go now." She fought back a sniffle. "Thanks for thinking of me."

He picked up the music sheet and squinted at it. "You can sort of sing, and I have a great idea."

Susan stood and dropped her sunglasses onto her nose. "You have an endless supply of incredibly stupid ideas, but I sure could use one."

"Want to make some music together?"

She paused with a warm smile. "We can make a lot more than music together. Any other bright ideas?"

"Yeah, got a couple, but first my clock needs reset." He stood and hoisted the backpack strap on his shoulder. "If you're not too busy tonight, we could go over to Stan's. I'll grill some hot dogs, and we'll watch TV. He has a DVD of the complete first season of 'Space Aliens.'"

He put his arm across her shoulders and pulled her tight. She put her head to his shoulder as they went out the door.

Erik Johnson

Avid history researcher as well as a sci-fi fan. Learning to write a novel is work, but it is satisfying work... whether or not something gets published. So many ideas to get down on paper!

A Deep Gaming Experience

by Stanley Griffin

Liam followed the synthesized voice of his GPS through Silverthorne, Colorado. He parked his old Chevy Suburban in front of the video game store, stepped out, and locked the door. The Friday morning sun shone bright in the sky. With each breath he took, the cold mountain air stung his lungs. Liam strolled into the welcoming warmth of the store.

Inside, an old man hunched over the counter reading a newspaper. A white scraggly hair and bearded man in his mid to late sixties. His tie-dyed T-shirt, and blue jeans gave him the look of an aged hippie.

"Good morning," the man said without looking up from his paper. "Let me know if I can help you."

An attractive young woman, with black shoulder length hair, blue gray eyes, in skinny jeans, and a powder blue ski jacket stood at the other end of the room. She smiled at him shyly, played with her hair, and went back to thumbing through the used games rack.

Liam smiled back before returning his attention to the old man. "Do you have 'Demon's Army Three'?"

The old man looked up. "No, not yet. It should be in Monday's shipment of games. Check with me then."

"That's okay." Liam said. "Me and some friends are staying at a hotel for the weekend. We'll head back to Denver Sunday night. I just hoped I could get some play time in. I need a new game. I've beaten all my others."

"Well," replied the old man as he folded the paper and placed it on the counter. "Then, let's see what we can do. You know, even the old games can be fun if you haven't played them. Maybe I have one that'd be a challenge for you."

"I doubt it," Liam scoffed. "I've played on every gaming platform out there. Nintendo, X-box, PlayStation, or PC. You name it and I can, or already have beaten it on the hardest levels."

"Really?" The old man sipped his coffee and smiled. "You must be the game king."

"Kind of," Liam replied. "I just have a knack for it. I can find the clues and get through the games faster than anyone else I know. Solving puzzles and coming up with new strategies is what gets my blood pumping."

"You drove up here just to game at the hotel?" asked the old guy. "Why aren't you skiing like most people?"

"It never interested me," Liam replied. "Tried it once. But the idea of throwing myself down a mountain on slats just seems crazy. My friends drag me along because I have that big old '79 Chevy Suburban out there. We call it 'The Beast'. " Liam pointed to the parking lot.

"It's hauled us to all the ski slopes in the state. No matter how bad the weather is, it gets us there. My friends all have these small and expensive cars they're afraid to drive in the snow. But my old Beast, she pulls the six of us and all our gear and never misses a lick. She's a tank."

"That's a bit inconvenient for you, isn't it?" the old guy muttered. "You're forced up here only to waste time while your friends are having fun."

"I don't mind," Liam added. "They pay for everything. Gas, food, beer, and hotel room. I spend my time playing games, milling around the stores, or going to the movies on their dime. When they're done, we go some place to eat and have some beers. That's where I get to hear them recount the day's adventures on the slopes. I drink a good craft beer and laugh at my friends' mishaps or bad attempts at picking up ladies."

He glanced at the pretty young woman still looking at games. "Besides, back in the hotel room, we'll spend half the night drinking beer and killing all manner of digital things on my Xbox."

"Sounds like fun, I guess," the old guy said. "I've been working on a new gaming system myself. I hope to market it in a few years to a big company like Microsoft."

"Really?" Liam walked to the counter, his interest suddenly peaked. "So what makes it better than the others?"

"Well, my system incorporates a kind of virtual reality with a First Person Shooter. By the way, I'm Karl Hilbert. I own this store." Karl held out his hand.

"Liam O'Connell." Liam took his hand for a quick shake.

"It's more of a first-person fantasy sword fighting game. Imagine, a touch of the holodeck from Star Trek with magic and swords. I'm building it in my basement. It takes a couple of computers tied together to run it. Still working on the hardware needs, and the graphics aren't the best."

"Do you need a beta tester?" Liam asked. "I've done lots of beta testing for several different companies. I'd love to help out on a virtual reality First Person Sword-er. That sounds cool!"

The young lady moved over to the counter. "Can I get in on that, Mister Hilbert? You told me you'd let me try it when it was ready. The two of us could go in and see what the game can handle." She turned to Liam and held out her hand. "Isabell Fergusson. I've been buying games from Mister Hilbert ever since he opened this shop three years ago."

"I don't know if it's ready for two players yet," Karl replied, then grinned widely. "But I'm a bit of a gambler." Karl reached under the counter and pulled out a black velvet bag. He opened it and dug around until he pulled out three twenty-sided dice. He laid them on the counter and said, "My Dungeons and Dragons dice." He smiled. "Yes, I still play the old school games. Now, I'll roll one of these. If you two can get within two points of my number. That's my number or two up or two down. I'll take you to my house for a few hours and let you try it out. Cecil, my assistant, gets here at eleven o-clock. He can run the store while I'm gone."

"I'm good with that!" Isabell said excitedly.

Liam looked at the three dice. One was clear green, one was clear blue, and one was red with gold flakes. "Sure, I'm game," He replied, pointing to the dice. "Ladies first."

Isabell reached for the blue die.

Liam took the green one.

Karl smiled and muttered, "How interesting." He took the red die, shook it in his fist and then let it roll on the counter. The die stopped on the number twenty. "Ouch! That cuts your chances almost in half. You'll have to roll an eighteen or better."

Isabell took a deep breath and began to shake her die.

Liam shook his as well and they released the dice at almost the same time. When the two dice came to a stop, both showed the number twenty.

Isabell jumped around with excitement.

Karl's face took on an expression of confusion, mixed with surprise and delight.

Liam pumped his fist into his side. "Yes! Way cool!" Then after a moment he asked. "Is there something wrong, Mister Hilbert?"

Karl replied, "No, I just never would have guessed you two could've done that. The odds of both of you rolling twenties are gigantic. Something like, one in eight thousand, I believe." He clapped his hands and rubbed them together. "So, it looks like you're going to try out my Deep Gaming Experience after all. Or the DGE, as I call it."

"Should be fun," Liam said excitedly.

Karl put his dice back in the bag, looked at his watch, and said, "It's nine forty-five. If you two want, you can wait in the coffee shop next door. Once Cecil gets here, I'll come over and get you. You can follow me to my house."

"Sounds great," Liam agreed.

Liam wiped up a coffee spill with his napkin. "So, you live around here?"

Isabell nodded after a sip. "Yes, I've lived here most of my life. I graduated from high school four years ago. Right now, I work as a clerk at Walmart. It's my day off, so I went to see if Mister Hilbert had anything new. And you—, what do you do?"

"I'm a software engineer," Liam replied. After a sip of his coffee, he continued. "That's why I'm so good at beta-testing games. I understand the code. That gives me an in-depth understanding of how the game functions."

"That so cool." Isabell drained her cup. "I wish I could do computers. I've tried. My brain just doesn't work that way."

"Well programming is not for everyone," Liam replied as he stood up. "But the rest can be learned. I'll teach you if that's okay. Hey, I'm going to get us a couple of fresh cups. I'll be back in a minute."

Isabell's lightly freckled nose and cheeks, gave her a playful look that Liam liked. Out of the corner of his eye, Isabell smiled at him as he paid for their refills. As he returned to the booth with their drinks, he kicked a small disposable lighter that had been dropped on the floor. He put down the coffees and went back and picked it up. He tossed it on their table. "Have you played any of the 'Elder Scrolls'?"

After a sip of her coffee. "Yes, but only once." She picked up the lighter and looked at it for a moment, then she slipped it into her pocket. "A friend of mine had the games on his PC. Another game I like to play is 'Mechwarrior'. But it won't play on my new PC. Sucks really."

I had never been good at talking with women. He thought to himself. *But with Isabell, I feel a connection between us.*

When Karl walked in, he ordered a coffee and stood next to Isabell. "Well, you two ready to give this a try?"

"Sure," Liam slid out of the booth. "We'll follow you."

"Isabell, you might want to ride with me or Liam," Karl said. "I live up in the hills and that little thing you drive might not get through the mega-potholes in my driveway."

"You can ride with me if you like," Liam exclaimed a bit louder than he probably should have. He blushed slightly. "The Beast can get anywhere."

She looked at him and smiled brightly. "I'd like that, and we can finish our conversation. Can we get another coffee to go?"

"Sure." Liam headed to the counter, trying to hide his excitement. "I'll drop you back at your car when we're done." He wasn't sure which excited him more, the idea of playing a new game, or spending more time with Isabell.

Liam and Isabell followed Karl's old Jeep until they turned up a long drive. Snow-packed in the shaded areas, with many deep muddy holes where the sun melted the ice. Several times Liam had to slow to a crawl to get through the deep ruts and not spill their coffees. As they pulled up to the house, Liam said, "He's well off the beaten path, ain't he?"

Isabell nodded. "I bet the quiet makes it easier to work. No noise to interrupt you."

"True enough, I guess," Liam said. They walked up to an a-frame style home, built into the slope of a hill. Its walkout basement was carved into the hillside, large retaining walls on both sides kept the hill back, leaving only one wall, and a sliding-glass door visible. A wooden deck jutted over it from a main floor doorway.

"I'm a bachelor," Karl said as he made his way up the side stairs. "So the house is a mess. Give me a moment and I'll open the basement door." A few moments later Karl opened dark curtains and pulled the glass door open.

Isabell and Liam stepped inside to see a large, unfinished room.

"Welcome to the DGE." Karl said with a wave of his hand. "You may want to keep your coats on. I don't have much heat down here."

In a corner against one wall, behind a sheer green curtain, stood metal shelves filled with computers. Lights on the top shelf shone brightly in the dingy gloom of the basement. In front sat a long plastic folding table. On it, a small control console with three monitors faced the wall.

Karl walked into the space at its narrow end, through a wooden screen-door, covered in the same sheer fabric. He stopped for a moment and typed on a keyboard.

The walls, ceiling, and floor were covered with matching green paint. Small cameras and projectors looked down from the ceiling at all angles. A white star polygon was painted in the middle of the floor with strange symbols that decorated each of its eight points.

"What's with the eight pointed star?" asked Isabell as she pointed to it. "You doing magic or something?"

Karl replied with a laugh, "It's just my compass." He reached under the table and then stepped from the control room with a black cloth bag. "The computer uses it to tell what direction you're moving. The symbols I created just because I didn't like looking at N,S,E, and W on the floor." He smiled and waved his hands in the air. "With the help of my computers here, I'm going to send you off on a magical journey to an alternate world." Karl laughed.

"A wise man once said," Liam muttered as he looked around the room, "one man's technology is another man's magic."

"A wise man indeed," Karl replied. He handed the black bag to Liam, and opened it. He pulled out Velcro bands with small orange balls on them. "You need one on each of your ankles, knees, shoulders, and elbows. The belted ones go around, your hips, and mid chest. This one goes on your head and the gloves, well you know."

"So these points mark where we are and what we are doing." Liam said. "Just like motion capture computer graphics. And the room is a giant green screen."

"Exactly," Karl replied with a note of enthusiasm. "The computers keep track of each point. Then it interprets it into a 3D coordinate in the game space. You may feel yourself often having to turn left or right. That's because this should be in a larger room than I have, like a small warehouse. To compensate for the small size of my basement, the computers will make you move around obstacles, forcing you to make corrections to prevent you from walking into the walls." Karl handed them each a visor. "You'll use these to see the game view heads-up display. That will show you the map, your mana, health, and experience bars. It also gives you a simulated three-dimensional view."

Karl moved back into the control room as they finished putting on the marker points. When the lights dimmed, a castle appeared on one wall. Liam looked around at the rough graphic details.

"Go ahead and put on the visors," Karl said as he worked at the console. "Then move to the center of the star. That's your spawning point."

Liam put on the visor and they moved to the star's center. The immersion glasses provided a rough3-D scene.

"Starting the program now," Karl said. "It'll take a few seconds to boot. While it does, I'll give you your first task. Go into the castle and locate the library. There you'll find a great big white book on a stand near a large window. It's called the Book of Antiquity. Open it to the last page, and read what it says. That will tell you what to do next. You got that?"

Isabell repeated, "Go in the castle, find the library, and read the last pages of the Book of Antiquity. Got it!"

"It's almost ready," Karl said. "The visors will go dark for a moment, and then there'll be a bright flash. After that, you can start."

The screens in the eye pieces went dark. A bright flash of light leaked in past the edges of the visor. When the light faded away, Liam found himself in the courtyard of a castle. Isabell stood next to him.

"Wow," Isabell said. "I thought Karl said the graphics weren't up yet. This is amazing! It's like really being there."

Stone walls encircled them. All around were unkempt decorative plants in large pots. Some distance away, stone stairs climbed to a set of doors in the castles wall. It stood well over five stories tall with windows that looked out on both the sides he could see. Under their feet was an exact replica of the Star Polygon complete with the strange symbols.

"What happened to our immersion goggles?" Isabell reached up and touched her face.

"I don't know," Liam said. He walked to a nearby stone sculpture of a warrior. He reached out and touched it. Cold stone met his fingers. "Something's wrong here, Isabell." Everything around him felt real.

Isabell was smelling a flower on a nearby rosebush. Not only were their visors not there, but all the motion capture points were also missing.

"This is great, Karl," Isabell said excitedly. "Even the flowers have smells! I've never played any games that had smells."

"We're not in a game," Liam said. "Feel the plant and you'll see this is for real."

Isabell reached out and touched the flower. "How did he do that?" She snatched her hand back. "It pricked my finger!" Her bright smile washed away, replaced by dread. "Liam, it drew blood! How can a computer game make you bleed?" Hugging herself, Isabell asked, "How do we get home?"

"I don't know," Liam put his arm around her. "But I won't let anything happen to you, I promise."

Isabell gave him a weak smile. "I thought this was going to be a game?"

"This is no game," Liam whispered. "It's too real to be a game! Like it or not, we've spawned in a new place, or world, or something."

Struggling with their new reality, they slowly explored the courtyard. Liam hoped to find a flaw in the scene that would explain everything. But each thing he encountered, just reinforced the fact they were in a real castle. They wandered around the courtyard for a time, then the last words Karl told them came to mind. *Find the library and look for the Book of Antiquity.*

Liam took Isabell's hand.

Quickly she turned to face him. Afraid that he had offended her, Liam let go of her hand.

Isabell smiled slightly. "That's okay." She blushed a bit. "I don't mind if you hold my hand."

"Sorry if I frightened you," Liam mumbled.

"That's okay, it's nice," Isabell replied. "I'm so scared right now it isn't funny. So it helps keep me from screaming out loud."

Liam took her hand once more, and started for the castle stairs. "Well, I guess we should go find that damn book Karl was talking about."

Isabell accompanied him up the stairs to the castle door. He opened one of the double doors onto a long hall. Four chandeliers hung from the ceiling. Tapestries and paintings hung on the teal painted walls. For the next couple of hours, they looked around the castle. The only sound was their footsteps echoing down the halls. A musty and dusty smell hung heavy in the air. Each door they opened gave the sensation of being frozen in time. In one of the bedrooms, they found a light green dress on a bed, as if waiting for its owner to put it on. It had gold trim and small, blue, glass beads that covered the sleeves and just above the hem.

Isabell touched it. "It's very pretty isn't it?"

"Yes," Liam answered. "You'd look good in it." He picked it up and held it to her. "The green would complement your eyes and it contrasts nicely with your hair. I think you'd look beautiful in this."

"You really think so?" Isabell asked with a weak smile.

"Sure," Liam said, trying to sound reassuring.

Her smile grew brighter. But Liam feared he hadn't been convincing. Her smile washed away quickly, replaced with a despondent expression. They opened a set of double doors and found the library. Inside was a round room, two stories high. Its walls were lined with dark wood shelves. Beside the door on each side, stairs led up to the second floor landing above the entrance, connecting to a walkway accessing the bookshelves on the second floor. Most of the shelves held books. But some had stacks of parchment, or scrolls. Three small tables with soft, dark brown, leather chairs were placed around each table. They all faced into the center of the room on a rich red and gold carpet. At its center, an ornate, large, blue and green shield with a gold Griffon standing on its hind legs with its front claws extended.

Directly across from the door, a massive floor to ceiling window filled the room with sunlight. Centered on the window stood a huge white stone pedestal. A very large white book sat open on it.

Liam leafed through the pages until he found the last entries. He read with Isabell standing beside him. "It talks about a new form of monster they called Daretharth. Apparently, these creatures walk upright and have coarse fur, long claws, and long teeth. They also eat human flesh. Here's a reference to a species of a great bird-like creature."

Isabell added, "Hey, one of the bird things was friends with the mage that lived here. And would let him ride on its back and fly him all around. Cool!"

Liam stood shocked as black marks appeared on the page below the last sentence. "Uh, look at that."

Isabell gasped and stepped back a little.

The marks became words, and then sentences. Liam scratched his head. "What tha…" he stopped in mid sentence.

Liam, and Isabell, this is Karl. Sorry I was forced to mislead you about the game. All that equipment you saw, Bogus. You two are the best I've found and I need your help. I made a mistake and if I'm to return to this world, I need the two of you to help me repair the damage. You may not be great warriors, but maybe you can think of something I couldn't. To start, go back to the star, stand in its center, and say these words out loud:"Reth Nae ThiBael." He will answer your call. Tell him you must speak with the queen. She will explain more.

"Karl, can you hear me?" Liam watched the book for more writing, but none came. His shaking hand found Isabell's and held it tight. After a few moments his voice shaky at first, "A-a self-writing book? Okay, that's a first for me."

"Do you think we should?" asked Isabell. Any hint of a smile was long gone. "I-I mean, go back to the star in the courtyard." She hugged herself once more. "This scares the shit out of me. Of all the horror films I've watched, this scares me more. And nothing has jumped out and tried to kill us yet."

Liam pulled her into his arms and held her while she cried for a few moments. He choked down the fear that clawed at him as well. When she stopped sobbing and looked up at him. She asked, "Do we call out these words? I don't know if I can even pronounce them right. I mean, '*Reth Nae, ThiBael,*' is that it?"

"I guess we need to." Liam turned for the door. "And that's as close as we can get to the right pronunciation. Shall we go?"

They moved to the center of the star, and Liam said, "Go ahead, say the words."

Isabell shouted, "*Reth, Nae, ThiBael.*"

The lines of the star glowed a fluorescent blue. "You are not Elkhazel," a voice replied. "Who are you?"

"I-I'm, Isabell and this is Liam," Isabell stammered as she talked to the disembodied voice.

"How did you get inside Elkhazel's private sanctuary?" the voice asked.

"We don't know how we got here," replied Liam. *What the hell, books that write themselves, and voices out of nowhere. Can this shit get any crazier?* Things had been happening so fast and furious, It was all new and strange. He just hoped he answered correctly. In too many games he'd played, the wrong answer was greeted with death. "We don't know how we got here, but we need to speak to the Queen."

"We will be there just before sundown." The blue faded from the lines.

Liam looked to the sky and guessed at the time. "My best guess is that sundown will be in three to four hours. Should we have another look around the castle? We may find some items we'll need for our quest. That's what we'd normally do in a game, right?"

"I guess." Isabell hugged herself, looking down at her feet. "But I don't mind telling you I'm scared as hell right now."

"I know," Liam said, trying to sound strong. "Me, too."

After searching around the castle, they stood upon the wall above the courtyard as the Sun neared the horizon. Green rolling hills moved out into distant trees. Sunlight glistened off a waterfall that cascaded from a cliff far in the distance. The slightest hint of a rainbow shown in the air just above it.

"What's that in the distance?" Isabell asked.

A high shimmering wall of air stood where she pointed. "I don't know," Liam said. "It kinda looks like a force field or barrier. It goes all the way around this place like it's meant to keep someone in or out."

A loud screech echoed overhead. They turned to see several large winged beasts flying in formation. As they got closer, Liam recognized their shape. His mouth dropped open for a moment and finally, he said, "Those are griffons, Isabell. Look, real griffons! And there are people on them!"

"Um, don't griffons, like, eat people?" Isabell asked as she stepped behind him.

"I guess these don't," Liam replied as the griffons and their riders landed in the gardens beyond the courtyard. "Let's go meet them."

They found a small gate in the short wall near the courtyard that led them into the gardens. Like the plants in the courtyard, the vegetation here had been neglected. Vines and branches crept into the walking paths.

Liam moved ahead of Isabell as they traversed the paths to the garden's center. His heart beat faster with each step they took. The seven griffons landed on a large flat gravel patch surrounded by a short planter wall. Each lion-like body was the size of a small horse, with a saddle on their backs. Their bird-like heads eyed Isabell and himself as if they were looking at their next meal.

Four guardsmen wore black, studded-leather armor. Each man moved with the confidence of a tried and true warrior as if every movement was planned out to coincide with the next. They surrounded a woman in a green shirt, blue loose-fitting pants, and white armor. Her hair had been light brown once, but now more gray had started to show through. Her eyes were a deep blue like the eyes of the magnificent white griffon standing behind her. Four more brown griffons stood behind them. Two rider-less animals waited, one griffon was light amber and the other black.

"I am Queen Essaerae of the Kingdom of Cushendall," the woman proclaimed. She looked them up and down. "How did you get into this castle? Your clothing is very strange. You can't be from my Kingdom. Who are you?"

"I'm Liam O'Connell." He gestured to Isabell "This is Isabell Fergusson. How we got here—I really don't know. But no, we're not from here. How far away—I can't tell you that either."

"This place is under my protection," the queen said. "It belonged to the wizard Elkhazel. I've placed enchantments around this place to prevent wizards or the Daretharth from using its magic point. How did you get here?"

The men beside the queen drew swords. The first two took a few steps closer towards Liam and Isabell.

Liam raised his open hands. "Look, your Majesty, we don't know how we ended up here. We were in our friend Karl's basement on a star just like the one in the courtyard."

"I do not know this Karl you speak of," the queen said. "Where is he?"

"Back home." He pointed towards the courtyard. "There was a bright flash of light, and when it went away, we were standing on the star here. The last thing he told us to do was to find the library and look at the last pages in the Book of Antiquity. It told us to call *'Reth Nae, ThiBael,'* and then someone would appear and we would talk to the queen—I mean, you."

"Reth Nae," the queen said as she stepped forward. "It means 'arcane whisper.' It is a communication spell that allows one to speak over a long distance. This is Thi-Bael." She pointed to the gold griffon. "When you stood on the magical point and said *'Reth Nae, ThiBael,'* you made a connection that let him speak with you."

The griffon stepped forward and sniffed the air around Liam and Isabell. "I smell Elkhazel on them. I'd know him anywhere."

It stepped closer and turned an eye towards Liam. "Where is Elkhazel?"

"Look, I don't know who this Elkhazel is." Liam heart raced. He wished the griffon would back off a little bit. He didn't like feeling as if the beast could eat him at any moment. "I only know this guy—Karl Hilbert. He owns a video game store. He had the same eight-pointed star painted on his basement floor. We were supposed to be play testing a game of his. It was supposed to be a new kind of gaming experience. But after this bright flash somehow we ended up here."

"It is late," Queen Essaerae said. "We will stay here until morning. Follow me."

Liam and Isabell followed the queen back into the castle. The guardsman walked behind Liam and Isabell, with the griffons following close behind. Queen Essaerae led them into the castle and down a hallway. Both sides were filled with paintings of men and women. When she stopped, she pointed to one of the paintings. "Is this the man you call Karl Hilbert?"

There was a painting of the old man from the game store. Red robes trimmed in some form of white fur. A long black staff held in one hand. A noble and po-werful expression on his face. Nothing at all like the aged hippy from the game store.

"That's him," Isabell said. "Only he doesn't wear those kind of clothes."

"That explains much," said the queen, hesitating a moment. "He must have used the magic star to send himself to your world. Afterwards, he sent you here. But why? I don't understand."

"The book said—" Liam changed his mind and started again. "I mean, Karl—from inside the book—said something about repairing a mistake he made."

"Let us go and have a meal," Queen Essaerae or-dered. "We can talk more as we eat."

They followed the queen into a feasting hall. A huge banqueting table filled the room. Except for a thick layer of dust, the table was ready for a feast. Empty plates, goblets, bowls, and utensils sat in their proper lo-cation, waiting for the servers to bring out the meal.

Queen Essaerae walked to the far side of the table. "Lady Isabell, if you would, follow me. Lord Liam, take the seat across from her." She sat at the head of the table. The four soldiers stood against opposite walls, two be-hind Liam and two behind Isabell. ThiBael and the all-white griffon lay down on either side of the queen's chair. The other griffons sat on the floor at the entrance of the hall.

"It seems that Wizard Elkhazel has sent you here to mend what he broke years ago," Queen Essaerae explained. "Isabell, you and Liam will never be able to go home unless you can find a solution to bring our people back."

Queen Essaerae waved her hands at the table and a strange wind blew the dust away. With another wave of her hand, steaming hot food appeared, and the goblets filled with wine. "There. We can eat while I explain what has happened."

Liam looked at Isabell. She glanced at the food in front of her, then back at Liam. He nodded. He was suspicious of the food as well.

"There is nothing wrong with the food, so eat," the queen ordered. She waited for several moments then, with a disgusted sigh, Queen Essaerae began to eat. After her first bite, she looked at each of them in turn. "If I had wanted you dead, my guards would have already seen to it. You would be occupying your graves by now. Poison is such a tacky way to kill someone. I much prefer it done quick and the bodies removed from my sight."

Liam took a bite and Isabell copied him. To his surprise, the meal was delicious. Each bite tempted him to continue feasting. Once he started, Liam didn't want to stop. Isabell washed down a mouthful of the meal with a sip from her goblet.

Queen Essaerae scrutinized them for a few moments, then she continued, "Years ago, I sent a young man named Saevel to visit West Water, a town on my northern border. He had been newly promoted to Captain. Unfortunately, he was killed in an ambush outside of town. Young Saevel was Wizard Elkhazel's only son. Maddened with grief, Elkhazel cast a spell on the northern town. In his anguish, he was unable to concentrate, and the spell went awry. It turned the population of that, and several other towns nearby, into the Daretharth. A tusked, muzzled, flesh-consuming monster that devours everything in their path. They quickly moved over the land, killing and eating everyone and everything in sight. My people and I refuse to kill our own kin, even if they have been transformed into mindless savages, so we created magically defended walls and strongholds like this one to keep them at bay."

"Karl," Isabell stumbled on her words. "I mean, Wizard what's-his-name, he couldn't turn them back?"

"No," the queen said solemnly. "Wizard Elkhazel tried for days and days but failed. I feared he still grieved over his son and didn't want to succeed. So I had no choice but to banish him from my Kingdom. Afterwards I employed every wizard I could, to place barriers across the narrow piece of land between the Daretharth and us. Then we worked at the task of changing them back. But none of us could make headway."

"Well," Liam said as he placed his fork on his plate. "If I'm to solve this mystery of what happened to your people, I need to go to this village. The answers must be there. But can Isabell stay here? It will be dangerous and I don't want anything to happen to her."

"If you go," Isabell scolded. "I'm going with you. Karl sent both of us because he felt it would take both of us to fix the problem. Plus, even the dice said both of us were to go! You're not leaving me behind."

"You cannot," Queen Essaerae replied coldly. She paused, wiping a tear from her eye. "That village is deep in Daretharth-held lands. I cannot, in good conscience, let either of you go into that kind of danger."

"Your Majesty," Liam said, "you said we can't go home until we find a way to change this. I can't do that until I find out what really happened. I understand the danger. But I can't help you—or us—-until I know the truth."

"I will not risk your lives, or the lives of my griffons, on this folly," Queen Essaerae said.

"I volunteer, my queen," ThiBael said. "Elkhazel was…" He paused, eyes cast down. "He's my closest friend. I hope to clear his name and see him back here."

"You can't carry both of them," Queen Essaerae replied.

"He won't have to, your Majesty," the black griffon said, standing up and walking to the end of the table. "I can bear and protect Lady Isabell."

"I see, KorMitore." The Queen looked at the griffon. Then she looked towards the white Griffon. "DaeCla, what does his mother say about this?"

"As his mother—" The white griffon stood and walked toward the table. "—I would not wish to see my son travel into danger. However if his father is to go, I can make an exception. ThiBael knows much about magic. If any could keep him safe, it would be my husband."

"I see," remarked Queen Essaerae. "KorMitore, you scored highest in flight and ground combat. Combined with your father's magical skills, the two of you should be formidable in battle." The queen looked back at ThiBael. "Do you think there is anything to be learned there? It has been more than three years."

"My queen." ThiBael bowed his head. "We won't know the answer to that until we get there. You know as I, Elkhazel is one of the most brilliant wizards of all time. If he feels these two can change this, I'm willing to risk my life and that of my son to see it through."

"Then eat," Queen Essaerae commanded after a pause. "Rest tonight, you will leave tomorrow after sunset. Flying high in darkness will give you the best chance of remaining unseen. I have only one request. If found, the body of Young Captain Saevel is to be brought back to the capital city. Long ago, I deemed it too dangerous to send anyone to try and find him. It would please the whole of the Kingdom if you could bring back one of their heroes." The Queen pointed to one of the guards. "Gather food and supplies for Lord Liam and Lady Isabell. Then make arrangements for all of us to have beds for tonight."

The man bowed and quickly walked from the room.

The room grew silent as they finished their meals. When they were done, Queen Essaerae stood. "I take my leave of you now. I'll not be here to see you off, I'm afraid. I must leave at daybreak to go home. I wish you all the best of luck. Understand me—you are to kill no Daretharth unless it is unpreventable. They are still my people and I'm sworn to protect them." She turned and left the room, followed by her guards.

Liam awoke to the sensation of falling like being in a dropping elevator. Cold air rushed past stinging his eyes as he tried to focus on the ground far below. All that was visible was darkness, broken by the coming dawn. The sun's full light was only half an hour or so away. "What's happening?" he asked with a start.

ThiBael leveled off his altitude. "I see something up ahead," ThiBael replied. "Just going down for a closer look. How did you like your sleep?"

Squinting from the wind, Liam shouted, "Sorry, just dozed a bit." He rubbed his eyes. "I don't see any-thing."

"You don't have the eyes of a griffon," ThiBael chuckled.

Liam looked around and saw Isabell astride Kor-Mitore to his left. She looked as sleepy as he felt. She was draped across KorMitore's neck, her head propped up on her arm.

"It looks like a wagon," ThiBael said, "just left abandoned on the roadway. We're still several miles from what used to be the Township of West Water."

"Let's check it out," Liam yelled over the rushing air.

"We'll circle the site until it's light enough," Thi-Bael yelled back to Liam. "I want to see what might be lurking in the brush. We don't want any unwanted atten-tion from the Daretharth."

They circled the spot several times until daylight filled the darkest shadows, before landing on the road. Liam unstrapped himself from the saddle and slid to the ground.

Isabell got down very slowly. She moved stiffly, pulling at the seat of her pants.

The scent of trees and wildflowers was all around them. Pine, elms, and ash trees surrounded them. Bushes grew on the roadside. The road itself was overgrown from lack of use.

"Look, father," KorMitore whispered. "The bones of the horses… still in their harnesses."

"It would appear that way, son," ThiBael replied. "And more bones scattered about. These seem to be human."

"Yes," Isabell said slowly and pointed to the back of the wagon. "This one's human all right and he's still in armor."

Liam ran to her side. There in the back of the wagon, lay the bones of a man in armor. His arms were crossed on his chest and a rusty sword lay horizontally under his flattened hands.

ThiBael reached in and pulled the blade free. "I know this sword. This must be the body of Captain Saevel. They must have been taking him home. But why is he still here and not devoured like the others?"

"The Book of Antiquity said the Daretharth eat humans," Isabell added.

"I know not what the book says," KorMitore replied. "But, from my own experience, I can tell you they eat anything they can kill. Humans, wild or domesticated animals, even their own dead."

"Maybe by the time they attacked these men, Saevel's body had spoiled too much to be eaten." Isabell said.

Liam reached down at Saevel's feet and picked up a weathered leather bag. He opened it and found a yellowed sheet of parchment. He gently removed it and read out loud:

"To my Queen Essaerae and the Wizard Elkhazel.

"I wish to add my sympathies to you in this time of sorrow and loss. It is my loss as well, for Saevel was my dearest friend for many years. I am having his body brought back to you in hopes it will give you some solace.

"I wish to also explain how Saevel died. When I heard it was he who would come to West Water for inspections, I was overjoyed. As a jest, I rode out of town with some of my men, and set up a fake ambush. It was only to give him a start and nothing more. But his horse jumped when we sprang the trap and threw him to the ground. Saevel hit his head on a rock and died in my arms moments later.

"If I had even a thought this might happen, I would never have played the trick on him. As I take full responsibility for the actions that day. I have placed myself in the custody of the Township of West Water's magistrate. I await your judgment.

"Your loyal servant, Lieutenant Belanor."

"That's why Wizard Elkhazel became so angry," ThiBael remarked. "If not for the horse throwing him to the ground, Saevel would have thought it a fun lark played on him that day. But, in Elkhazel's rage, he found it to be a crime. That the people of the town would let something like this happen."

"Why didn't he ride a griffon?" asked Isabell.

"Saevel was a strong and courageous man, to be sure," ThiBael said. "He had only one fear—great heights. Queen Essaerae always tried to get him to take a griffon on his missions. But he never could last more than a few moments before he demanded to be put back on the ground."

"We should take his remains back with us," Kor-Mitore added. "It would help with the queen's grieving."

"Wait," Isabell said. "I thought Saevel was Elkha-zel's son. That's what the queen said."

"Yes," KorMitore said. "But he was her son as well. Elkhazel is the queen's husband. She puts on a strong and disconnected facade when faced with Saevel's death. Queen Essaerae doesn't want anyone to think her weak."

"I heard her crying last night before she fell asleep," ThiBael said. "Your appearance has opened a wound that's not fully healed."

"A wound in us all," KorMitore whispered.

Silence fell on the group as Liam looked through the remains of the bag. He tried to think of the next step. After a moment, he asked, "Can you find this place again?"

"Yes, why?" ThiBael asked.

"Let's make our way to the town and see what's there," Liam said. "We'll stop here on our way back, wrap his bones in a blanket and take him home with us.

But right now, we can't be tied down with him. And heaven forbid, we might lose him along the way."

"You have a valid point," ThiBael said. "Shall we move on?"

Liam helped Isabell get back on KorMitore.

"I'm so not liking this saddle," Isabell said as she walked stiffly back towards KorMitore. "The inside of my legs and butt hurt like hell."

"Sorry," KorMitore replied. "But it can't be helped right now. We'll need to find someplace safer, my father can heal your wounds then."

Once he had Isabell safely in the saddle, Liam climbed back on ThiBael and strapped himself in. His time in the saddle had left him hurting, but not too bad. After a brief moment, ThiBael took a few steps down the road and leapt gracefully into the air. His wings pushed hard against the air at first to gain lift. Liam rode the rise and fall of ThiBael's back with each stroke of his wings. After they gained sufficient altitude, then he slowed and let the air currents help him rise higher.

An hour or more went by. Then a seashore came into view off to Liam's left and ThiBael turned, following it for some time. The remains of a village appeared hidden in the trees up from the shore.

"We'll fly out to sea just over the coast line. With the sun behind us the Daretharth are less likely to be alerted to our presence," ThiBael said as he banked away from shore.

The buildings hadn't been maintained in several years. Some had holes in their thatched or slate roofs. On the streets, what could only be Daretharth wandered about. Human-like, they had tusked muzzled heads that look like a wild boar and were covered in a coarse brown fur like a bear. Clad in crude leather and bone armor, they carried stone-headed clubs and spears for weapons.

"Can we land outside of town?" Liam asked ThiBael. "We need to see what's going on."

ThiBael and KorMitore circled around and landed in a clearing about half a mile inland from town. Liam slid from the saddle and ran to help Isabell to get down. "I'm going to sneak into the village to have a look around. Isabell, you need to stay here. This is going to be dangerous."

"How stealthy can you be?" ThiBael whispered. "The Daretharth hunt by both sight and smell. One hint of your scent on the wind and the Daretharth will be on you for a feast."

Before Liam replied, Isabell interrupted, "You tried that shit back at the castle. We're in this together. You aren't leaving me behind."

"Having two humans close together will guarantee your demise," KorMitore remarked. "They can smell out their prey better than we can."

Liam looked down at the mossy ground. "How in the hell can I get in there then? I need to find out what's going on."

ThiBael sat on his haunches. "I don't have a spell that will prevent you from being seen, heard, or smelled. The town is overrun by Daretharth. You heard the queen. We're not to kill them. If something goes wrong, we'll have to kill many of them to save you."

"Silence," KorMitore whispered. "Something moved in that brush." He pointed with one talon.

Looking at the bush, a movement caught Liam's attention. A large dark gray cat bounded from beneath the leaves. It moved towards them until it came to Isabell, it turned around, fur and tail fluffed up, and hissed back the way it had come.

"I smell Daretharth," KonMitore said.

The cat ran behind them and disappeared into the brush.

"Look Out," Isabell yelled as she dove into Liam, knocking him down just as a spear past over them.

Three Daretharth ran into the clearing. Their tusked muzzled noses sniffed at the air. Two held stone-headed clubs, the other a spear. That one stopped just long enough to throw it.

ThiBae sent a bolt of magic that hit the spear making it land just short of Isabell, its intended target.

KorMitore moved in and grabbed the spearman by the neck. He picked it up and shook it like a ragdoll. With the other front talon, he raked down its chest, ripping flesh and bone.

Liam got up from under Isabell, pulled the spear from the ground, and prepared to defend her.

ThiBae charged the other two Daretharth. As he moved towards them, the Daretharth split up. One continued to charge at him from his front, while the other moved to flanked the griffon.

With its back to him, Liam ran at the flanking Daretharth, driving the spear deep into its spine.

ThiBae gripped the first Daretharth with his front talon, while ripping its head off with his beak. Then he turned and swiped at the second, disemboweling it.

Liam pulled the spear loose and let his victim fall.

"Thank you." ThiBae said. "I didn't know it was gravely wounded already."

"Hay." Liam drove the bloody end of the spear into the ground. "I wounded it, and you finshed it off. I got no problems with that."

"What a nasty taste." ThiBae flicked his tongue in and out of his beak.

"Why do you think I didn't bite them?" KorMitore remarked. "I know better."

Liam turned to Isabell. "I told you it would be dangerous."

"Shut up." Isabell raised her open palm to him. "I saved your ass, I don't want to hear it"

The two griffons laughed at Isabell's comment. Then ThiBae got serious. "The queen won't be happy. But it couldn't be helped, they attacked us."

With that, the cat walked out from the brush. Timidly, it moved towards them until it came to Isabell. She sat down and held out her hand. It smelled her hand several times then rubbed against it. Slowly, Isabell petted the cat and it purred loudly. After several minutes, it climbed into Isabell's lap and laid down.

"It must have been someone's pet," Isabell said while she stroked it. "Poor thing's been on its own for so long. But it still remembers that humans were nice to it."

"It was probably someone's barn cat." ThiBae flicked his tongue out a few more times. "From the look of it, she's been quite successful both as a mouser, and hiding from the Daretharth."

"Father." KorMitore pointed a talon at the cat. "Can you use that spell to communicate with this cat? You know, the one you showed me when I was younger. When we were hunting and you talked with that eagle to find our game."

"What good would that do?" ThiBael cocked his head for a moment as if studying the cat.

"She could tell us what went on here," KorMitore answered. "If she was here when it happened, she would know what occurred."

"True," ThiBael closed his eyes and raised one front talon towards the cat. A light blue glow encircled the cat for a few moments. When it faded, ThiBael said, "What is your name, feline?"

Isabell stroked the cat and asked, "Do you understand us, little one?"

The cat hissed, jumped from her lap to a tree, and climbed to the lowest branch. Its hair stood up straight with its tail fluffed out.

"Don't be frightened, my friend," ThiBael said smoothly. "We just need to talk to you."

"How is it, I—I can understand you?" the cat growled. Her voice was rough, but obviously female.

"I placed a spell on you that lets you understand us," ThiBael said. "The spell will fade in a few weeks."

"What is your name?" Isabell asked again.

The cat laid down on its perch and licked at its fur on its front paws. It reminded Liam of the Cheshire cat from the Alice in Wonderland cartoon.

She stopped licking. "My humans called me Ravenna."

"Ravenna," Isabell said. "That's a pretty name."

ThiBael asked. "Ravenna, can you tell us what happened here three years ago? How did the humans change into these creatures?"

Ravenna said. "The humans weren't changed. They were eaten."

"Over three years ago, there was a burst of rogue magic," KorMitore countered. "That magic changed them into Daretharth. We know of the magic and where it came from."

"Well, I was just beyond a kitten here three years ago," Ravenna remarked with a low growl. "But I watched as my humans were eaten. I was in the loft of the barn, laying in the sun, minding my own cares." The cat shook itself. "When I heard their screams, I went to the loft door. There they were, outside their small home. The man tried to push the woman into the home, but she was hit in the head before he could. She fell just outside the door. The man used an ax to defend her. He even killed two of the beasts. But when the ax became lodged in the skull of one of them, he too went down. Your monsters dragged them to the middle of the yard and devoured them. I can show you—my home is not far from here. I still live there."

"Is it safe?" Liam asked. He didn't want to inadvertently stumble into another group of Daretharth. They were a little tougher than he'd expected. Isabell and luck had been on his side to defeat the last one. He felt Isabell would be there again if he need her, but would he run out of luck. He really didn't want to find out.

"The house is far from the main road." Ravenna gestured behind her. "The Daretharth, as you call them, mostly stick to the main roads anymore. So long as you don't start a fire, you should be safe. They would track the smell of smoke."

"Then take us there," ThiBael said. "We'll make plans for what to do next."

Ravenna jumped down. "Follow me."

Liam tailed Ravenna through the forest. Isabell walked only a few steps behind him, while the two griffons moved with them on each flank. Ravenna made little sound as she ran through the dead leaves that covered the ground. To Liam's astonishment, the two griffons made only slightly more. But no matter how he tried, the sound of his own footsteps seemed to echo through the trees. The snap of hidden twigs made him jump as if it was a gunshot. The scent of damp earth wafted up as his feet uncovered the ground.

After only a few moments, Ravenna said, "Watch the fence here." She disappeared into some brush. Then she added, "You'll have to climb over."

A split rail fence lay hidden in the bushes. Liam climbed over and helped Isabell to the other side.

KorMitore flew over the fence and landed quickly, scouting the area behind the brush. "I see a small house and barn."

ThiBael jumped the fence at a low place and they started walking to the house.

"Maybe we can stay here tonight?" Isabell said. "I really don't want to get back in that saddle for a little while. My butt hurts."

"Let us get inside," ThiBael said. "Then I'll help you with that."

"Watch where you walk," KorMitore said in a low voice as he pointed with his beak at the tall grass in front of them.

Strewn around the yard between the house and barn were the remains of the people that had called this place home. The bones were white with age and many lay partially hidden by the overgrown vegetation that was trying to reclaim the quaint little cottage.

"Ewww!" Isabell exclaimed. "I don't want to step on them."

Liam held her hand as she tip-toed her way through the yard. Riding in the griffon's saddle must have been hard for her. Her legs seemed stiff and sore as she weaved her way through the bones, wincing with every step. On several occasions, he had to pull her back from the brink of falling when she tried at the last moment to change the place to put her foot because of a bone on the ground.

"I just stepped on a part of them." Isabell hopped to one side. "I hope they don't get mad at us."

"This way," Ravenna said. The door stood slightly open and she squeezed into the room.

KorMitore pushed his way in first. A few moments later, he said, "It's uninhabited. You can enter."

Inside, Liam found a quaint little home. Across from the door was a cold, empty hearth. On his left was a table with two benches. Ravenna jumped to the bench, then to the table.

"This is the first time in a long time I've come in here," Ravenna said sadly. "I mostly stay in the loft. Too many memories here."

With the two griffons in the small home, it was a little cramped. KorMitore squeezed passed ThiBael and moved towards the door.

"Now, Isabell," ThiBael said, "let me help you. I have a healing spell that should ease your discomfort."

Isabell looked at him for a moment. "I--I don't normally let people I don't know do first aid on me. But it hurts so bad—I'm willing to try anything."

He placed his closed talon above Isabell's back pocket.

"Oh shit!" Isabell squealed. "This tingles all over!" She grabbed the table as an amber glow grew around her butt and legs. When it was done, Isabell sat down at the table. "Okay, that magic shit freaks me out! You just don't know how that shit freaks me out." After several moments she added, "But, it helped a lot. Thanks."

"You are welcome," ThiBael said and bowed before her.

As Liam settled across from Isabell, she asked, "Why is it you don't seem to be hurting as much from riding in those saddles?"

"I grew up on a ranch outside of Alamosa," Liam said. "I spent a good part of my life in the saddle. I'm sore, but not too bad."

ThiBael squatted at the end of the table while KorMitore stayed at the door.

"Ravenna, you said the Daretharth killed all the humans here?" asked Liam.

"Yes," Ravenna said. "They came from the north. Swarmed into the village like a strong wind. Killed everything in their way. They would have eaten me if I weren't so good at hiding." She paused then added, "More and more come through every day. I sometimes hide up high in a tree by the main road. I've watched them walking by in groups of ten to fifteen. They stay in the village for a time, then move on."

"That makes a lot of sense," ThiBael said absentmindedly.

"What do you mean?" asked Liam. He really wanted to understand some of what was going on. With all the magic and everything he felt more than a little bit lost. He wasn't sure how he was going to be the hero of the story and not be let in on something that was going on.

"Well, obviously Elkhazel's rogue magic didn't change the humans," ThiBael said as he put one front talon on the table. "We've been trying to change them back to their 'normal form.' But it never worked. So it reasons if they were never humans in the first place, a change spell couldn't change them back into humans. But what are they and where are they coming from?"

"And what happened to Elkhazel's rogue spell?" asked Liam.

"I talked with another cat once," Ravenna muttered. "He said he saw them moving down from the ice river way north of the village."

"Ice river?" Isabell asked.

"You must mean the glacier at SiksinNeneweth-Bay," ThiBael said. He tapped the table with his talon, much like a human would tap a pencil when thinking about something. "That bay is the northern most point in the Kingdom. It's dominated by a four-mile-wide glacier that empties into it. They can't be landing ships there. It's far too dangerous."

"The other cat told me they walked across the frozen sea," Ravenna said.

"But even in the harshest of winters," ThiBael said, "the glacier calves off massive chunks of ice. That prevents the bay or even the waters around there from freezing over completely. That's why it's so dangerous. I have seen ice the size of castles fall from that glacier."

"Then that's where we need to go next," Liam said. "Something has changed there, and the Daretharth are using the ice to make their way into the kingdom."

"There are only a few more hours until dark," KorMitore remarked from the door. "We should stay here until dawn. It's too treacherous to fly into the northern lands after dark."

"My son's right," ThiBael said. "The mountains and the air currents between here and there are dangerous at the best of times. We should travel in daylight."

"Will you take me with you?" asked Ravenna. "I've missed having a human to call friend. When I saw you two in the woods, I almost didn't believe my eyes. I won't be any trouble."

"Of course we will," Isabell said.

"We will leave at first light." ThiBael added.

By noon, Liam looked down from ThiBael's back. He stood on top of SiksinNeneweth glacier looking down at the bay. With every breath, the cold air stung his lungs. A puff of white escaped with each exhale. Below him, three groups of Daretharth walked along the frozen bay.

"I see tracks from other groups weaving around the small ice mountains trapped in the bay," ThiBael said

"What's that out there moving on the ice?" asked Ravenna, her head poking out from inside Isabell's jacket.

Far out to sea, the ocean broke against the ice a little more than a few miles out. On the ice, many more lines of dark spots made their way towards land.

"That would be more Daretharth," KorMitore replied. "I'd guess over a hundred moving in small groups into Cushendall."

"It's cold up here," Isabell whispered. She rubbed her gloved hands together trying to warm them up. "I wish I had brought my snow suit."

"Me too," Liam said. "Right now, we'll just have to deal with the blankets we got from the farmhouse. They help some." Liam pointed to the cat looking at him from her jacket. "Besides, you have Ravenna in your coat to keep you warm."

"That's true," Isabell said. She pulled at the crude coverings wrapped around her legs. "It was a great idea to use the old blankets and cut them into pants. Better than nothing."

"I feel a strange magic here," ThiBael said. "This is where Elkhazel's rogue magic went. It's holding back the glacier. Preventing it from calving off ice. The pressure built under this spell is tremendous."

"If we can release the pressure," KorMitore said. "It would destroy the ice bridge that lets the Daretharth cross into our Kingdom."

"Yes," ThiBael said. "But how far will it explode? It's had over three years to build up tension."

"It can't be helped," Liam said. "Releasing it should stop the Daretharth from continuing to invade your Kingdom. This glacier stopped them from moving into this land before." Liam looked at ThiBael. "Can you break the spell?"

"I can," ThiBael replied.

"Why is it that your people have never seen the Daretharth before?" Isabell asked. "I mean, you've said yourself that you've been here many times before."

"I don't know," ThiBael answered. "From the looks of them, they appear to be nomadic. Moving from place to place as their food runs out. It must have been just bad timing that Elkhazel's rogue magic stopped the glacier. They were in the vicinity to take advantage of the ice bridge. Somewhere out there beyond the horizon must be another land where the Daretharth originally called home."

"Then break the spell," Liam said. "We'll pick up Saevel's bones and head back to the queen. Once we tell her about the Daretharth and that they're not her subjects, she can send your armies and re-take your lands." He pointed first to Isabell then to himself. "Then hopefully, we can go home." Deep inside, he really hoped this was going to work. He wanted to get back to a world he knew and understood.

Isabell frowned. "But that would mean the extinction of the Daretharth on this land."

"Look," Liam said. "Let's not talk about whose right it is to live here. The people of this Kingdom have the right to defend it. This is an invasion, and the Daretharth have weapons and armor. They've shown an intent to do the people of Cushendall harm. Hell, they intend to eat them."

"But they've been here for years now," Isabell argued. "It seems to me that they have a clam to this land as well."

"The Cushendall," ThiBael said, "have lived and worked here not just a few years, but for generations upon generations. Besides, its up to the queen to decide their fate."

"True enough, I guess," Isabell answered back.

"Then get ready," ThiBael said. "When I release this spell, the ice we're standing on will explode far out beyond the bay. How far, even I can't tell you that."

ThiBael and KorMitore walked up to the very edge of the glacier and jumped off.

Cold wind rushed passed Liam's face chilling him even more. They lifted up into the sky and circled around towards the sea. As they turned to face the glacier, ThiBael raised one of his taloned front feet. From it, a long line of reddish orange light struck the glacier face. At first, it was only a spot, but it grew slowly until it almost touched the land on each side.

A cracking sound tore through the glacier, followed by a series of explosions that ripped through the air. In seconds, ice blasted far beyond the bay and deep out to sea. With each new detonation, more pieces fell, breaking holes in the ice shelf. Within moments, massive slabs of ice began to move farther out to sea. Some had Daretharth clinging to them, while some fell or were hurled into the frigid waters. Immense slabs tilted up on their edge from the weight of the falling ice. When the explosions subsided, ThiBael and KorMitore dropped down to look at the large areas of the bay, now cleared of the ice bridge.

The griffons rode the rising currents of air as they watched the calving ice. Suddenly, a massive explosion shattered the face of the glacier. Huge chunks of ice flew higher than before. ThiBael and KorMitore worked to dodge the in-coming debris. Liam could only hang on for dear life as ThiBael rolled over to avoid an ice missile.

Pain sliced through his skull as a smaller slab struck Liam in the head, leaving him dazed by the impact. Liam found it impossible to hold on. After a moment, a sensation of falling took him. Confused, Liam wondered why the freezing water rushed upwards towards him. Or was it he that rushed towards the water? He could not bring his thoughts together to understand what was happening.

The sudden splash of ice cold water that should have cleared his mind, but it only confused him more. Liam floated face down on the water for a few seconds, then slowly slipped below the surface, as darkness enveloped him.

Liam awoke gradually. He opened his eyes to see nothing but darkness. *Am I dead?* Slowly, his memories came back to him, one by one, like waves lapping at a shore. Each swell brought more memories, more pieces of what had happened to him. The sound of a cough broke into his consciousness and he heard the crackle of burning wood. He moved a bit. Pain lanced through his head.

"Well, I think I felt our lifeless swimmer move under here."

Light spilled into his eyes as the huge black wing of KorMitore folded back in place. Cold air assaulted him, and Liam shivered violently, turning into the wing for warmth. He screamed when a claw sank deep into his leg. A cat bolted out from where it was laying on his legs.

Ravenna ran to Isabell's side. "He almost rolled over on me!" she cried. "And all I was doing was trying to keep him warm."

"Why am I naked?" Liam asked. He didn't want to move to much and expose himself to everyone around him.

"Here, you should cover up." Isabell threw him a blanket.

"Sorry, Ravenna," Liam apologized to the cat as he caught the blanket. "I didn't know you were there. But I ask again, why am I naked?"

"You fell into the bay," Isabell said. "I had to get your wet clothes off before you froze to death. Just stay covered up. I have a fire going to dry them out." After a moment she added, "I was a Girl Scout. I learned some things about frost bite and hypothermia."

"Girl Scout," Liam said as he hastily wrapped the blanket around him. "I guess that means you know how to get a fire started by rubbing sticks together?"

"No," she said with a grin. "Never passed that one. Lucky for you, I picked up that lost disposable lighter you found. I had it in my pocket all this time."

"Yes, very lucky," ThiBael said. "How do you feel? You took a nasty bump to the head."

"Okay, I guess," Liam answered. "But what happened?"

"I thought the built up pressure had dissipated," ThiBael said. "But one last explosion caught us off guard. I tried to dodge the fragments, but you got hit by a sizable piece. When you let go of the handles, you fell. I think the blanket pants may have allowed you to slip from the straps more easily as well."

"I fished you out of the water," KorMitore added. "You're heavier than you look, by the way. I almost didn't make land with the two of you."

KorMitore added. "Well, as soon as we get your clothes dry we must get back home, Our work here is done. It will be sundown in a few hours. We'll rest until day break, then we must get back and tell the queen of this."

Queen Essaerae stepped back from Saevel's grave. She turned and faced Liam. Beside him stood Isabell with Ravenna in her arms. Beside them ThiBael, and KorMitore waited silently.

"I thank you for bringing Saevel home to me," Queen Essaerae said and wiped tears from her eye. "I wondered what happened to his body, but could never bring myself to send out a search party. Any party would have had to fight their way to him. I feared they would be killing my people. But now I know my people are dead. We've already started the war to take back our lands. As we speak, my armies push from the magical bastions against the Daretharth. For too long we've cowered before them. Many griffons fly in support. This gives us a small advantage."

She walked away and ordered, "Liam and Isabell, follow me. The rest of you, stay here."

Liam looked at Isabell who shrugged.

Ravenna jumped from Isabell's arms and ran to the shade of a tall plant. "I'll wait for you here, Isabell."

Liam and Isabell followed the queen. She led them through the gardens to the Star Polygon. There she sat down on a stone bench and sighed.

"You have completed a great undertaking," Queen Essaerae said. "And for me and my people, I'm grateful. I thank you once more for my son. But you must return to your world. Even if you wished to stay, I would have to stop you. This is not your home."

She paused. "But I have one more task to ask of you before you go. Would you be willing to take on this task?"

"What is it, Queen Essaerae?" Isabell asked before Liam could speak.

Queen Essaerae smiled weakly and said, "Please, upon reaching your world, tell my husband to return to me. I've missed him dearly. With my son back, I can move beyond my grief to what lies ahead."

"We will, your Majesty," Isabell said.

"We will, Queen Essaerae," Liam said as he took Isabell's hand. "We'll send him back to you the moment we get there. I'm just glad we could help you and your Kingdom."

"Thank you," Queen Essaerae said with a wave of her hand. "Now go, before it's too late."

Liam and Isabell walked the few steps to the center of the Star Polygon. There they turned to wave goodbye. A bright flash of light engulfed them, and Liam covered his eyes with one hand and held on to Isabell with the other. When the light died away, he looked around. "We're back in Karl's basement."

"You mean Wizard Elkhazel's," Isabell corrected with a smile.

"Okay, they're one and the same," Liam said as he looked around. The basement appeared much as it had when they'd left it, but Karl wasn't there. The place was deserted. Even the computers on the shelf had been turn off. "But where is he?"

"I don't know," Isabell took his hand and pulled him towards the stairs. "Let's check upstairs. He could be there."

Liam followed as they both ran for the staircase. Taking the steps two at a time, they bounded up to the main floor. There they found a stark house that held few furnishings. But on a table in the front of the living room windows stood an open book. "That looks like a smaller copy of the Book of Antiquity," Liam said. They slowly moved towards it.

When they reached the book, Liam said, "Look, these are the words we saw write themselves onto the page of the Book of Antiquity."

"Yes," Isabell said excitedly and squeezed his hand. "That means he wrote them here, and we read them there?"

Just then, words began to write themselves on the page.

Liam and Isabell, I can't thank you enough. You have saved me from exile, brought my son's body back to us, and allowed me to be with my queen once more. Now that I'm back, I'll help her reclaim our Kingdom. You two are much alike, you know. I hope you'll have a long and happy life together. Goodbye and thank you, Karl Hilbert a.k.a. Wizard Elkhazel.

The book faded into nothing right before their eyes.

Liam said, "I guess we'll never see him again."

"No, but he's where he wants to be." She smiled. "And we helped him get there."

A sense of peace filled him, as Liam pulled Isabell into his arms and held her close. "Yes, we did." Isabell wrapped her arms around him and hugged him back. Then to Liam's amazement, she kissed him.

Stanley Griffin

Born in Lubbock Tex. Stan joined the U.S Army right out of high school, and came to Ft Carson on his first duty assignment. He fell in love twice here. Once with the mountains and the land as a whole, then second to his wife Patricia. They came back to Colorado Springs after his career in the Army. He has written one Novel called "Earth Seed Four", a Novelette called "Oracle Lake" and a short story called "The Last James", and He is working on another Novel called "The Treachery of Zethus".

Colorado Springs Fiction Writers Group

Critique Groups
The four critique groups are the backbone of CSFWG. The groups are designed to give an author honest feedback on a story or poem, providing both praise and suggestions for improvement. Visitors are always welcome, but only members may submit works for critique.

Workshops
CSFWG offers workshops on a variety of subjects requested by our members. All workshops are free and open to the public.

Write-Ins
CSFWG offers weekly write-ins at Montague's Coffee House every Monday from 1 pm to 6 pm. All write-ins are free and open to the public, though we suggest supporting Montague's Coffee House with a food or drink purchase as a 'thank you'.

Brainstorming Sessions
CSFWG hosts monthly brainstorming sessions the first Thursday of every month at Montague's Coffee House. This event is free and open to the public.

Anthologies
With the release of the first anthology, <u>An Uncommon Collection</u>, CSFWG took the next step in encouraging creativity and drive in its members. The bi-yearly anthology only accepts the best stories on a theme from the members of CSFWG. The theme for the anthology scheduled for release in 2016 is 'A Colorado State of Mind'.

About the Editor

Kari Wolfe

Kari Wolfe is a Colorado author and editor, owned by a one-eyed cat named Jacq and has a daughter who is on the autism spectrum. Both want all of her attention, albeit in different ways, but she manages to scratch out stories in her spare time. Kari. is an avid reader. Having learned on her own to read when she was three, she has never not had a book in her hand. In the winter while her mate and daughter are skiing, you'll most likely find her with a book in one hand, a hot toddy in the other, escaping into whatever world she's come across. Or she'll have her fingers on her laptop keyboard, pounding out the next story or thoughts that come to mind. Her dreams include self-sufficiency from writing and riding and owning her own horses. If not writing and/or taking care of her daughter, you'll find her down at the barn, grooming and learning as much as she can.